I saw him. My heart skipped a beat.

He had a sturdy, chiseled jaw, a strong nose, and a square forehead. He looked rough around the edges, from the trace of stubble on his jaw to the short, tousled dark hair. Rough, masculine, and arrestingly sexual. His eyes, smart and clear under the thick, dark eyebrows, evaluated everything he saw with calm precision, but deep inside those blue irises, a cold fire glowed. The same kind of lethal fire you would see in the amber eyes of a tiger, predatory yet irresistible. It compelled you to stare, even though you knew that if you caught his gaze, that icy fire would swallow you whole. He pulled me like a magnet. Every female instinct I had went into overdrive.

Oh wow.

I looked into his blue eyes. No, I was wrong. He wasn't a tiger. He was a dragon, regal and deadly, and he was coming for me.

By Ilona Andrews

ILONA ANDREWS

BURN FOR ME

A HIDDEN LEGACY NOVEL

AVON

An Imprint of HarperCollinsPublishers

This is a work of fiction. Names, characters, places, and incidents are products of the author's imagination or are used fictitiously and are not to be construed as real. Any resemblance to actual events, locales, organizations, or persons, living or dead, is entirely coincidental.

AVON BOOKS
An Imprint of HarperCollins*Publishers*
195 Broadway
New York, New York 10007

Copyright © 2014 by Ilona Gordon and Andrew Gordon
Untitled excerpt copyright © 2015 by Ilona Gordon and Andrew Gordon
ISBN 978-0-06-228923-0
www.avonromance.com

First Avon Books mass market printing: November 2014
First Avon Books mass market special printing: June 2014

Avon Trademark Reg. U.S. Pat. Off. and in Other Countries, Marca Registrada, Hecho en U.S.A.
HarperCollins® is a registered trademark of HarperCollins Publishers.

Printed in the U.S.A.

10 9 8 7 6 5 4 3 2 1

To our awesome daughters,
who make it all worthwhile,
and the rest of our family,
who drive us crazy.

Acknowledgments

Writing a manuscript is a solitary endeavor, but creating a book isn't. We would like to thank the following people for helping us bring this story to you.

We are grateful to:

Erika Tsang, for her firm and witty editorial guidance. Thank you so much for making this book better and for bearing with odd phone calls asking if we should "cut this part."

Nancy Yost, our agent, for her unwavering belief in our modest talents and her support. We know how difficult we can be and we appreciate your professional expertise and your friendship. We would also like to thank Sarah, Adrienne, and the staff of NYLA for all of their hard work.

Thomas Egner, the Art Director; Richard Jones, the artist; and Patricia Barrow, the cover designer, for their fantastic work on the book cover.

Karen Davy, Managing Editor, and Rhea Braunstein, interior designer, for turning a manuscript into a beautiful book.

Judy Gelman Myers, for her attention to detail and help in purging mistakes and inconsistencies.

Shannon Daigle, Denise Gray, Cindy Wilkinson, Nicole Clement, Amanda Ferry, and others, for the generous gift of their time and expertise as they proofread the manuscript. All errors of fact and grammar are due to our own shortcomings.

Jeaniene Frost and Jessica Claire, for their friendship and guidance, and to J. S. You are right. It is so much better when there is a family.

Well, here it is, our new book. Thank you, dear readers, for taking a chance on it. We hope you will like it.

In 1863, in a world much like our own, European scientists discovered the Osiris serum, a concoction which brought out one's magic talents. These talents were many and varied. Some people gained ability to command animals, some learned to sense water from miles away, and others suddenly realized they could kill their enemies by generating a burst of lightning between their hands. The serum spread through the world. It was given to soldiers in hopes of making the military forces more deadly. It was obtained by members of fading aristocracy, desperate to hold on to power. It was bought by the rich, who desired to get richer.

Eventually the world realized the consequences of awakening godlike powers in ordinary people. The serum was locked away, but it was too late. The magic talents passed on from parents to their children and changed the course of human history forever. The future of entire nations shifted in the span of a few short decades. Those who previously married for status, money, and power now married for magic, because strong magic would give them everything.

Now, a century and a half later, families with strong hereditary magic have evolved into dynasties. These families—Houses, as they call themselves—own corporations, have their own territories within the cities, and influence politics. They employ private armies, they feud with each other, and their disputes are deadly. It is a world where the more magic you have, the more powerful, the wealthier, and the more prominent you are. Some magic talents are destructive. Some are subtle. But no magic user should be taken lightly.

 **Prologue**

"I can't let you do this. I won't. Kelly, the man is insane."

Kelly Waller reached over and touched her husband's hand, looking for reassurance. He took his hand off the wheel and squeezed her fingers. Strange how intimate a touch can be, she thought. That touch, fueled by twenty years of love, had served as her rock in the nightmarish storm of the past forty-eight hours. Without it, she would have been screaming.

"He won't hurt me. We're family."

"You told me yourself he hates his family."

"I have to try," she said. "They'll kill our boy."

Tom stared straight ahead, glassy eyed, guiding the car up the curve of the driveway. Old Texas oaks spread their wide canopies over the grassy lawn, sprayed with drops of yellow dandelions and pink buttercups. Connor wasn't taking care of the grounds. His father would've had the weeds poisoned . . .

Her stomach churned. A part of her wanted to go back and somehow undo the events of the last two days. A part of her wanted to turn the car around. It's too late, she told herself. It's too late for regrets and what ifs. She had to deal with the reality, no matter how terrifying it was. She had to act like a mother.

The driveway brought them to a tall stucco wall. She raked her memory. Sixteen years was a long time, but she was sure the wall hadn't been there before.

A wrought-iron gate blocked the arched entrance. This was it. No turning back. If Connor decided he wanted her dead, her magic, what little of it there was, wouldn't be enough to stop him.

Connor was the culmination of three generations of careful marriages aimed at bolstering the family's magic and connections. He was supposed to have been a worthy successor to the fortune of House Rogan. Much like her, he hadn't turned out the way his parents had planned.

Tom parked the car. "You don't have to do this."

"Yes, I do." The dread that hung over her mugged Kelly, setting off a wave of overwhelming anxiety. Her hands shook. She swallowed, trying to clear her throat. "This is the only way."

"At least let me come with you."

"No. He knows me. He might see you as a threat." She swallowed again, but the clump in her throat refused to disappear. She never knew if Connor could read people's thoughts, but he was always aware of emotions. She had no doubt they were being watched and probably listened to. "Tom, I don't think anything bad will happen. If something does, if I don't come out, I want you to drive away. I want you to go home to the kids. There is a blue folder in the cabinet over the small desk, the one in the kitchen. On the second shelf. Our life insurance policies are in there, and the will . . ."

Tom started the engine. "That's it. We're going home. We'll deal with it ourselves."

She jerked the car door open, jumped out, and hurried to the gate, her heels clicking on the pavement.

"Kelly!" he called. "Don't!"

She forced herself to touch the iron gates. "This is Kelly. Connor, please let me in."

The iron gate slid open. Kelly raised her head and stepped inside. The gate glided shut behind her. She walked through the arch and up the stone path that wove its way through the picturesque copse of oaks, redbuds, and laurels. The path turned, and she stopped, frozen.

The large colonial beast of a house with white walls and distinguished colonnades was gone. In its place stood a two-story Mediterranean-style mansion, with cream walls and a dark red roof. Had she gone to the wrong property?

"Where is the house?" she whispered.

"I demolished it."

Kelly turned. He stood next to her. She remembered a thin boy with striking pale blue eyes. Sixteen years later, he stood taller than her. His hair, chestnut when he was younger, had turned dark brown, almost black. His face, once angular, had gained a square jaw and hard masculine lines that made him arrestingly handsome. That face, suffused with power, harsh but almost regal . . . It was the kind of face that commanded obedience. He could've ruled the world with that face.

Kelly looked into his eyes and instantly wished she hadn't. Life had iced over the beautiful blue irises. Power stirred deep in their depth. She could feel it just beyond the surface, like a wild, vicious current. It bucked and boiled, a shocking, terrifying power, promising violence and destruction, locked in a cage of iron will. A chill ran from the base of Kelly's neck all the way down her spine.

She had to say something. Anything.

"Dear God, Connor, that was a ten-million-dollar house."

He shrugged. "I found it cathartic. Would you like some coffee?"

"Yes. Thank you."

He led her through the doors into a lobby, up a wooden staircase with an ornate iron rail, to a covered balcony. She followed him, slightly dazed, her surroundings a vague smudge until she sat down on a plush chair. Beyond the rail of the balcony, an orchard stretched, the trees weaving their way around ponds and a picturesque creek. Far at the horizon, the bluish hills rolled, like distant waves.

She smelled coffee. Connor was standing with his back to her, waiting for the coffeemaker to fill their mugs.

Establish a common ground. Remind him who you are. "Where is the swing?" she asked. It had been the favorite hangout of the Rogan kids. That's where they'd gone when he'd had to ask her advice, back when he was twelve and she'd been the cool older cousin Kelly, twenty and wise in all things teenager.

"It's still there. The oaks grew and you can't see it from the balcony." Connor turned, set her cup in front of her, and sat down.

"There was a time you would've floated the cups over," she said.

"I don't play games anymore. At least not the kind you remember. Why are you here?"

The coffee mug was burning her fingers. She set it

down. She hadn't even realized she'd picked it up in the first place. "Have you watched the news?"

"Yes."

"Then you know about the arson at First National."

"Yes."

"A security guard burned to death. His wife and their two children were visiting him. All three are in the hospital. The security guard was an off-duty police officer. The security camera footage identified two arsonists: Adam Pierce and Gavin Waller."

He waited.

"Gavin Waller is my son," she said. The words sounded hollow. "My son is a murderer."

"I know."

"I love my son. I love Gavin with all my heart. If it was my life against his, I would die for him in an instant. He isn't an evil person. He's a sixteen-year-old child. He was trying to find himself, but he found Adam Pierce instead. You have to understand, kids idealize Pierce. He is their antihero—the man who walked away from his family and started a motorcycle gang. The bad boy charismatic rebel."

Her voice turned bitter and angry, but she couldn't help it.

"He used Gavin to commit this atrocity, and now a police officer is dead. The officer's wife and their two children were burned very badly. They will kill Gavin, Connor. Even if my son walks out with his hands in the air, the cops will shoot him. He is a cop killer."

Connor drank his coffee. His face was perfectly placid. She couldn't read it.

"You don't owe me anything. We haven't spoken in twenty years, not since the family disowned me."

She swallowed again. She had refused to follow their instructions and marry a stranger with the right set of genes. She'd told them she wanted to be in control of her own life. They'd obliged and thrown her out like a piece of garbage . . . no, don't think about that. Think about Gavin.

"If there was any other way," she said, "I wouldn't bother you. But Tom has no connections. We don't have power, or money, or great magic. Nobody cares what happens to us. All I have now are our childhood memories. I was always there for you when you got in trouble. Please help me."

"What is it you want me to do? Do you hope to avoid his arrest?"

She detected a hint of cynical disapproval in his voice. "No. I want my son to be arrested. I want a trial. I want it to be televised, because after Gavin spends ten minutes on the stand, everyone will recognize exactly what he is: a confused, foolish child. His brother and sister deserve to know that he isn't a monster. I know my son. I know that what he's done is tearing him apart. I don't want him to die, gunned down like an animal, without ever having a chance to tell the family of the people he killed how deeply sorry he is."

Tears wet her cheeks. She didn't care. "Please, Connor. I'm begging you for my son's life."

Connor drank his coffee. "The name is Mad Rogan. They also call me the Butcher and the Scourge, but Mad is the most frequently used moniker."

"I know you—"

"No, you don't. You knew me before the war, when I was a child. Tell me, what am I now?"

The pressure of his gaze ground on her.

Her lips trembled and she said the first thing that popped into her mind. "You're a mass murderer."

He smiled, his face cold. No humor, no warmth, just a vicious predator baring his teeth. "It's been forty-eight hours since the arson, and you are just now here. You must be really desperate. Did you go to everyone else first? Am I your last stop?"

"Yes," she said.

His irises sparked with electric, bright blue. She looked into them, and for a split second she glimpsed the true power that lay inside him. It was like staring into the face of an avalanche before it swallowed you whole. In that moment she knew that all of the stories were true. He was a killer and a madman.

"I don't care if you're the devil himself," she whispered. "Please bring Gavin back to me."

"Okay," he said.

Five minutes later, she stumbled down the driveway. Her eyes watered. She tried to stop crying but couldn't. She had accomplished what she'd come here to do. The relief was overwhelming.

"Kelly, honey!" Tom caught her.

"He'll do it," she whispered, shell-shocked. "He promised he would find Gavin."

 **Chapter 1**

All men are liars. All women are liars, too. I learned that fact when I was two years old and my grandmother told me that if I was a good girl and sat still, the shot the doctor was about to give me wouldn't hurt. It was the first time my young brain connected the unsettling feeling of my magic talent detecting a lie to the actions of other people.

People lie for many reasons: to save themselves, to get out of trouble, to avoid hurting someone's feelings. Manipulators lie to get what they want. Narcissists lie to make themselves seem grand to others and themselves. Recovering alcoholics lie to safeguard their tattered reputations. And those who love us most lie to us most of all, because life is a bumpy ride and they want to smooth it out as much as possible.

John Rutger lied because he was a scumbag.

Nothing about his appearance said, Hey, I'm a despicable human being. As he stepped out of the hotel elevator, he seemed like a perfectly pleasant man. Tall and fit, he had brown, slightly wavy hair with just enough grey on his temples to make him look distinguished. His face was the kind of face you would expect a successful, athletic man in his forties to have: masculine, clean-shaven, and confident. He was that handsome, well-dressed dad at the junior football league yelling encouragements at his kid. He was the trusted stockbroker who would never steer his clients wrong. Smart, successful, solid as a rock. And the beautiful redhead holding hands with him was not his wife.

John's wife was named Liz, and two days ago she hired me to find out if he was cheating on her. She had caught him cheating before, ten months ago, and she'd told him that his next one would be his last.

John and the redhead drifted across the hotel lobby.

I sat in the lobby's lounge area, half hidden behind a bushy plant, and pretended to be absorbed in my cell phone, while the small digital camera hidden in my black crocheted purse recorded the lovebirds. The purse had been chosen precisely for its decorative holes.

Rutger and his date stopped a few feet away from me. I furiously shot birds at the snide green pigs on my screen. Move along, nothing to see here, just a young blond woman playing with her phone by some shrubbery.

"I love you," the redhead said.

True. Deluded fool.

The pigs laughed at me. I really sucked at this game.

"I love you too," he told her, looking into her eyes.

A familiar irritation built inside me, as if an invisible fly was buzzing around my head. My magic clicked. John was lying. Surprise, surprise.

I felt so sorry for Liz. They had been married for nine years, with two children, an eight-year-old boy and a four-year-old girl. She showed me the pictures when she hired me. Now their marriage was about to sink like the *Titanic*, and I was watching the iceberg approach.

"Do you mean that?" the redhead asked, looking at him with complete adoration.

"Yes. You know I do."

Magic buzzed again. Lie.

Most people found lying stressful. Distorting the truth and coming up with a plausible alternative version of reality required a good memory and an agile mind. When John Rutger lied, he did it to your face, looking straight into your eyes. And he seemed really convincing.

"I wish we could be together," the redhead said. "I'm tired of hiding."

"I know. But now isn't the right time. I'm working on it. Don't worry."

My cousins had run his lineage. John wasn't connected to any of the important magical families whose corporations owned Houston. He had no criminal history, but still something about the way he carried himself set me on edge. My instincts said he was dangerous, and I trusted my instincts.

We also ran a credit check. John couldn't afford a divorce. His record as a stockbroker was acceptable but not stellar. He was mortgaged up to the gills. What wealth he had was tied up in stocks, and divvying them up would be expensive. He knew it too and took pains to cover his tracks. He and the redhead had arrived in separate cars twenty minutes apart. He'd probably let her leave first, and, judging by the tense line of his back, this open display of affection in the lobby wasn't part of his plan.

The redhead opened her mouth, and John bent down and dutifully kissed her.

Liz would pay us a thousand dollars when I brought her

the proof. It was all she could get her hands on without John knowing about it. It wasn't much, but we weren't in a position to turn down work, and as far as jobs went, this one was simple. Once they walked out of the hotel, I'd leave through the side exit, notify Liz, and collect our fee.

The hotel doors swung open and Liz Rutger walked into the lobby.

All my nerves came to attention. Why? Why don't people ever listen to me? We had expressly agreed that she wouldn't do any sleuthing on her own. Nothing good ever came of it.

Liz saw them kissing and went white as a sheet. John let go of his mistress, his face shocked. The redhead stared at Liz, horrified.

"This isn't what it looks like," John said.

It was exactly what it looked like.

"Hi!" Liz said, shockingly loud, her voice brittle. "Who are you? Because I'm his wife!"

The redhead turned and fled into the depths of the hotel.

Liz turned to her husband. "You."

"Let's not do this here."

"Now you're concerned with appearances? Now?"

"Elizabeth." His voice vibrated with command. Uh-oh.

"You ruined us. You ruined everything."

"Listen . . ."

She opened her mouth. The words took a second to come out, as if she had to force them. "I want a divorce."

I've been working for the family business since I was seventeen, and I saw the precise moment adrenaline hit John's system. Some guys get red-faced and start screaming. Some might freeze—those are your fear biters. Push too far and they will go crazy. John Rutger went flat. All emotions drained from his face. His eyes opened wide, and behind them a hard, calculating mind evaluated the situation with icy precision.

"Okay," John said quietly. "Let's talk about this. It's more than us. It's also the kids. Come, I'll take you home." He reached for her arm.

"Don't touch me," she hissed.

"Liz," he said, his voice perfectly reasonable, his eyes focused and predatory, like the hard stare of a sniper sighting his target. "This isn't a conversation for the hotel lobby. Don't make a scene. We're better than that. I'll drive."

There was no way I could let Liz get into his car. His eyes told me that if I let him gain control of her, I would never see her again.

I moved fast and put myself between them.

"Nevada?" Liz blinked, thrown off track.

"Walk away," I told her.

"Who is this?" John focused on me.

That's right, look at me, don't look at her. I'm a bigger threat. I body-blocked Liz, keeping myself between them.

"Liz, go to your car. Don't drive home. Go to a family member's house. Now."

Muscles on John's jaw bulged as he locked his teeth.

"What?" Liz stared at me.

"You hired her to spy on me." John shrugged his shoulders and turned his neck like a fighter loosening himself for a fight. "You brought her into our private life."

"Now!" I barked.

Liz turned and fled.

I raised my hands in the air and backed away toward the exit, making sure the camera in the hotel lobby had me in plain view. Behind me the door hissed as Liz made a break for it.

"It's over, Mr. Rutger. I'm not a threat."

"You nosy bitch. You and that harpy are in it together."

At the desk the concierge frantically mashed buttons on a phone.

If I'd been on my own, I would have turned and run. Some people stand their ground no matter what. In my line of work, a stint at the hospital, coupled with a bill you can't pay because you're not working, cures that notion really fast. Given a chance, I'd run like a rabbit, but I had to buy Liz time to get to her car.

John raised his arms, bent at the elbow, palms up, fingers apart, as if he was holding two invisible softballs in his hands. The mage pose. Oh shit.

"Mr. Rutger, don't do this. Adultery isn't illegal. You haven't committed any crimes yet. Please don't do this."

His eyes stared at me, cold and hard.

"You can still walk away from this."

"You thought you could humiliate me. You thought you'd embarrass me." His face darkened as ghostly magic shadows slid across his skin. Tiny red sparks ignited above his palms and flared. Bright crimson lightning danced, stretching to the tips of his fingers.

Where the hell was the hotel security? I couldn't take him down first—it would be an assault, and we couldn't afford to be sued—but they could.

"Let me show you what happens to people who try to humiliate me."

I dashed to the side.

Thunder pealed. The glass doors of the hotel shattered. The blast wave picked me up off the floor. I saw the chair from the lounge fly at me and I threw my hands up, curling in midair. The wall smashed into my right shoulder. The chair hit my side and face. Ow.

I crashed down next to the shards of a ceramic pot that

had held a plant two seconds ago, then I scrambled to my feet.

The red sparks ignited again. He was getting ready for Round Two.

They say a hundred-and-thirty-pound woman has no chance against an athletic two-hundred-pound man. That's a lie. You just have to make a decision to hurt him and then do it.

I grabbed a heavy potsherd and hurled it at him. It crashed against his chest, knocking him off balance. I ran to him, yanking a Taser from my pocket. He swung at me. It was hard and fast, and it caught me right in the stomach. Tears welled in my eyes. I lunged forward and jammed the Taser against his neck.

The shock surged through him. His eyes bulged.

Please let him go down. Please.

His mouth gaped open. John went rigid and crashed like a log.

I knelt on his neck, pulled a plastic tie from my pocket, and wrestled his hands together, tying them up.

John growled.

I sat next to him on the floor. My face hurt.

Two men burst from the side doors and ran to us. Their jackets said security. *Well, now they show up. Thank God for the cavalry.*

In the distance police sirens blared.

Sgt. Munoz, a stocky man twice my age, peered at the security footage. He'd watched it twice already.

"I couldn't let him put her into the car," I said from my spot in the chair. My shoulder hurt and the handcuffs on my hands kept me from rubbing it. Being in close proximity to cops filled me with anxiety. I wanted to fidget, but fidgeting would make me look nervous.

"You were right," Munoz said and tapped the screen, pausing on John Rutger reaching for his wife. "That right there is your dead giveaway. The man's caught with his pants down and he doesn't say, 'Sorry, I fucked up.' He doesn't beg for forgiveness or get angry. He goes cold and tries to get his wife out of the picture."

"I didn't provoke him. I didn't put my hands on him either, until he tried to kill me."

"I see that." He turned to me. "That's a C2 Taser you've got there. You do know range on those things is fifteen feet?"

"I didn't want to take chances. His magic looked electrical to me, and I thought he might block the current."

Munoz shook his head. "No, he was enerkinetic. Straight magic energy, and trained to use it, courtesy of the U.S. Army. This guy is a vet."

"Ah." That explained why Rutger went flat. Dealing with adrenaline was nothing new to him. The fact that he was an enerkinetic made sense too. Pyrokinetics manipulated fire, aquakinetics manipulated water, and enerkinetics manipulated raw magical energy. Nobody was quite sure what the nature of that energy was, but it was a relatively common magic. How in the world did Bern miss all this in the background check? When I got home, my cousin and I would have to have words.

A uniformed cop stuck his head in the door and handed my license back to Munoz. "She checks out."

Munoz unlocked my cuffs, took them off, and handed me my purse and camera. My cell and my wallet followed. "We have your statement, and we took your memory card. You'll get it back later. Go home, put some ice on that neck."

I grinned at him. "Are you going to tell me not to leave town, Sarge?"

Munoz gave me a "yet another smart-ass" look. "No. You went up against a military-grade mage for a grand. If you need the money that bad, you probably can't afford the gas."

Three minutes later I climbed into my five-year-old Mazda minivan. The paperwork described the Mazda's color as "gold." Everyone else said it was "kind of champagne" or "sort of beige." Coupled with unmistakable mom car lines, the minivan made for a perfect surveillance vehicle. Nobody paid it any mind. I once followed a guy for two hours in it on a nearly deserted highway, and when the insurance company later showed him the footage demonstrating that his knee worked just fine as he shifted gears in his El Camino, he was terribly surprised.

I turned the mirror. A big red welt that would mature into one hell of a purple bruise blossomed on my neck and the top of my right shoulder, like someone took a handful of blueberries and rubbed it all over me. An equally bright red stain marked my jaw on the left side. I sighed, readjusted the mirror, and headed home.

Some easy job this turned out to be. At least I didn't have to go to the hospital. I grimaced. The welt decided it didn't like me grimacing. Ow.

The Baylor Investigative Agency started as a family business. We still were a family business. Technically we were owned by someone else now, but they mostly left us alone to run our affairs as we saw fit. We had only three rules. Rule #1: we stayed bought. Once a client hired us, we were loyal to the client. Rule #2: we didn't break the law. It was a good rule. It kept us out of jail and safe from litigation. And Rule #3, the most important one of all: at the end of the day we still had to be able to look our reflections in the eye. I filed today under Rule #3 day. Maybe I was crazy and John Rutger would've taken his wife home and begged her forgiveness on bended knee. But at the end of the day, I had no regrets, and I didn't have to worry about whether I did the right thing and whether Liz's two children would ever see their mother again.

Their father was a different story, but he was no longer my problem. He made that mess all on his own.

I cleared the evening traffic on I-290, heading northwest, and turned south. A few minutes later I pulled up in front of our warehouse. Bern's beat-up black Civic sat in the parking lot, next to Mom's blue Honda Element. Oh good. Everyone was home.

I parked, went to the door, and punched the code into the security system. The door clicked open, then I let myself in and paused for a second to hear the reassuring clang of the lock sliding home behind me.

When you entered the warehouse from this door, it looked just like an office. We built walls, installed some glass panels, and laid down high-traffic beige carpet. That gave us three office rooms on the left side and a break room and large conference room on the right. The drop ceiling completed the illusion.

I stepped into my office, put the purse and the camera on the desk, and sat in my chair. I really should do a write-up, but I didn't feel like it. I'd do it later.

The office was soundproof. Around me everything was quiet. A familiar, faint scent of grapefruit oil in the oil warmer floated to me. The oils were my favorite little luxury. I inhaled the fragrance. I was home.

I survived. Had I hit my head on the wall when Rutger had thrown me, I could've died today. Right now I could be dead instead of sitting here in my office, twenty feet from my home. My mom could be in the morgue, identifying me on a slab. My heart pounded in my chest. Nausea crept up, squeezing my throat. I leaned forward and concentrated on breathing. Deep, calm breaths. I just had to let myself work through it.

In and out. In and out.

Slowly the anxiety receded.

In and out.

Okay.

I got up, crossed the office to the break room, opened the door in the back, and stepped into the warehouse. A luxuriously wide hallway stretched left and right, its sealed concrete floor reflecting the light softly. Above me thirty-foot ceilings soared. After we had to sell the house and move into the warehouse, Mom and Dad considered making the inside look just like a real house. Instead we ended up building one large wall separating this section of the warehouse—our living space—from Grandma's garage so we didn't have to heat or air-condition the entire twenty-two thousand square feet of the warehouse. The rest of the walls had occurred organically, which was a gentle euphemism for We put them up as needed with whatever material was handy.

If Mom saw me, I wouldn't get away without a thorough medical exam. All I wanted to do was take a shower and eat some food. This time of the day she was usually with Grandma, helping her work. If I was really quiet, I could just sneak into my room. I padded down the hallway. *Think sneaky thoughts . . . Be invisible . . .* Hopefully, nothing attention-attracting was going on.

"I'll kill you!" a familiar high voice howled from the right.

Damn it. Arabella, of course. My youngest sister was in rare form, judging by the pitch.

"That's real mature!" And that was Catalina, the seventeen-year-old. Two years older than Arabella and eight years younger than me.

I had to break this up before Mom came over to investigate. I sped down the hallway toward the media room.

"At least I'm not a dumb ho who has no friends!"

"At least I'm not fat!"

"At least I am not ugly!"

Neither of them was fat, ugly, or promiscuous. They both were complete drama queens, and if I didn't break this party up fast, Mom would be on us in seconds.

"I hate you!"

I walked into the media room. Catalina, thin and dark-haired, stood on the right, her arms crossed over her chest. On the left Bern very carefully restrained blond Arabella by holding her by her waist above the floor. Arabella was really strong, but Bern had wrestled through high school and went to a judo club twice a week. Now nineteen and still growing, he stood an inch over six feet tall and weighed about two hundred pounds, most of it powerful, supple muscle. Holding a hundred-pound Arabella wasn't a problem.

"Let me go!" Arabella snarled.

"Think about what you're doing," Bern said, his deep voice patient. "We agreed—no violence."

"What is it this time?" I asked.

Catalina stabbed her finger in Arabella's direction. "She never put the cap on my liquid foundation. Now it's dried out!"

Figured. They never fought about anything important. They never stole from each other, they never tried to sabotage each other's relationships, and if anyone dared to look at one of them the wrong way, the other one would be the first to charge to her sister's defense. But if one of them took the other's hairbrush and didn't clean it, it was World War III.

"That's not true . . ." Arabella froze. "Neva, what happened to your face?"

Everything stopped. Then everyone said something at once, really loud.

"Shush! Calm down; it's cosmetic. I just need a shower. Also, stop fighting. If you don't, Mom will come here and I don't want her to—"

"To what?" Mom walked through the door, limping a little. Her leg was bothering her again. Of average height, she used to be lean and muscular, but the injury had grounded her. She was softer now, with a rounder face. She had dark eyes like me, but her hair was chestnut brown.

Grandma Frida followed, about my height, thin, with a halo of platinum curls stained with machine grease. The familiar, comforting smell of engine oil, rubber, and gunpowder spread through the room. Grandma Frida saw me and her blue eyes got really big. Oh no.

"Penelope, why is the baby hurt?"

The best defense is vigorous offense. "I'm not a baby. I'm twenty-five years old." I was Grandma's first grandchild. If she lived until I turned fifty, with grandchildren of my own, I'd still be "the baby."

"How did this happen?" Mom asked.

Damn it. "Magic blast wave, wall, and a chair."

"Blast wave?" Bern asked.

"The Rutger case."

"I thought he was a dud."

I shook my head. "Enerkinetic magic. He was a vet."

Bern's face fell. He frowned and marched out of the room.

"Arabella, get the first-aid kit," Mom said. "Nevada, lie down. You may have a concussion."

Arabella took off running.

"It's not that bad! I don't have a concussion."

My mother turned and looked at me. I knew that look. That was the Sgt. Baylor look. There was no escape.

"Did paramedics look at you at the scene?"

"Yes."

"What did they say?"

There was no point in lying. "They said I should go to the hospital just in case."

My mother pinned me down with her stare. "Did you?"

"No."

"Lie down."

I sighed and surrendered to my fate.

The next morning I sat in the media room, eating the crepes and sausages Mom made for me. My neck still hurt. My side hurt worse.

Mom sat at the other end of the sectional, sipping her coffee and working on Arabella's hair. Apparently the latest fashion among high schoolers involved elaborate braids, and Arabella had somehow cajoled Mom into helping her.

On the left side of the screen, a female news anchor with impossibly perfect hair profiled the recent arson at First National, while the right side of the screen showed a tornado of fire engulfing the building. The orange flames billowed out the windows.

"It's awful," Mom said.

"Did anybody die?" I asked.

"A security guard. His wife and their two children came by to drop off his dinner and were also burned, but they survived. Apparently Adam Pierce was involved."

Everyone in Houston knew who Adam Pierce was. Magic users were segregated into five ranks: Minor, Average, Notable, Significant, and Prime. Born with a rare pyrokinetic talent, Pierce had Stainless Steel classification. A pyrokinetic was considered Average if he could melt a cubic foot of ice under a minute. In the same amount of time, Adam Pierce could conjure a fire that would melt a cubic foot of stainless steel. That made Pierce a Prime, the highest rank of magic user. Everybody wanted him—the military, Home Defense, and the private sector.

A wealthy, established family, the Pierces owned Firebug, Inc., the leading provider of industrial forging products. Adam, handsome and magically spectacular, was the pride and joy of House Pierce. He'd grown up wrapped in tender luxury, had gone to all the right schools, had worn all the right clothes, and his future had had golden sparkles all over it. He'd been a rising star and the most eligible bachelor. Then, at the ripe age of twenty-two, he'd given them all the finger, declared himself a radical, and gone off to start a motorcycle gang.

Since then Pierce had been popping up in the news for one thing or another, usually involving cops, crime, and antiestablishment declarations. The media loved him, because his name brought ratings.

As if on cue, Pierce's portrait filled the right side of the screen. He wore his trademark black jeans and unzipped black leather jacket over bare, muscled chest. A Celtic knot-work tattoo covered his left pectoral, and a snarling panther with horns decorated the right side of his six-pack. Longish brown hair spilled over his beautiful face, highlighting the world's best cheekbones and a perfect jaw with just the right amount of stubble to add some scruff. If you cleaned him up, he would look almost angelic. As is, he was a tarnished poseur angel, his wings artfully singed with the perfect camera shot in mind.

I'd seen my share of real biker gangsters. Not the weekend bikers, who were doctors and lawyers in real life, but the real deal, the ones who lived on the road. They were hard, not too well kept, and their eyes were made of lead. Pierce was more like the leading man playing a badass in an action movie. Lucky for him, he could make his own background of billowing flames.

"Hot!" Arabella said.

"Stop it," Mom told her.

Grandma Frida walked into the room. "Ooh, here is my boy."

"Mother," Mom growled.

"What? I can't help it. It's the devil eyes."

Pierce did have devil eyes. Deep and dark, the rich brown of coffee grinds, they were unpredictable and full of crazy. He was very nice to look at, but all of the images of him looked staged. He always seemed to know where the camera was. And if I ever saw him in person, I'd run the other way like my back was on fire. If I hesitated, it would be.

"He killed a man," Mom said.

"He was framed," Grandma Frida said.

"You don't even know the story," Mom said.

Grandma shrugged. "Framed. A man that pretty can't be a murderer."

Mother stared at her.

"Penelope, I'm seventy-two years old. You let me enjoy my fantasy."

"Go Grandma." Arabella pumped her fist in the air.

"If you insist on being Grandma's little stooge, she can do your hair," Mom said.

"We will return to the investigation on the arson after the break," the news anchor announced. *"Also, iconic downtown park infested with rats."*

The image of Bridge Park popped on the screen, its life-size bronze statue of a cowboy on a galloping horse front and center.

"Should Harris County officials resort to drastic measures? More after the break."

Bern walked into the room. "Hey, Nevada, can I borrow you for a moment?"

I got up and followed him out. Without saying a word, we went down the hallway and into the kitchen. It was the closest place where Mom and Grandma wouldn't overhear us.

"What's up?"

Bern ran his hand through his short, light brown hair and held out a folder. I opened it and scanned it. John Rutger's lineage, biography, and background check. A line stood out, highlighted in yellow: Honorable Discharge, Sealed.

I raised my finger. "Aha!"

"Aha," Bern confirmed.

Usually employers liked hiring ex-servicemen. They were punctual, disciplined, polite, and capable of making quick decisions when needed. But combat mages sent the typical HR manager running in the opposite direction. Nobody wanted a guy stressing out in their office when he had the ability to summon a host of bloodsucking leeches. To circumvent this issue, the Department of Defense started sealing records of some combat-grade personnel. A sealed record didn't always mean combat-grade magic, but it would've given me a nice heads-up. I would've approached Rutger's situation from an entirely different angle.

"I screwed up." Bern leaned against the counter. His grey eyes were full of remorse. "I had a modern history exam. It's not my strongest class, and I needed at least a B to keep the scholarship, so I had to cram. I gave it to Leon. He ran the lineage and the background check, but forgot to log in to the DOD database."

"It's okay," I told him. Leon was fifteen. Getting him to sit still for longer than thirty seconds was like trying to herd cats through a shower.

Bern rubbed the bridge of his nose. "No. It's not okay. You asked me to do it. I should've done it. You got hurt. It won't happen again."

"Don't sweat it," I told him. "I've missed stuff before. It happens. Just make it a point from now on to check DOD. Did you get a B?"

He nodded. "It's kind of interesting, actually. Do you know that story about Mrs. O'Leary's cow?"

I used to really like history. I even thought of getting a minor in it, but real life got in the way. "Didn't she knock over a lamp in the barn and start the Great Chicago Fire sometime in the 1860s?"

"In October of 1871," Bern said. "My professor doesn't think the cow did it. He thinks it was a mage."

"In 1871? The Osiris Serum had barely been discovered."

"It's a really interesting theory." Bern shrugged. "You should talk to him sometime. He is a pretty cool guy."

I smiled. It had taken me four years, including every summer, to limp my way to a criminal justice degree, because I'd had to work. Bern got an academic scholarship because he was smarter than all of us combined, and now he was doing well. He even liked at least one of his classes outside his major.

"There is more," Bern said. "Montgomery wants to see us."

My stomach did a pirouette inside me. House Montgomery owned us. When savings and the money from the sale of our home hadn't been enough to cover Dad's medical bills, we'd sold the firm to Montgomery. Technically, it was mortgaged. We had a thirty-year repayment term, and every month we squeaked by with the minimum payment. The terms of our mortgage practically made us a subsidiary of Montgomery International Investigations. Montgomery had taken very little interest in us up to this point. We were too small to be of any use to them, and they had no reason to bother us as long as the check had cleared, and our checks always cleared. I made sure of that.

"They said ASAP," Bern said.

"Did it sound routine?"

"No."

Damn it. "Don't tell Mom or Grandma."

He nodded. "They'll just stress."

"Yes. I'll call you as soon as I find out what this is about. Hopefully we just forgot to file some form or something."

I was almost to the door when he called, "Nevada? John Rutger's wife wired the money. A thousand dollars, as agreed."

"Good," I said and escaped. I needed to brush my hair, make myself presentable, and hightail it across town to the glass towers.

Really, how bad could it be?

 **Chapter 2**

$\mathcal{T}$he asymmetrical glass tower of Montgomery International Investigations rose above the neighboring office buildings like a shark fin of blue glass. Twenty-five stories tall, it gleamed with hundreds of tinted cobalt windows. It was meant to impress and fill you with awe at House Montgomery's magnificence. I tried to scrounge up some awe but got only anxiety instead.

I walked through the door to the gleaming elevator, passing through a metal detector. The message from Montgomery said seventeenth floor, so I entered the elevator when the doors whooshed open, pushed the button with 17 on it, and waited as the car shot upward with a whisper.

What the heck could they possibly want?

The doors opened, revealing a wide space punctuated by a receptionist's desk made of polished stainless steel tubes. At least twenty-five feet separated the glossy dark blue floor and the white ceiling. I stepped out before the elevator closed. The walls were pure white, but the enormous wall of cobalt glass windows behind the receptionist turned the daylight pale blue, as if we were under water. It all felt ultramodern, pristine, and slightly soulless. Even the snow-white orchids on the receptionist's desk did nothing to add any warmth to the space. MII might as well have wallpapered the place with money and been done with it.

The receptionist looked up at me. Her face was flawless, pale brown, with big blue eyes and artfully contoured pale pink lips. Her tomato red hair was wrapped in an impeccable French twist. I could see each one of her long eyelashes, and not one had as much as a hint of a clump. She wore a white dress that really wanted to be a sleeve.

The receptionist blinked at my bruised face. "May I help you?"

"I have an appointment with Augustine Montgomery. My name is Nevada Baylor." I smiled.

The receptionist rose. "Follow me."

I followed. She was probably the same height as me barefoot, but her heels added about six inches. She clicked her way around the curving wall.

"How long does it take?" I asked.

"I'm sorry?"

"How long does it take you to get dressed for work in the morning?"

"Two and a half hours," she said.

"Do they pay you overtime for that?"

She stopped before a wall of frosted glass. The white feathers of frost moved and slid across the surface in hypnotic pattern. Here and there a fine thread of pure gold shone and melted. Wow.

A section of the wall slid aside. The receptionist looked at me. I stepped through the opening into a vast office. We must've been in a corner of the fin, because the wall to the left and straight ahead consisted of blue glass. A white, ultramodern desk grew seamlessly out of the floor. Behind the desk sat a man in a suit. His head was lowered as he read something on a small tablet, and all I could see was a thick head of dark blond hair styled into a short and no doubt expensive haircut.

I approached and stood by a white chair in front of the desk. Good suit, in that color between grey and true black people sometimes call gunmetal.

The man looked up at me. Sometimes people with talent in illusion minimized their physical flaws with their magic. Judging by his face, Augustine Montgomery was a Prime. His features were perfect, in the way Greek statues were perfect, the lines of his face masculine and crisp but never brutish. Clean-shaven, with a strong nose and a firm mouth, he had the type of beauty that made you stare. His skin nearly glowed, and his green eyes stabbed at you with sharp intelligence from behind nearly invisible eyeglasses. He probably had to have protective detail when he left the building to fend off all the sculptors who wanted to immortalize him in marble.

The glasses were a masterful touch. Without them, he'd be a god on a cloud, but the hair-thin frames let him keep one foot on the ground with us mere mortals.

"Mr. Montgomery," I said. "My name is Nevada Baylor. You wanted to see me?"

Montgomery valiantly ignored the purple tint of bruises on my face. "Sit down, please." He pointed to the chair.

I sat.

"I have an assignment for you."

In the five years they'd owned us, they had never given us an assignment. Please let it be something minor . . .

"We'd like you to apprehend this man." He slid a photograph across the desk. I leaned forward.

Adam Pierce looked back at me with his crazy eyes.

"Is this a joke?"

"No."

I stared at Montgomery.

"In light of recent events, the Pierce family is concerned about Adam's welfare. They would like us to bring him in. Uninjured. Since you are our subsidiary, we feel you're perfectly suited to this task. Your portion of the fee will amount to fifty thousand dollars."

I couldn't believe it. "We're a tiny family firm. Look at our records. We aren't bounty hunters. We do small-time insurance fraud investigations and cheating spouse cases."

"It's time to expand your repertoire. You're showing a ninety percent success rate with your cases. You have our complete confidence."

We showed a 90 percent success rate because I didn't take a case unless I knew we could handle it. "He's a Prime pyrokinetic. We don't have the manpower."

Montgomery frowned slightly, as if bothered. "I'm showing one full-time and five part-time employees. Call your people in and concentrate on it."

"Have you checked the DOBs on those part-time employees? Let me save you the trouble: three of them are under the age of sixteen, and one is barely nineteen. They are my sisters and cousins. You're asking me to go after Adam Pierce with children."

Montgomery clicked the keys on his keyboard. "It says here your mother is a decorated army veteran."

"My mother was critically injured in 1995 during operations in Bosnia. She was captured and put in a hole in the ground for two months with two other soldiers. She was presumed dead and rescued by pure chance, but she suffered permanent damage to her left leg. Her top speed is five miles per hour."

Montgomery leaned back.

"Her magic talent is in her hand-to-eye coordination," I continued. "She can shoot people in the head from very far away, which will do absolutely nothing, since you want Pierce alive. And my own magic . . ."

Montgomery focused on me. "Your magic?"

Crap. Their records said I was a dud. ". . . is nonexistent. This is suicide. You have twenty times the resources and manpower we do. Why are you doing this to us? Do you think we have any chance at all?"

"Yes."

My magic buzzed. He just lied. The realization hit me like a load of bricks dumped on my head.

"That's it, isn't it? You know bringing Pierce in will be expensive and difficult. You'll lose people, trained, skilled personnel in whom you've invested time and money, and in the end it will cost more than whatever the family is paying you. But you probably can't turn House Pierce down, so you're going to give this to us, and when it ends in disaster, you can show them our records. You can tell the Pierces that you assigned it to your best outfit with six employees and a ninety percent success rate. You've done all you can. You expect us to fail and possibly die to preserve your bottom line and save face."

"There is no need to be dramatic."

"I won't do it." I couldn't. It was impossible.

Montgomery clicked a couple of keys and turned his computer monitor toward me. A document with a section highlighted in yellow filled the screen.

"This is your contract. The highlighted section states that turning down an assignment from MII constitutes a breach of contract, with the payment due in full."

I clenched my teeth.

"Can you pay the balance of the loan in full?"

I wished I could reach across the table and strangle him.

"Ms. Baylor." He spoke slowly, as if I were hard of hearing. "Can you pay the balance in full?"

I unlocked my jaws. "No."

Montgomery spread his arms. "Let me be perfectly clear: you do this or we will take your business."

"You're not giving me a choice."

"Of course you have a choice. You can take the assignment or vacate your premises."

We'd lose everything. The warehouse was owned by the business. The cars were owned by the business. We'd be homeless. "We've always been on time with payments. We never caused you any trouble." I pulled my wallet out of my purse, slid out the picture of my family, and put it on the desk. It was taken a couple of months ago, and all of us barely crowded into the shot. "I'm all they have. Our father is dead, our mother is disabled. If something happens to me, they have no means of support."

He glanced at it. A shadow of something crossed his face, then it went blank again. "I require an answer, Ms. Baylor."

Maybe I could just half-ass it. It went against the grain, but I had to do what I could to survive. "What if the cops catch him first?"

"Your business is forfeit. You have to bring him in, alive and before the authorities get their hands on him."

Damn it. "What happens if I die?"

Augustine raised his hand, moving the text up on

his screen. "You're the licensed investigator in the firm. When we purchased the firm, we invested in your ability to earn. Without you, we have no interest in your enterprise. Under the terms of your contract, your assets will be written off as a loss. We'll confiscate any cash and liquid assets, those would be stocks, money market instruments, and so on that the business holds, and write off the loan."

"What about the agency's name?"

He shrugged. "I'm sure we can come to an agreement."

I was carrying a million dollars in personal insurance. I paid for it out of my own paycheck, because I was paranoid that if something happened to me, the family would end up destitute. Short term, I was worth more dead than alive. With a million dollars, Bern could stay in school, nobody would be evicted, and if they were, there was enough money to keep the family afloat. Mom could buy out the name and hire an investigator.

"Yes or no?" Augustine asked.

On one end of the seesaw my family, on the other, possibly my life.

"Yes," I said. "You're a terrible person."

"I'll just have to live with myself."

"Yes, you will. Write an addendum to the contract that in the event of my death, my family can buy out the agency's name for a dollar, and I will go after Pierce."

"A dollar?"

"If I die, my family gets the firm back. Take it or leave it."

"Very well." Montgomery's fingers flew over the keyboard. A piece of paper slid out of the printer. I read it, signed on the line, and watched him write his name in an elegant cursive.

Montgomery tapped his tablet. "I've emailed Pierce's background file to you. Once again: you must apprehend Adam Pierce before the police take him into custody or your loan is forfeit."

I got up and walked, leaving the picture of the family on his desk. He should have to look at it. My hands shook. I wanted to turn around, march back, and punch him.

I kept walking until I was out of the building. Outside the wind fanned me, pulling at my clothes. I pulled my cell phone out of my pocket and dialed Bern.

"Drop whatever you're doing. I need everything on Adam Pierce."

"We're going after Pierce? Are you serious?"

"Look in our inbox."

"Holy shit."

"I need his lineage, his full background, his criminal record, who he went to school with—everything. Every scrap of information you can find. The more we know the better."

"Do you want me to tell Aunt Pen?"

Oh, Mom would just love this development. "No. I'll do it. Call Mateus for me."

When I said that all of our part-time employees were children, I didn't lie. But occasionally, when we needed muscle, we hired free agents on a one-job basis. I had a feeling none of them would touch any job involving Pierce with a ten-foot pole, but it was worth a try.

"How much should I offer?" Bern said into my ear.

"Ten grand." It was about three times what we normally offered. It was also the entirety of our rainy day fund. We could take a loan if we had to.

"We can't pay that much."

"We can if we apprehend Pierce. Tell him payment on delivery."

The phone clicked as Bern put me on hold. I walked to my car.

Where the hell would I even start?

Another click. "He laughed."

In his place I'd laugh too. "Try the Cowboy."

Click. Click. "No. And that's a quote."

"Asli? Bump it up to fifteen." Asli was expensive as hell, but she was worth every penny, and I haven't known her to back down.

I reached my Mazda and leaned against the grill.

"She says she's busy with something else."

Argh. These were my top three. Why did I have this vision of all of our freelancers running away from us like a pack of scared rabbits? "Okay. Start running the background on Pierce, please."

I hung up. The panic that first welled inside me in Augustine's office crested and drowned me. I let it pull me under.

If we failed, MII would call in the loan and take everything. We would literally walk out of our home with nothing but a black plastic bag filled with clothes and whatever toiletries each of us could carry. Grandma would have no place to run her business. I would have no business at all. I could start over, but it would take time and money. I built on the name and foundation that my parents had created. Personal referrals accounted for 90 percent of our jobs. We would be on the street, all seven of us. We would lose our health insurance. We would still have our other debts. Our savings might put a roof over our heads and food in our mouths for a month or two, but then what?

Bern would drop out. There was no way he wouldn't.

He would drop out and take any job he could get, whatever would buy us another week in a cheap motel or another meal. I saw his future, and it was going up in flames.

And my sisters . . . We'd just gotten back to normal after the chaos of dad's illness. We'd just stabilized. The therapy worked, everyone was back on track, and the kids finally had some routine. If this happened . . . It felt like someone had taken an ice-cold knife and stabbed it into my stomach to gut me.

No. This wouldn't be happening. They would not do this to my family. They would not take everything I'd worked so hard to build. No. Just no.

I breathed in and out, exhaling anger.

Think. It's a skiptrace. I had done skiptraces. This wasn't my first rodeo.

Private investigators tended to specialize. Some developed financial profiles and dealt with asset searches. Some took surveillance cases. Others performed background checks. We did a little bit of everything, and I had done my fair share of skiptracing. This was just another skiptrace. Except if I found him, he would sear the flesh off my bones. And the family might still end up on the street, when MII took our house. At least they would get the business name back.

This probably wasn't the most productive line of thinking.

This mess, as my father used to say, was way above my pay grade. I wasn't even sure where to start. I could go to First National and look at the burned-out wreck. I had handled exactly four arson cases before, all in connection with insurance, and I knew the scene really wouldn't tell me anything. I didn't need to determine if Pierce committed the arson. I just had to find him.

Pierce had killed a cop and hurt his family. Right now every cop in the Houston metro area was champing at the bit, hoping to put a bullet in Pierce's handsome head. I bet the cops had a file on Pierce that was a mile thick. That file would be an awesome place to start, except they wouldn't let me look at it. First, I was a civilian, and second, I was in competition with the cops. In the crime novels, a PI is either an ex-cop or has some cop buddies who owed him a favor and who happily provided him with the department's files, while carrying on about how it could cost them their job. I had no cop buddies. I tried to avoid them as much as possible. My dad had been friendly with a couple of people, but both of them worked in the Financial Crime Unit, not in Homicide. Besides, right now nobody except Montgomery, me, and Bern knew that I was looking for Pierce. If I put myself on the cop radar, they would start paying attention to what I was doing, which would make finding Pierce harder.

Around me downtown Houston hummed with life. The skyscrapers, some glass and steel, some towering monoliths of stone, rose around me. The cobalt building of MII loomed to the left, looking even more like a shark fin. I could almost imagine the pavement cracking, breaking open in huge slabs, and a colossal shark head bristling with razor-sharp glass teeth emerging to swallow me whole. In front of me, traffic inched up the busy street. A red Maserati convertible pulled out of traffic and drove down the Metrorail tracks toward the hospital. The driver, a young guy in a black T-shirt, was putting on cologne. Dumbass.

Above him a large flat-screen billboard mounted on the wall of a stone tower flashed with advertisements. A news segment came on, and an image of a woman in a business suit filled the screen. She was in her late thirties, athletic, attractive, with medium brown skin and a dark wealth of curly hair, currently pulled back from her face into a knot. Everyone in Houston knew her name. Lenora Jordan, Harris County District Attorney. When I was fourteen years old, she walked into the street to face George Kolter. She was fresh out of law school and he was a seasoned fulgurkinetic Prime. He could shoot lightning from fifty feet away, he stood accused of child molestation, and he had decided at the last moment that he wasn't going to trial. Lenora Jordan walked down the courthouse steps, like a gunfighter from the Old West, summoned chains from thin air, and bound George Kolter to the pavement. The whole thing had been recorded and played by every news outlet. It was epic. Every girl in my grade wanted to be Lenora when she grew up. She was incorruptible, powerful, and smart, she had no fear, and she didn't take shit from anyone. I had no doubt that if Pierce was apprehended and received his day in court, she would destroy him while making sure that his constitutional rights were perfectly preserved.

I wasn't Lenora Jordan, no matter how much I wanted to be. If I did run into Pierce by some chance, I couldn't dramatically bind him. I couldn't make him do anything against his will either. I would have to somehow convince him that it was in his best interests to come with me.

I pulled my phone out, downloaded the background file on Pierce, and opened it. Most people accumulated identifiers: DOB, SSN, last known address, driver's license number, place of employment, all the things that tied them down and made them relatively easy to track. About 75 percent of the time, their idea of being off the grid meant hiding out at their cousin's house. And 90 percent of the time, their mother, no matter what she claimed, could get hold of them within minutes.

Pierce's file provided me with a date of birth, place of birth, Social Security number, parents' names and address, and his education. Elementary school, middle school, high school, Stanford University, bachelor of arcane science in materials science and engineering, minor in philosophy, 3.9 GPA. Applied and was accepted into a graduate program for a master's of materials science and engineering, dropped out two months into it. Current residence: unknown. Current job: none. Awesome.

Arrest record. Aha. Adam Pierce had been arrested six times in the past sixteen months. Busy boy. Let's see, public intoxication, vandalism, resisting arrest—surprise-surprise, loitering . . . loitering? That must've been one pissed-off cop.

Let's see, Facebook. I scrolled through half a dozen Adam Pierces. Nothing smelled genuine. That's okay, he was probably a short burst social network kind of guy. I flicked to the Twitter app and searched for Adam Pierce. His Twitter account had been inactive for the last forty-eight hours. I followed him and clicked through his photos. Adam on a bike. Adam with his shirt off. Adam and a bunch of pretty-looking bikers in front of a bike shop. The photo showed a section of the sign: *-aves Custom Cycles*. I saved the photo on my phone.

I opened a writing app and began typing what I knew about Pierce.

Vain. Terminal fear of T-shirts or any other garment that would cover his pectorals.

Deadly. Doesn't hesitate to kill. Holding him at gun-point would result in me being barbecued. Whee.

Likes burning things. Now here's an understatement. Good information to have, but not useful for finding him.

Antigovernment. Neither here nor there.

Hmm. So far my best plan would be to build a mountain of gasoline cans and explosives, stick a Property of US Government sign on it, and throw a T-shirt over Pierce's head when he showed up to explode it. Yes, this would totally work. If only.

Likes to be arrested. It probably made him feel tough. Adam Pierce, the rebel. He didn't like jail though. His first arrest happened to be on Sunday, and he spent the night in jail. The five subsequent arrests showed bail posted within hours after booking.

Famous. That was both in my favor and not. Being famous would make it harder to hide, but if he was recognized, the 911 boards would light up like fireworks and cops would be on him faster than I could blink. But being famous also would mean many false sightings. Especially if the cops offered a reward. People would see him here, there, and everywhere.

Handsome. With devil eye bonus.

Rich.

Rich. Adam Pierce was rolling in money. This morning when I saw him on TV he was wearing a designer jacket and posing against a bike that looked like something out of a science fiction movie and probably cost a lot more than my car. He was a spoiled rich boy, and spoiled rich boys didn't deal well with lack of money. They might slum for a little while, but they liked their toys and their creature comforts. The key concept of running any sort of enterprise, criminal or civil, was work. Given Adam Pierce's track record, work was something he detested.

Someone had posted those bails for him. Where was his money coming from?

I scrolled through the file. Pierce had an incentive trust fund. He could draw money only while he was in college pursuing a master's degree or after obtaining it. According to the file, the family had cut him off cold turkey. A note marked ASM—probably Augustine Something Montgomery—read, *Confirmed with the family. Stressed importance of financial incentive as means of bringing him in.*

I called Bern. "Hey, have you pulled Pierce's record?"

"Does ice float?" Bern's voice had a measured cadence to it, which usually meant he was doing about six other things on the computer screens while talking.

"Who posted his bail?"

"One of his college buddies. Cornelius Maddox Harrison."

Quite a name. Someone's parents had ambitions.

"I'm emailing his home address now," Bern said. "You can catch him at the house. According to his tax return, he's a stay-at-home dad."

"Thanks. I'll swing by his house now."

"Wait," Bern said, his voice suddenly flat.

Uh-oh.

"Can you come by the house instead? I need to show you something."

"This doesn't sound good."

"It isn't good," Bern said.

How could it possibly get any worse?

I found Bern in the Hut of Evil, otherwise known as our computer room. Soundproof and equipped with its own air-conditioning unit, the room occupied the space at the north of the warehouse, directly behind the offices. It was raised five feet off the floor, like a house on stilts, because Bern found it convenient to mess with the wiring underneath it. We used to joke that if the warehouse got flooded, we'd all race to the Hut of Evil to stay dry. From the outside, it looked like a separate tiny house within the larger space of the warehouse, complete with a ten-step stairway leading to it. At first we called it the House of Evil, but over the years it somehow became the Hut of Evil.

I climbed the stairs and knocked on the door.

"Come in," Bern called.

I went inside and shut the door. The air here was at least five degrees cooler. Bern sat ensconced among four different monitors on swiveling mounts. Three computer towers blinked with red, white, and green lights. Across from him, Leon's station, a smaller desk with a triple monitor, stood empty. He and the girls were in school.

Bern turned to me, his handsome face tinted with blue by the glow of the largest monitor. There was always something a little comical about seeing his big frame next to the computer screens. The keyboards and monitors seemed too small for him.

"What did you find?" I asked.

"While I was talking to you, I ran the background check on the kid implicated in the arson."

"Gavin Waller."

Bern nodded. "I pulled his lineage."

In our world, lineage was everything. The magical families owned corporations, and most major cities were divided into family territories. Some families influenced only a few city blocks, others controlled entire neighborhoods. Your last name and your family tree could open doors or get you killed. If the family became prominent enough, it was considered a house. House Montgomery. House Pierce.

"Gavin's father is Thomas Waller. His mother is Kelly Waller. Neither is magically significant." Bern paused.

I waited. Bern stored information in logical chains. When asked something, he would start at the beginning of the chain and pull it all out link by link until the relevant information finally emerged. If the house were on fire, Bern would begin by describing how he went to get the box of matches to light the candle that started it. Trying to hurry this process up wasn't only futile, it was counterproductive. Interruptions derailed Bern. He would get back on track in his methodical way, and he couldn't understand why you jumped up and down and foamed at the mouth in sheer frustration while he took his time doing it.

"Kelly Waller's maiden name was Lancey."

Mhm.

"Her father was William Lancey."

Mhm.

"Her mother was Carolina Rogan."

Mhm. Wait, what? "Rogan? As in House Rogan?"

Bern nodded. "Mad Rogan is Kelly Waller's cousin. That makes him Gavin's first cousin once removed."

My legs decided that this would be a fine time to go on strike. I landed in a chair.

The United States hadn't officially declared war in the last seventy years. Instead it got itself involved in armed conflicts, peacekeeping actions, and armed interventions, which, for all intents and purposes, were wars without having a scary label attached to them: Europe, the Middle East, and then the so-called South American Wars, which broke out when the discovery of magically potent mineral deposits in Belize destabilized the neighboring region. Mexico, already a magical powerhouse, invaded tiny Belize. Honduras, Nicaragua, and Brazil formed a coalition to oppose the invasion. Both the United States and the United Native Tribes joined the anti-Mexican co-alition, even though the territories of the Dakotas, Wyo-ming, and Montana were nowhere near the border and even though UNT usually went against the USA in just about every policy decision. Everyone paid lip service to the brave soldiers of Belize, but the true reason was clear: nobody wanted Mexico, the magical juggernaut, to be more powerful than it already was.

The war was terrible. In the end Mexico relinquished its hold on Belize, but the ripples of that invasion spread through South America. Armed conflicts flared and died down across half a dozen nations. Mad Rogan made his name in those conflicts. He was off the charts even for the Primes. Nobody knew exactly what he was capable of, but everyone knew the name. Mad Rogan. The Butcher of Merida. *Huracan.*

The chances of us succeeding in apprehending Adam Pierce were already close to zero. If Mad Rogan decided to take an interest, it would knock us right into the negative.

"What do we know about Mad Rogan?"

Bern pushed a key on his keyboard. A grainy video filled the monitor. I remembered watching it once, a long time ago, while still in high school. I had gotten bored with it back then, because nothing really happened in the first two minutes, and hadn't finished.

A young man with longish dark hair and pale eyes, his face smudged by static, standing in the middle of an empty four-lane road, silhouetted against an overcast sky, padded with gray clouds.

". . . *Carla will float you,*" a measured female voice said. "*No worries. We know you're up to it.*"

"This was taken somewhere in Mexico," Bern said. "Most people agree it was probably Chetumal. You can catch a glimpse of an ocean in one of the frames."

I raked my brain, trying to find something about Chetumal. A port city on the tip of Yucatán, one of the hubs of Mexico's robust international trade. Thriving economy. It suffered in the war.

"This was his trial run. He wasn't even commissioned yet. This video was the only one that got out onto the Internet. They cracked down hard after that."

The man shrugged. He was pale and painfully young, younger than Bern. It might have been the lousy quality of the video, but he looked scared. The camera zoomed in on his face. His blue eyes were so sad, almost mournful and filled with power.

"How old is he?"

"It's his senior year of college. He's nineteen. He graduated from high school early and did his bachelor's in three years. He was brilliant."

"He also had the best tutors money could buy." House Rogan was wealthy. I wasn't sure what exactly they did, but Mad Rogan was a fourth-generation Prime.

"*It's time,*" the woman's voice said. "*Remember, this entire sector has been evacuated. This is just property damage. No doubts, Connor. You are doing the right thing.*"

Sure he was. Someone must've talked to him at college, someone from the military with many bars on his or her shoulder, and he must've listened, because they flew him out to Chetumal to see what he could do.

Rogan started down the road, a lone figure in a grey hoodie, walking along the yellow line toward the high-rises. A hundred feet. Two hundred. Rogan kept moving. He was almost to the buildings.

"*What is he, half a mile out?*" a male voice asked off-screen.

"*He's giving us safe space,*" the original woman speaker said.

"*How much safe space does he need?*"

"*As much as he wants.*"

Rogan kept moving.

"*Is he still in range?*" the woman asked.

"*I can levitate him from here, ma'am,*" a second woman with a higher voice said, "*but if he walks any farther, we'll have to close the distance.*"

Levitating a person without causing serious internal injury was a very specific branch of telekinetics. Levitators were highly prized, and once it became apparent that a child had this particular brand of magic, that's all they did. A regular telekinetic could lift or throw a person, but he or she would likely be dead even before landing.

Rogan stopped. He was two buildings into the block. On his left, a huge rectangular complex of dark stone rose eight floors high. On his right, a white tower spiraled toward the stormy sky.

"*Finally,*" the male voice said.

Rogan regarded the towers of glass and stone. He stood motionless, as if overwhelmed by the sheer size of the buildings.

Moments dragged by, towing a convoy of minutes.

"*Oh come on,*" the male voice said.

Rogan leaned back. The wind stirred his long, dark hair.

"*Let it rip,*" the first woman murmured.

The video blurred for a moment. I held my breath.

Nothing.

"*And?*" the male voice asked. "*You told me he was some sort—*"

The white tower on the right slid to the side like a cut tree.

This couldn't have been happening. Nobody could cut through a building.

Cracks streamed up the tower. On the left, thin puffs of grey dust shot out of the office complex windows. The building held together for one long, torturous second. The front of it sagged and plunged down, tons of bricks and stucco plunging, like the waters of Niagara Falls. Thunder pealed as thousands of tons of rock, steel, and concrete crashed onto the street.

Oh my God. My insides went cold. The sheer power. A human being couldn't contain that much power.

Offscreen, people screamed. Their cries had no words, only the raw, primal sounds of intense human terror.

The tower collapsed. Dense smoke, churning with grey and black dust, billowed like a tsunami from both buildings, clashing in the middle of the street right over Mad Rogan. Six feet on both sides of him the blast waves broke, rolling back as if bouncing from an invisible wall. Debris crashed into the barrier and ricocheted into the street. He stood enveloped in a funnel of clear, calm air.

Wind swirled Rogan's dark hair. He turned his hands palms up.

The recording blurred. To the left and right, the buildings adjacent to the rubble, a red tower and a brown apartment high-rise, fractured and fell. The sound was deafening.

"*Stop him!*" the man screamed.

"*He can't be stopped,*" the original woman howled

over the roar of the falling buildings. "*He can't hear us or see us! We have to wait it out!*"

Mad Rogan's feet left the ground. He rose two feet above the pavement.

"*It's not me,*" the levitator screamed. "*It's not me, I can't reach him!*"

The recording blurred.

The camera trembled. The heavy truck parked on the left slid toward it.

"*Jesus Chri—*" a man yelled.

The recording stopped midword.

Bern and I stared at the dark screen. I sat, shell-shocked, not sure what to do next. I've studied many Primes. I've never seen one who could do that. This was inhuman.

"I think we should reconsider getting involved," Bern said.

"It's too late," I told him. My voice sounded dull. "I took the job."

We looked at the screen some more.

"We can't tell Mom," I said.

"Oh no, no, we really can't." Bern clicked the video off and went to erase the browser history.

"Leon?" I guessed.

"Mhm. He likes to snoop, and he'll blow our cover."

The video disappeared, but my dread didn't.

"What kind of magic was that?"

"The consensus is, he's an inorganic telekinetic."

"Telekinetics move things. They don't cut buildings in half."

"He does," Bern said.

"What's Mad Rogan doing now?" I asked.

"He left the military four years and eight months ago.

Nobody has seen him since. By all indications, he became a shut-in. The chatter on the House groupie forums says he was horribly disfigured in the war."

"Yes, and he's waiting for just the right woman to come and love him as he is."

Bern gave me a small smile. Primes, like any celebrities, had their admirers, especially the young, handsome, male, unmarried Primes. They spawned a whole subculture on Instagram, Tumblr, and Vine. They even had their own social network—Herald. Most of the content consisted of photos of Primes, fanart and fanfiction, often with a romantic bend, and wild speculation about who was going to marry whom and what sorts of powers their kids could possibly have. Usually powers carried over from generation to generation, but when two different magic bloodlines mixed, there was always a chance for some mayhem.

"Does he love his cousin?" I asked.

"The Lanceys disowned Kelly Waller when she turned twenty-two."

Wow. Being thrown out of the family was the worst kind of punishment. Having financial support severed was hard enough, but being disowned also cut you off from all family contacts and connections. It made you an outcast. You couldn't go to your family's friends or to your family's enemies, because neither would trust you. Members of the Houses almost never suffered being disowned, even when they were complete screwups. Case in point, Adam Pierce probably murdered a man and injured a woman and two children, and his House was falling over itself trying to bring him back into the fold. Members of a House were simply too valuable. The Lanceys weren't the main branch of House Rogan, but still.

"Why would they do that?"

"I don't know," Bern said. "But she hasn't had any contact with either Rogans or Lanceys. Three years ago her bakery went under."

Rogan had gotten out almost two years prior. "He didn't help her?"

Bern shook his head. "Also, she and her husband, Thomas, repeatedly borrowed against their house for Gavin's tuition. They've been hanging by a thread for the last two years."

"How much did she need to keep the bakery open?"

"According to her bankruptcy filing, eighty-seven grand would've paid off her debts."

Eighty-seven grand would have been chump change to Mad Rogan. He was the head of the House. Poor Kelly Waller. All my life I knew that my parents loved me unconditionally. Oh they let me suffer the consequences of my mistakes, but they always loved me. I could go on a wild shooting spree and murder a dozen people, and my mother and my grandmother would be horrified, but they would fight for me to the bitter end. They would be confounded, but they would still love me, and get me the best attorney, and cry when I would go to the sacrificial chair. If my father had still been alive, he would have done the same. Ms. Waller's family jettisoned her out, and they didn't lift a finger to help her no matter how desperate she got. It was tragic and painful for her, but encouraging for us.

I phrased my question carefully. I would need Bern in my corner for this investigation. "Have you seen any indications that Mad Rogan is taking an interest in what happens to Gavin?"

"No."

"Neither did Montgomery, or it would be in the file. Look, he didn't bail her out during a bankruptcy, when it would've cost him next to nothing. This arson smells so bad, everyone is running away from it as fast as they can. Nobody wants to be Adam Pierce's friend right this second, let alone help Gavin Waller. We might be okay."

Bern sighed. "What happens if we back off?"

"MII will call in our loan. We will default. They will seize all of our professional assets, including the warehouse and any equipment we have claimed as exemptions on our tax returns, which includes two of the cars, the weapons, the office equipment, and everything in this room."

"We would be homeless and penniless," Bern summarized.

"That's about right."

Bern's eyebrows came together. His face went hard, his grey eyes turned to steel, and for a second I got a hint of what kind of man my cousin would become in a few years: determined and unflappable, like one of those medieval knights in armor. "That's fucked up."

"Yes."

"Did you . . ."

"I explained our situation. They don't care. They don't want to offend House Pierce, and we look good on paper, so they are giving it to us, knowing we will fail. We are the cheapest option for them."

"Let's do it," Bern said. "Let's get Pierce and shove him down their throats so they'll choke on him."

Yes. "Thanks."

"Always." Bern grinned. "We are family."

 **Chapter 3**

Cornelius Maddox Harrison lived in Royal Oaks, which was slightly strange. I would've expected an address inside the Loop.

Houston was defined by three roads, which circled it in rings. The first road, closest to the city center, was known as the Loop. Inside the Loop lay the central business districts—the downtown—and the pricey "it" neighborhoods like River Oaks, University Towne, and a chunk of Bellaire. If you moved out about five miles or so from the Loop, you'd cross the Beltway, the second ring. Ten miles more and you would hit a stretch of Grand Parkway, the third ring, which was still in the process of being constructed. Royal Oaks lay just outside the Beltway, in the Westside.

Houston was an odd city, which was in the habit of devouring smaller towns and turning them into neighborhoods. We had no zoning laws, so business centers sprung up organically where they were needed, with residential areas clustering around them. Most of the city was sectioned off into territory of this or that House. It didn't affect normal people much. House members took interest in other House members. We were the small fries.

House Harrison wasn't large or powerful enough to claim its own territory, but they were comfortably wealthy. Cornelius Harrison was the second son of Rupert and Martha Harrison. His older sister and brother likely would inherit the reins of the family. His sister lived in University Towne, his brother lived close to his parents in River Oaks, but Cornelius had moved all the way outside the Beltway. Not that he was slumming it, I reflected, driving down the long street. Giant houses sat here and there on generous, artfully landscaped lots next to an immaculate golf course. The noise of the city had receded. We could've been in the middle of some resort miles from any metropolis. Each small mansion probably cost about two million and up. It's good to be rich.

My GPS chimed at me. I pulled up to a sprawling mansion. Two stories high under a roof of clay shingles, the house looked like it was a movie prop: the walls perfectly clean, the yellow stone steps devoid of any debris, and the plants flanking the walkway trimmed with precision usually reserved for bonsai. I parked the car in the driveway, walked up to the door, pulled out my ID, and rang the bell.

A few seconds later the door swung open and a short trim man in his late twenties regarded me with solemn blue eyes. His dark blond hair was cut short, his jaw was clean shaven, and his face had a slightly absentminded expression, as if he was thinking about something completely abstract when you interrupted and now struggled to remember what it was.

I smiled, trying to project trustworthy and nonthreatening. "Mr. Harrison?"

"Yes?"

I handed him the ID. My name alone would get me nowhere, so I decided to shoot with the biggest gun I had. "My name is Nevada Baylor. I work for Montgomery International Investigations. I was hired by House Pierce to find Adam Pierce."

Cornelius Harrison grimaced and passed the ID back to me.

"May I ask you a few questions?"

He shrugged. "Sure. Come in."

I followed him into a large foyer. The marble floor with inlaid mosaic gleamed with polish. A curving staircase led to the top floor on the left, guarded by an ornate wrought-iron rail. Cornelius turned to me. "Foyer, library, or kitchen?"

"Kitchen, please." People felt comfortable and relaxed in the kitchen, and the more relaxed Cornelius was, the more information I'd be able to pull out of him.

We crossed the formal dining room into a large kitchen lined with cherry cabinets and equipped with granite countertops. The kitchen opened into a sunny family room. By the window, crayons and pages from a coloring book depicting roosters with big tails lay scattered on the breakfast table. The roosters were decorated in a rainbow of colors.

Cornelius picked up the pages, arranged them into a neat stack, and set them aside. "Something to drink?"

"No, thank you." One learned very quickly to never eat or drink in the house of a magic user you didn't know. I didn't relish sprouting feathers or being turned into a goat.

We sat at the breakfast table. I set my digital recorder on the table, pushed the record button, and said, "Thursday, October twenty-fourth, interview with Cornelius Harrison."

Cornelius regarded me. He had smart eyes, calm and sardonic. I focused.

"For the record," he said, "I don't really want to answer your questions, but I fought with Christina Pierce before, and I have no desire to repeat the experience."

I waited for my magic to click. It didn't come. Cornelius was telling the truth. No love lost between him and Adam Pierce's mother. I made a mental note in case I'd need it later.

"How long have you known Adam?"

"Since we were very young children," Cornelius said. "Four or five."

True. "Are you his friend?"

Cornelius laughed quietly, a humorless, dry sound. "Are you a member of House Pierce?"

"No," I said.

"So you're hired help?"

"Yes," I said.

"Are you doing this job under duress?"

"Yes. How did you know?"

Cornelius smiled. "Because nobody in their right mind would go after Adam unless they had no choice. Also because that's the way House Pierce operates. They use both carrot and stick at the same time. You're hired help, and I assume at some point you will be paid. I was hired help, but I received no compensation. Quite the opposite. My mother and Christina Pierce went to college together. At some point it was decided that Adam needed a boyhood companion." He sank an ocean of sarcasm into those two words. "I was volunteered for the job. Nobody asked me or Adam if we were happy with the arrangement."

"Were you happy with it?"

Cornelius leaned forward a little and said, pronouncing the word with crisp exactness, "No."

True. "Why not?"

"Because I had the designated role of Adam's keeper, even though we were roughly the same age. I was the ugly friend who makes a woman look better at a party: less powerful, less wealthy, less significant. When Adam got in trouble, I was supposed to step forward and take the responsibility for the act. Except Adam reveled in rubbing people's noses in things he did. If he broke something, he would step forward and claim it like it was some worthy deed. Then I received the lion's share of the punishment because I 'failed to help him make good choices.' This arrangement continued until college, where he and I finally went our separate ways. I do not count Adam among my friends. He is somebody I used to know."

"And yet you posted his bail six times."

Cornelius sighed. "After college I took some steps to separate myself from my family. I love them, but they tend to use me, and I've decided I don't like being used. When my grandfather died, he left some money to me, which I used to purchase this house. For my sister, this would be a spare residence, one of several. For me and my wife, this is our home. This will likely be the only house we have, and we plan to pass it on to our children."

His voice told me he was proud of it. He probably thought his house was modest. To me it was a palace. It was all in the frame of reference.

"I took steps to become largely independent of my family," he continued. "However, at the time of Adam's first arrest, his mother was in a position to influence my wife's employment. I was given funds and asked to post his bail."

"Why go through the trouble? Why didn't House Pierce bail him out?"

"Because he publicly turned his back on them." Cornelius grimaced. "His bad boy image would take an unrecoverable hit if it became known that his mommy and daddy put up the money to spring him out of jail."

"But you, being the 'boyhood' companion, were safe."

Cornelius nodded.

This was beginning to look like a dead end.

A hint of movement on the stairs made me turn. A Himalayan cat, its fur cream and chocolate, ran down the stairs, followed by a raccoon and a white ferret.

"Excuse me," Cornelius said.

The three animals ran to his feet and sat, staring at him.

"I take it Matilda is awake."

Three heads bobbed in unison.

Cornelius rose, took a sippy cup with a bright red top out of the refrigerator, and washed it under the faucet. The raccoon stood up on her hind legs. Cornelius held the cup out.

"Take the juice to her and entertain her until I come up."

The raccoon took the juice into her dark paws and ran up the stairs on her hind legs. The cat and the ferret followed.

"You are an animal mage." They were so rare that I'd only met one before.

"Yes. I'm not a Prime, so you shouldn't worry about me summoning a pack of wild wolves to rip you to shreds."

"Why did you wash the cup?"

"Because if I don't, Edwina will wash it for me. It's instinct, and she can't help it. Unfortunately, she can't distinguish between the water from the sink and the water from the toilet, as both smell clean to her. Are we finished?"

"Just a few basic questions. Do you know where Adam Pierce is?"

"No."

True. "Do you have a way to contact him?"

"No."

True.

"Does he have any friends or acquaintances with whom he keeps in touch?"

"Not from his old life. I'm his only link. He wasn't unpopular—he was too handsome and wealthy—but he didn't form any lasting friendships."

"Do you have any information that could help me find him?"

"Direct factual information, no. But I can tell you that Christina would never allow her golden boy to suffer discomfort. One way or another, she is supporting him somehow. My advice is to follow the money."

"End of interview." I turned off the recorder and pulled out my business card. "Thank you so much, Mr. Harrison. If you happen to speak with Adam Pierce, please give him my number. He allegedly murdered a police officer. His family is worried about him, and I'm his best chance at surviving this mess."

"You're not going to ask me if I think he did it?" Cornelius asked.

"Honestly, I don't care. My job isn't to prove that he's innocent. I just have to bring him in in one piece."

"Very well." He walked me to the door, opened it, and hesitated. "Ms. Baylor, if you speak to House Pierce, they will claim that Adam was an exemplary human being until he went to college, where he somehow got all these radical ideas into his head. They have most people convinced of it."

He cleared his throat. "Our elementary school was less than five blocks from my house. When we were in third grade, we were given permission to walk home, with our bodyguard following us at a discreet distance. We would stop at a shop on the way. The first three times we did, Adam stole. Nothing much, a candy bar, a drink. He wasn't subtle about it. He just took it and walked out of the store, as if he was proud of the act. The fourth time, a relative of the owner grabbed his hand and took the candy bar away from him. Adam burned him. He burned him so badly that by the time the bodyguard got there, the man's skin had bubbled on his face. I still remember the smell. This acrid, terrible stench of human flesh cooking. House Pierce tried to say that Adam was a child who was completely terrified and lashed out on instinct. They threw enough money at the family, and the whole matter was swept under the rug. But I was there, and I saw his face. Adam wasn't scared. He was furious. He was punishing the man because he dared to prevent him from stealing."

Cornelius leaned toward me slightly, his eyes serious. "He would've burned that man to death over a candy bar. Adam takes what he wants, and if you tell him no, he will hurt you. That's the kind of person you're dealing with. I won't say good luck, but take care."

By the time I left Cornelius' modest palace, the sun had rolled close to the horizon. I sat in my car for a while and surfed the net. A quick search of my inbox revealed no new developments, but a search of motorcycle-related businesses within Houston city limits led me to Gustave's Custom Cycles. The picture of the business looked a lot like the backdrop in Pierce's Twitter shot. Gustave's

Custom Cycles was clear across town. By the time I got there, it would be close to getting dark.

Let's see what was around there . . . Steel Steed Bar and Grill on one side of the shop, Rattlesnake Body Art on the other. If the bikers had a mall, this would be it. That meant that Gustave's shop was open after dark and would have a steady stream of customers and visitors who came there to be social. If I went there now, I'd have an audience. They all knew each other and I would be coming in as an outsider, asking them to rat out someone they considered a friend. I could talk to the same guys one on one at their jobs during the day and they would be polite and calm. But get them all together, let them soak in a couple of beers, and group machismo kicked in. They would look for trouble, and if trouble walked in in the shape of a young woman with uncomfortable questions, they would rise to the challenge. Best-case scenario, they would catcall and posture and run me off. Worst-case scenario, someone would get hurt. There was no need for that. I could just as readily speak to the owner of Gustave's tomorrow morning, bright and early, when everyone would be sober.

I started the engine and went home. Adam Pierce had evaded capture for twenty-four hours. He would have to evade it until morning.

The traffic was murder. Unlike predictions of weather men and market analysts, Houston's world-famous traffic was 100 percent reliable—it never failed to show up and clog the roads. I drove through it, inching forward and avoiding drivers who barreled into the seemingly solid wall of cars as they switched lanes, and thought about Adam Pierce. He hadn't turned himself in. Nothing on the Twitter feed. Bern was scouring the Internet for any hint of him and Gavin Waller, and Bern was exceptional at what he did. So far he had turned up nothing.

Why torch the bank? Was it a bungled robbery attempt? It wasn't a political statement, otherwise Adam would've left some sort of loud declaratory message. Up yours, oppressors, or something along those lines. Was it a drunken prank that got out of hand? What was Gavin's role in all of it? I really hoped the boy would come out of this alive, if not for him, then for his mother's sake. Kelly Waller's financial record showed a life of sacrifice for her children. Whatever Gavin's sins were, Adam Pierce was older than he was by almost ten years. He was the ringleader.

How the hell was I going to convince Pierce to come in? John Rutger was nowhere near a Prime, and he'd tossed me against a wall. Too bad I couldn't spit fire. Wait, that wouldn't really help me. Too bad I couldn't spit ice? Theoretically, if you did spit ice, you wouldn't be able to spit much. A human body held only so much water. Now if I could summon binding chains . . . Pierce would probably melt them. Would molten metal burn him if he was the one who melted it?

Mad Rogan's image popped into my head. There was something about those blue eyes looking into the camera. Not exactly sadness, but a kind of self-awareness, underscored by a slightly bitter smile. Almost as if he knew he was a human hurricane and regretted it, but he wouldn't stop. I was probably reading too much into it. How in the world did they contain him in the military? I'd seen firsthand the damage that war did to people. If a Prime snapped, hundreds of soldiers would die.

Forty-five minutes later, when I finally pulled in front of the warehouse, I was tired of the question marks and thinking in circles. And I was really hungry. The moment

I stepped into the hallway, the scent of freshly baked biscuits, barbecue sauce, and spicy meat swirled around me. Cinnamon, garlic, cumin . . . mmmm. I pulled my shoes off and let the scent carry me into the kitchen. A note and two plates with pulled pork and biscuits waited for me on the island. The note said, "Nevada, I called it an early night. Help yourself and please take a plate to your grandmother or she'll forget to eat again."

My mother called it an early night when she missed Dad and didn't want us to see her cry. I understood. It was five years, but I missed Dad, too. I could close my eyes and imagine him rummaging through the pantry, complaining that someone ate the steak he'd been saving and he was now reduced to eating unnatural things like salad and croutons. Mom was always the hard one. When Dad was around, she laughed. She still laughed now. Just not as often.

I gobbled up my food, rinsed the plate, stuck it into the dishwasher, and took the second plate and a glass of iced tea to the back of the warehouse. Once you passed through the main wall, no hint of our living space remained. It was all motor pool: sealed concrete floor polished to a shiny dark smoothness, tools on the walls, armored vehicles, some with small guns, some with tank-like barrels, crouching in the gloom, and the Grandma smell: gas, engine oil, and gunpowder.

A midsize armored track vehicle sat in the middle of the floor, bathed in the glow of the floodlights. Grandma Frida's skinny legs in jeans stuck out from under the vehicle. To the right, Arabella lounged on the gutted shell of a Humvee covered by a dark green tarp. I had grown up just like this. When I would get home after school, Mom and Dad would still be gone, so I'd grab a snack and go hang out with Grandma in her shop. You could tell Grandma anything. She said that vehicles spoke to her if she let them. Children did too. She never judged, and even if you cursed or admitted to doing something terminally stupid, she would never tell Mom and Dad. I vented most of my fears and worries here. Then it was Bern's and Catalina's turn, then Arabella's and Leon's. We all were busy now, so we didn't visit as much, but at least once a week one of us would end up hanging out here, spilling our guts and shaking our fists.

"Dinner!" I called.

Arabella scooted further up the tarp. She looked glum. Something didn't go well at school.

Grandma slid from under the vehicle and sat up. "Grub. Yes. Hungry."

I handed her the plate and nodded at the vehicle. "What's his name?"

"Thiago." Grandma touched the metal. Her eyes grew distant for a second—her magic making the connection to the inner workings Thiago's engine. "Wolf-Spider class. He seems like a Thiago to me."

Mech-mages like my grandmother were rare. Some made guns, others worked in civil engineering, but all shared a magical connection to things of metal and moving parts. For Grandma Frida, it was armored things that moved. It didn't matter if they rolled, crawled, or floated. She lived and breathed the deep-voiced rumble of their engines and the smoky odor of their guns. Tanks, field artillery track vehicles, personnel carriers, she loved them all. Luckily, many of the Houses maintained private security forces, and she had a steady supply of clients.

"Is your mom okay?" Grandma asked. "She was in a funk earlier."

"She's fine," I told her. "She just misses Dad, that's all. I've got a question for you."

"Shoot!" Grandma said.

"In the military, how do they keep mages in line? If one of them snaps, wouldn't they nuke their whole unit?"

"Shockers," Grandma Frida said. "Also referred to as joy buzzers, the shakers, squid shivers."

"Squid shivers?"

"A squid is a navy grunt," Grandma said. "The navy was the first to use the shockers, because it quickly found out that mages and ships don't always mix well."

Made sense. If you set fire to the ship or summon a swarm of poisonous flies, there was nowhere to go.

"It's some kind of device they implant into your arms. Completely invisible from the outside, but it lets you shock anyone with magic. Hurts you like hell, but it hurts whoever you grab even more. Seriously nasty gadgets. People used to die from those."

"People who got shocked?" I wondered if Mad Rogan ever got shocked . . . okay, I needed to stop obsessing over those eyes. I was a freshman in high school when that recording was made. He probably didn't even look the same anymore. He definitely wasn't the same nineteen-year-old. He'd been through six years of war. War chewed people up and spat out the gristle. If I kept going this way, I'd end up on Herald, trawling for Mad Rogan fanfic. *We made love as the city fell around us, raining down concrete in chunks of despair* . . . Yeah, right.

Grandma nodded. "The shocked and people who did the shocking. A shock works two ways. First, you have to prime it with your own magic, and only then it hits the other guy as you make contact. It sucks a good chunk out. If it takes too much magic, your body gives out and it's curtains. First generation of trials had a mortality rate of over thirty percent. By the time Penelope enlisted, they had done a lot better with them. You wouldn't believe the stuff they've got now. I know a guy who can implant one."

That didn't surprise me. "Is it illegal?"

"Oh yes." Grandma grinned. "And you might die from it. You want a set?"

"No, thanks."

"You sure?" Grandma winked at Arabella. "You wouldn't need a Taser anymore."

"No, I'm all good. Besides, the plan is to avoid being in a situation where I have to use the Taser in the first place."

"Aha."

"For example, I had a chance to interrogate an owner of a biker shop late at night and I decided instead to come home."

Grandma Frida set the plate down and picked up the five-foot-long breaker bar used to break track on the vehicles. In the right hands, it could disable a tank, and Grandma Frida was an expert. "I don't understand you, Neva. You're twenty-five years old. Where is your sense of adventure? When I was your age, I was half a planet away from the place I was born. You're just so . . . sensible."

Arabella perked up, sensing blood in the water. I had to nip this in the bud, or the teasing would never end. She who showed weakness to teenagers would be picked on to death. True fact of life.

"I have a family full of quirky people. Someone has to be sensible so all of you can enjoy being reckless weirdos."

"You have to live a little." Grandma fitted the track bar into the cog on the track. "Go out with a bad boy. Run headfirst into a fight. Get roaring drunk. Something!"

A guilt trip. Unfortunately for Grandma, I grew up with four younger siblings. Guilt tripping was sometimes the only reason anything got cleaned in our house. "Grandma, why don't you knit?"

"What?"

"Why don't you knit? All grandmas knit."

Grandma leaned into the track bar. The track split open and crashed to the floor with a loud clang. She stared at me with big blue eyes. "You want me to knit?"

Arabella snickered.

"If you look in the dictionary under *grandmother*, you'll see a little old lady with two knitting needles and a ball of yarn." I pretended to stir imaginary spaghetti with two imaginary chopsticks. "Sometimes I sit and think, if only my grandma had knitted me a hat or a scarf . . ."

"We live in Houston, Texas!" Grandma wiped her hands with a rag. "You'd get heat stroke."

"Or a stuffed animal. I would've cuddled with it at night." I sighed heavily. "Oh well. I guess that's never going to happen."

Arabella giggled. Grandma pointed the breaker bar at her. "Quiet in the peanut gallery."

I gave them a nice, sweet smile. "Well, I'm going now. You two have fun. I have to work tomorrow."

 **Chapter 4**

Gustave's Custom Cycles occupied a rectangular steel building with corrugated metal walls. It was exactly two hundred feet wide and eight hundred feet long, manufactured by Olympia Steel Buildings, delivered to the site and assembled there four years and seven months ago. Bern had pulled up the city permits for me.

Before I went to bed last night, I spent hours reading the background file on Adam Pierce and whatever Bern had been able to dig up during the day. I read interviews with Adam Pierce's parents and teachers, tabloid articles, credible gossip on Herald, and what little Adam's college friends said about him. I read his speeches. Adam liked making speeches, especially after giving his family the finger, and the message wasn't so much anarchy but right of might. If you can take what you want, you should be able to do so, and government and law enforcement shouldn't be able to prevent you because they have no right to exist. He threw around terms like *negative liberty* and quoted Hobbes.

I knew about Hobbes only because my major had

required some political science courses. Hobbes was a seventeenth-century English philosopher best known for his belief that without political community, man's life was solitary, poor, nasty, brutish, and short. Adam had found a different sentiment from Hobbes: "A free man is he that, in those things which by his strength and wit he is able to do, is not hindered to do what he has a will to." He repeated it on at least three occasions. Adam felt society hindered his freedom by not letting him do what he wanted to do. Unfortunately for him, if what he wanted to do was set people on fire, he was out of luck. The rest of us wouldn't stand for that.

I now knew more about Adam Pierce than I ever wanted to. He was smart, at times cruel, and easily bored. He wouldn't trust me no matter what I did. Establishing some sort of friendship was out of the question. If I tried to be earnest and sincere, he'd laugh; if I tried to use reason, he would yawn. My only chance was to be interesting. I had to catch his attention and hold it.

The Twitter picture of him in front of the bike shop kept bugging me. A real biker didn't let just any mechanic put hands on his bike. No, real bikers picked their mechanics carefully. There was a good deal of trust involved. So last night I looked into Gustave's Custom Cycles, and when a couple of red flags went up, I asked Bern to help. He found a number of interesting things. This morning I ate breakfast, put on my jeans and comfortable running shoes in case I had to run for my life, and drove to the motorcycle shop. Adam wanted amusement out of life. I was about to tap him on the shoulder. I just had to do it hard enough for him to turn around.

The building looked older than either of its neighbors. The corrugated walls had suffered some dents over the years. Someone had painted the front facade solid black and airbrushed a hell bike on it: huge, shiny, and framed in billowing flames full of grinning red skulls.

The parking lot held two vehicles, both Dodge trucks, one white, one black. Good. I wouldn't have to do my show-and-tell in front of the whole class. I parked next to the white truck, grabbed my business fake-leather folder, and walked into the office. Nobody was manning the counter, so I rang the bell and waited.

The door swung open and a man in his early thirties shouldered his way in. Tall and lanky, he looked spare; not underfed but dried like jerky under the sun. He wore a T-shirt smudged with oil and faded old jeans. His skin was a rich olive brown, about a shade or two darker than my own. He'd shaved his head, but a short, carefully shaped beard hugged his jaw. I recognized him from the image Bern had dug up during his research—Gustave Peralta, the owner.

He saw me and blinked. I clearly wasn't someone he'd expected. "How can I help you?"

"My name is Nevada Baylor. I'm looking for Gustave Peralta."

"Call me Gus," he said. "What can I do for you?"

I passed him my business card.

"Private investigator." He frowned. "That's new."

"I was hired by House Pierce to find Adam Pierce."

"Can't help you," Gus said. "Haven't seen him in the last six months."

An annoying magic click. A lie.

"He hasn't visited the shop in the last week?" The Twitter photo was shared this Monday.

"Nope."

A lie.

"Gus . . ."

"Mr. Peralta. I have nothing to say to you. You can show yourself out." He turned to leave.

I opened the folder and pulled a piece of paper out. "This is the printout of your payments received."

He stopped and turned on his heel toward me.

I put a second piece of paper on the counter. "This is the printout of your outgoing payments. And this is your payroll."

He grabbed the paper off the counter. "Where did you get this?"

"We hacked your office computer."

"That's illegal!"

I shrugged. "I told you, I'm not the cops."

He reached for his cell phone. "How about I'll dial nine-one-one right now and report this?"

I smiled. "Let me get to the end, and if you still want to call the cops, I won't stop you. If you look over here where I drew a small star? This shows a payment in the amount of nine thousand nine hundred and ninety dollars labeled 'Motorcycle repairs.'"

The righteous anger died down a little in Gus's eyes. "So what?"

"This is a recurring payment that's coming out of Christina Pierce's personal account." Mrs. Pierce was a wild guess. The best we'd been able to do was determine that the payment had been made from an account owned by someone within House Pierce. Adam's mother seemed like a safe bet.

"So? I did some work for Adam back then, and he was low on cash. His family makes payments."

"No, Mr. Peralta. You and I make payments. Adam Pierce walks in and says, 'I'll take one of each color' and throws down his Visa Black Card. If you look right here, in your payroll, you will see a gentleman by the name of Reginald Harrison listed as an independent contractor. You will also see that Reginald Harrison is paid nine thousand nine hundred and ninety dollars in cash. The nine thousand nine hundred and ninety dollars number is very interesting because the IRS pays attention to any cash transaction in the amount of ten thousand dollars or above."

"So what? Reginald works for me."

Lie. "Reginald Harrison's net worth is close to twenty million dollars, so I very much doubt that. He does have a younger brother, Cornelius Harrison, a very nice man, who happens to be Adam Pierce's childhood friend. You're washing Adam's money. His family makes a payment and you pass it on to Adam in cash, while Reginald claims it on his taxes. You receive five hundred dollars in compensation via the second payment, two days later, once Adam gets his money."

Gus crossed his arms.

"The payments are made on the seventh of each month. That means the next payment is in two days and Adam Pierce will visit you to pick up his pocket change. I'm guessing you didn't mention this to the nice detectives who interviewed you."

If I'd had the manpower, and if I'd been confident that Houston's finest wouldn't find Adam for two more days, I would have laid a lovely trap. But Adam would burn through anything I could throw at him, and the manhunt had reached hysterical levels. Talking Adam into surrendering to his House was still my best and only strategy. To do that, I had to show that I wasn't lying.

"He didn't do it," Gus said. "Adam is a stand-up guy."

"I don't care," I said. "Right now most of the city's police force is foaming at the mouth hoping to blow his brain over the nearest sidewalk. You're a reasonable man. Honestly, what do you think his chances are of getting out of this alive?"

Gus grimaced. "Look, I don't know where he is."

True. "I just want to bring him home safe to his mother. She loves him. He is her baby boy. She doesn't want to lose him to some trigger-happy SWAT sniper." I pushed my card across the counter. "Tell him I came by. That's all I'm asking."

$\mathfrak{T}$he shark fin of Montgomery International Investigations rose among the towers of Houston's downtown, still as menacing as ever. I stuck my tongue at it. It didn't seem impressed.

I parked and marched to Augustine Montgomery's office. The immaculate receptionist spoke into her headset and motioned me to follow.

"So how long did it take you to figure out which shade of liquid foundation would cover up your bruise?" she asked.

"About half an hour. Did it work?"

"No."

Touché.

Augustine Montgomery, still impossibly beautiful, raised his eyes from his tablet. "I am not a terrible person."

"Yes, you are. The note in the file states that House Pierce cut off Adam financially. They are still giving him money. His mother is probably the culprit."

Augustine leaned back and braided his long fingers into a single fist. If their shredder stopped working, they could just dump the paper over his head and his marble-perfect cheekbones would slice it to ribbons on the way down.

"I was assured that all financial ties were severed."

I put the printouts of Gustave's business hijinks on Augustine's desk. He studied them for a long moment. "Do I want to know how you got these?"

"No."

Augustine motioned to me. "Stand here."

I came over and stood next to him.

"Say nothing," he said. "I want you to understand that if this information is in error, the consequences for you will be serious."

His fingers flew over the keyboard. A large monitor came to life, showing an office backdrop and a trim man in a business suit at a desk. Peter Pierce, Adam's older brother. The traces of Adam's beauty were definitely there, in the dark eyes, the bold line of the nose, and the shape of the mouth, but Peter lacked the pretty-boy smolder that turned Adam into the darling of the media. Peter was at least ten years older, and he radiated "respectable" the way his young sibling radiated "edgy."

"Augustine," Peter said. "Have you found him yet?"

"We're working on it."

We meant me, and Peter saw my face. I was now irrevocably connected to the search for Adam.

Augustine leaned back. "I have reason to believe House Pierce is still supplementing his income. I can't stress how important the financial incentive is to bringing him in safely. If you keep giving him play money, he will keep taking his chances."

Peter waved his hand. "Yes, yes, we must make it as nasty for him as possible. I remember the lecture. I assure you, no payments have been made to him."

Augustine ran through the transfer for him.

"Give me the account number," Peter said.

Augustine typed it in. A computer chimed on Peter's side. He peered on another monitor to his left and shook his head, his expression grim. He pushed a few keys on the keyboard. "Mother?"

"Yes?" an older female voice said on the other end of the line.

"You have to stop funneling money to Adam."

"Oh, please, it's an insignificant amount."

"He can't have money, Mother. We've discussed this."

"But then he will be poor. This is ridiculous. Do you want your brother to be poor, Peter? Why do all of you have to make it so unpleasant for him?"

Augustine kept his face perfectly neutral.

Unpleasant. That was a good word, especially considering that right now a widow with two children was getting ready to bury the charred corpse of her husband.

"Perhaps you want him to be like the dirty migrants begging for a dollar by the traffic lights?"

Charming. If I never met Christina Pierce, it would be too soon.

"Yes," Peter said. "I want him to be poor and desperate. So desperate that he comes to us for help."

"Absolute and utter . . ."

Peter waved at us and pushed a key on his keyboard. The feed stopped. We both looked at the screen for a blink or two.

"So, if I make less than nine thousand nine hundred and ninety dollars per month, does it mean I can legitimately beg at intersections?" I couldn't help myself.

Augustine took his glasses off and rubbed the bridge of his nose.

"Do your clients know that you hire dirty migrants?"

"Stop," Augustine said. "Christina Pierce is a third-generation Prime. She hasn't been poor a day in her life. It colors her mind-set."

"If I do track Adam Pierce down, are you going to provide me with support?"

"It depends on the situation."

Lie. "I stand by my earlier statement. You will have to live with yourself."

I walked out of his office. My cell phone rang midway through the lobby. An unfamiliar number. I took the call.

"Nevada Baylor."

"Adam Pierce," a male voice said. He sounded just like I thought he would, with a slightly sardonic voice, the kind that would fit a self-aware spoiled rich boy to a T.

I had to bait the hook just right. My heart was beating too fast. Deep breath. I could do this.

"Gustave tells me you derailed my money train."

"Yes, I did. Your brother and your mother are having a conversation about it right now. Does she have something against migrant workers?"

He chuckled. "She probably meant vagrant. So you want to find me?"

"*Want* is the wrong word. I'm forced to find you. I don't particularly want to."

"Who's forcing you?"

Got you. "What are the chances of you surrendering to me?"

He laughed again, a distinct male chuckle. "Come see me and we'll talk about it."

Score. "Sure. Where?"

"Mercer Arboretum, Shade Bog Garden. In half an hour."

He hung up.

Half an hour. Mercer was twenty miles north of downtown. Twenty miles in Houston traffic might as well have been sixty. Bastard.

I double-timed it to the car, texting Bern on the way. He would still be in class. *"AP just called my cell. Meeting in half an hour, at Mercer Arboretum."*

No response.

Bern could track my phone anywhere, but tracking wouldn't do me any good if Adam turned me into burnt ends. Half an hour would give me just enough time to get to Mercer Arboretum. Not enough time to wrangle any backup. Besides, backup wouldn't do me any good.

I jumped into my Mazda and drove out of the parking lot like my wheels were on fire. *Be interesting. Convince him to turn himself in. Don't get killed.*

I walked into Mercer Arboretum exactly twenty-nine minutes after the call. A two-hundred-and-fifty-acre botanical garden, Mercer was a welcome spot of green shade popular with magical heavyweights. There was something about gardens, and especially flowers, that drew magic users to them even if their magic had nothing to do with plants. I felt it too. All around me flowers bloomed, trees spread their vast canopies, insects fluttered from leaf to leaf, birds sang . . . It was like being wrapped in a cocoon of life, suffused with a simple happiness of existing.

I wasted twenty seconds at a gift kiosk, turned north, and hurried down the trail, my purchase folded in my hand. Men and women passed me, some speaking quietly, some deep in thought. Expensive clothes, beautiful faces, some so flawless that illusion magic had to be involved.

There was a point where a human being became too perfect and lost whatever sexual allure they might have been born with. They became untouchable and almost sterile, like plastic mannequins in store windows. Many Primes understood this and left some imperfections, like Augustine Montgomery, but a lot of mages of lower caliber didn't. Considering how many magic users I passed, this might turn out to be a wild-goose chase. Adam Pierce was too well known, and this place was too public.

The winding path turned into a boardwalk flanked by a black iron rail. The points of the rail bent out toward the nature in arches, as if straight, man-made lines had no business here. Trees crowded in. The air smelled of moisture, that unmistakable wetlands scent of mud and water plants. A bog stretched on both sides of the trail, a few inches of water the color of tea surrounded by thriving green plants and brilliant red irises. The path veered slightly, crossing over the bog, and brought me to a bench. A low stone wall flanked the bench on both sides. On the wall sat Adam Pierce.

He perched, cross-legged, his legs stretching the black leather of his pants. He was wearing a jacket over a black T-shirt. His hair fell over his face in a ragged wave. A complicated magic circle, drawn in black and white chalk, marked the boardwalk and the wall around him. Three rings within each other, three half circles facing outward, their backs touching the middle ring. Spider-thin perfectly straight lines crossed back and forth within the circles, forming an elaborate pattern. Half circles out meant containment. He was holding in his power.

Years ago when aristocrats were expected to serve in the military, they began practicing with swords as soon as they could walk. Now Primes practiced drawing arcane symbols. If I had to duplicate whatever he had drawn, I would need a picture for reference, a ruler, a pair of compasses to make those circles, and a couple of hours. He probably drew it freehand in a few minutes. It looked perfect.

He was capable of incredible precision and control. Come to think of it, the way he sat, the way he posed during interviews with his best angle to the camera, indicated that he had practiced in front of the mirror. Maybe Adam the Chaotic Rebel was just for show. Maybe everything he did was calculated. Wouldn't that be just the icing on top of this Cake of Awful? I would have to tread this treacherous water very carefully.

Adam glanced up. Brown eyes took my measure. He looked just like he did in all those photographs. Okay. Now I needed to not get fried as I talked his handsome ass into surrendering.

I went over to the bench. As I passed by him, heat washed over me, as if I had stepped too close to a bonfire. He had made the containment circle and then filled it with heat. I had my Taser in my bag. I could probably shoot him from here, but even if the Taser hit and he went down, getting anywhere close to him was out of the question. The heat would peel the skin off my fingers. Then the shock would wear off, and I would be dead.

I sat down.

Adam Pierce smiled. His face lit up, suddenly boyish and charming, but still a little wicked. So that's why his mother gave him anything he wanted.

"Nevada. Such a cold name for such a sunny girl."

Aren't you smooth? Nevada meant "snow-covered" in Spanish. I was anything but.

Grandma Frida's parents came to the US from Germany. She was dark haired and light skinned naturally. Grandpa Leon was from Quebec. I didn't remember much about him except that he was huge and dark-skinned. It caused some issues for both of them, but they loved each other too much to regret it. Together they made my mother, with dark hair and medium brown skin. We didn't know a lot about Dad's family. He once told me that his mother was a terrible person and he didn't want anything to do with her. He looked part Caucasian, part Native American to me, with dark blond hair, but I never asked. All of those genes fell into the melting pot, boiled together, and I came out, with tan skin, brown eyes, and blond hair.

My hair wasn't silvery blond but a darker, tupelo honey kind of blond. I almost never burned in the sun, just got darker, while my hair turned lighter, especially if I spent the summer swimming. Once, when I was seven, a woman stopped my grandma and me as we were walking to my school. She tried to chew Grandma out for dying my hair. It didn't go well. Even now people sometimes asked me which salon did the coloring job. *Nevada* didn't exactly fit me. There was nothing wintery about me, but I didn't care what he thought about it.

I shook my left hand, unfolding a Mercer Arboretum gift T-shirt, black with a sage green Mercer logo on it. "For you."

"You bought me a T-shirt?" He raised one eyebrow.

Every nerve in my body was shivering with tension. Steady. "You keep forgetting to put one on, so I thought I'd bring you one. Since we're having a serious discussion."

He leaned forward, his beautiful face framed by soft hair. "Do you find my chest distracting?"

"Yes. Every time I see that panther with horns, it makes me laugh."

Adam Pierce blinked.

Didn't expect that, did you? "Just out of curiosity, why horns?"

"It's Mishepishu, an underwater panther of the Great Lakes. It's revered by Native American tribes. It has the horns of a deer, the body of a lynx, and the scales of a snake."

"What is it famous for?"

"It lives in the deepest reaches of the lakes, where they guard copper deposits. Those who cross their waters must pay it tribute."

"And if the tribute isn't paid?"

Adam smiled, giving me a small flash of teeth. "Then Mishepishu will kill you. One moment the waters will be placid, and the next you will see your death glaring you in the face."

So Adam thought of himself as Mishepishu. He ruled, and those who crossed his waters had to pay him tribute. Full of himself didn't begin to describe it.

Adam was looking me over in a slow, evaluating way. "I don't believe my mother hired you."

"Why not?"

"She hires for appearances. Those jeans cost what, fifty dollars?"

"Forty. I got them on sale a couple of years ago. I wore them especially for going to see Gustave."

"Why?"

"Because I needed him to trust me and I wanted to show him that I'm a working person, just like him. I'm not 'them.' I'm not the Man. I don't even know the Man, although he does occasionally pay my bills. If I went to see your mother, I would've worn my Escada suit. It cost sixteen hundred bucks, so your mother wouldn't be impressed, but at least she wouldn't dismiss me as a beggar right away."

Adam's eyes narrowed. "I've looked you up. You're small potatoes, Snowflake."

Pet names? Ugh. "Our firm has an excellent reputation."

"Why would you spend a grand and a half on a suit? Isn't it like half of your monthly paycheck?"

I forced my voice to be casual and light. "See, this is how I can tell you've never been poor. Are you poking at me, or are you genuinely curious?"

He leaned back. "I'm curious. When I start poking at you, you'll know."

I let the innuendo fly by, pretending I didn't get it. "When you're wealthy, you have the luxury of wearing whatever you want. You're rich. If someone does attempt to judge you by the way you're dressed, you would find it amusing and rub their nose in it. When you're poor, your ability to land the job you need or accomplish some social task often depends on what you wear. You have to cross that threshold from supplicant to 'one of us.' It's amazing how doors can open once people stop looking down on you. So you save up, buy one outrageously expensive outfit, and wear it to every special occasion for years as if it's your everyday clothes. I have two, an Escada and an Armani. Once in a blue moon, a large insurance company or a wealthy member of some House wants to hire us, so I wear one to get the job and the other to deliver results, because I like to be promptly paid. The rest of the time they hang in my closet wrapped in two layers of plastic, and my sisters know that to touch them is to face a penalty of horrible death."

Adam laughed. It was the rich, self-indulgent laugh of a man who didn't have a care in the world. "I like you, Snowflake. You're genuine. Real. Why are you on this job?"

"Because our firm is a subsidiary of Montgomery International and if I don't bring you in, they will take away the business I worked years to build. My family will be homeless."

Adam laughed again. Something about my family being homeless must've been hilarious.

"How much do you weigh?"

"That's an odd question. About a hundred and thirty pounds."

He shook his head. "You don't lie at all, do you?"

When an occasion called for it, I lied like he wouldn't believe. "People lie too much, because it's easier. I don't lie unless I have to. Adam, you know you can't evade the cops forever. When they find you, it won't be 'put your hands on the back of your head and kneel so we can cuff you.' It will be a bullet to the brain."

He leaned his elbow on his knee and rested his chin on his fist. "Mhm."

"If they don't find you within the next couple of days, they will offer a reward. Then any junkie on the street will be gunning to turn you in. The only logical way out of this situation is turning yourself in to your House."

"Why? So I could rot the rest of my life in a cage?"

"I seriously doubt House Pierce will let you rot in a cage. Your mother clearly adores you. She'll move heaven and earth to keep you out of prison. You have money and power on your side. And anything is better than being dead."

He focused on me. "Do you think I did it?"

I was beginning to think he did. I forced a shrug. "I don't care. My job ends with bringing you in."

He unfolded himself from the wall and touched the chalk with his foot, smudging the perfect line. Heat shot upward in a column. My heart was beating too fast. I tasted metal in my mouth. Adrenaline had kicked in. If he fried me now, I couldn't do a thing about it.

Adam shrugged off his leather jacket. A whiff of burned fabric polluted the air. Scorched patches appeared on the T-shirt. It melted, turning into ash, and Adam shrugged it off. The sun played on his sculpted chest and washboard abs, highlighting every smooth curve and every hard contour of muscle with golden glow. It was good Grandma Frida wasn't here. She would have had a heart attack for sure.

Adam reached over and plucked the Mercer T-shirt from my hand. He pulled it on, shrugged on the leather jacket, and grinned at me.

"Adam . . ."

"I'll think about it, Snowflake." He winked at me.

I pulled out my cell phone and snapped a picture of him.

He stepped over the stone wall and guided a motorcycle from behind a bush.

He'd taken a motorcycle into Mercer. Into this calm, tranquil place where even bicycles were restricted to only a few trails.

Adam saddled the bike and roared off at breakneck speed.

Well, that went about as well as I had expected.

My hands shook. My body still hadn't realized the danger had passed. I took a deep breath, trying to calm down.

In front of me the bog spread, a green and brown labyrinth of mud and water. Suddenly it seemed depressing. I wanted flowers, color, and sunlight. I got up and walked south, heading toward the gardens.

I'd failed. Logically I'd known I wouldn't be able to talk Adam into turning himself in on the first try, but I still had hoped. I was good at talking to people.

Well at least he hadn't fried me. That was good. I pulled out my cell phone, sent the picture of Adam Pierce to Augustine's inbox, dialed MII, and asked for Augustine.

"Yes?" his cultured voice said into the phone.

"Check your inbox."

There was a tiny pause. "Why is he wearing a Mercer Arboretum T-shirt?"

"I bought it for him to cover up the Native American water panther on his chest. He refuses to come in. His exact words were 'Why? So I could rot the rest of my life in a cage?' I think I can get him to meet with me again, but I need some assurances from the family. He doesn't want to go to prison."

"I'll see what I can do." Augustine hung up.

I kept walking. Adam probably did commit the arson. I had no idea what would possess him to torch the bank, but the way he danced around it, flirting with the question, suggested he had something to do with it. Of course, he could just have a persecution complex, let himself be blamed for something he didn't do, and revel in his victimhood. In any case, whether he did it or not, I had to deliver him to his family. Even spoiled rich boys were entitled to due process. My job ended with him in his mother's loving arms. What House Pierce did with him afterward wasn't my problem.

The path brought me to the center of the gardens, to a

rectangular plaza surrounded by towering trees. A long water-curtain fountain stretched across the far end of it, a pale concrete beam supported by ten-foot-tall Doric columns. When you came close, water would spill down from it in a cascade of glittering drops, which fell into three narrow basins. Rectangular flower beds and carefully bordered stretches of vibrant green grass dotted the plaza. Several benches sat on the edges. They looked so inviting. I walked over to the bench under a wooden pergola and landed. I just wanted to sit here for a minute.

Being scared took a lot of energy. Now I was tired and kind of flat.

People milled around the plaza. To the right of me two women chatted on a bench. The one on the left had long silver-blond hair that fell down to her chest without any hint of a curl. She wore a peach teardrop dress that stopped midthigh and probably cost about as much as my best professional suit. Her tan was golden, her makeup bright and flawless. Her dark-haired friend had chosen a pearl-colored asymmetric top with a soft feminine ruffle and a pale grey pencil skirt. Both wore high-heeled shoes so delicate that they looked like they would break if any actual weight rested on them.

They saw me. Both looked me over with identical expressions of attractive women evaluating another young woman in their orbit. Judging by the raised eyebrows and the brunette's stifled sneer, my faded jeans, plain blouse, and beat-up Nikes failed to make an impression. They went on chatting. Probably critiquing my lack of taste and money. They dismissed me as a peasant, I dismissed them as shallow, and we were all happy like that.

Past the women a couple of men lingered midway down the plaza. Both wore light-colored loose pants, expensive shirts, and designer sunglasses. Both were groomed to within an inch of their lives, and the perfection of their faces signaled money and magic.

The men were discreetly checking out the women, while the women pretended not to notice. It was an old dance. Eventually the men would break the ice and the women would pretend to be surprised but receptive. They looked like they could reasonably belong together.

A dark-haired man walked out from one of the side trails into the plaza. He wore jeans and a plain black T-shirt and carried something that looked like a roll of fabric in his hand. His T-shirt stretched tight across his broad shoulders. Muscle corded his arms, the powerful, supple muscle of a fighter, built by practice to punch and rip through his opponents. He stepped lightly, his stride sure and unhurried, like a huge jungle cat, an apex predator out for a prowl in his domain. There was no hint of submission anywhere in his body. He walked like he didn't know his spine could bend.

I leaned forward, trying to see his face.

The two illusion-smoothed men simultaneously moved out of his way.

I saw him. My heart skipped a beat.

He had a sturdy, chiseled jaw, a strong nose, and a square forehead. He looked rough around the edges, from the trace of stubble on his jaw to the short, tousled dark hair. Rough, masculine, and arrestingly sexual. His eyes, smart and clear under the thick, dark eyebrows, evaluated everything he saw with calm precision, but deep inside those blue irises, a cold fire glowed. The same kind of lethal fire you would see in the amber eyes of a tiger, predatory yet irresistible. It compelled you to stare, even though you knew that if you caught his gaze, that icy fire would swallow you whole. He pulled me like a magnet. Every female instinct I had went into overdrive.

Oh wow.

He didn't simply walk into the plaza. Those eyes told me that the moment he stepped foot into it, he owned it. I knew I should've looked away, but I couldn't. I just sat there, shocked, and stared.

The two women saw him and stopped talking. He cut right through the layers of civilization, politeness, and social snobbery to some preternatural female sense that said, "*Dominant male. Danger. Power. Sex.*"

Why couldn't I find someone like that? Why couldn't he be my guy? If he ever talked to me, I probably wouldn't be able to string words together into a sentence.

The man was looking at me.

Wait. There were two other attractive women in his way, both brightly dressed, better styled, and telegraphing "available" with every cell in their bodies. They were roses, and in my current getup, I was a daisy. He should've looked right over me. I was pretty, but not that pretty.

He was looking at me like he knew who I was.

My brain took a quarter of a second to process that fact before spitting back a cold rush of alarm. Stay or go?

I wasted another precious second trying to listen to my instincts and my magic. My gut feelings were almost always right.

Stay or go?

I looked into his blue eyes. No, I was wrong. He wasn't a tiger. He was a dragon, regal and deadly, and he was coming for me.

This was bad. Bad, bad, bad. I had to go. Now.

I jumped right off the bench and made a beeline for the

trail leading out of the park. He made a slight adjustment to his course, heading for me.

I sprinted down the trail. The greenery flew by. People stared at me. The trail turned and I chanced a glance back.

He was running full speed toward me and gaining.

I dashed forward, squeezing every drop of effort out of my body. The air turned hot in my lungs. My side hurt. The path turned again and I shot out into the open plaza with the gift shop. The entrance was only a hundred yards away.

I felt the magic behind me. It swelled, furious and unstoppable, like a cataclysm.

I glanced back.

He was twenty-five yards behind me.

I wouldn't make it to my car.

Too far for a Taser, and I didn't want him any closer. I pulled my .22 Ruger Mark III out and flicked the safety off. I had practiced with this gun every other week. I would hit him.

"Stop. I *will* shoot you." I didn't want to shoot him. I had no idea who he was. I had no idea what he could do. I didn't want to fire a gun in this crowded place. I didn't want to kill him.

He kept walking. I *felt* him coming closer. I've never felt magic like that in my whole life. It was like trying to stand in the path of a tornado. Fear shot through me, turning the world crystal clear and sharp.

"Help me!" I yelled.

Nobody moved. There was a plaza full of people and nobody moved.

Damn it. I raised the gun, barrel up and to the left over the trees, and fired a warning shot.

He threw the roll of fabric at me. I saw a flash of blue silk and then my arms were pinned to my body by a crushing force, my gun flat against my leg. The fabric clamped me, like a straitjacket.

Strong arms grabbed me. Something pricked my neck. My legs went soft and I fell over. He caught me and picked me up as if I weighed nothing.

The world was turning fuzzy. I wanted to yell at the top of my lungs, but instead a weak whisper came out. "Help . . ."

"Hey!" A man in a cowboy hat moved toward us.

"I wouldn't advise it," the man told him, his voice like ice.

The cowboy froze.

The man shifted me in his arms and I saw his eyes up close, blue eyes, on fire with magic and tinted with self-awareness.

Oh my God. My lips were too puffy to speak. "Meh . . . ma . . . mad . . ."

"Mad Rogan," he said.

Someone shut off the sun, and I fell asleep.

 **Chapter 5**

I opened my eyes. A pale ceiling stretched above me. I sat up. Folds of blue silk slid off my body, slippery over my skin.

I was in the middle of the floor in a large rectangular room. No windows interrupted the dark walls. Two floor lamps placed in the corners spilled soft yellow light into the room, not so much banishing the darkness but gently diluting it. The floor was smooth polished concrete. Lines crossed it, circles, triangles, and arcane symbols drawn in chalk, charcoal, and pure intense blue, which could only come from grinding lapis lazuli into powder. The lines glowed with gentle radiance, some parts of the pattern flat on the surface of concrete, some floating a few inches above it. I followed its flow with my gaze to a circle ringed in symbols. Someone sat inside the circle. I looked up.

Mad Rogan stared at me with his blue eyes. They opened wide, like two windows into the depth of him, and magic glared back at me. Monstrous, shocking magic, a living darkness filled with flashes of intense light and power. I might as well have looked into the heart of a supernova. I forgot to breathe. My heart tried to run away without the rest of me. My hands shook.

I jerked back and fell. Something was holding me to the floor. I pulled the silk away. Two steel cuffs enclosed my ankles. Metal rods secured the cuffs, disappearing into the concrete. I strained. My feet didn't move at all.

"You chained me to the floor." My voice trembled, and I hated it.

The demonic, inhuman thing that was Mad Rogan tilted his head, watching me. He sat cross-legged. He wore only dark loose pants that flared at the bottom. His feet were bare. His torso was bare too. Supple, hard muscle corded his frame. Carved biceps stood out on his arms, like living steel. His powerful chest slimmed down into flat planes of hard, ridged stomach. Pale stripes of scars crossed his bronze skin. He wasn't just toned. He had the kind of body that was meant for combat: strong, flexible, hard, and fueled with explosive power. If Adam Pierce were present, he would perish in a fit of jealousy.

I forced my brain to work. Thin blue lines marked his skin, blending into glyphs. He had written arcane symbols on his chest and stomach. He was amplifying his power, which was dangerous to his health. Why? Why could he possibly need more power if he already forced all the air out of this big room with his presence?

"What gives you the right to grab me off the street and chain me in your dirty basement?"

"Do you know what this is?" His voice matched him, deep and slightly raspy. If dragons existed and could talk, they would sound just like him.

I strained my neck, trying to get a sense of the pattern in the scattering of symbols and lines. I was locked in a circle ringed with several larger concentric circles.

Straight lines fanned through the circles, connecting to a triangle. The "top" point of the triangle contained a smaller circle, where Mad Rogan sat. Lines of runic script and arcane characters wound through the pattern, glowing with magic. My insides went cold. Acubens Exemplar, named after the "Claw" star in the Cancer constellation.

When my parents discovered the nature of my magic, we had a long talk, and my father explained to me that there was only one profession for someone with my talents. I could be an interrogator. No matter what other things I wanted to do, once my talent became known, either the military or the civilian authorities would pressure me into becoming a human lie detector. They would keep the pressure on until I gave in. I would witness torture and see horrible things done in the name of the greater good, and it would destroy my chances at a happy life. He told me that when I was old enough, I could always make the choice to become an interrogator, but until then, my ability needed to stay secret. To make his point, he made me watch a documentary on the Spanish Inquisition. I was only seven years old, but I understood. That horrible life could be my future.

When I was twelve, I began rebelling against everything my parents stood for, and I studied interrogation techniques and spells. Acubens Exemplar was one of the most potent. It took days of careful preparation to set up, and there was a very narrow window in which it could be used before the magic it accumulated dissipated, but it was almost completely foolproof. Like the claw of the crab for which it was named, the spell would allow a telepath to put crushing pressure on the person trapped in its center. The spell would amplify the pressure until the victim's will broke and they revealed whatever secret they had been trying to hide.

"Acubens Exemplar requires a telepath." I was grasping at straws. "You're a telekinetic."

The lines around Mad Rogan pulsed brighter. Okay. So he was also a telepath. Or he had some sort of will-related magic.

"I want to know everything you have on Adam Pierce," he said. "His location, his plans, his family's plans for him. Everything."

I crossed my arms. "No. First, I was hired to find Adam Pierce, and my client has an expectation of confidentiality. Second, you attacked me and then chained me to the floor." I tried to rattle my cuffs to underscore the point, but they remained completely immovable.

Mad Rogan fixed me with his blue eyes. There it was again, the predatory, merciless power. Alarm squirmed through me. He *was* a dragon in human skin, powerful, ruthless, and dangerous. My mind locked, struggling to come to terms with it. The muscles in my legs and arms tensed; my chest tightened. I wanted to scream at the top of my lungs to just vent the fear out of my body.

"I don't want to hurt you," he said. "I want the information."

True.

"Forcing you gives me no pleasure."

True. "If you don't like forcing me, you should let me go."

"Tell me what I want to know, and you can walk out of here."

"No. It would be unethical and unprofessional."

He was a Prime telekinetic. Sometime Primes had secondary talents, but they were never as strong as their primary magic. Telepathy was will based. My magic was also will based, and in all of the time I had been alive, I had never met a person on whom it hadn't worked. I grabbed onto that thought and used it to steady myself. He might be a dragon, but if he tried to swallow me whole, I'd make him choke. I scooted forward, trying to get as comfortable in my restraints as I could, and licked my dry lips. "Okay, tough guy. Let's see what you've got."

Mad Rogan shrugged his shoulders. Magic pulsed from him, running down the lines of magic, turning them brighter, like fire traveling along a firing cord. Pressure clamped me, squeezing my mind in an invisible vise. I clenched my teeth. He was strong.

I pushed back. His eyes narrowed.

"Adam Pierce." He would keep repeating the name. The more he repeated it, the harder it would be not to think about it, and the harder the spell would grind against my defenses.

I braced myself against the pressure. He wouldn't break me. "Eat dirt and die."

The pressure crushed my mind, pushing against it like an impossibly heavy weight. It felt like my head was locked inside a giant lead bell, and it kept growing tighter and tighter, compressing my skull. The relentless assault of magic had turned into a steady, terrible pain. It hurt to think. It hurt to move. Time had dissolved into ache in my mind.

The heat from all the energy rushing back and forth through the spell had turned the room into a sauna. Sweat slicked my skin. I had pulled off my T-shirt ages ago. I would've stripped off my jeans too if I could've gotten them over the cuffs.

Across from me, Mad Rogan sat motionless in the circle. A damp sheen beaded at his hairline and slicked his chest and carved biceps. The blue runic script covering his body still held, but some symbols were beginning to smudge. The effort of crushing my will was wearing him out. In the soft illumination of the room, he looked barely human, a feral, predatory creature of some arcane magic. I would've loved nothing more than to walk over there and kick him right in the face. As it was, I glanced at him anytime the pressure got to me, and a fresh jolt of fear kept me going.

The pressure ebbed slightly. He was tired.

"You're rich, right?" My voice came out rough.

"Yes."

"Couldn't you spring for air-conditioning in the room?"

"I didn't expect to sit here for hours. But if you're too hot, feel free to take the bra off."

I gave him the finger.

"What are you?" he asked.

"I'm the woman you chained in your basement. I'm your captive. Your . . . victim. Yes, that's the right word. All of that education. How come nobody ever explained to you that you can't just kidnap people because you feel like it?"

He grimaced. "You had a full second to shoot me."

"I don't just shoot strangers unless my life is clearly in danger. For all I knew, you could've been a cop assigned to Pierce's case. If I fire, I have to be prepared for the possibility of killing my target. Besides, discharging a firearm into a crowd is irresponsible."

"A .22 will bounce off wet laundry on the line. Why even carry it?"

I leaned back. Something in my spine popped. "Because I don't shoot unless I mean to kill. A large caliber will tear a hole through the target and exit, possibly striking innocent bystanders. A .22 will enter the body and bounce around inside it, turning your insides into hamburger. Small-caliber gunshots to the chest and skull are nearly always fatal. Had I known you were going to pull a pretty ribbon out of your sleeve like some two-bit magician, tie me up with it, and indulge your mental torture fetish in your basement, I would've shot you. Many times."

"Two-bit magician?"

"Men like you enjoy being flattered."

The muscles on his arms bulged. Magic clamped me, hard and painful. The familiar fear flooded me in a slow wave. I was really tired.

"I've broken Significant mages in this trap," he said, his voice matter-of-fact.

True.

"I'll break you."

"You will try."

The pressure on my mind skyrocketed. The magic turned into a beast, chewing on me. Its teeth ripped a quiet moan from me. I stared at him, channeling all of my anger into my defenses.

Blood slipped from his nostrils and slid down his face.

"Give up," he growled.

"You first."

It hurt. The weight was so heavy. My defenses quaked. My hands were shaking.

Mad Rogan growled like an animal. It hurt him too.

Adam Pierce, Adam Pierce, Adam Pierce . . . The name resonated through my mind like the toll of a church bell. I wanted to clamp my hands over my ears, but it wouldn't help. The sound and pressure were everywhere. The magic devoured my barriers, seeking its prey.

My thoughts began to dissolve, slipping away from me. He was almost through.

Adam Pierce, Adam Pierce, Adam Pierce . . .

The basement swam around me. The walls turned liquid.

My mind boiled under pressure. I had to give in. I had to feed the beast to save myself.

I couldn't betray my client. He couldn't win.

Feed the beast. Feed it something secret, something I kept buried so deep in my soul that I swore never to let it out.

No, I can't.

The magic ripped apart the inner walls of my mind.

I can't.

My defenses burst, and with one last effort I shoved my deepest secret in front of the beast. It snapped my guilt into its jaws and tore it out. The words spilled out of me in a rush.

"When I was fifteen years old, I found the letter from our physician with my father's diagnosis on it. He caught me and made me promise not to tell anyone. I kept his secret for a year. I'm the reason why my father died when he did. If I had told Mom, we could've started treatment a year earlier. I'm responsible. I didn't tell. I didn't tell anyone to this day, because I'm a coward."

The magic shot through the Acubens Exemplar like a blast wave. The glowing lines pulsed with brilliance and vanished, exhausted, all of their power expended in trying to rip my secret out of me.

I slumped over on the floor, my face cold. The lack of pressure was pure, distilled bliss. I felt so light.

Mad Rogan walked over to me, moving carefully, and swore.

"Fuck you too," I told him.

He knelt by my feet. How the hell could he even move after this? I heard metal clanging. He lifted my head and put something to my lips.

I clamped my teeth together.

"It's water, you stubborn idiot," he snarled.

I tried to shake my head, but he forced my mouth open. Water wet my tongue. I swallowed, fighting the fog.

Fatigue wrapped me, or maybe it was some sort of blanket. Then we were in a car. It was dark outside.

The car stopping. Car door swinging open. Mad Rogan carrying me. Warehouse door. Cold cement.

The door opening.

Mom.

I woke up in the living room. Someone had left the table lamp on. It glowed with soft electric light, and the room looked so cozy, with its dark blue-green walls and warm yellow lamps. I snuggled into the throw someone had put over me. I'd had a really ugly nightmare.

I stretched. The muscles of my legs and arms cramped. Ow, ow, ow.

Not a nightmare. Mad Rogan really did chain me in his basement.

I sat up. Everything hurt. My back felt like it had been beaten up by a sack of potatoes.

That bastard. I'd file a police report, except nobody would believe me, and explaining how I'd held him off inside the spell would make things really complicated. That's okay. I would find some way to get even.

Voices floated to me from the kitchen. Mother. She

sounded upset. I squinted at the clock on the Blu-ray player. 11:45 p.m. Given a chance, we argued until we turned purple in the face and passed out from the effort, but this was late for a fight even by our family's standards. I pushed myself upright and staggered toward the voices.

My mother's voice cut through the night. ". . . Pierce? Irresponsible and stupid. Stupid, Bernard!"

Right. We'd been busted. After that ass dropped me off at my doorstep, my mother must've leaned on Bern for explanations, and he must've broken down and told her everything.

I pushed my way into the kitchen. Bern sat at the table, his face a somber mask. Next to him Leon was pushing a marble back and forth on the table with a chopstick and trying his best to look like he didn't care about anything. Catalina and Arabella sat together. Catalina's face had shut down, the way it usually did when something really stressful happened between adults. Arabella looked like she wanted to punch something. Both they and Leon should've been in bed. Grandma Frida nursed a coffee, her eyes red. I felt a rush of guilt. I'd made my grand-mother cry.

"I can't believe you," my mother snarled.

"You can stop yelling at him," I said. "It was my call."

Mom spun around. We stared at each other.

"Tomorrow you will go to MII," she said. Her voice was quiet, but it had about as much give in it as a steel beam. "You'll tell them you're off this job."

I braced myself. I'd known this moment would come sooner or later, and I'd been dreading it. "No."

My mother squared her shoulders. "Fine. Then I will do it."

Mother had lost her license four years ago. She blamed

herself for it. If anything happened to me, she would blame herself as well. I didn't want to do this. I didn't want to stir up all that guilt and heartache, so I tried to keep my voice as gentle as possible. "You don't have the authority to speak for the firm. The agency is in my name."

The kitchen went so quiet you could hear a pin drop. Catalina's eyes were as big as saucers.

My mother's face turned into a cold, flat mask.

"The decision is mine," I said. "I'm the one licensed. We are going after Pierce."

"How are you going to contain him?"

"I don't have to contain him. I met him and I'm talking him in."

"How is that working for you?" Mother asked. "Because you looked half dead when I found you on the doorstep."

"That wasn't Adam Pierce. That was Mad Rogan."

Mother recoiled. Leon made a choking noise.

"I thought he was out," Bern said.

"He's in. Apparently he does care about his cousin."

"Are you out of your mind?" Mother's voice cracked like a whip. "Do you have any idea what kind of fire you're playing with?"

"Yes, I do."

"It's just money."

"It's not just about money." My voice went up. "It's about our family. I won't let them push us around just because they feel like it. I won't let them uproot us. They don't get to do it."

"Nevada!"

"Yes, Mother?"

"We can start over!"

"And how long will that take? Without equipment,

without a house, without our client database? You know most of our business comes from word-of-mouth recommendations, and those recommendations are for Baylor Investigative Agency. MII will take our name. When our phone is disconnected, and our website is down, people will assume we're out of business and move on. It will take years before we rebuild. The answer is no."

"It's not worth your life!" my mother snarled. "If you're doing this out of some misguided obligation to your father . . ."

"I'm doing it for us and for me. When I took over, the business had slowed to almost nothing. I built this agency on the foundation you and Dad made. It's my business now because I worked my ass off for six years to get it running. I sacrificed for it, and I love it. I love what I do. I love our life. It makes me happy and I'm good at it, and nobody, not you, not Grandma, not MII, or Pierce, or Mad Rogan is going to take it away from me!"

I realized I was screaming and clamped my mouth shut.

Shock slapped Mom's face. The kids sat frozen. Bern kept blinking.

Grandma Frida set her coffee cup down with a clink. "Well, she is your daughter."

Mother turned and walked out of the room.

I faced the kids. "Bed. Now."

They took off.

Bern got up. "I'm going to go too."

I landed next to Grandma Frida. I felt all raw inside. Fighting with Mom was always difficult. She used to drive me insane. I would scream and she would counter with these perfect, logical arguments. And then I grew up and realized how brittle she was.

Grandma glanced at me. "You look like hell."

"Mad Rogan sedated me, kidnapped me, chained me in his basement, and then tried to pry information out of me with a spell."

Grandma Frida blinked. "Did you give him what he wanted?"

"No. I broke his spell."

Grandma Frida looked into her cup. "Your mother will get over it. She knew you'd butt heads sooner or later. Hell, if you didn't, I'd take you to have your head examined. Your mother survived in that hole in the ground for two months. She's more resilient than you give her credit for."

That didn't make me feel any better. "Grandma . . ."

"Yes?"

"When you said you knew someone who could install shockers, did you mean it, or were you kidding me?"

Grandma Frida set her coffee back down. "You're not serious, are you?"

"I wouldn't ask if I wasn't."

"That bad?"

I had been beaten up before and I'd been shot at four times. But what happened today bothered me more. "When I get into a fight, I know I can cause damage. When I am shot at, I can shoot back. But this . . ." My hands curled into fists as I struggled to find the words. "I had no chance. His magic was off the scale. I felt it when he picked me up. It was like looking into an outer space shot of a supernova. It made me feel helpless. Vulnerable. Like nothing I did would even make a dent in him."

Grandma sighed.

He could've killed me. He could've cut my head off while I was chained up, and there was nothing I could've done about it. I caught myself before I told that to my grandmother. "I need a way to have a fighting chance."

"You can walk away."

I shook my head. "Oh no. No. Maybe before he attacked me, but not now."

"You have to be very sure, darling. Once they go in, they stay in forever."

"How likely is it to kill me?"

"Less than one percent of the bindings go wrong, and if Makarov installs them, you won't have an issue. But bindings aren't your biggest problem. It's using those bastards. Do it wrong, and it will kill you."

"Then I'm sure." The next time Mad Rogan came near me, he would be in for a hell of a surprise.

"Let me make a call." Grandma rose.

I got up and went to look for my mother.

I checked the living room, the media room, and the hiding room, which had started out as a spare bedroom but had turned into another hangout room. I checked the door to Mother's bedroom and found it locked. Knocking didn't seem to produce any result. Calling "Mom . . ." in a sad, conciliatory voice didn't work either. I gave up and headed to my bedroom.

When I was picking out the spot for my bedroom, I wanted privacy. There was a time about seven years ago when I couldn't get away from my sisters no matter how hard I tried. When we moved into the warehouse, my parents took that into account and built me a small loft apartment. My bedroom and bathroom sat near the top of the warehouse, on top of the two storage rooms. My bedroom faced the street and my bathroom, along the same wall, was right against the separating wall that segregated our living space from Grandma's motor pool. A wooden staircase led to a landing, which connected to my loft by a sturdy folding ladder. If I wanted, I could stow the top ten steps, making my bedroom unreachable.

I climbed the stairs up and flicked on the light. Generally the warehouse had no windows, but when we set up the bedrooms, if you wanted a window, one was installed for you, and I had wanted a window. I had wanted two, actually, one in the bathroom, overlooking Grandma's garage, so I could glance out and see the back entrance, and one in the bedroom running the entire length of the room. If I lay on my bed, I could look out of my window at the city. The city could also look back at me, so I invested in pleated blinds in addition to two sets of curtains, one gauzy and white, the other thick opaque white. I had left the blinds drawn up and the opaque curtains open, and the night unrolled past the glass in all its dark glory. If I'd still had a screen, I'd have opened the window and let the night in. But I had managed to accidentally push it out a month ago when I'd been cleaning the window, and getting it back at that particular moment had proved to be too frustrating. If I opened the window now, I'd let in the night and a swarm of mosquitoes.

Let's see, I had blackmailed a mechanic; called my employer, who was probably a Prime, a terrible person—again; met with a pyrokinetic Prime and gotten kidnapped by a telekinetic Prime; gotten into a fight with my mother; and made the decision to have a weapon that could possibly kill me implanted in my arms. Some day I'd had. Too many Primes all around.

I was tired and threadbare, as if today had worn holes in me. I didn't want to think about anything, most of all about what I had to give up to break Rogan's spell. I just wanted to numb myself somehow and go to sleep. I had a bottle of nonprescription sleeping pills in my medicine cabinet, but they gave me nightmares.

I can't believe I've been obsessing over his eyes. I can't believe I thought he was hot when I was watching him walk toward me. I should've known right then he was trouble. A man like that didn't just take a stroll through botanical gardens. I saw a tiger with glowing eyes and teeth as big as my fingers, and instead of running for my life, I sat there and admired how handsome he was while he got close enough to pounce.

Something bounced off my window. I jerked back. Too small for a bat. Too dark outside for a bird. What in the world . . .

I unlatched the window and pulled it open. A small fireball shot at me from the street. I leaped back and slammed into the bookshelves six feet behind me.

The fireball landed on my rug, still on fire. Aah! I kicked it across my bedroom floor into the bathroom, onto the tile. Then I raced after it, yanked the shower door open, grabbed the detachable shower head, and drowned the flames.

A charred tennis ball.

Well, wasn't that lovely? I pulled a pair of scissors out of a drawer, stabbed the tennis ball, and marched to the window, carrying my trophy. Adam Pierce stood on the street below me.

I scraped the tennis ball off on the outside of the window. It fell to the asphalt below.

"What the hell is wrong with you? Are you trying to kill me?"

"If I was trying, you'd know. Come talk to me."

"It's one o'clock in the morning."

"It's two, but who cares." He waved at me. "Come on. I've got something to show you."

To go or not to go? If I went, he would learn that when he said "Jump," I did. But if I didn't go and he was thinking of surrendering, I would kick myself for losing this opportunity. I had to make up my mind fast. If my mother saw him in her current state, she'd shoot him in the eye. God, that would be all I needed right now. Ugh.

"There's a tree over there, behind the wall." I pointed to an old oak behind a four-foot-high stone wall. "Wait for me behind it."

He put his foot out and bowed with a flourish. "Yes, my lady."

I climbed downstairs, grabbed the keys in case someone decided to lock me out, and made a beeline for the tree. I hopped over the wall. He was waiting where I told him to be, behind the tree, shielded from the house by the massive trunk. His motorcycle leaned against the wall. I came over and sat next to him on the mulch around the tree.

He grinned. "Why here? Scared your mother will see me?"

"Scared she will shoot you. My mother isn't feeling charitable toward you at the moment."

"It's like that, huh?"

"It is."

He peered at my face, picked up a fallen branch, and lifted it up. The branch burst into bright orange flame. "What happened to you? You look like hell."

"I have competition and he wasn't nice."

"I'm popular, what can I say." The flame vanished, and he blew ash from his fingers.

"Yes, let's make it all about you."

He startled.

"Did you come to surrender?" I asked.

"No."

I sighed. "What will it take for you to see the light?"

"I don't know." He shrugged and grinned. "Try sleeping with me. It might convince me."

Did he just hit on me? Yes, he did. "No, thanks."

He leaned back on his elbow, his black leather pants tightening over his legs, and smiled. It was his famous "come-hither" smile, the one the media loved to broadcast, the kind of smile no woman who'd gone through puberty would ignore. It promised things, wild, wicked, hot things. It probably almost never misfired. Well, he was in for a surprise.

"If you're really hard up, I can introduce you to my grandmother. She's a fan."

Adam blinked.

"She doesn't typically sleep with pretty young things, but she would make an exception in your case. You might even learn a trick or two."

He finally regained his ability to speak. "Your grandmother?"

I nodded.

He laughed. "Well, at least she would die happy."

"Don't flatter yourself."

"It's not flattery. It's a fact." He leaned over to me. "I can set your sheets on fire."

I had no doubt of that. "Will I be burned to a crisp?"

"Kiss me and you'll find out."

No, thanks. "Your family is worried about you."

"You're fun. I like fun. I like new and exciting. Did I tell you that your voice is hot, Nevada?"

The way he said my name was almost indecent. He

couldn't have sunk more invitation into it if he'd stripped in front of me.

"When you talk, it makes me think of fun things I could do to you. With you."

Good catch there.

"And your skin is like honey. I wonder how you taste."

Bitter and tired. "Mhm."

He reached over to touch a strand of my hair. I pulled back. "You don't have the touching rights."

"How do I get those?"

Stop being a self-absorbed spoiled baby. "You get those if I fall in love with you."

He stopped. "In love. You're serious?"

"Yes." That would shut him up.

"What is this, the sixteenth century? Should I write you a sonnet next?"

"Is it going to be a good sonnet?"

He leaned back on the grass and swiped his thumb across his phone. "Watch this."

The screen turned white. The pale background shattered, breaking into individual pieces and flying off in a complicated pattern. A woman appeared on the screen. She was older, probably past fifty, although it was hard to tell her exact age. A navy business suit hugged her pencil-thin frame. Her makeup was expert, her caramel hair styled with artful precision into a loose, yet formal, hairdo. Her heart-shaped face, big dark eyes, and narrow nose gave her away. I was looking at Christina Pierce.

"I got a message from my mother," Adam said. "Emailed to my private address from a public location and encoded with the family encryption. Very cloak and dagger."

He pushed Play. Christina Pierce came to life.

"I have a plane on standby ready to take you to Brazil,"

she said. Her voice had the overtone of a Georgia accent, but there was nothing soft about it. "It's a non-extradition country. This is the house." A picture of a mansion replaced her image: white walls, tropical greenery, and an infinity pool, dark blue silhouetted against the lighter blue of the ocean. Christina reappeared. "While you're gone, someone else will take the blame. You can return in as little as a year to a clean record and a tide of public support and sympathy for you being wrongfully accused. A year in paradise, Adam, with your every need attended. You have my word that you won't spend a single minute in jail. Think about it."

I'd asked Augustine for reassurance. House Pierce had obliged.

"My mother says she loves me." Pierce studied her image. "Love is control. People say they love you when they want to run your life. They wedge and pound you into a shape they find comfortable, and when you try to escape, they hog-tie you with guilt. My family figured it out years ago. We've been marrying and breeding for profit for over a century. No love involved."

"I don't see it that way."

"The only reason you're sitting here under this tree is because my mother twisted Montgomery's arm, and he twisted yours by threatening your family. If it wasn't for them losing their house, would you have taken this job?"

"Probably not. But in the end the choice was mine."

"Why? You don't owe them anything. You didn't ask to be born. They dragged you into this world kicking and screaming, and now they expect you to conform. Well, I say fuck 'em."

You didn't ask to be born . . . In some ways he was still fifteen years old inside and as volatile as the fire he made.

"Look, at least you have your parents," I said. "My dad's gone. Nothing can bring him back."

He tilted his head. "What is it like?"

"It hurts, still. He was in my life for so long and now he's just not there. My mother loves me. She'd do anything for me. But my dad was the one who got me. He understood why I did things. We tried so desperately to keep him alive, but he still died, and our world collapsed. I was older, but my sisters were young, and it hit them really hard."

Adam shrugged. "I have a father. I never had a dad. He's diligent. If my mother explained to him that a football game or a piano recital needed to be attended, he would make sure to show up. He was present but not there. I don't know what he loves, but I know he likes money. My oldest brother works for the company. My other brother is in the military, building those vital business connections. My father talks to both of them. He starts taking an interest in his kids when we start making money. Until then we belong to Mother."

"At least she cares enough to worry about you. She must love you."

"She indulges me. There is a difference. Indulgence implies tacit disapproval. The House is doing well. Her professional life is healthy; she has an IQ of 148 and could do her job in her sleep. Our finances are robust, and my father would never embarrass the family by a scandal. I'm her excuse to be emotional. Every time I do something that shakes their palace, she can grab the lion's share of attention with her dramatics. If it wasn't for me, what would she bitch about? I make it a point to be a disappointment as often as I can."

Wow. "Have you ever just accidentally stumbled into meeting their expectations?"

"I went to college. When I started my master's, I realized that it would never be enough. All my life the House would expect me to climb the ladder of their expectations. Get a degree. Make money. Marry right. Produce intelligent, magically gifted children. Make more money. They had me for twenty-four years. That's all they get." Adam leaned toward me. "Look, bottom line is, parents and sisters is something you do when you're five. I'm giving you a shot at being free. Shoot your family the bird and come away with me."

I'm a known fugitive who likes to set people on fire. Come away with me so we can have hot sex while the entire city is trying to shoot me in the head. If I get bored, I'll barbecue you for my amusement. Sure, let me get my shoes.

"It's not a good idea."

"What if I pretend I'm in love?" Adam flicked his fingers and a tiny flame flared above his hand. He held it like a candle to my face. His eyes, fringed in thick eyelashes, were so dark that they turned into two bottomless pools. "I guarantee nobody would find us. The cops can look for a thousand years, and they still won't get me."

He was really pushing the whole run-away-with-me thing. I played dumb. "Are you just leading me on?"

"Me? No."

Lie. He was lying to me. Why?

"I really am in lust, I mean, in love, with you."

Well, the lust part was true. I had to play it cool. "Do you have any intention of letting me bring you in?"

"I'm considering it."

Lie. Damn it.

"Nevada," he purred. "Come on, sunny girl. Live a little."

Cornelius's words came back to me. *Adam takes what he wants, and if you tell him no, he will hurt you.* He wanted acceptance. He wanted to be reassured he was special. If I outright rejected him, the sting of that rejection could turn into hate in a blink. I had to bring him in and not end up like that security guard.

"Forget your family and jump off the cliff with me. We'll fly away."

I leaned over and kissed him on the cheek. "Not tonight. Maybe one day, if I grow wings."

I got up and walked toward the warehouse.

"They're pulling you down and you're letting them," he called after me.

"Don't get killed, Adam," I called over my shoulder. "I still have to turn you in."

 **Chapter 6**

ad Rogan and I stood on the edge of a cliff. Below us, the ground plunged so far down that it was as if the planet itself had ended at our feet. The wind tugged at my hair. He was wearing those dark pants again and nothing else. The hard muscle corded his torso, fueled by an overpowering, almost savage strength. Not the mindless brutality of a common thug or the cruel power of an animal, but an intelligent, stubborn, human strength. It was everywhere: in the set of his broad shoulders, in the turn of his head on a muscular neck, in the tilt of his square jaw. He turned to me and his whole body tightened, the muscles flexing and hardening, his hands ready to grip and crush, his eyes alert, missing nothing, and blazing with the brilliant electric blue of magic. I could picture him getting his sword and walking alone onto the drawbridge to defend his castle against a horde of invaders with that exact look on his face.

He was terrifying, and I wanted to run my hands down that chest and feel the hard ridges of his abs. I was some special kind of idiot.

Magic roiled about him, ferocious and alive, a pet monster with vicious teeth. He moved toward me, bringing it with him. "Tell me about Adam Pierce."

I reached over and put my hand on his chest. His skin was burning hot. The muscle tensed under my fingers. An eager electric shiver ran through me. I wanted to lean against that chest and kiss the underside of that jaw, tasting his sweat on my tongue. I wanted him to like it.

"What happened to the boy?" I asked. "The one who destroyed a city in Mexico? Is he still inside?"

"Nevada!" My mother's voice cut through my dreams like a knife.

I sat straight up in my bed.

Okay. Either I was way more messed up inside, or Mad Rogan was a strong projector and could shoot images straight into my mind. Either way was bad. What happened to the boy . . . I needed to have my head examined.

"Neva?"

"I'm up." I got out of bed and swung the door open. My mother stood on the landing. "Your grandma brought her specialist over. You're really going through with this?"

I raised my chin. "Yes."

"Why?"

"Would you go to war without your gun?"

"Is it war now, Nevada?"

I sat on the stairs. "Okay, so you were right. It is a little bit about Dad, and it is a lot about keeping a roof over our head. This is our home. I will do almost anything to keep it. Also I negotiated with MII, and if I die, you get the name of the agency back for one dollar."

Her face twisted. "I don't care, Nevada. Sweetheart, I don't care. I want you to be okay. None of it is worth losing you. I thought we were a team."

"We are."

"But you didn't tell me. And you got Bern to cover it up."

I sat on the steps. "I didn't tell you because you would do exactly what you did last night. You'd order me not to do it. We are a team, but you're my mother. You will do everything to keep me safe, and there is a point where it's my decision to stay safe or not."

My mother considered it. "Okay. Point made."

"He came here last night," I said. "Adam Pierce."

"Here?"

I nodded.

"What did he want?"

"He wanted me to go away with him. He's playing me somehow, and I don't know what his game is yet. We need to make sure the alarm is set every night. I don't trust him." I rubbed my face. "I'm really deep in this mess now."

"By choice," Mother said.

"Does it really matter? I don't think I could get out even if I wanted to. It's scaring me. Mom, I can't even . . . Mad Rogan was . . ." I raised my hands, trying to make the right words come out.

"Like standing in a hurricane," my mother said.

"Yes. Like that. I just want a level playing field. I love you. Please don't be mad at me."

"I love you too. If you think you need a level playing field, then go for it. You're an adult. It's your decision. But I have a problem with it. With all of it."

She walked away. Great. She was still mad at me.

I found Grandma and her "specialist" in the garage part of the warehouse. Makarov turned out to be a sparse, fit man in his early sixties. He had started balding, and his silver hair was cut short. He sat in a folding chair talking to my grandmother, a heavy metal box about two feet by two feet sitting next to him, while a dark-haired man my age, who looked like a carbon copy of Makarov forty years ago, waited nearby.

Grandma saw me and waved me over.

"So this is the kandidat." Makarov's voice was spiced with a Russian accent. "How old are you?"

"Twenty-five."

"Height?"

"Five feet five inches."

"Weight?"

"One hundred and thirty pounds."

"Heart problems?"

"No."

"Blood pressure, migraines, any of that?"

"I get a headache once in a while, but migraines not that often. Maybe one every six months or so."

Makarov nodded, smart green eyes appraising me. He tapped the box with his foot. "This is *murena*. Means 'moray eel' in Russian. It's not a fish. Some say plant, some say animal, a really primitive one. It's a thing. We call it *murena* because of what it does. The moray eel will hide in its lair. You never even know it's there. It sits quietly underwater until a fish swims by, and then pow!" He grabbed a fistful of air. "It shoots out and bites the fish. It has a second mouth inside its throat, and that mouth shoots out and sinks onto the fish with hooked teeth." He raked the air, holding his fingers like talons.

I wasn't nervous before, but he was getting me there.

"That's what you will be like. Nothing visible from the surface. Walk through any detector. And then pow!"

"Pow sounds good." Sort of.

"Now the drawback. The fine print." Makarov leaned

forward. "First, nobody knows what the hell this is. We reached into magic and pulled them out and nobody on the planet can tell you what they are and where they come from. We don't know what long-term consequences are. We know that we had them implanted in three generations, and so far nothing. I have them in me. I don't hear voices or get wild urges to murder people. But there is always a possibility."

"I can live with that."

"Two, one kandidat in a hundred and twelve rejects *murena*. They don't always make it. That's why Szenia is here." He nodded at the blond man. "He is a trained paramedic. But if your heart stops, it stops. Eh." He spread his arms.

"Eh" was not the reaction I was looking for.

"Three, the way this works. *Murena* feeds on your energy. You've got to prime it with your magic. It's going to hurt. It will hurt like a son of a bitch. But when you touch the other guy, it will hurt him more." He grinned. "But do it more than a few times in a row, you're going to see red floating thing in your eyes. They call it the glow-worm. That's your body's way of telling you to stop. Do it again, the veins in your head will blow up and"—he made a sharp noise, drawing his thumb sideways across his neck—"no need to bother with nine-one-one. You're going to die right there."

"How do I prime it?"

"It's mental. I will show you once they are in."

"What happens when I hurt someone?"

Makarov narrowed his eyes. "Depends on how much power you've got and how badly you want them hurt. You control it. It's certified nonlethal and meant for behavior modification, not straight self-defense. Any kandidat up to Notable magic rank is pretty safe. You hurt the bad guy, he stops what he's doing, rolls around on the ground for a bit while you're kicking him in the ribs, but at the end, both of you go home. Significants have been known to send people into convulsions."

"What about Primes?" my mother asked.

I almost jumped. I hadn't heard her come in.

"No Prime had one in them, as far as I know. Primes don't need them. They have their own magic, and they are busy doing things with it rather than herding recruits through boot camp or babysitting mages on the battle-field." Makarov looked at my mother. "Haven't seen you for a while, Sergeant First Class. How's the leg?"

"Still there, Sergeant Major."

He nodded. "That's good to hear."

"You kill my daughter, you're not walking out of here," Mother said.

"I'll take that under consideration." Makarov turned to me. "So, yea or nay?"

"How much is it going to cost us?" I asked.

"That's between you and your grandmother. I owe her a favor."

I took a deep breath. "Yea."

Makarov got up and took a marker out of his pocket. "Good. Did you eat?"

"No."

"Even better."

Thirty minutes later, every inch of my arms was covered with arcane marks. Szenia took my vitals, then brought in a large chair, and he and Makarov strapped me to it.

"Is it going to hurt?"

"You bet."

Sergeant Major had a lousy bedside manner.

He pulled out a cardboard box of kosher salt from Szenia's bag and drew a simple circle around the chair. "Just in case."

"In case of what?"

"In case *murenas* get snippy." He set the metal box in the circle of salt, put a large, old-fashioned key into the lock, and opened it with a click. A faint scent of cinnamon floated into the air.

The box's top slid aside. Makarov barked something in a language I didn't understand. His left hand turned blue, as if coated in glowing, translucent light. His fingers lengthened, the knuckles becoming large and knobbed. Claws slid over his nails. He reached into the box with his new demonic hand and withdrew a thin ribbon of pale green light. It had no legs, no head, no tail. Just a strip of light about seven inches long and an inch wide. It wriggled in his fist.

Makarov chanted, bringing it closer.

Maybe this wasn't such a good idea.

Makarov slapped the light onto my exposed left forearm, right between the glyphs on my skin. It felt like boiling oil. I screamed. The light sprouted tentacle-like roots and bit into my skin. Pain lanced me like a scalpel dipped in acid. I fought against it, but it burrowed its way into my skin, into my flesh, sinking deeper and deeper. I jerked in the chair, trying to get it off me. If only I could get my hand free, I would claw it out of me.

My mother turned away, her face contorted.

The pain seared the inside of my arm, ripping another scream out of me. Magic clamped my body. It felt like an elephant had landed on my chest. I kept screaming until it finally slid into my bone and settled there. I slumped against my restraints, exhausted.

The ache subsided. Sweat drenched my forehead.

Makarov raised my chin with his right, human hand and peered in my eyes.

"Alive?"

"Alive," I ground out.

"Good. Now the right arm."

It felt like forever before they finally undid the restraints. The marks on my skin had faded, as if absorbed by the magic. My arms still ached, as if I had done too many push-ups or carried something really heavy the day before, but the soreness was nothing compared to the way it had first felt. I'd take the soreness any day.

"We're going to do a little demonstration now." Makarov motioned to Szenia. The blond man came to stand next to me.

"Picture power flowing down from your shoulder into your right hand."

I pictured a wave of green light sliding down inside my arm into my fist.

"Wait for it. The first time always takes a little longer."

I stood there, picturing a viscous glow and feeling stupid.

Something shifted inside my arm. Nothing happened on the surface, but I felt a faint prickling at my fingertips.

"Ready?" Makarov asked.

"Yes."

"Give Szenia a little love tap."

I reached over and grasped Szenia's shoulder. Blinding pain shot through my arm straight into my chest. Thin streaks of lightning danced over my arms, piercing through my skin. Szenia's eyes rolled back in his head. The pain crushed me, and I doubled over. The ache reverberated through my skull, rattling my teeth. Ow.

Makarov shoved me back. I let go, and Szenia crumpled to the floor. Thick white foam slid out of his mouth. His legs drummed the ground. Oh no.

Makarov dropped to his knees and slid his demon hand straight into Szenia's chest. The convulsions slowed. Slowly Makarov withdrew his clawed fingers. Szenia opened his eyes.

"Szivoi to, geroy?" Makarov asked.

The blond man nodded.

Makarov turned to me, looked at my face, then turned to Frida. "I've got to talk to you."

They marched to the other end of the warehouse. I got Szenia a bottle of water from Grandma's fridge and propped him up so he could drink. "I'm so sorry."

"That's okay." He took the bottle and drank in long, greedy gulps. "That stung a bit. I'll just lay here for a while." He lie back down.

Across from us Makarov and Grandma Frida were arguing. Makarov was pointing at me. I strained, trying to hear. Something about "should've told me."

Makarov did an about-face and marched toward me. Grandma trailed him. The Russian closed the distance between us, his jaw set. "You listen to me and listen good. Don't use this on anyone below Significant level, you hear me? You could kill somebody, and I don't want their souls on my conscience."

He picked up his box and walked out. Szenia rolled to his feet and followed him.

Grandma Frida watched him go, her arms crossed on her chest.

"What's going on?" my mother asked.

Grandma Frida shook her head. "Crazy Russian. Never mind. Just be careful with the shockers, Neva."

My teeth still hurt. "I wasn't planning on randomly buzzing people on the street with them."

My cell phone rang on the table. I never went far without it, even in the house. I picked it up. An unlisted number. Oh goodie.

"Nevada Baylor."

"I need to talk to you," Mad Rogan said into the phone. "Meet me for lunch."

My pulse jumped, my body snapped to attention, and my brain shut down for a second to come to terms with the impact of his voice. I'd slap myself except my mother and grandmother already thought I was nuts, and hurting myself would get me committed for sure.

"Sure, let me get right on that." Hey, my voice still worked. "Should I bring my own chains this time? Or do you have bigger plans, and this is some sort of freaky murder foreplay"—why did the word *foreplay* just come out of my mouth?—"and I'll end up cut up into small pieces inside some freezer at the end? I can just spray myself with mace and shoot myself in the head now and save you the trouble."

"Are you done?" he asked.

"Just getting started." I was so brave over the phone.

"Lunch, Ms. Baylor. Concentrate. Pick a place."

"You seem to be under the impression that I work for you and you can give me orders. Let me fix that." I hung up.

Grandma looked at my mom. "Did she just hang up on Mad Rogan?"

"Yes, she did. Did you know that Adam Pierce showed up at our house last night?"

Grandma's eyes went wide. "He was here?"

"She met him outside."

Grandma swung toward me. "Did you take any pictures?"

My phone beeped. Unlisted number again. I answered it.

"I'm not a man of infinite patience," Mad Rogan said.

I hung up.

"Pictures or it didn't happen!" Grandma declared.

I scrolled through my phone and pulled up the shot of Adam Pierce in a Mercer T-shirt. "There you go."

Grandma grabbed the phone. It beeped. She answered it. "She'll call you back. Nevada, can I email Adam's picture to myself?"

"You have to hang up first."

She hung up and clicked the phone, typing with her index fingers. "Arabella is going to flip."

My mother sighed.

Grandma passed me the phone. "Here's your phone back."

Another beep.

"Yes?"

His voice was quiet and precise. "If you hang up on me again, I will slice your car into small pieces and hang them on your roof like Christmas wreaths."

"First, destroying my property is a crime, just like kidnapping me is a crime. Second, how exactly is mincing my car into small pieces supposed to convince me to come to lunch with you? Third, if you're close enough to slice my car, I'm close enough to shoot you in the head. Can you deflect bullets if you don't know they're coming?"

"I'm trying to be reasonable," he said. "Come to lunch with me and we can exchange information or . . ."

"Or what? My mother and grandmother are right here.

Shall I pass the phone to them so you can threaten them with terrible things if I don't agree to lunch?"

"Will it do any good?"

"Probably not."

"What would make you feel safe?" he asked.

"An apology would be a start."

"I apologize for kidnapping you," he said. "I promise not to kidnap you before, during, or after lunch. This is a business conversation. Where would you be comfortable meeting me?"

Comfortable? The memory of his magic was still burning my brain. There was no such thing as being comfortable where he was concerned. I could meet him in the middle of city hall, surrounded by SWAT, and he could nuke them and me without breaking a sweat. But I would have to talk to him. He wanted to meet me, and he would get what he wanted one way or the other.

"Ms. Baylor?"

"Hold on. I'm trying to figure out a place where nobody will recognize us."

"If you prefer, I can acquire a windowless creeper van, and we can huddle in it and have greasy takeout."

Huddle? "Tempting, but no. Takara, in an hour . . ."

He hung up.

I rolled my eyes.

"Is this a good idea?" Mother asked.

"I don't know. He mentioned exchanging information, so he might have something to trade. I don't think avoiding him will work. He won't take no for an answer. I can meet him on my terms or on his. I've tried his and I don't like them. Besides, Makarov said not to use shockers on anyone with low magic. Mad Rogan is a Prime." I made grabbing motions with my fingers.

"Mom?" Mother turned to Grandmother.

"What?"

"She's going to lunch with her kidnapper!"

"Take a picture for me," Grandma said.

"This family will put me into an early grave," my mother growled. "I'm coming with you. Mother, lock the doors and set the alarm. We'll take the van and the Barrett."

"Would the Barrett be enough?" Grandma Frida asked. "Isn't he supposed to bounce bullets off of his chest?"

"It fires .50 cal at twice the speed of sound. It will hit him before he ever hears the shot." My mother crossed her arms. "I'd like to see him bounce that off his chest."

 **Chapter 7**

$\mathcal{T}$akara's website described it as an Asian bistro, which in reality meant that they specialized in beautiful sushi and had a couple of traditional Chinese and Korean dishes on the menu. It occupied a large, modern building, all heavy brown stone and big windows. As I walked through the door, an eight-foot-wall fountain greeted me. The color palette was creamy beiges, soothing greens, and rich browns with a touch of metallic bronze here and there. The colors, the gentle sound of water, and the tasteful decor were soothing, yet the hostess in front of me and the three sushi chefs behind the counter looked distinctly freaked out.

I looked over the dark brown tables and saw Mad Rogan, wearing a grey suit over a white shirt opened at the collar. He sat toward the back, by the oversized bamboo shoots in a tall black floor vase. I knew the table. It let you look outside through the window, but the passersby couldn't really see you clearly. It was the least noticeable table on the floor, but now it might as well have been in the middle of the room. Mad Rogan was extremely difficult to ignore. The place was empty, except for two young women and a middle-aged couple, and all four pretended their hardest not to watch him.

My mother was parked across the parking lot, barely two hundred feet away. Her Barrett sniper rifle had an effective range of just over a mile. Her magic ensured that she didn't miss. My knees were still shaking. This was a dumb idea.

A hostess in a tight black dress forced a smile at me. "Ms. Baylor? Right this way, please."

I followed her. All this adrenaline primed my magic, and I could almost feel it pouring out of me like an angry swarm of electric bees ready to buzz. I was wearing old jeans, a charcoal blouse, and my best pair of running shoes. If I had to run for my life again, I was all set.

Mad Rogan rose to his feet, a fluid motion. A waiter appeared, as if by magic, and held the chair out for me.

Mad Rogan didn't touch my chair. He should've pulled it out, but he stayed right where he was. It could have been deliberate because he felt I didn't deserve the courtesy, but members of Houses lived and breathed etiquette.

"Did you do something to my chair?"

"No."

My magic snapped like a whip. Lie.

I turned to the table by the window. "I like the table over there better."

The waiter froze, petrified, unsure what to do.

I stepped toward the window table, pointed to the chair facing the parking lot, and looked at the two of them. "I'm sitting here."

Mad Rogan moved the fingers of his left hand half an inch. Faint red smoke puffed out of the carpet, forming a shape of a magic circle centering on my former chair, and dissipated into the air. He had laid a trap, and I had almost sat down into it. Bastard.

I pulled out my new chair. The rules of politeness dictated that he sat across from me, which would put the back of his head to the window and give my mother a lovely target. Mad Rogan took a step toward my chosen table. It slid back across the carpet out of the window's view as other tables glided aside, making room. The chair jerked out of my hand and followed. The three other chairs chased mine and arranged themselves around the table. He put his hand on the chair that let him watch both the door and the window, then invited me with a casual gesture. "Your table."

Grrrrr. This wouldn't go well.

I sat down.

He did also.

We glared at each other across the table.

The waiter hovered next to us, a nervous look on his face. "Welcome to Takara. What can I get you to drink?"

"Unsweetened tea with lemon," I said. "And could you please bring me some fake sugar with it?"

"Same," Mad Rogan said. "No lemon."

"Appetizer?" the waiter asked.

Mad Rogan glanced at me. "Your pick."

"Carpaccio."

"Great, I'll get that right out." The waiter took off, visibly relieved.

The Scourge of Mexico and I resumed our glaring. His eyes seemed to change color depending on the light. Yesterday, when he was in the circle, they were dark, almost indigo. Today they were a light, clear sky blue. My mind flashed right back to the cliff in my dreams. I stomped on that thought. I had no idea what sort of telepath he was.

The last thing I needed was to have him pluck an image of his half-naked glory out of my head.

"Do you have any ID?" I asked.

"ID?"

"You told me you were Mad Rogan, but how do I know you are who you say you are."

He broke apart his pair of chopsticks, rubbed them against each other, and held one at eye level, thicker end toward the ceiling. He opened his fingers. The chopstick remained suspended above the table. Impressive. I knew this game. We all played it in elementary school to identify our magic. If you could move the chopstick off the table, you were telekinetic. If you could lift the chopstick and hold it steady, you were a high-precision telekinetic and people would come to talk to your parents and offer scholarships for the commitment to future employment. They would pay for your education, and you would work for them for a decade or two in return.

Mad Rogan casually unrolled his napkin. A paper-thin slice of wood, so thin it was translucent, shaved itself off the top of the chopstick and floated down. Holy crap.

Another slice peeled off. The middle-aged couple stopped eating. The man's mouth hung slack. The woman visibly strained to swallow. Shivers ran down my spine. This couldn't be happening. Moving a table was one thing. It was bulky and heavy and required a lot of power to move, but this was on a different level. No telekinetic had that much control.

Mad Rogan placed the napkin across his lap. The chopstick spun in place. The wooden slivers rained down, landing in a perfect circle around it, like a ring of tiny petals.

The waiter came out of the back, carrying our drinks, and froze in the middle of the floor.

The first circle filled up with wooden shavings, and a second ring, wider, formed around it. The remaining half of the chopstick landed in the center of the two rings and split into four slivers with a loud crack.

I remembered to breathe.

The man from the middle-aged couple pulled out three twenties, tossed them on the table, and grabbed the woman's hand. They hurried out at a near run.

That was the scariest thing I had seen in a long time. How was it even possible that he could do this? If he did that to a human being, it would be horrifying.

Mad Rogan looked at me.

I had to say something, do something. Anything.

I pulled out my phone and took a picture of the table.

His eyebrows crept up a tiny bit.

"For my grandmother." I put the phone on the table and smiled at the waiter. "He broke his chopstick. Could you get us another set?"

The waiter nodded, hurried over to the table, set our drinks and carpaccio down, and escaped without saying a word. Mad Rogan picked up a tiny white dish usually used for soy sauce and casually swept the wooden slivers off the table with his hand.

"I would've settled for a driver's license." This was so not a good idea. He was freakishly powerful.

"A driver's license can be counterfeited. Nobody in the continental United States can duplicate this."

And so modest too.

The shorter of the women with auburn hair rose, walked over to our table, and placed a card on it. Her fingers shook a little. "My name is Amanda. Call me."

She walked back to her table, aggressively swaying on her heels.

I snagged a pink slice of rare New York strip drizzled with tangy sauce. Mmm, delicious. "That was ballsy. You've chased off two diners, caused the other two to lose their minds, and scared our waiter. Would you like to go in the back and terrorize the kitchen staff as well?"

"You started it with the table."

"Was I supposed to sit down in your trap?"

His face was completely serious. "Yes. It would've made you more agreeable and let us both get out of here faster."

"Well, I didn't." I almost slapped myself. How was that for a clever comeback? Not.

The waiter reappeared with chopsticks. "May I take your order?"

"Bulgogi," Mad Rogan said.

I ordered a simple salmon roll, and we both tore identical pink packets of fake sugar and dumped them into our drinks.

"Here is what I know," Mad Rogan said. "Your name is Nevada Baylor. You're the only licensed investigator in a small firm, which is currently a subsidiary of MII. MII runs security for several venues owned by House Pierce. House Pierce hired MII to bring their prodigal son home, and you drew the short straw."

I stole another piece of meat and chewed. It was delicious, and it kept me from talking and saying anything I might regret later.

"I'm not interested in Adam Pierce," he declared.

True. "Could've fooled me. Now I'm insulted. You kidnapped and tortured me for someone you're not even interested in."

The dragon refused to be amused. "I'm interested in finding Gavin Waller. Preferably alive."

True, but I had figured it out already. "Gavin has vanished off the face of the planet. His Twitter is inactive, his Instagram hasn't been updated, and there have been no sightings of him since that night. He's either hiding or dead."

Mad Rogan nodded. "Agreed."

"But Adam is loud and flashy, so you decided it would be easier to find Adam and make him tell you where Gavin is. I understand all that. Explain the kidnapping part."

"It's not relevant."

I paused with the slice of carpaccio halfway to my mouth. "You do understand that you grabbed me off the street like some serial killer? I thought you might seriously hurt me. It made me scared and upset. I was in fear for my life. This is extremely relevant to me."

Mad Rogan sighed. "Fine. I looked into Gustave's shop and found a series of large deposits from House Pierce."

I nodded. "I did as well."

"I came to discuss the deposits when I saw you inside. You're young, attractive, and blond. Adam's type."

"You thought I was Adam's groupie?" I'd be offended, but it was a waste of time.

"Yes. I thought you were delivering the cash to him. I tailed you to MII. Given their business ties, if the Pierces wanted to funnel money to Adam, using MII would've been a logical step. I saw you come out of the building and talk on the phone, then I followed you to Mercer."

My magic came on high alert. It wasn't a lie exactly, but it felt off to me.

"How?"

"How what?"

"How did you follow me to Mercer?"

"I tailed you."

Lie. My magic bounced up and down like a giddy toddler. Lie, lie, lie. Even if it didn't, I'd still know he was lying. I always checked to see if I was being followed. It was a habit. The traffic had been too heavy for him to tail me effectively anyway. He'd watched me enter MII and leave my car in the parking lot. He'd done something to my vehicle. *Aren't you a sly devil?* That's okay. Two could play that game.

"I was searching the gardens for you when I heard that idiot's motorcycle." He grimaced slightly. Adam Pierce wasn't his favorite person. If Adam got one of my cousins accused of murder, I wouldn't be a fan either.

"So instead of talking to me, asking for my credentials, or doing any of those things a normal person would do, you decided to assault me and chain me in your basement?"

He shrugged, a slow, deliberate movement. "It seemed like the most expedient way to obtain the information. And let's be honest, you weren't exactly harmed. I even took you home."

"You dumped me on my doorstep. According to my mother, I looked half dead."

"Your mother exaggerates. A third dead at most."

I stared at him. Wow. Just wow.

Our food arrived. Record time.

"I have no idea where Adam is hiding." I grabbed a piece of salmon roll, smeared some wasabi on it, and stuffed it in my mouth.

"I realize that now. Also the fact that you're meeting him alone, without any means to capture him, indicates that House Pierce hired MII and you to talk him into surrendering himself into their tender embrace." He leaned forward. His blue eyes focused on me, his gaze direct and difficult to hold. "MII employs combat-trained mages. Why would they send you? What are you? You're something. Not a telepath, but something."

Wouldn't you like to know? I chewed enthusiastically. *Mmm, mmm, yummy sushi. Sorry, can't talk with my mouth full.*

"What's your take on Adam?" he asked.

I kept chewing, playing for time and trying to think of the right words.

"I promise I won't share."

I sipped my tea. "Adam is volatile and chaotic. Every emotion is intense. He craves attention and desperately wants to be seen as cool, almost like a teenager. He likes a challenge, so when someone isn't instantly knocked off their feet with his sheer awesomeness, he'll work to prove that he's awesome. But, like a teenager, he is self-absorbed and can be cruel. He hates rejection, and his need to impress can flip into hate fast. He's smarter than he lets on, persistent, and dangerous."

"But you think you can talk him into surrendering himself to his House?"

"It's possible." I had captured his attention, which was in my favor, but he was lying to me, which wasn't. "I cut off his money. Combined with the manhunt, it should put enough pressure on him. He's flirting with the idea. What's your take on Adam?"

"A spoiled rich brat with too much free time, a daddy complex, and a sadistic streak a mile wide."

Okay. We were on the same page then.

Mad Rogan leaned slightly forward, focused on me. "What if I told you that he's stringing you along?"

"What makes you think that?"

He took a small tablet out of the inner pocket of his

suit and passed it to me. I took it, careful not to touch his fingers.

"A show of good faith," he said.

True. A video was paused on the screen. I flicked it on with a swipe of my finger. A recording of the street in front of First National Bank, probably from a security camera. Was that the video the cops had? "How did you get this?"

"I have my ways."

On the screen, two figures, one tall, the other shorter and slighter, walked into the camera's view and stopped before the glass-and-marble facade of the bank. The taller figure, in a familiar leather jacket, set down a metal canister, pulled out a piece of chalk, and crouched, drawing on the asphalt. I couldn't see what he was drawing, but my money was on a magic circle.

Thirty seconds later, the man spread his feet to shoulder width and raised his arms, elbows bent, fingers of the hands toward each other as if he were holding a large, invisible ball. The other figure opened the canister and began carefully pouring a thick, viscous liquid in front of the first man. A fire dashed through the stream, a quiet, golden flame contained in the invisible sphere between the first man's hands. The shorter man kept pouring. The fire blazed brighter and brighter.

"Napalm B," Mad Rogan said. "It's a thickening agent that makes jellied gasoline."

"I know. Benzene, gasoline, and polystyrene." Grandma Frida had outfitted more than one House vehicle with a military-grade flamethrower. Napalm B also burned for almost ten minutes and generated temperatures that beat even Adam Pierce's fire. It was one of the worst things humankind had ever invented.

Mad Rogan raised his eyebrows. I must've surprised him.

The ball of fire between the man's hands had grown to the size of a basketball. It churned and roiled, a furious inferno contained by magic. The flame brightened to yellow, then blazed with white. The taller man turned, and I saw his face, lit up by the glow of the fireball. Adam Pierce.

The shorter man—probably Gavin Waller—raised his hands palms out and pushed. The fireball vanished. The windows of the bank shattered, and flames shot out. First National exploded from the inside out. The fire roared like an enraged grizzly.

That's right, Gavin Waller was a short-range teleporter. Adam and Gavin stared at the flames, two dark silhouettes against the inferno.

Gavin's image looked slightly distorted. The next second, the distortion disappeared.

Wait a minute.

I rewound the video a few seconds. Two minutes thirty-one seconds, thirty-two, thirty-three, thirty-four, thirty-five, missed it. Thirty-two, pause.

Gavin's silhouette stood frozen on the screen. He was holding something rectangular, and it was bulging out on the left side. I zoomed in closer. A box. He was holding some kind of box. When did he get it?

I rewound the video back. The box popped into Gavin's hands a millisecond after the fireball disappeared. "What is Gavin Waller holding? He teleported something into his hands."

"A safe-deposit box."

"What was in the box?"

"Nobody knows." Mad Rogan grimaced. "They pulled

it out, took something out, and put it back. Adam pressurized the napalm B, and when the magic was no longer containing it, it exploded. The bank employees are still sorting through the wreckage. Part of the vault melted."

So this wasn't a political statement. This was a theft, and the arson was just a cover-up. Adam had torched a bank, killed a man, and injured his family just so he could steal something. And he had needed Gavin to teleport his fireball directly into the vault, because coming through the front door would have meant all sorts of alarms going off. By the time he would have made his way to the vault, half of Houston's finest would have surrounded the bank.

"Gavin isn't a strong teleporter," Mad Rogan said. "Someone had to have tagged the right safe-deposit box for him. Someone had gone to that bank and marked the box so Gavin could pull it out with his magic and stick the fireball in its place. That someone wasn't Adam Pierce or Gavin himself. The point is, this was planned. Pierce pulled off a perfect heist, covered his tracks, and hasn't said a word about it. Why?"

The heavens opened, and the realization fell out and hit me on the head. "He isn't done. Adam has an almost pathological need for attention. If he was done with his scheme, he would take a bow. He would go out in a blaze of glory, or let himself be arrested, or turn himself in to his House with a giant show. He wouldn't be able to resist making a statement one way or another. Instead he's hiding. And he's using me to keep his family at bay. As long as I report that I'm making contact and he's listening, they'll think there is a chance he'll turn himself in. They won't try to capture him. They will concentrate on slowing down the manhunt. I'm making it easier for him to keep going on with his plan."

"You don't sound surprised," he noted.

"I knew he was leading me on. I just didn't know why. Now I do." I gave him a bright smile to rub it in. "Thank you for solving the mystery for me."

Mad Rogan leaned back, his muscular body resting against the chair. "You're an experienced investigator. You want Adam Pierce, and he is open to making contact with you, but you can't talk him in and you have no means to subdue him. I want Gavin Waller. I have money and power on my side, but I can't find him. Lead me to Adam, and I will help you deliver him to House Pierce."

"You think you can contain Adam Pierce?"

He nodded, his face confident. "Yes. I can't guarantee he'll be undamaged after I'm done, but I give you my word he will be alive."

I folded my napkin and put it on the table. "Thank you for a lovely lunch. The answer is no. I already have an employer."

"You've been employed to find Pierce, not Waller." Mad Rogan flicked his fingers across the tablet. An electronic check appeared on its surface. "Type in a number."

I could type in a number large enough to pay off my mortgage to MII. It was tempting. So, so tempting. But you don't jump into the cage with a wild bear because he's offering you some of his honey. Right now Pierce and I were just talking. Once Mad Rogan got involved, it would escalate to an open confrontation, and the kind of power he and Pierce threw around meant I could—no, would— get hurt. My life meant nothing at all to either of them. "No, thank you."

His eyes narrowed. "You're still upset about the basement."

"Yes, but my personal dislike of you has nothing to

do with my decision. This is a purely professional choice. You've broken the law by kidnapping me, and although you apologized, your apology wasn't sincere. It was a means to an end. You've rearranged the restaurant, someone else's property, to accommodate your personal needs, you lied to me during this conversation, and you tried to trap me into a spell after assuring me that I wouldn't be harmed."

"I assured you that you wouldn't be kidnapped."

"You are incredibly powerful, and you have a blatant disregard for laws and moral constraints. I'm guessing that you don't think anything you ever do is wrong. That makes you very dangerous and a huge liability in my line of work. You will break laws and kill to get what you want, and if I manage to survive, I'll be left with the fall-out. So the answer is no."

"This isn't wise, Nevada. I take care of my employees."

The sound of my name coming from him derailed me for a half second. Trading being in debt to MII for servitude to House Rogan. No, thank you. At least with MII there were rules. There was a legal, binding contract, and what they were doing to us was underhanded but within the bounds of that contract. My value to them was tied to my ability as an investigator. My value to Rogan was tied to me somehow getting him together with Adam Pierce, and Rogan wasn't bound by any rules. I had no business getting in bed with him.

In bed.

With Mad Rogan.

My mind conjured him naked on dark sheets. I slammed the door on that thought so fast that my teeth shook.

I pulled two twenties out of my pocket and put them on the table. "I don't have any reason to trust a word you say."

He leaned forward. His body tensed, his muscles flexing under his clothes. His face turned predatory. All of that civilized veneer tore, and here he was, a dragon in all of his terrible glory.

"Do not walk away from me." His voice vibrated with power. "You're in over your head. Adam Pierce, House Pierce, and MII are out of your league. I'm offering to become your ally. Don't make me into an enemy, or you will regret it."

"And this is exactly why it's a no." I rose. "And the next time you choose to project into my dreams, do keep your clothes on."

He smiled. It was a very male, self-aware smile, not just sexual but carnal. The predatory look in his eyes turned ravaging. I felt the need to grab a napkin and hold it in front of me like a shield.

"I can project, but I would have to be next to you to do it."

Oh crap.

His voice turned smooth and sensual. A man had no right to sound like that. "Tell me, what wasn't I wearing in your dreams?"

I rose, turned my back to him, and walked out.

The sound of his laughter caressed my back, almost like a sexual touch.

Keep walking, keep walking, keep walking. That was dumb. I just had to get that last word in. Would it have killed me to keep my mouth shut?

My phone beeped. I answered it.

"Drawbridge Security," a brisk female voice said into the phone. "We're showing a fire alarm at your residence."

Grandma set the fire alarm off again. She'd test fuel or use some tool, and the alarm service called in a panic every couple of months. I had left them standing instructions to let the phone ring for at least a minute before calling the fire department. Sometimes Grandma took the time to put the fire out before answering.

"Did you let the phone ring?" I was almost to the door.

"We did. We're registering two separate alerts, the workshop and the front door."

Front door. The hair on the back of my neck rose. "Call the fire department now!"

I sprinted out the door and across the parking lot.

The van was already idling. I jerked the driver's door open and jumped inside. "Our house is on fire!"

My mother snapped the rifle case shut, dropped into the passenger seat, and buckled. I stepped on the gas, and the van shot out of the parking lot. Mom dialed the house.

"Anything?" I took the corner too fast. The van careened and fell back in place, the springs screeching.

She put it on speaker. Ring . . . Ring . . . Ring . . .

"Is it the workshop?"

"The front door."

We turned onto a side street. A slow-moving Prius blocked the lane. The line of cars in the opposite direction made it impossible to pass. Screw this.

I turned the wheel to the right. The van jumped the curb with a thud. I tore down the sidewalk.

Ring . . . Ring . . .

The Prius flew by. I dropped the van back into the lane.

Ring . . .

I made a sharp left. The warehouse loomed in front of us. It looked intact.

I screeched to a halt before the front door.

My mother swore. A huge chain blocked the door. Someone had cut holes in the walls and the door, strung an industrial-size chain through it, and locked it with a padlock. What the hell?

I stepped on the gas and drove around the warehouse to the workshop side. An identical chain blocked the back door. Damn it. I mashed the garage door opener attached to the visor. The massive door didn't move. Disabled.

We had no tools that would cut the chain. Everything was inside the warehouse.

"Smoke," Mother said.

A puff of black smoke escaped from the vent near the roof.

Grandma was inside. She could be burning to death.

"Ram it?"

"Go." My mother braced herself.

I reversed, speeding backward down the street. The garage door would be the weakest point. It was an industrial garage door, reinforced from the inside, but it was still weaker than the walls. I'd have to hit it pretty hard. I aimed for the pale rectangle of the door and stepped on the gas. The van rocketed forward, picking up speed.

Mad Rogan stepped between the van and the garage door.

I slammed on the brakes, but there was not enough time to stop. I would hit him. I saw him with crystal clarity—his body, turned sideways to me, his striking face, his blue eyes—as the van skidded at him.

He raised his hand.

The van hit a cushion of air, as if we plowed headfirst into viscous honey. We slid to a soft stop a foot before his fingertips.

Mad Rogan faced the garage door. It clanged and crashed to the ground. Smoke billowed out, black and oily.

I jumped out of the van and ran inside. The smoke scoured the inside of my nose and scraped against my throat like fine-grade sandpaper. My eyes watered. The acrid stench choked me. I coughed and stumbled, trying to see through the dark curtain.

A human shape lay prone on the floor. Oh no.

I lunged forward and fell to my knees. Grandma Frida lay on her stomach. I flipped her, grabbed her by her arms, and pulled her across the floor. Mad Rogan congealed from the smoke, picked my grandmother off the floor, and headed for the exit.

The smoke ate at the inside of my mouth. It felt like someone filled my throat with crushed glass, and it was cutting into me. My head swam. I stumbled after Rogan, trying to find the exit. Suddenly the smoke ended and I shambled into fresh air. My lungs felt like they were on fire. I bent over and coughed. It hurt like hell.

Mad Rogan lowered my grandmother to the ground. Mom dropped by her. We couldn't lose her. Not yet.

"Grandma," I croaked.

"We've got a pulse, but it's weak." My mother pulled my grandmother's mouth open and began doing CPR.

Please don't die. Please don't die, Grandma.

My mother began chest compressions. Tears rolled down my cheeks. Grandma Frida was always there for us. She was always . . . What would we do . . .

A fire truck rolled into the street.

Grandma coughed. A word came out, creaky, like an old door. "Penelope."

Oh God. Oh thank you. Relief washed over me like a cold shower. I exhaled.

"Mom?" Mother asked.

"Get off of me."

My stomach constricted. I crouched, trying to get a hold of myself. Mad Rogan's shoes came into view. Mad Rogan. The man who told me I would regret it if I walked away from him and who now conveniently showed up to be the hero. The fear and nausea boiled together into anger inside me. We almost lost Grandma Frida. Someone came into our house, someone chained our doors shut, and then someone tried to kill her. Someone did this, and I would make them pay. The fury drove me up. I stared into Rogan's eyes. Something broke inside of me like a chain falling apart. My magic shot out, savage and raging like an invisible thundercloud, and locked onto Mad Rogan.

He strained, his teeth gritted. I felt him fighting me, but my anger was whipping my magic into a frenzy. I had questions. He would answer them, damn it.

I spoke and heard my own voice, inhuman and terrible. "Did you order someone to hurt my grandmother?"

His will fought mine, steel-hard and unyielding, but I was too angry. He refused to bend, so I chained him in place and squeezed.

He unlocked his jaws. The answer was a growl. "No."

Truth.

I compelled him to answer. I had no idea how I was doing it, but I would do it some more. "Did you order someone to set this fire?"

"No."

Truth.

"Did you set it yourself?"

"No."

Truth.

My hold was slipping. He was too strong. It was like trying to twist a railway tie into a knot. "Do you know who did?"

"No."

Truth.

I released him. He moved. His strong fingers fastened on my wrist, sending an electric shiver of alarm through me. His face was terrifying. His voice was suffused with quiet, barely contained aggression. "Don't do that again."

I should've been scared, but my grandmother had almost died and I was too furious and too tired to care. "Don't like when the shoe is on the other foot? Let go of me."

He opened his fingers.

There were only two people in my life right now who could have done something like this arson, and I had just eliminated one. *Parents and sisters is something you do when you are five. They're pulling you down and you're letting them.* No. Adam couldn't be this stupid, could he? Did that bastard actually try to kill off my family?

Paramedics loaded my grandmother into an ambulance. It must've come while I'd been interrogating Mad Rogan. The first responders tried to keep the oxygen mask on my grandmother's face. She wasn't having it. My mother walked over to me.

"The last thing she remembers is getting the lug wrench. There is blood on the back of her head."

"Someone hit her." I would make them pay.

"Looks that way. I'm going to ride with her to the hospital."

"I'm good," I told her. "Go."

She gave Mad Rogan an evil eye and climbed into the ambulance.

A fireman emerged from the workshop. The smoke had mostly dissipated. The fireman nodded at the inside of the warehouse. "Looks like someone left a lit cigarette near a can of gasoline. Ought to be more careful."

"Thank you, we will." I turned away from him to hide my expression. Unfortunately that put me face-to-face with Mad Rogan. An unspoken question hung in the air as the fireman walked away.

"My grandmother doesn't smoke," I said quietly. "All gasoline is stored in the metal cage. All munitions are stored in the other cage. Before I left for lunch, the warehouse had no chains on its doors."

An SUV pulled up. Two men in dark pants and dark polo shirts exited. One was in his forties, dark-skinned, his short hair barely touched with grey. He was carrying a large, dark suitcase. The other man looked Latino and was about ten years younger. They moved like soldiers. I'd been around enough of them to recognize the walk, the unhurried but efficient stride of people who had a definite objective and had to get to it. They halted a few feet away.

"These are mine," Mad Rogan said. "They're arson specialists. If you give them permission, they will examine your warehouse."

I nodded. I still didn't trust him, but he had nothing to do with the arson.

"Go ahead," he said.

The two guys went inside the warehouse.

I was suddenly so tired. My eyes were burning. My throat still hurt.

Mad Rogan raised his hand. A bottle of water landed into it. He handed it to me. "Rinse your mouth and eyes. Don't swallow."

I opened the bottle, gulped, swished the water inside my mouth, and spat. The scratching subsided.

The younger of the men reappeared in the warehouse door and nodded to us. We started toward him.

"Thank you for saving my grandmother," I said.

"You're no good to me if you're burying a relative instead of looking for Pierce. I did it for a completely selfish reason," he said.

Lie.

We walked inside. The older of the men was kneeling by the melted gasoline container. Soot covered the concrete floor. The suitcase lay open in front of him. Inside, vials and test tubes rested in a protective cushioning of foam.

Mad Rogan took in the canvas-covered vehicles. His eyebrows rose. "Is that a tank?"

"Technically that's a gun on tracks. Mobile field artillery. That's a tank in the corner. His name is Romeo."

Mad Rogan shook his head in disbelief.

We reached the older man. He held up a test tube so I could see it, then used a small wire tool to scrape some of the soot off the floor. He lowered the tool into the test tube and shook it. A small clump of soot fell into the glass. The man added a few drops of a clear solution in a plastic bottle. The soot turned blue, then slowly changed color to pale purple.

"They used a party buster," the older man said. "It's a military-grade, slow-burning, smoke-producing compound. They mixed about four gallons of it with half a gallon of gasoline and lit it up. The woman who was loaded into the ambulance, where was she when you found her?"

"On the floor, facedown," I said.

"She's lucky," the younger man said. "Floor was the safest place, plus the high ceiling helped. This stuff is designed to clear personnel from buildings without doing structural damage. You stay too long in it, you die."

"Whoever did this knew what he was doing," the older man said. "Party buster is expensive and hard to get without a clearance. Most civilian arson inspectors don't test for it, and it dissipates quickly. Mixing it like that will make the incident look just like a normal gasoline fire. One more thing. I talked to the firemen. They say a cigarette was the point of origin. I've been doing this a while and I'm telling you now, a lit cigarette may have been here, but it wasn't what started the fire. The container melted from the back and top down. Someone put a strong heat source against the back of it. Like a blowtorch."

Or Adam Pierce's hand.

"Thank you," I said.

The two men rose and walked out.

Mad Rogan looked at me, his expression neutral, waiting.

"Thank you," I repeated. "I'm very grateful for your help. I would like you to leave now."

He turned on his heel and left.

I marched to the corner of the motor pool and opened the cabinet, where the old computer sat waiting. Bern had networked the entire house a long time ago. I tapped the arrow key. A prompt ignited on the screen and I typed in my password. The graphic of the security screen appeared. I clicked the rear camera and rewound back an hour. Grandma Frida puttering around the shop . . . I fast-forwarded ten minutes, another ten . . .

A blurry dark figure appeared in the doorway. The image went black.

I checked the outside camera. It went black without capturing anything at all. I rewound back to the image of the figure. It could've been a man or a woman. I couldn't tell.

I turned around and went back to the door. The security camera was mounted about fifteen feet off the ground. It was gone. In its place was a melted mess of metal and plastic. The camera was too high for the direct flame and if the fire had burned that hot, my grandmother would be dead. No, this was done by a precise strike of a pyrokinetic. Only one pyrokinetic had come in contact with me in the past week. Adam Pierce had attacked my family.

I looked around the warehouse, at the burn stain on the floor, at the melted container, and I imagined my grandmother lying here on concrete, facedown, dying slowly in her favorite place. Whatever willpower held me together broke. I leaned against the nearest vehicle and cried.

 **Chapter 8**

By the time Bern picked up my mother and grandmother from the hospital, I had cleaned up the garage, made dinner, and spent hours marinating in the fact that my actions had almost gotten my grandmother killed. I replayed the conversation with Adam in my head half a dozen times. The melted camera was far from definitive evidence, but my gut said he did it. My instincts almost never steered me wrong.

I'd tried calling back on Adam's number. It was no longer in service. He must've used a prepaid phone and then tossed it.

If I hadn't taken this job . . . I folded that thought very carefully and used it as fuel for the angry fire I was stoking inside. Guilt did me no good right now, but anger gave me all of the determination I needed. I would find out if he did it, even if it meant I'd turn the city upside down. And if he did do it, there would be hell to pay. I might not have combat magic, but I would make it my mission in life to bring him down. Nobody hurt my family and got away with it.

At two o'clock, the kids barged into the house, a full two hours ahead of schedule. Catalina's friend and her mother happened to drive past our place on their way to a doctor's appointment and saw the fire trucks. The friend texted Catalina, who saw the text after class and immediately texted Mom. Mom told her that Grandma was in the hospital but everything was fine. Catalina called Bern, got her cousin and her sister out of school, and drove home like a bat out of hell, because that's how our family rolled.

I served them late lunch and sketched the situation out. It took them fifteen minutes to calm down and another fifteen minutes to be convinced that none of this should be shared on Facebook, Instagram, or Herald.

We were about done with food when Grandma came through the door looking like she wanted to punch somebody. My mother followed, limping. Today must've done a number on her leg.

"They wanted her to spend the night, but she won't do it," Mom said.

"Grandma!" Arabella waved her arms. "Why aren't you in the hospital?"

"I have things to do," Grandma squeezed through her teeth.

"Like what?" Lina blocked her way.

"Catalina, do *not* mess with me right now." Grandma's eyebrows came together. "I'm going to get a blowtorch and repair the walls, and then I'm going to install an observation post for your mother so she can shoot the next sonovabitch who tries to break in here."

My mother pinned me down with her stare. "What did the firemen say?"

"They said Grandma shouldn't have been smoking next to a gasoline container."

Grandma Frida spun toward me. If looks could burn, we'd all be incinerated.

"Mad Rogan's arson guys said someone mixed a military-grade antipersonnel compound with some gasoline and applied a heat source to it."

"Mad Rogan?" Bern asked.

At the table Leon suddenly came to life and put his phone down. "Mad Rogan?"

"Mad Rogan had nothing to do with the arson," I said.

"How do you know?" Leon asked.

"I know," I said. "I asked. I monitored his experts too, and they weren't lying."

"Mad Rogan was here?" Leon pointed at the table. "Here? And nobody told me?"

"A thousand pardons, Your Majesty," Arabella said. "Everybody was too busy trying to save Grandma."

Leon ignored her. "Did he do anything while he was here?"

"He cut down the garage door," I told him.

Leon jumped off his seat like his butt had springs.

"Sit," Mother said.

He landed back in the chair. Apparently my younger cousin was a secret Mad Rogan fan.

"How sure are you that this was done by Adam Pierce?" Mother asked.

"I'm pretty sure," I said. "I'll be one hundred percent sure after I ask him face-to-face."

My mother put a small box on the table. Ten orange pills rested inside. "So find him and ask."

"I'd like nothing better." I swiped the pillbox off the

table. Looked like I would be going to the bad part of town tonight. It was just past three o'clock. Plenty of time before it got dark. "I might have to get backup. The kind you won't like."

"Do whatever you have to do," my mother said.

"Better you get Pierce, than us," Grandma Frida said. "Because if Pierce shows up here again, we won't be playing around."

"After we're done, we'll put what's left of him into a plastic grocery bag and you can take it to his family," Mother promised. "And Nevada? If you're even thinking of beating yourself up over what happened, forget it."

"You were doing your job," Grandma Frida said. "You didn't cause this to happen. They started it, whoever they are. They will regret it, because we will finish it."

"Thank you." It didn't kill the guilt, but right now guilt wasn't as important as finding Adam and finding out if he was responsible.

I headed out of the room. I'd need to get my Ruger.

Behind me, Mom said, "Let's talk about safety. Nobody goes anywhere alone . . ."

I went to the cage, unlocked it, and took out my P90. The pills were for Bug. It was barely three in the afternoon, but I'd need backup to go see Bug, even in daylight. Bug lived in Jersey Village, or, as it was better known, the Pit. I could call one of the freelancers except that right now most of them ran from us like we were on fire. It would also cost me an arm and a leg. Going into the Pit was bad for your health.

I split the pills, putting seven into a plastic bag and three in the jar to take with me. I might need to go see Bug more than once. Three would do for the first visit.

There was one person who could give me all the

backup I needed and then some. I scrolled through my phone to Mad Rogan's number. This was insanity, but the stakes had changed. Before, Adam was just talking. Now there was a chance he'd turned violent. If he had tried to burn my grandmother to death, nothing would stop him from incinerating me the moment I said something he didn't like. And if I did find Adam Pierce, I had no way in hell to contain him.

I hesitated with my finger over the number.

This was a bad idea. Mad Rogan was violent, ruthless, and brutal. All of the things I normally avoided in my job. I had a feeling he had no brakes, and that scared me. If he went off the rails and started slaughtering people, there was very little I could do about it. I didn't want to be responsible for any deaths. Nor did I want to be left holding the bag when the dust from his rampage cleared and cops came asking questions. He had expensive lawyers. I didn't.

The way my body came to attention when he was near scared me too. He turned me on by just looking at me. Having sex with him would be an experience I would never forget, and some insane part of me wanted that experience. I wanted to see him naked. I wanted to have all of that overwhelming masculine intensity focused on me. I'd never before had a reaction like that to a man.

I couldn't trust Mad Rogan. Not just because he was likely a sociopath but also because he was a Prime and head of an old House. To him I was a peon. If he needed a bullet shield in a fight, he'd use me without any hesitation. I was the hired help, the means to an end, and I had to draw some strict lines in the dirt for him and for myself, or I would come out of this crushed or not at all. And if I gave him any hint of being vulnerable, whether it was my love for my family, my pride, or my irrational craving to find out what his hands on my skin would feel like, he would use it against me.

Not to mention that I had locked him in place with my magic and pulled the answers out of him. Considering that I was still alive and uninjured, he'd handled it awfully well. That was something I would need to research. My magic was rare and information about it was sparse, mostly because the few people who had it worked in classified positions. I had done my best to learn as much as I could, but I had never seen any mention of that particular magic. It had come out of nowhere.

I stared at Mad Rogan's number. Was there any other way to do this?

If Adam turned on me, any freelancer I took with me, even if I took two of them, would end up dead. I would end up dead. Adam thought he could use me; so did Mad Rogan. The best way to deal with them was to use them right back. I had to throw the two Primes at each other and wait quietly on the sidelines until the dust settled.

I took a deep breath and pushed the keys. He answered on the second ring.

"Yes?"

Hearing his voice was like being caressed. Chains, I reminded myself. Basement. Psycho. Boundaries. Boundaries were good. "I thought about your offer."

"I'm aflutter with anticipation."

Psycho who likes to mock me. Even better. "I don't want your money. I don't want to be employed by you. But I would like to have a partnership. I want to be very clear: I wouldn't be working for you. I would be working with you on equal footing toward a common goal. And I have conditions."

"I'm listening."

"One, you don't kill anyone unless they make a clear attempt to murder us."

There was a long pause. "I'll try."

"Two, you promise to apprehend and deliver Adam Pierce to his House alive."

"I can't promise you that. I can promise that I'll do everything in my ability to keep him alive, within reason, but if that moron decides to jump off Baytown Bridge, there won't be much I can do to save him."

Technically it was true. Human bodies reacted oddly to the loss of gravity and free fall. Even if Mad Rogan caught Adam with his magic half a second after he jumped, Adam would still die of internal bleeding. That's why levitators had their own classification and weren't just lumped together with other telekinetics.

"Fine. Promise me that you will do everything you can to help me return him alive to his family."

"Sure."

These promises probably weren't worth diddly squat.

"Third, I want you to protect my family while we're doing this. I need to know that I can count on that protection."

"Of course. That's the nature of our agreement. Would you like me to station some people to keep an eye on your home?"

"Yes. They have to come to the front door, and they have to introduce themselves to my family, or someone might accidentally shoot them."

"Done." His voice was crisp. "My turn. This is a professional partnership, and I expect you to treat it as one. If you hear from Adam, if he calls you, if he comes to your house, the moment that meeting or conversation is over, I want to be informed of it. Not the next day, not when it's convenient, but immediately after. You'll disclose all information related to this matter, including the terms of your contract, the state of your relationship with Adam, and anything you know about Gavin Waller."

"Fair enough."

"You also won't depart on any expeditions without discussing it with me. I don't want to get a text 'Hi, going after Pierce' and then watch cops fish you out of Buffalo Bayou the next morning."

"I'm touched." Not really.

"I would have to start the investigation from scratch. If you die, it will be very inconvenient."

I rolled my eyes.

"Do we have a deal?" he asked.

"Yes. I'm going to Jersey Village to look for Adam Pierce. Would you like to come?"

"I'll pick you up in ten minutes."

I hung up. So this is what making a deal with the devil felt like. Too late for regrets now. I sighed and packed an extra clip.

A Range Rover slid into the parking lot in exactly ten minutes. It was a large vehicle, gunmetal grey, slick, but solid. The passenger door swung open and I saw Mad Rogan in the driver seat. He'd traded the suit and shoes for faded jeans, a pale grey T-shirt, and heavy, dark boots. The effect was staggering. The suit had toned him down, smoothing harshness with a veneer of wealth and civilization. Now he was all rough edge and rugged strength. He looked like he needed some jungle ruins to explore or some bad people to hit with a chair. Trouble was, he was the bad people.

His magic lay coiled about him, a violent pet with vicious teeth.

I would have to get in and sit next to him, with only a few inches of distance between us. I would have to enter his space. I couldn't do it. I couldn't get into this car.

"I have one more condition," I said.

He simply looked at me.

"Do not read my thoughts." He didn't need to know what was in my head. He just didn't.

He smiled. "Not a problem."

I took the passenger seat and put my backpack in the space in front of it. Okay. I was in. I just had to say the bare minimum and keep my thinking to myself.

"I can't read thoughts," Mad Rogan said. "But I find that most of the time I don't need to."

And that did not sound ominous. Not at all. I buckled up.

The Range Rover shot down the side road. The window glass looked really thick and tinted. This wasn't the cheaper bullet-resistant version. This was the heavy-duty bulletproof glass with six-centimeter safety glazing and a layer of polycarbonite on the inside to keep the window from shattering. You could fire an AK-47 at it at close range and the glass would crack but remain completely smooth on the inside. This kind of glass also weighed a ton. I touched the window controls. The window crept down, whisper quiet, and back up. Grandma Frida would be proud. A normal window lifter wouldn't be able to raise the window back up. He'd had custom window lifters installed. The vehicle was likely armor-plated too.

"What's the rating on the armor plates?"

"Hard ammo. It's a VR9 vehicle."

Holy crap. The Range Rover wouldn't just stop a bullet from a handgun or an assault rifle. It would stop an armor-piercing round from a machine gun. That much armor meant a crap load of extra weight, but the car glided like a skater across the ice, which required reinforced suspension and custom dampers. This vehicle wasn't retrofitted with armor. It was built to be armored from the ground up.

To top it off, it looked just like any other high-end Range Rover on the road. Most people didn't realize that armored cars weren't just about being the most bulletproof. It was also about discretion. No car was completely damage proof, not even a tank, and the best strategy to keep your occupant safe was to not get shot at in the first place. That required the vehicle to be as close to the non-armored equivalent as possible so it would blend in with other cars on the road. There were always idiots who wanted flashy armored monstrosities that looked like something out of a postapocalyptic movie. They wanted to make a statement. Unfortunately, their statement said, Here I am, shoot me. People who actually required protection opted for quiet quality like this, the kind that came at a heart-stopping price and said volumes about their owners.

Mad Rogan didn't give a crap about what the rest of us thought about him. He had no need to impress; he wanted the best, and he would pay premium price as long as he got it. Somehow that didn't make me feel any better.

"What's in Jersey Village?" he asked.

"Bug. He's a surveillance specialist. I have something he wants, and I'm going to have him find Adam Pierce for us. We have to do it now, before Adam shows up at my house again, because my mother has threatened to deal with him and then send what's left of his body to his House in a plastic grocery bag."

"Your mother seems confident," he said.

"Do you know what a Light Fifty is?" I asked.

"It's a Barrett M82 sniper rifle."

"My mother was looking at your head through the

scope of one while we were eating lunch. We need to find Adam Pierce before my mother shoots him or my grandmother runs him over with a tank. Or before he incinerates our home and my family with it."

"As we discussed, I have a team guarding your warehouse. If he shows up anywhere near it, we'll know. Now your turn. I'll have the information now," Mad Rogan said. "All of it."

I started at the moment MII called us, told him very briefly that MII hired us to find Adam Pierce, and ran through my investigation, skipping unimportant details such as mortgaged businesses and dreams featuring him being half naked. Volunteering was for suckers, and he wouldn't get any information out of me unless it was absolutely necessary.

He grimaced. "Augustine finally caved in."

"You know him?"

"Yes. We went to college together. I'm not his favorite person."

"Why?"

"I've seen him without his magic." Mad Rogan shrugged his muscular shoulders. "Augustine always had an overdeveloped sense of loyalty to his House. He struggled with it. I told him back then that if he wasn't careful, he'd end up in an office dancing to his family's tune."

"Is that why you joined the military? To get away from your family?" And why did I ask that?

"I joined because they told me I could kill without being sent to prison and be rewarded for it."

True. Holy shit. I was trapped in a car with a homicidal maniac. Awesome.

"You have a strange look on your face," he said.

"I just realized I shouldn't be in the same vehicle with

you. In fact, I shouldn't have called you in the first place, so I'm trying very hard to rewind time."

He grinned. *I've amused the dragon. Whee.*

"Would you rather I lied to you? Not that I would bother, but even if I did, there is no point in it, is there?"

I didn't answer. Keeping my mouth shut was an excellent strategy.

"Does Augustine know you're a Truthseeker?"

He'd figured me out. I wasn't really surprised, not after I'd pinned him down and wrenched the answers out of him. "What my employer knows or doesn't know about me is none of your business."

He chuckled, a genuine, rich laugh.

"What's so funny?"

"Augustine prides himself on his powers of observation and being an excellent judge of character. He thinks he's Sherlock Holmes. He used to try to make brilliant deductions by noting what people wore and how they acted. He has a Truthseeker on staff and he has no idea. He's likely been looking to employ one for ages." Mad Rogan chuckled again. "The irony, it's delicious."

I kept my mouth shut. Hopefully he wouldn't ask me anything else.

"Truthseeking is the third rarest magic talent. Why not make a living from it? Shouldn't you be in some office with a two-way mirror asking uncomfortable questions?"

"That's not covered under our agreement."

He glanced at me, his eyes dark. "Would you rather talk about your dream?"

"No."

"Considering that I was featured in it, I think I deserve to know the particulars. Were my clothes missing because we were in bed? Was I touching you?" He glanced at me.

His voice could've melted clothes off my body. "Were you touching me?"

I shouldn't have gotten into his car. I should've taken a separate vehicle.

"Cat got your tongue, Nevada?"

"No, we weren't in bed. I was pushing you off a cliff to your death." I pointed at the highway. "Take the next exit and stay in the right lane, please. We'll need to make a right."

He chuckled again and took the exit.

The Range Rover rolled down a gentle stop at the end of the exit ramp, and we turned right onto deserted Senate Avenue. At some point it was a typical suburban street, two lanes on each side, divided by a flower bed and decorative trees. A field with grass mowed short stretched on the left. An equally shorn lawn lay on the right, a curving drive cutting through it to permit access to a one-story brick building. A large sign rose on the right, set on a sturdy metal pole.

YOU ARE LEAVING HOUSTON
METRO AREA

A second sign in bright yellow yelled at us with big black letters.

FLOODING AHEAD
TURN AROUND
DON'T DROWN

"Make a right here." I pointed at the driveway.

Mad Rogan turned. The driveway brought us to a

drive-through at the brick building, blocked by a solid metal bar. Another sign said Private Security Area Parking. $2 per hour, $12 per day maximum.

"Let me do the talking," I said.

"Be my guest."

The drive-through window slid open and a woman looked at me. She was short and muscular, with dark brown skin and glossy black hair put away into six neat cornrows. A tactical vest hugged her frame, and a Sig Sauer lay in the desk next to her.

"Hi, Thea." I showed her my ID.

"Haven't seen you for a while," Thea said. "Who's the prince in the driver seat?"

"A client."

Thea's eyebrows rose. "You're taking a client into the Pit?"

"There is a first time for everything."

Thea leaned forward a little and gave Mad Rogan her tough stare. "Okay, client. Standard warning: you have left the Metro Houston area. You are entering territory controlled by House Shaw. This is a limited-security area. If you proceed past the red line at the end of this parking lot, you may be a victim of a violent crime, such as mugging, assault, rape, or murder. House Shaw patrols the water, and if they observe you being a victim of such a crime, they will render aid, but by crossing that red line you acknowledge that House Shaw has a limited ability to assist you. This conversation is being recorded. Do you understand the warning that has been given to you?"

"Yes," Mad Rogan said.

"Your consent has been recorded and will be used as evidence should you attempt to seek any damages or hold House Shaw liable for any harm happening to you in the

Pit. Getting in is easy, getting out is hard. Welcome to the anal sore of Houston. Have fun, kids."

She popped a paper ticket from the machine on the side of her desk and handed it to Rogan. He took it. The bar rose and he steered the vehicle into the deserted parking lot. He drove to the far end and parked by the foot-wide red line drawn on the pavement. A hundred yards beyond the line, a bayou spread. The murky water the color of green tea lay placid. On the left, the top floor of a once-two-story office building stuck out of the mire. Once-decorative trees stood half submerged next to sunken wrought-iron streetlamps.

Jersey Village used to be one of those small suburban towns Houston was in the habit of swallowing whole as it grew. A boring bedroom community northwest of downtown, Jersey Village slowly grew a robust mini-downtown, with several large tech companies building their offices here. It would've continued to exist in happy obscurity if it hadn't been for the infamous Mayor Bruce. Mayor Thomas Bruce, better known as Bubba Bruce, somehow managed to get himself elected on the platform of being a fun guy to have over to your backyard barbecue. Once in office, Bubba Bruce desperately tried to leave his mark on Houston. He really wanted to build an airport, but since Houston already had one, Bubba decided to build a subway. He was told that Houston was built on marshes and ground moisture would be an issue. Bubba Bruce insisted. He planned to use mages to "push" the groundwater out of the construction areas. Despite vocal opposition to the project by people much smarter than him, he went ahead with it.

Twelve years ago, a cadre of mages broke the ground on the first metro station here, in Jersey Village. They spent a month setting up their spells and finally activated their complicated magic. The water left the area. Without it, the weight of the town proved to be too much, and Jersey Village, which sat atop an empty oil field, promptly sank into the ground. An hour later the water came back with a vengeance, aided by nearby bayous and underground streams. In twenty-four hours, Jersey Village turned into a swamp. Two days later, Mayor Bruce was kicked out of office.

Over the next year the city tried unsuccessfully to drain the area. The suburbanites had cashed in their insurance and fled, while criminals, drug addicts, and homeless squatted in half-flooded buildings. Finally the city council, exhausted by lawsuits and failed attempts to drain the area, gave up and excised the entire flood zone from the Houston metro area, because it was single-handedly doubling Houston's crime rate. Now private firms patrolled the area. The task of keeping the Pit from completely degenerating into a lawless zone came bundled with some lucrative municipal contracts, so over the years it bounced from House to House. Right now House Shaw was looking after the Pit. They were doing just enough to keep the contract.

Over the last decade, Jersey Village had become the last stop. Magic-warped, gangsters, most wanted—they made their lairs here, hiding from the light in the abandoned offices. The Houses didn't care, as long as they didn't get out. The last time I had come here, I'd taken Aisha for backup. It had cost me a grand, and both of us had barely gotten out.

I checked my gun in its shoulder holster and stepped out of the car. Mad Rogan exited on his side. A rickety dock led the way into the Pit, veering off between the buildings. I started down the bridge. Mad Rogan strode next to me.

Bayous had their own primeval beauty, a kind of grim, timeless elegance, with dark, calm water and enormous cypresses, buttressing the shore with their bloated trunks. Jersey Village had none of it. It looked just like a flood zone where the water hadn't gone away. Here and there the top of a rusted car poked through the dirty water. Some smaller buildings had burst, warped by the flood, spilling moldy trash into the open. Pale green scum floated on the surface. The Pit was ugly and it smelled even worse. Like sticking your head down an old half-drained fish tank.

"Lovely place," Mad Rogan said.

"Wait until you meet the natives."

A sardonic smile curved his lips. "Will there be a welcome party?"

"Probably."

He stopped and held his arm out, blocking me. The water in front of us parted. A clawed hand reached out, grabbing the slimy support of the bridge, and a nude woman pulled herself up onto the wooden planks. Her skin was a mottled green. You could play xylophone on her ribs. She blinked at me, her eyes dull and empty.

"How's life, Cherry?" I asked.

"How the fuck do you think it is? You bring me meat?"

I reached into my backpack and pulled out a plastic container with two big raw chicken drumsticks in it, the thigh meat on. "Bug still alive?"

"Yeah. He's in his old digs, in Xadar building. Stay away from the main bridge. Peaches and Montrel are in a turf war."

That meant Peaches did away with his former boss. Not good. I passed the container to Cherry. She grabbed the chicken leg and bit into it with triangular crocodile teeth. I stepped around her and kept walking. Mad Rogan followed me.

"A friend of yours?"

"I met her about two years before," I said. "She's magic-warped."

"I can see that."

Magic was a funny thing. Almost a century and a half ago, when the serum that granted magic powers was first developed, some people took it and gained power, while others turned into monsters. Now, generations later, all of us still carried the potential to become twisted. Sometimes when people tried to augment their power, their magic reacted in terrible ways and they became like Cherry—warped.

"What happened to her?" he asked.

"I don't know. Her arms have track marks, so she was likely a junkie at some point. Probably sold herself to some institute or House for experimental augmentation and it didn't go well. I bring her chicken to trade for information."

"It's a rare treat for her?" he asked.

"Yes."

"Then you didn't get a good deal. She didn't tell you anything to justify the chicken."

"She told me that Peaches killed Basta and took over the Southside. Montrel has the Northside, and he can be reasonable, but Peaches is batshit crazy and there is no way we can avoid him, because there are only a handful of ways in and out of here, and Xadar building is in the Southside."

"You could've gotten more out of her."

I turned to him. "What's your point?"

Mad Rogan loomed next to me. "You bring her chicken because you feel sorry for her."

"Yes. Why is that a problem?"

"I don't judge," he said. "You're allowed your compassion."

Oh great. *Thank you for permission.* "You're doing that thing again."

"What thing?"

"The one where you think you can tell me what to do."

The bridge split and we turned right, away from the main route. Ahead, office buildings stuck out of the water like islands of concrete and brick. The roofs bristled with metal poles supporting tangles of wires. Above the second floor, a wide yellow line crossed each building with words stenciled in yellow: No power below this line.

Mad Rogan's magic brushed against me and I fought an urge to jump back.

"As I said, I don't judge," he said. "If you had kicked her in the face instead of giving her chicken, I'd need to know. If you had hurled the chicken into the water and made her swim for it, I'd need to know that too. The more information I have, the better I can anticipate your actions when it will matter. For example, if a starving man pulls a gun on you and you get the upper hand, you will likely let him go because you will feel sorry for him. That's the kind of person you are."

"And what kind of person are you?"

His face was hard. "The kind who shoots first."

The bridge curved behind the office buildings. We walked past the first half-sunken giant of concrete. Ahead, the bridge ended abruptly. I stopped.

"Damn it."

"We'll have to take the main bridge?" Mad Rogan asked.

I reached into my light jacket, pulled my gun out of the holster, and put it in my pocket. Mad Rogan watched me with a slightly amused expression. We turned left, picking our way across a rickety, narrow bridge until it spat us out into the open space between the office buildings. Here the ground rose slightly. Over the years, the Pit's inhabitants had dumped piles of gravel, concrete, and brick chunks onto it until a narrow rectangular island had formed. Wooden bridges thrust from it, curving in all directions. Directly in front of me, men and women peered from the windows of an abandoned building. To the right, a group of people crowded around something.

I stepped onto the island. The group parted and a tall man strode out. He was skinny and pale, his arms and legs too long for his body. Limp reddish hair framed his face, the tangled strands the exact color of a ripe peach.

"Peaches?" Mad Rogan murmured next to me.

"Yes."

"Anything I need to know?"

"He summons swarms of poisonous swamp flies."

It's a known fact that child molesters look just like normal, ordinary people. Peaches looked like you would imagine a child molester might look. His face wasn't unpleasant, but there was something deeply unsettling in his gaze. Something sick and creepy. It rolled over you like old oil from a fryer.

Peaches pointed over my shoulder at Mad Rogan. "Hey you! You! What the fuck are you doing in my house?"

On his left, a tall man jerked a Glock up. A woman in a black tank top and dirt-smeared jeans next to him raised a Chiappa Rhino. The distinct barrel was a dead giveaway. Just what we needed.

"We don't want any trouble," I said. "We're just passing through."

"Trouble? I *am* fucking trouble, bitch!" Peaches waved his arms. His face flushed. He was building himself up. If he'd been a wild turkey, he would have puffed out all his feathers. He'd work himself up to violence in a minute. Mad Rogan must've set off some alarm in Peaches' brain that told him something was to be gained by humiliating him. "You think you can just come through here with your bitch?"

Mad Rogan didn't answer.

"You· mute, punk? You mute?" Spittle flew from Peaches' lips. He closed the distance.

My heart sped up. My knees trembled slightly from the rush of adrenaline.

Peaches looked like he was about to ram Mad Rogan with his chest. Mad Rogan looked at him. It was a cold, emotionless stare. Peaches decided that two feet of space was close enough. "You're in my place now! I am in charge here!"

His hand barely missed me as he flailed around. I took a step back.

"Don't you fucking move! Shoot her if she moves."

The man on the left clicked the safety off his Glock.

Peaches leaned closer. "I tell you what, if I was in a good mood, I'd fuck you up and send you back without your bitch, but I'm in a bad mood. I'm in a bad mood, punk. I'm gonna shoot your bitch right here and then I'm gonna put you in a hole. You worth money, punk, because you look like you worth money."

I could shoot Peaches from where I stood. I'd shot through my pocket before. I would have to kill him though, because if he lived, the flies he summoned would turn me into a cluster of boils. Aiming through a pocket was tricky.

Mad Rogan smiled a big, wide, conciliatory grin and raised his hands. "Hey, hey. No need to get worked up. Look, no gun. I can see you're the man. You're in charge here."

"That's right!"

"You're a businessman, right?" Mad Rogan kept smiling, his expression pleasant and placating. "Let's talk, like two businessmen." He invited Peaches to a bridge stretching back the way we came. "Let's just calm down for a minute and talk, right, buddy?"

"Talk money, punk." Peaches moved with Mad Rogan onto the bridge.

Mad Rogan strolled next to him. "I can see you own all of this and you being in charge and all . . ."

Mad Rogan grabbed Peaches by the throat, kicked his feet out from under him, and hurled him into the water as if the tall man weighed nothing.

Several things happened at the same time: I yanked my gun out and took a shooter stance; the barrels of the man's Glock and the woman's Chiappa fell off the guns as if sliced off by a razor blade; and Peaches splashed in the water. We all stopped moving, me with my Ruger pointing at the group, and the two shooters staring blankly at their disfigured firearms.

The larger man opened his hand and let the Glock's remains fall to the ground.

"I'll fucking kill you!" Peaches howled, rising to his feet, up to his hips in water. Dark green dots swirled around him. A swarm of fat flies shot out of his hands, curving around him like a shawl.

Mad Rogan flicked his fingers. The wall of the nearest

building broke off in one long, twenty-foot slab, slid off the building, and crushed Peaches.

Oh my God.

Mad Rogan turned to face the crowd. Behind him a large crack split the building's side, and bricks and mortar rained down onto the first chunk. Nobody screamed.

The last brick fell onto the pile. It was so quiet you could hear a pin drop.

"Now we know," Mad Rogan said, his voice cold. "I'm in charge. I'm in charge of you. I'm in charge of the guy next to you. I'm in charge of the ground you're standing on. When I'm gone, I don't care who is in charge. When I leave here, you can fight and kill each other over who is running things while I'm not here. But let's be clear: when I'm here, when you see me, I'm in charge."

The woman lowered her disfigured gun to the floor. The rest of Peaches' people stood motionless.

"Are there any questions?" Mad Rogan asked.

A short man in a tattered Dallas Cowboys jersey raised his hand slowly. The woman in the tank top grabbed his hand and pushed it down.

"Okay then. You may go."

By the time I took three breaths, the island was clear.

"Which way is your expert?" Mad Rogan asked me.

 **Chapter 9**

"You killed Peaches." I stepped over the gap in the bridge.

"Of course I killed him."

I opened my mouth and closed it.

"Okay," Mad Rogan said. "This is distracting you, and I need you to function, so let's fix this. Which part of what happened is upsetting?"

I opened my mouth again and closed it again without saying anything. Peaches would've attacked us, possibly killed us, so what Mad Rogan did was justified. It was the sheer sudden brutality of it. It was the way he did it, without any hesitation. One moment Peaches was there, and then he vanished. No trace of him remained. He was crushed out of existence. He was . . . dead.

"Let me help," he said. "You've been taught all your life that killing another person is wrong, and that belief persists even in the face of facts. Not only would Peaches have killed us given the chance, but this way I only had to kill one person rather than kill half a dozen of his followers. I saved several lives, but your conditioning tells you I've done the wrong thing. I didn't. He started it. I finished it."

"It's not that. I was getting ready to shoot him in the head." But when you shot someone, there was a slight chance they might live. There would be a body. What he did was so complete and sudden that I needed a couple of moments to come to terms with it.

"Then what is it?"

"It's the . . ." I struggled for words. "Splat."

Mad Rogan glanced at me, his eyes puzzled. "Splat."

"Yes."

"I had briefly considered impaling him with one of those steel poles from the roof, but I decided it would be too graphic for you. Would that have been preferable?"

My mind conjured up Peaches with a steel pole sticking out of his stomach. "No."

"I really would like to know," he said with genuine curiosity. "The next time I kill someone, I'd like to do it in a way that doesn't freak you out."

"How about you don't kill anybody for a little bit?"

"I can't make that promise."

Small talk with the dragon. How are you? Eaten any adventurers lately? Sure, just had one this morning. Look, I still got his femur stuck in my teeth. Is that upsetting to you?

Ahead Xadar building loomed, top three stories above the water, its faded green sign grimy and stained with swamp algae. The tangle of wires on the roof looked like a black spiderweb. Somewhere inside, Bug sat in the center of this web, wrapped in his hysterical brand of crazy. I stopped.

"Don't kill Bug," I said. "I'm dead serious."

Mad Rogan smiled.

"I mean it. Do not murder Bug. If you kill him, our deal is off."

"Fine," he said.

I resumed my walking.

"Maybe you should make me a list of people I can kill and ways in which they're allowed to die," he said.

"You are not funny."

"I'm very funny. Just ask Peaches."

We reached the building and climbed through a large second-story window. A damp, musty smell emanated from the commercial rug. Slugs crawled across the fallen cubicles. An old motivational poster hung on the wall. It showed a mountain climber hanging by his hands off a cliff. The caption said Break the Boundaries. The glass was cracked.

"Don't touch anything," I said. "He has the whole place booby-trapped."

I followed a narrow path between the cubicles, stopped before a camera mounted in the corner, and held up the vial of orange pills.

An intercom somewhere close crackled with static and a scratchy male voice said, "Stay there. I'll send Napoleon." The static cut out.

"Have you ever killed someone?" Mad Rogan asked me.

"No. I saw a man die once." I shouldn't have said that.

"How did it happen?"

I glanced at him and stopped. He was focused on me, as if I was about to tell him the most intriguing thing in the world and he was prepared to absorb every word. Even his magic hovered around him, anticipating. For a few moments I had Mad Rogan's undivided attention, and it wasn't frightening. It was . . . flattering. As long as I told him things, he would keep looking at me just like that, and that alone was enough incentive to compel most women to tell him anything he wanted. And if I did tell him things, he would likely use them against me in some way.

He was still waiting. Oh what the hell.

"My dad wanted me to get a taste for the different areas of PI work, so when I was sixteen, I interned with a repo agent. He worked with his two sons. Our first few runs were great. We'd find the vehicle, sneak up, and tow it off, like spies on some secret operation in a movie. It was exciting. The guys told me how people try to scam the banks out of money, so we were doing a good thing."

My lips had gone dry. It still bothered me after almost a decade.

"What happened?" he said, his blue eyes welcoming. A man had no right to be this fiercely sexual without even trying.

"We were trying to repossess a truck from a small suburban home, when a woman came out of the house. She was holding a toddler, and her eyes had this hollow look. She said, 'Take it. I can't afford to put gas into it anyway.' The expression on her face was terrible. I should've quit right there. I should've called my dad and asked him to come and get me. But I was trying to do the right thing. My dad got me this job, and I was going to do it, even if it sucked.

"The guys just attached the tow, and then this man tore out of the house with a rifle and started shooting at us. No warning. We couldn't even get into our truck. We just hunkered down behind it. The woman was screaming, but he kept firing at our truck. Doug called the cops. They got there fast. The man shot at the police cruiser, and the cops gunned him down. I saw the bullets hit him in the chest, and then he collapsed. More kids ran out of the house, and everyone started crying and screaming. I remember cops led his wife away and she kept trying to tell them that he was a good man and wouldn't do something like this. I found out later he lost his job four months before that and his house had gone into foreclosure. My dad came and got me, and I never had to go back." For which I'd thanked my lucky stars every morning for a month. "Your turn. First person you ever saw die."

"I was seven," he said, his voice intimate and quiet. "I was practicing spells, and my grandfather was watching me. He had dozed off in a chair, the way he usually did. Suddenly he clutched his head, groaned, and fell down. I ran to him, but he wasn't breathing. He had a brain aneurysm. I ran downstairs and told my grandmother that Grandfather died. She told me that laziness was the worst trait in a man, and making up lies to get out of practice wasn't much better. Then she told Gerard, her servant, to take me to the study and lock me in there. I sat on the floor for two hours looking at my grandfather's corpse."

Oh God.

A faint noise came from the hallway. A small dog trotted into view. He was squat, with huge, triangular ears and a pushed-up muzzle that said that somewhere in his ancestry there was an adventurous French bulldog. The origin of the rest of his DNA was a mystery. He was solid black, his coat fuzzy and wiry, and he moved like he owned the place.

"Hey, Napoleon," I said.

Napoleon regarded me with solemn dark eyes from his cute gargoyle face. Then he turned around and padded into the hallway.

"A dog guide," Mad Rogan said.

"Yes. Be careful. Bug likes to string clear fishing line around. If you pull one, bad things will happen."

"What kind of bad things?" he asked.

"Exploding kind."

We followed Napoleon through the maze of hallways up to the third floor. A heavy steel door barred our way. I took the Taser out of my backpack.

"No killing."

"I'll be on my best behavior," Mad Rogan assured me.

The door clanged and opened, revealing a room lined with monitors. They sprouted from the walls and ceiling on narrow mounts, like rectangular electronic flowers blooming among vines of cables. In the middle of this digital jungle, in a broken circle of keyboards thrusting from the walls, a man sat on a rotating platform. His clothes, a grimy, dark, long-sleeved T-shirt and a pair of fatigue pants that had seen better days, hung on his slight frame. His disheveled dark hair, dragged rather than brushed from his broad, high forehead, competed with his clothes to see which lasted without washing the longest. A small nose and a small mouth combined with a triangular jaw made his face look top-heavy. His big eyes with brown irises burned with a manic intensity. His hands shook.

"Give it to me." He jumped off his chair. He was about my height and weighed maybe twenty pounds less. "Give me."

I raised the Taser. "Work first."

He bounced in place. "I need it. Give it to me."

"Work first."

"Give! Give, give give gimme . . ." He was moving too fast, jittery, shaking. His words began to blend. "Giveit-tomebitch give giveme need-need-need . . ."

"Work first."

"Fuck!" Bug spun on his foot. "What?"

"Adam Pierce. Find him."

He held up a finger. "To take the edge off. One. One!"

I passed the vial to Mad Rogan, keeping the Taser on Bug. He'd made a lunge at me before. "Please give him one pill."

Mad Rogan opened the jar. A pill rose in the air. Wow. The man's control was crazy.

The pill floated to Bug. He snatched it out of the air, yanked a knife from the sheath on his belt, put the pill on the table, and sliced a third off. His fingers trembled. He swiped the smaller section of the pill off the desk and slid it in his mouth. Bug froze, standing on his toes, his hands straight down, as if he'd been about to take flight. The shaking stopped. He became completely and utterly still.

Mad Rogan glanced at me.

"Equzol," I told him.

Equzol was a military drug designed to level you out. If you were sleepy, it would keep you awake; if you were hyper, it would calm you down. When you took it, the world became clear. You saw everything, were aware of everything, reacted fast, but nothing freaked you out. It was issued to snipers and convoy drivers. They would take it to keep from overcorrecting or giving in to fatigue, and once it wore off, they'd sleep for twenty hours straight. It was a classified substance, but my mother still had connections.

Bug opened his eyes. The strange, jittery hysteria was still there, but it receded, curling down for a rest deep inside him.

"They're quiet," he said softly and smiled.

I nodded at the jar. "Adam Pierce."

Bug slid into his seat and pulled up the sleeves of his dark, grimy, long-sleeved shirt. Dozens of tiny dots marked his forearms, each a tiny individual tattoo blending together into an arcane design. His hands flew over half a dozen keyboards as if he'd been a virtuoso pianist. Tranquil sounds of trance music filled the space. The screens scrolled too fast to follow, the images flickering. He was tapping into the security cameras on the streets. I'd seen him do it before, and he was expert at it.

Mad Rogan's face had hardened into a cold, determined expression. His eyes turned merciless.

"What is it?" I asked quietly.

"He's a swarmer," he ground through his teeth.

"Yes."

"How long?"

"How long has he been one?"

"Yes."

"Three years. He was bound to a swarm two years into his enlistment, and he's been out of the Air Force for one."

Mad Rogan stared at Bug. "He should be dead. Their life expectancy after the binding is eighteen months."

"Bug is special."

Swarmers were surveillance specialists. They were bound by magic to what they themselves described as swarms. Swarms had no physical manifestation. They lived somehow inside the swarmer's psyche, letting him or her split his attention over hundreds of independent tasks, like a river splitting into narrow streams. Swarmers processed information at a superhuman speed. Most of them had the binding done in the military, and most of them didn't live two years past that. Those who volunteered for the procedure were either terminally ill or tempted by a huge bonus payable to their families. Bug somehow survived. It might have been his deprivation chamber, or maybe he was just better suited for it than most, but he lived, got out of Air Force, and hid here, away from everyone.

Mad Rogan locked his teeth. It made his jaw look even more square.

"Does it bother you?" I asked.

"It bothers me that they do this to soldiers, squeeze everything they can out of them, and then discard them like garbage. People know this goes on and nobody gives a shit. Acceptable losses." He said the word like it burned his mouth.

So some part of the dragon was human after all.

My cell phone beeped. Unlisted number. Again. I answered it.

"Yes?"

"Hello, Snow," Adam Pierce purred into my ear.

I fought an urge to scream into the phone. "Hi, Adam." I put him on speaker. "Did you decide to turn yourself in?"

Mad Rogan went from icy anger to predatory alertness in a blink.

"Depends. Are we still in lust? I mean in love. Funny how I keep making that mistake."

"Depends," I said. "Do you want to meet so we can talk about it?"

"Not right now," Adam said. "I'm busy tonight. Maybe later."

"Found him," Bug pressed a key on the keyboard.

The screen flickered and showed the same image from different angles. Adam Pierce stood on the corner of a busy street, holding a phone to his ear. Faded jeans hugged his ass and long legs. He wore his trademark black leather jacket and black boots. A tall building ten floors high rose in front of him, its dusky, smoke-colored glass crossed by stripes of bright yellow. To the left, another building, a tall, narrow tower, offered silvery windows to the rays of the evening sun.

"Were you looking for me?" Adam asked. "So sweet."

"You sure you don't want to meet?"

"Yeah. Turn the TV on. I've got something to show you."

The phone went dead. On the screen Adam tossed a cell phone onto the street, shrugged off his jacket, revealing bare, muscled back, and let the jacket fall to the ground. His face was plastered over every local news broadcast at least once a day and here he was, in broad daylight, taking his clothes off in public. Somebody would recognize him and call the cops for sure. Damn it.

Adam strode into the intersection, oblivious to traffic. Tires screeched as a dark sedan swerved, desperately trying to avoid plowing into him. He raised his head. The air around him shimmered, rising. A stray paper receipt carried by the wind fluttered by and burst into white-hot flame before raining down in a powdery ash.

A ring of fire ignited on the asphalt around him. The bright orange flames rushed outward, spreading in a complex pattern. An arcane circle blazed into life. He must've painted it on the asphalt with some kind of fuel.

"What is it?" I asked.

"I don't know," Rogan growled. "It's fire-attuned. I can tell you it's a high-level circle. He's about to offload a lot of power."

Adam leaned back. The tightly defined muscles flexed and bulged under his skin. He spread his arms wide, his biceps trembling with the strain. His body froze, every muscle tight, every tendon ready. The panels of a green jaguar parked on the street a few feet away began to melt.

"Where is this?" Mad Rogan asked.

"Corner of Sam Houston Drive and Bear Street," Bug said.

About ten minutes from us, off Sam Houston Parkway. Around Adam, traffic stopped. People got out of their cars and stared.

"Zoom in," Mad Rogan ordered.

Bug touched a key. The camera zoomed in on Adam. His eyes were gone. In their place a blazing yellow inferno glared at the world. A translucent new shape overlaid Adam's body, shining here and there with deep, fiery orange. His hands spouted foot-long, angular phantom claws, as if he had put on a pair of demonic glass gloves. Translucent curved spikes burst from his spine.

"Goddamn moron," Mad Rogan snarled. "I know what this is."

Brilliant, white hot fireballs formed between Adam's opened fingers, churning with red and yellow.

"It's Hellspawn," Rogan said. "House Pierce-specific high spell."

High spells were the result of generations of research and experimentation, and Adam Pierce was about to use one of them to cause havoc in the middle of the city. Right now House Pierce was collectively having fits.

Adam opened his mouth and vomited a torrent of fire at the dark building. Glass shattered, raining down. The fire punched through the building. Part of the flames shot straight up, melting glass in a column of fire.

People screamed. Fire alarms wailed. The towering column of fire shot higher, an unbridled power of a Prime running wild.

A fire engine came down the street, swerved to avoid

Adam, and pulled into the parking lot of the silver high-rise. Odd.

"Are you seeing this?" I asked.

"Yes." Rogan focused on the fire engine.

The doors of the fire engine opened. People in fire-fighter suits jumped out and moved toward the building in a determined way.

I thought out loud. "Why evacuate that building instead of the building he's burning? Can you zoom in?"

Bug struck a quick staccato on the keys. Three of his screens zoomed in on a firefighter crew.

Two of the people carried fireman axes. The other three people were carrying rifles. There was no conceivable reason for the firemen to carry rifles. When people faced the prospect of being trapped in a burning building, they panicked. That's why we spent a great deal of time training children to never question what a man in a fireman suit said. We were conditioned from a very early age to not think but just blindly obey whatever order the fireman gave us, because he was there to save us. If a fireman said to evacuate, we would run for the nearest exit.

As if on cue, the doors of the building opened and people in business clothes rushed out.

Mad Rogan's face turned grim.

Adam Pierce was a diversion. The real target was located in that building, and the "firemen" with rifles were going after it.

The screens turned dark.

"Shit fire and save the matches," Bug swore. "Someone took out the street-level cameras. Let me get a different angle . . ."

The screens flickered, still dark.

"No cameras on the other side of the block either." Bug's eyebrows came together. "Dickfuckers."

Mad Rogan grabbed my hand. "Now we really have to go. Come on."

"Equzol first!" Bug yelled.

I tossed him the jar. He snapped it out of the air. "Napoleon, out!"

Napoleon jumped off the pillow and bounded out of the room. I chased him.

Mad Rogan rattled off a phone number at Bug. "Get eyes inside that building, and I'll get you twice as many of your happy pills."

We ran through the hallways, careful not to trip on anything. Mad Rogan put his cell to his ear. "I need the list of businesses in a high-rise on the corner of Sam Houston Drive and Bear Street. Blueprints, ownership, send me everything."

"Think Adam's a diversion?" I almost ran into a pile of chairs.

"If he is, it's a good one."

We burst out onto the wooden bridge. Something flashed in an empty window in the building across from us, reflecting the sun. I grabbed Mad Rogan's arm and yanked him toward me. A shot rang out.

"Where?" Mad Rogan growled.

"Top floor, left corner."

A chunk of concrete the size of a basketball shot out from the pile of rubble and rocketed into the dark window. A muffled scream echoed through the building sounding a lot like "Ow!"

We ran down the bridge.

"Crown Tech," a calm male voice said from Mad Rogan's cell. "Emerald Drilling, Palomo Industries, Powell

Piping Technologies, Bickard, Stang, and Associates, and Reisen Information Services Corporation."

Mad Rogan hung up.

"Does that tell you anything?" I asked.

"No."

Ahead, a pattern crossed the bridge, drawn in chalk and coal. It hadn't been there when we had come the other way. Mad Rogan frowned. The boards with the pattern broke. A flash of vile-smelling green mist shot into the air. He jumped over the gap. I followed.

"I think they're trying to kill me," he said.

"You came into the Pit and punked them in their own territory. Of course they are trying to kill you. Get used to it."

The bridge shuddered under our footsteps. We ran through the island and onto the bridge leading out.

Ahead, sun reflected in a long, horizontal spark right at the level of Rogan's throat.

"Wire!"

"I see it." He pulled a knife out of his jeans and slashed at the wire. It snapped, the two ends coiling to the sides. We ran down the bridge into the parking lot and jumped into the Range Rover. Mad Rogan peeled out of the parking lot so fast that the car almost banked. I grabbed onto the door handle out of sheer self-preservation.

"If he is using Hellspawn, we might not be able to get him," Mad Rogan said.

"What?"

"Hellspawn creates null space."

"In English?"

"The amount of magic he's using is so high that the boundary of the circle he's in doesn't exist in our physical realm."

"How can it not exist? What does that—" A tiny grey body shot in front of the Land Rover. "Squirrel!"

Mad Rogan swerved to the side, trying to avoid the suicidal beast. The SUV hit a curb and jumped. For a terrifying second, we almost flew, weightless. My heart leaped into my throat. The heavy vehicle landed back on the pavement with a thud. The squirrel leapt into the grass on the other side.

I remembered to breathe. "Thank you for not killing the squirrel."

"You're welcome, although now I want to go back and strangle it." Mad Rogan took a ramp onto the interstate. "Back to arcane circles. The boundary of the circle is where our physical reality meets the arcane realm, the 'place' where we reach to get swarms for swarmers, for example. It's a small hole in our space. Nothing can penetrate the circle while the null space is active. You can stand on the street and lob grenades at Pierce, and they'll just bounce off."

We'll see about that.

While the Land Rover hurtled down the interstate, an imaginary conversation between Adam and me played in my head. *Hi, Adam. Did you set fire to my house? Did you try to kill my grandmother?* They said I had to bring him in alive. They didn't say anything about what condition he had to be in.

Maybe I could do it again, that thing I did with Mad Rogan—lock Adam in place and make him answer me. I bet I could. Just thinking about Grandma Frida made me shake.

Mad Rogan took the exit, and I glanced at the clock. Four minutes. We made it in record time.

Ahead the street rolled out, devoid of traffic. In the

middle of the intersection, Adam Pierce spat a torrent of white-hot flames at the building. Two wrecks that used to be cars slowly melted a couple dozen feet from him.

Mad Rogan slammed on the brakes, and the Land Rover screeched to a halt.

"Get us closer, please." I reached for my gun.

"Too hot. Look."

The pavement just outside Adam's circle had turned dark and soft. He was melting the road.

I jumped out of the car. Heat bathed me, blocking my way like a wall.

A car door clanged as Mad Rogan leaped out of the vehicle. A metal pole holding up a streetlight snapped in half and flew like a spear toward Adam Pierce. The pole hit the circle and ricocheted, spinning back at us through the air. I gulped. The pole reversed and punched the invisible boundary of Adam's magic circle, grinding against it.

Mad Rogan grimaced.

The pole clattered to the pavement.

"Null space," he said. "Come on."

I could see Adam. He was right there. Argh.

"Nevada! We're wasting time."

Right there.

But the firemen and Adam were working together. If we got what the firemen were after, Adam would come to us.

We spun around and hopped back into the Land Rover. Mad Rogan took a sharp turn left, circling the buildings, heading for the silver tower. He drove up to the front steps and parked the car, then we got out. The moment I stepped onto the stone steps leading to the door, a blinding headache gripped my brain and squeezed like a vise, tighter and tighter. I took another step up the stairs. The doorway wavered in front of me, distorted. The pain scraped the inside of my skull. I had an absurd feeling that my brain had swelled like an overinflated water balloon and was about to pop.

"They have a mage blocking the door." Mad Rogan backed away onto the pavement and jogged right, looking at his phone.

I followed him. As soon as I left the stairway, the headache vanished. That was a nice power to have. If I'd had that power, I wouldn't have had to build retractable stairs to my room.

In the distance sirens wailed. The emergency responders were on their way, which meant the fake firemen in the building would speed up whatever they were doing so they could get away before Houston's finest showed up in force. We had to find a way in, and we had to find it now.

Since the firemen left someone covering the front entrance, it was highly likely they were still on the first floor. Their team was small. If their goal was on a different floor, they wouldn't have left anyone covering the front entrance; they would've all gone to that floor instead. But they left a guard, so all of them were probably on the first floor, and they were armed, which meant they would probably defend the side entrances. That left us with windows, but the bottom floor of the tower was solid stone, and the first row of windows started about eighteen feet off the ground.

"They'll expect people coming through the side exits," I called out.

"That's why we're not going through the side exit." Mad Rogan showed me a blueprint on his phone. "There are five ways to access the lobby, front entrance, two side exits, elevator, and an internal stairway."

"Perfect." They'd evacuated the building, so they wouldn't expect us coming from the internal stairway. "Now we just have to get into the building itself."

Mad Rogan pointed at a pair of green industrial-size Dumpsters. They slid across the pavement toward us. The first Dumpster bumped into the wall. Mad Rogan strained. The second Dumpster rose in the air and landed on top of the second one, hanging off one side. Together, they were just tall enough to let us reach the second-floor windows.

I grabbed onto the first Dumpster and climbed up. Black and white bags filled it nearly to the brink, and I had to cross to get to the second Dumpster. I stepped down and sank in to my knees. The top bag popped, and a metric ton of old lasagna spilled onto my pants. The stench of soured spaghetti sauce washed over me. Ew. Of all the trash from this whole giant building, I had to step on a bag from the food court. Damn it.

Well, they'd definitely smell me coming.

I mashed my way through the bags to the second Dumpster, climbed up, pulled out my gun, and hit the butt of the gun against the glass. It shattered. I knocked the shards in and climbed inside.

A conference room: a long table, chairs, and a flat-screen TV on the wall. Mad Rogan climbed in behind me, pulled out his phone, and showed it to me. A text message from a blocked number with a video clip. He clicked the link. A grainy video filled the screen, showing a lobby of a building, with a polished greyish floor and two rows of wide columns. At the top of the screen the glass front entrance spilled sunlight onto the floor. A man in fireman's gear leaned against the wall near it, a rifle in his hands. Below him, on the right, another gunman leaned against a marble column. A little lower still on the left, right past the elevators, three people stood by the wall. One held his hand against the marble, the other swung an axe, hitting the wall below, and the third covered them with the rifle. The clip stopped, barely five seconds long. Bug had come through.

Whatever it was they wanted was in the wall. The man with the hand on the marble had to be a sniffer. Sniffers had higher sensitivity to magic, and they could find a magical object even through stone.

"The stairway will put us here." Mad Rogan pointed to the left bottom corner of the screen.

We'd be in full view of the three gunmen. "Are you bulletproof?"

"No, but the metal door that blocks the staircase likely is. Do you have your Ruger?"

I pulled the gun out of its holster.

"I'll hold the door as a shield, but you'll have to fire."

"Why can't you just slice them to pieces like that chopstick?"

"Because my telekinetic magic doesn't work on living things. I can throw something metal fast enough to slice an opponent to pieces. I can hurl a board at him, because cut wood is dead. I can choke him with his own clothes if they are loose enough. But I can't simply throw a body."

Oh. "So the best way to fight you is to strip naked and attack?"

His eyes flashed with a wicked light. "Yes. You should try it and see what happens."

Well, I did walk right into that one.

"I could try to slice the barrels off their guns, but considering the distance, I would need several seconds to aim, and they would likely shoot us. So, I'll provide a shield, but the rest is up to you. I'm a less than mediocre shot."

I leaned back. "Humility? I had no idea you had it in you."

"No," he said. "Honesty. I'm not very good with a gun. I don't typically carry one."

The pile of rubble that had buried Peaches flashed before me. Not that he ever needed one. "Good that I brought mine, then."

"Nevada," Mad Rogan said.

The sound of my name coming from him short-circuited my brain. All of my thoughts stopped. Damn it. I had to get over this, and fast.

"These men are well trained."

Of course they were. They'd positioned themselves so that every entrance was covered by at least two intersecting fields of fire. No matter where we entered, at least two of them could shoot us from different angles.

"If we walk in there, they'll shoot us. They won't hesitate—they'll do it on instinct. It's second nature to them, a reflex, like stopping before a red light."

"Mhm." It's good that he was here to explain it to me. I would've never figured it out on my own.

"You have to shoot them back. Is it going to be a problem?"

"There is only one way to find out," I said.

He nudged the door open. An empty hallway lay before us. We ran down the hallway, passing the elevators. I stopped and mashed the down button. A diversion never hurt.

The elevator doors slid open with a chime.

"Good idea." Mad Rogan stepped in, pushed the button for the lobby, and stepped out.

We jogged to the end of the hallway where a large sign said EXIT. Behind us, the doors of the elevator chimed as it began its descent to the lobby. With luck, they would all be looking at the elevator instead of the stairs.

We ran down the stairwell. My blood was rushing through my veins, my heart pounding too loud and too fast.

If I didn't shoot them, they would shoot me.

I'd never killed anyone before.

The stairs ended in a large door. A grey-haired man in a dark security guard uniform sprawled facedown on the landing in front of it. The back of his head was one huge, red, wet hole. No, they didn't hesitate to shoot. Not at all. They killed this man. Probably someone's father, someone's grandpa . . . This morning he got up, ate his breakfast, and came to work, and now he lay here face-down, alone and cold. He would never get up again. He would never speak, never hug anyone, never smile again. They killed him and left him here.

I had to stop Adam Pierce. Not only because I would lose everything if I didn't, not only because he tried to kill Grandma, but because right now he was outside, spitting fire and not caring how many people he would hurt. The fastest way to stop Adam would be to get the thing he was after.

I was doing the right thing.

Mad Rogan stepped to the door, his feet shoulder-wide, his hands raised.

I wasn't ready. I wasn't ready . . .

"Aim for the center of mass," he whispered.

Center of mass my foot.

"Ready?" he whispered.

No. No, I wasn't. I took the safety off the Ruger. The firearm felt so heavy in my hands. Heavy and cold. "Go."

The door shot forward, six inches above the floor, and rotated, turning horizontal, like the top of a table.

Three gunmen, one directly in front, one on the right by the elevator, the third on the left by a column.

The gunmen swung away from the elevator and toward us. I sighted the one by the elevator—it felt slow, so impossibly slow—and squeezed the trigger. The gun barked. The bullet ricocheted from the elevator doors with a metallic clang. I corrected a hair and fired the second shot. The gunman's head snapped back. I swung left and fired at the second man by the column. The first shot took him in the neck, the second in the lower part of the face, right in his mouth.

The third gunman opened fire. The door spun, vertical again, like a shield. Bullets hammered against it.

Mad Rogan grabbed my hand and pulled me toward a column on our left. I ran with him, shielded by the door, and pressed my back to the cold marble. The hail of bullets followed us.

The whole thing must've taken a second, maybe two.

I just killed two people. Don't think about it, don't think about it . . .

Mad Rogan gaped at me, a look of utter shock on his face. I'd laugh if I could.

"My mother's a former sniper," I squeezed out. "I know how to shoot properly."

The bullet stream changed direction. The gunman was walking toward us.

The door spun around the column, hovering in front of us.

"Cover me." Mad Rogan winked at me.

I leaned left and fired at the couple by the wall in

short bursts. Boom-boom-boom. They ducked behind a column. The woman-sniffer jerked a handgun up and returned fire. Bullets tore through the air next to me. I hid behind the column, stuck my gun out, and shot in her general direction. Boom-boom-boom. Out. I ejected the magazine, pulled the spare from the pocket, slapped it in, and thumbed the release forward. Ten more rounds. That's all I had. The next time I went anywhere with Mad Rogan, I'd bring one of those bandoliers action stars wore when they routed terrorists from jungles.

Mad Rogan lunged to the left.

I fired again, the gun spitting bullets and thunder. Boom, boom. Eight rounds.

Someone screamed. The rifle fire vanished, cut off by the sound of shattering glass. Mad Rogan ducked behind the column next to me.

"Where's the door?" I asked.

"Outside."

I leaned out from behind the column. The man pulled something out of the wall. The woman spread her arms, snapping into the familiar mage pose. Oh no, you don't. I fired at her twice, the bullets piercing the air in rapid twin bursts. A dense curtain of smoke shot up in front of her and my bullets vanished. I was down to six rounds.

There was a side entrance right behind them. They were about to split.

Bullets tore out the curtain of fog, too wide, chipping the wall behind me. The man and the woman couldn't see through the smoke either.

Mad Rogan raced to the side entrance.

Ahead the man shot out of the smoke, knife in one hand. Mad Rogan rammed straight into him. He blocked the man's right arm with his left forearm and jabbed the heel of his right hand into the man's nose. The man staggered back. Mad Rogan snapped a kick. His foot smashed into the man's side, right against his liver. The fireman clutched at his side and fell to the floor.

Okay, fighting him, naked or no, was a terrible idea.

A bullet tore past me. I shied back. The woman leaped out of the smoke and crashed into me. The barrel of her gun yawned at me, dark and impossibly large. The world shrank to that barrel. I grabbed her wrist and hung on, throwing all my weight into it, trying to wrestle the gun from her. She jerked me toward her and swung her right hand. Pain slashed my forearm. I caught a glimpse of knife. I struck at her face with the gun, but she twisted out of the way and slashed my side. An icy burn lashed my ribs. She was stronger and better trained. For a fraction of a second our stares connected, and I saw cold calculation in her eyes. She would kill me.

Some instinctual switch flipped inside me. Magic burst into pain in my shoulder, rolled down into my fingertips, and exploded into frothy lightning on the woman's hand.

The woman's eyes rolled back in her head.

It hurt. It hurt so much. My chest shuddered. It felt like every nerve in my arm snapped loose, frayed with agony.

The woman shook in my grip. The magic linked us, the pain binding us together into one.

I unlocked my fingers, severing the connection.

She crashed to the floor. Her feet drummed the ground. Foam slid from her mouth. She shuddered one last time and lay still.

"You're full of surprises," Mad Rogan growled next to me.

The pain receded, a dull echo of the burning agony. My right arm was red with blood.

"Are you okay?" he asked me.

The woman on the floor didn't move. It didn't look like she was breathing. Jesus. I dropped by her and felt for a pulse. Nothing. I didn't mean to . . . No, I guess I did.

Mad Rogan reached over and gently raised my arm to look at the two-inch-long cut. "Shallow. You'll live."

My lips had gone numb. I made my mouth move. "Thank you, Doctor."

He held up a large piece of jewelry studded with small pale stones, each about the size of a pomegranate seed. It looked like two elongated oval loops, one on top of each other, as if a child had tried to draw a hamburger and had forgotten to draw the top half of the bun. A straight piece, studded with the same stones, ran vertically through the center of the two loops. In the center, the straight piece widened into a ring about as big as my index finger and thumb touching. If it was a brooch of some sort, it was the strangest design I had ever seen.

"Is this what they were after?"

Mad Rogan nodded.

"What is it?"

"I have no idea," he said. "Why don't you ask him?"

I looked past him to where the last firefighter slumped against the wall, clutching at his side. Okay. I could do that. It didn't require me to kill anyone.

I walked over and crouched by the fireman. His breath was coming out in ragged gasps.

"What did you do to him?"

"I kicked him in the liver and then broke two of his ribs. He'll live if paramedics get here in the next ten-fifteen minutes."

I held up the piece of jewelry. "Is this what you came here for?"

He stared at me. I focused, trying to re-create the lasso of magic that had clamped Mad Rogan and squeezed the answers out of him. Nothing happened.

"Compel him to answer," Mad Rogan said.

"I'm trying."

Mad Rogan picked up the knife the woman had dropped. "We can always go to Plan B."

"Give me a minute."

"Nevada, you're wasting time." His voice turned cold and precise. "Be useful for a change."

Useful? You asshole.

"I'm tired of dragging around your dead weight."

Nothing stirred inside me.

"Do something, don't just sit there."

"Has anybody told you that you're a colossal asshole?"

Mad Rogan grimaced. "Apparently anger isn't your trigger, and we don't have time to figure out what it is. Oh well."

He jabbed the knife into the man's leg. The fireman screamed. I winced.

"Is this what you came here for?" Mad Rogan barked.

"Yes."

True.

"Is it magic?" I asked.

"No."

"Lie," I said.

Mad Rogan yanked the knife out and jabbed it into the man's leg again. The man howled.

"I'll keep cutting you until your leg turns into hamburger," Mad Rogan told him, his voice light. "Then I'll put a tourniquet on it and start on your other leg. Answer her questions, or you'll never walk again."

"Are you working with Adam Pierce?" I asked.

"No."

"Lie."

Mad Rogan stabbed the man's leg again.

"What does it do?" I asked.

The man stared at me.

Mad Rogan jabbed his leg again, methodically, calmly, the knife going in and out, in and out . . .

The man cried out, "It opens the gate to enlightenment!"

"True."

Mad Rogan glanced at me.

I spread my arms.

"What time is it?" the man groaned.

I looked at the electronic clock above the elevator. "Five thirty-nine. No, wait, five forty."

The man smiled. "Three . . ."

Mad Rogan spun around.

"Two . . ."

Mad Rogan lunged at me, knocking me off my feet.

"One . . ."

An enormous fireball erupted from the side entrance. Orange flame boiled, raging toward us. Heat bathed my face.

That's it, flashed in my head. *I'm dead.*

The floor surged up and swallowed us whole.

 **Chapter 10**

I was lying on my side. Darkness surrounded me.

A hard arm was wrapped around me. Someone's body pressed against my back, curled around mine.

"Am I dead?"

"No," Mad Rogan said.

Mad Rogan was spooning me. The thought blazed through my head. I tried to scoot away. My chest met hard rock. My back met an equally hard surface, which had to be his chest. There was nowhere to scoot away to.

"What's happened?"

"Well, they must've rigged an explosive device to cover their exit. It detonated."

"I get that. Explain the not dying part." And the spooning part. He was touching me. Oh my God, he was touching me.

"There was no time to escape, so I broke through the floor and pulled it on top of us."

His voice was quiet, almost intimate. He sounded so reasonable, like it was just an ordinary thing. I broke through some solid marble and then built it into a shelter over us in a split second. No big. Do it every day. Just thinking about the amount of magic it would take to do this made me shiver.

"There was an explosion," Mad Rogan said. "Some debris fell on top of us. I had to shift things around, but it's relatively stable now."

"Could you shift things around so we could escape?"

"I'm spent," he said, his voice the same measured calm. "Shifting a few thousand pounds of rock drained me. I need time to recover."

So there was a limit to his power. Good to know that occasionally he was mortal. "Thank you for saving me."

"You're welcome."

My brain finally digested his words. "So we're trapped underground with the building on top of us." We were buried alive. Fear welled in me.

"Not all of the building. I'm reasonably certain it's still standing. I activated the beacon, so my crew is en route. It's just a matter of getting us out."

"What if we run out of air?"

"That would be unfortunate."

"Rogan!"

"We've been here for about fifteen minutes. There is probably about twenty cubic feet of air here, about what you would find in an average coffin."

I would kill him if I ever got out of here.

"There are two of us and your breathing's elevated, so I would estimate we'd have about half an hour. If we weren't getting the air from somewhere, we would be feeling the CO_2 buildup already."

I clamped my mouth shut.

"Nevada?" he asked.

"I'm trying to conserve oxygen."

He chuckled into my hair. My body decided this would be a fine moment to remember that his body was wrapped around mine and his body was muscular, hard, and hot, and my butt was pressed against his groin. Cuddled up by a dragon. No, thank you. Let me off this train.

"If you keep wiggling, things might get uncomfortable," he said into my ear, his voice like a caress. "I'm doing my best, but thinking about baseball only takes you so far."

I froze.

We lay still and quiet.

"What is that smell?" he asked.

"It's my jeans. A bag of food court trash broke when I climbed through the Dumpster."

A minute passed. Another.

"So," he said. "You come here often?"

"Rogan, please stop talking."

He chuckled again. "The air isn't stale. We're getting oxygen."

He was right—the air wasn't stale. At least we wouldn't suffocate. Unfortunately that left all the other problems, like being buried alive and being wedged against him.

"Can you turn so you're not pressed against me?"

"I could," he said, his voice amused. "But then you would have to lie on top of me."

My brain said, "NO." My body went, "Wheee!"

I gave up and lay still.

And waited.

Buried.

With tons of debris on top of us.

If something gave, we'd be crushed. I strained, listening for the slightest noise of things shifting overhead.

Crushed.

With our bones cracking like eggshells under the weight of stone and concrete and . . .

"Why did you enlist in the Army?"

"Simple question, but a complicated answer," he said. "When you're a Prime, especially an heir Prime, your life stops being your own once you graduate from college. Certain things are expected. Your specialty is predetermined by your family's needs. It's understood that you will complete your education, work to further the family interests, select a mate whose genetic pedigree is most likely to produce gifted children, marry, and have said children, at least one but no more than three."

"Why not more than three?"

"Because it tends to complicate the family tree and division of assets. It's that same old version of go to the right school, marry the right person, land the right job. Except in our cases magic dictates everything.

"The system allows for certain leeway, but not much. Instead of working on advanced weapons systems like my father, I could've moved into the nuclear reactor business. Instead of marrying Rynda Charles, I could've married her sister, or I could've imported a bride the way my father did."

When we got out of here, I'd have to look up Rynda Charles just to see what she looked like.

"My course was predetermined. I was the only child and a Prime. Somewhere around my eighteenth birthday, I realized that I was burning through my free time faster than my peers. If I ever hoped to break free of my extremely comfortable gilded cage, I needed to find someone strong enough to block my family's influence. The military fit the bill."

My memory resurrected his words. *I joined because*

they told me I could kill without being sent to prison and be rewarded for it. "And you got to kill people."

"Yes. Let's not forget that. Was your father in the military too?"

"No. Dad never went in. Military tradition in our family runs mostly through the female side."

He was doing that thing again. I couldn't even see his face and I knew he was doing it, that attentive focused listening, which made you want to keep talking and talking just to have the benefit of his attention. His hold shifted around me slightly, his body cradling mine. Don't think about it, don't think about it, don't think about it . . . If I concentrated on it too much, he might sense it. I still had no idea what sort of telepath he was or what abilities he had.

"You didn't go in either," he said.

"My father died when I was nineteen. Someone had to run the family business. My mother couldn't do it, because . . . for various reasons. Everybody else was too young."

"What was wrong with your father?"

Something inside me shrank, twisting into a cold, painful ball. "He had a rare form of cancer. It's called malignant peripheral nerve sheath tumor. MPNST."

How I hated these five letters.

"He had sarcomas, malignant tumors that formed around his nerves. They were so close to his spine that the doctors couldn't surgically take them out. When all of the traditional treatments failed, we moved onto experimental therapies. He fought for four years, but eventually it dragged him down." And the last year had been so horrible.

"And you blame yourself?" His voice was soft.

"No. I didn't give him cancer. I didn't even know exactly what he was diagnosed with. I had just read a letter from his doctor I didn't fully understand. He caught me and made me swear to not talk about it. I should've told my mother."

"Why didn't he want anyone to know?"

I sighed. "Because my father knew he was terminal and his chances of recovery were nonexistent. It was never about curing the cancer. It was about buying him a little bit more time. He knew it would come at a huge emotional and financial cost. My father always wanted to take care of the family. He . . . he weighed the costs and heartache of going through treatment against a couple years of his life and decided it wasn't worth it. When we finally found out, my mother was so angry at him. I was angry at him. Everyone panicked. We pressured him to go into treatment."

"Exactly what he didn't want." He said it as if he understood.

"Yes. We bought him three years." There was so much more to it. My father had poured his life into building the agency. In his mind he saw it as the means to provide for us, even for our children. A family business. We'd mortgaged it to MII to get the money for the experimental therapy. By that point control of the agency had passed to me and my mother as joint owners, with me owning 75 percent of it and my mother holding a 25 percent stake. We never told my father where the money came from. It would've killed him faster than any cancer. There was so much guilt to go around already. We kept drenching each other with it in bucketfuls.

No matter what happened, I would keep the agency alive.

Something scratched the stone above us.

I jerked.

"Easy." Mad Rogan pulled me closer to him, his arms shielding me.

His phone chimed.

His phone chimed! He had a signal. We couldn't be that deep underground.

Mad Rogan swiped across it. "Yes?"

A curt female voice asked, "Major?"

"Here," Mad Rogan said.

"Apologies for the delay, sir. We had to convince the first responders to grant us access to the scene. We're directly above your signal. It doesn't look too bad. You're under two shattered columns."

For a supposed recluse, he sure employed a lot of people, and those people spoke in very familiar tones. He hired ex-military or ex-law enforcement. Probably both.

"Did the cops get Pierce?" I asked Rogan.

"Pierce?" he asked.

"Disappeared," the woman replied.

How could he have disappeared? He was in plain view, belching fire at a tower from the middle of an intersection, and the cops had been en route. They would've converged on him like a pack of wolves. How in the world did he get away?

"Permission to begin the excavation, sir?" the woman asked.

"Granted," Rogan said.

"Stand by."

A muted mechanical whine of some sort of motorized saw cut the quiet above us. A tiny trickle of concrete dust fell on my face. I squeezed my eyes shut.

"Well, I knew they had to come and get us eventually,"

Mad Rogan said. "But you can't say we didn't have an awesome time."

I rang the doorbell. "You really don't have to wait with me."

"I do," Mad Rogan said. "I must deliver you to your loving mother's arms, or she might shoot me."

She might shoot both of us anyway. It was almost eight o'clock. It took Mad Rogan's people over an hour to pull us out, and the police detained us for questioning for another hour. We lied. Waiting to be cut out had given us a long time to get our story straight. Neither Mad Rogan nor I was associated with Adam Pierce in any way, so we both claimed to be in the building on business. The explosion had nearly obliterated the bodies, and when I asked Mad Rogan about the fact that bullets from a gun registered to me were in the bodies and in the wreck of the lobby, he told me he would take care of it. So I didn't mention shooting anyone, he didn't mention slapping anyone with the door, and I learned one crucial difference between a normal person like me and a Prime. When cops called Mad Rogan "sir," they meant it. He told them what happened and nobody doubted it. I had never been treated with deference by the police before. Today I was, simply because he was there. I wasn't sure what to think about that.

Mad Rogan's people had locked the jeweled ornament in a small metal case and taken it to his vault. I hadn't fought him on it. If Adam and whoever was working with him decided they wanted it back, Mad Rogan's private army was much better equipped to fight them off. I'd taken several pictures of it and emailed them to Bern.

The door swung open. I braced myself.

I had examined my reflection in the Range Rover's

side mirror, and I knew exactly what I looked like. The shallow knife scratch at my hairline had bled all over my face. The blood smears had combined with rock dust, black, oily soot from the explosion, and fire-retardant foam, which had dripped all over me when Mad Rogan's people had finally pulled us out of the hole. My hair had turned into a frizzy mess, and the foam cemented it together. To top it all off, the lasagna on my pants had ripened and now emitted an odor usually emanating from day-old roadkill. I was bloody, filthy, and soot-stained, and Mad Rogan didn't look any better.

My mother stared at me, then at Mad Rogan, then at me again.

I raised my hand. "Hi, Mom."

"Inside," my mother ordered. "You too."

"He doesn't need to come inside," I said. I didn't want Mad Rogan anywhere near my family.

"He's covered in blood. At the very least, he can wash it off."

"I'm sure he has a very nice shower at his house," I said.

"Actually, I would be very grateful for a chance to clean up." Mad Rogan touched his forehead. His fingers came away bloody and stained with soot. Suddenly he looked young and disarming, like one of my cousins when they were in trouble. "And a bite of food if you could spare some." If he laid it on any thicker, he'd be ready to audition for Oliver. My mother couldn't possibly buy this.

"You don't even have any clean clothes." I was grasping at straws.

"I do," Mad Rogan said. "I always carry a change of clothes in my car."

"Inside," Mother said.

I knew that tone. It meant the argument was over.

I walked in. Mad Rogan got a duffel out of the Range Rover and followed me. Mother closed the door behind us. I led him through the office into the hallway. He surveyed the warehouse from left to right, starting with the media room and the kitchen; the girls' bedrooms built on top of each other, Catalina's painted pure white on the outside, Arabella's charcoal and covered with her attempts at graffiti, mostly involving her name; Grandmother's rooms, the guest suite; my bedroom and bathroom above the storage room in the corner, Mother's suite, the boys' rooms; and finally, the Hut of Evil. Mad Rogan's eyes widened.

"If you harm anybody in my family, I swear I will murder you," I told him.

"I'll keep that in mind."

I led him to the guest suite.

It took three shampoos and a lot of scrubbing, but when I left my room, I was clean. The air smelled of bacon and pancakes. Suddenly I realized I was starving.

I walked into the kitchen and found Mad Rogan in it. He sat at the table, dressed in a blue Henley shirt and jeans, sipping coffee out of a mug with a little grey kitten on it. His dark hair was combed back from his face. His jaw was once again clean shaven. *I am a polite, nonthreatening kind of dragon with excellent manners. Horns are hidden, tail is tucked away, fangs covered. I would never do anything cruel, like stab a man with a knife about ten times to get him to answer a question.*

Somehow this new, on-his-best-behavior version was scarier than witnessing him calmly breaking a man with his bare hands. After what we'd been through, I would've expected him to hole up somewhere dark, eating raw meat, chain-smoking, guzzling some sort of ridiculously tough drink, like whiskey or kerosene or something, and thinking grim thoughts about life and death. But no, here he was, charming and untroubled, sipping coffee.

Mad Rogan saw me and smiled.

And my mind went right into the gutter.

How was it that he was sitting in my kitchen?

My mother turned away from the stove and held out a plate of pancakes. I took it from her and set it on the table next to a platter of bacon. Mad Rogan pushed the second mug of coffee toward me. It had an orange kitten on it.

Grandma Frida strode into the kitchen, followed by Lina and Arabella. "I smell bacon! Penelope, did you know there is a handsome man in our kitchen?"

Oh Lord, here we go.

My mother made some sort of noise halfway between a cough and a grunt.

"Well," Grandma Frida said, "introduce us, somebody."

"Grandma, Mad Rogan. Mad Rogan, Grandma," I squeezed out.

Arabella's eyes got really big. She grabbed her phone and started texting. "Leon's going to pee himself."

"Quit it," Lina growled and sat in the chair next to me. Grandma took a chair next to Rogan.

"How are you feeling?" he asked her.

"Fine, thank you." She gave him a big smile.

I passed a plate to Rogan and sat across from him.

Leon ran into the kitchen and stopped, his gaze fixed on Mad Rogan. Bern bumped into him, nudging him into the room. "If you're not getting bacon, get out of the way."

Arabella grabbed three pieces of bacon from the plate. "Mine!"

"Bacon hog," Lina told her.

"Settle down, there is more bacon." Mom pulled another broiling pan full of bacon out of the oven. I grabbed a pancake, wrapped bacon in it, and bit. It was fluffy and delicious, and for no apparent reason it made me want to cry.

"By the way," Arabella said, "you might get a call from school. I forgot to mention it before."

Mother paused. "Why?"

"Well, we were playing basketball and I guess I pulled on Diego's jersey. I don't even remember doing it. And Valerie decided it would be a good idea to snitch on me. I mean, I saw her walk over to the coach and pull on his sleeve like she was five or something. I even asked Diego if he cared, and he said he didn't even notice. It's a sport! I was into it."

"Aha," Mother said. "Get to the call-from-school part."

"I told her that snitches get stitches. And Coach said that I made a terrorist threat."

"That's stupid," Lina said, pushing back her dark hair. "It's not a threat, it's just a thing people say."

"Snitches do get stitches." Bern shrugged.

"Your school is stupid," Grandma Frida said.

"So he said I had to apologize and I refused, since she snitched on me, so I got sent to the office. I'm not in trouble, but they want to move me to third-period PE now."

Well, it could've been worse. At least she didn't hurt anybody.

Silence claimed the table. Across from me, Mad Rogan was cutting the pancake into precise pieces and devouring it with a familiar efficiency. When my mother had come home on leave, she'd eaten like that. She was leaning against the island now, watching him.

"You're Mad Rogan!" Leon burst out.

"Yes," Mad Rogan said, his voice calm.

"And you can break cities?"

"Yes."

"And you have all this money and magic?"

"Yes."

Where was Leon going with this?

My cousin blinked. "And you look . . . like that?"

Mad Rogan nodded. "Yes."

Leon's dark eyes went wide. He looked at Mad Rogan, then glanced down at himself. At fifteen, Leon weighed barely a hundred pounds. His arms and legs were like chopsticks.

"There is no justice in the world!" Leon announced.

I giggled and almost choked on my pancake. Mother cracked a smile.

"Can you play guitar too?" Leon asked. "Because if you can, I'll go kill myself right now."

"No, but I can sing a little," Mad Rogan said.

"God damn it!" Leon punched the table.

"Calm yourself," Bern told him.

"You shut up. You're the size of a Sasquatch." Leon pointed at Mad Rogan. "Are you seeing this? How is this fair?"

"He's fifteen," I told Mad Rogan. "Fair is very important right now."

"You have time," Mad Rogan said.

"Yeah . . ." Leon shook his head. "No, not really. I can't sing for sure, and I'll never look like that."

"I'm a product of calculated selective breeding," Mad Rogan said. "I was conceived because it would be good for my House to have an heir and because my parents' genes ticked the right set of boxes. You were probably conceived because your parents loved each other."

"According to our mother," Bern said, "he was conceived because she was too wasted to remember a rubber."

Mad Rogan stopped chewing.

"I was conceived because my mother skipped bail. Her boyfriend at the time threatened to call the cops on her, so she had to do something to keep him from doing it," Bern said helpfully.

Awesome. Just the right kind of information to share.

"Aunt Gisela isn't the best mother," I said. "There's one in every family."

"What do you do?" Leon leaned forward. "You left the Army and disappeared. How come?"

"Leon," Mother warned.

"Is it because of the war?" Lina asked. "People on Herald say you have PTSD and you became a hermit like a monk because of it."

"Either a hermit or a monk, not both," I corrected out of habit.

"Herald also said he was disfigured." Arabella made big eyes.

"Yes, I'm a hermit. Mostly I brood," Mad Rogan said. "Also I'm very good at wallowing in self-pity. I spend my days steeped in melancholy, looking out the window. Occasionally a single tear quietly rolls down my cheek."

Arabella and Lina snickered in unison.

"Do you also brush a white orchid against your lips?" Arabella put in.

"While sad music plays in the background?" Lina grinned.

"Perhaps," Mad Rogan said.

"Do you have a girlfriend?" Grandma Frida asked.

I put my hand over my face.

"No," Mad Rogan said.

"A boyfriend?" Grandma Frida asked.

"No."

"What about . . ."

"No," Mom and I said in unison.

"But you don't even know what I wanted to ask!"

"No," we said again together.

"Party poopers." Grandma shrugged.

"It's nine o'clock," Mom said. "Go on."

Leon pointed at Mad Rogan. "But Mad Rogan!"

"But you have a sixty-seven in French," she said. "You'll regain your staying-up privileges when you pass."

"But!" Leon waved his arms.

"Don't make me carry you," Bern rumbled.

"Dibs on the shower," Arabella jumped up.

The girls left the room and dragged Leon with them. Grandma Frida, Mom, Bern, Mad Rogan, and I remained.

My mother leaned forward. "Nevada is going after Pierce because we have no choice as a family. I don't know what this is about for you. I don't know if it's pride, or if you're just bored. I know you kidnapped Nevada. You scared her and tortured her. If you hurt my child again, I'll end you, Prime or not."

Nice, Mom. I'm sure he's scared.

Mad Rogan smiled without showing his teeth. The familiar cold, predatory look slid into his eyes, the dragon waking up and showing his true colors.

"Thank you for inviting me into your lovely home and offering me this delicious meal." His voice was calm and measured. "Because I'm your guest, I feel some small degree of obligation to you, so I'll make it perfectly clear, Sergeant. I know who you are. I've seen your service record, and I consider you to be a potential threat. If you threaten me again, I'll change your threat status to definite, and I'll act on it."

He'd seen my mother's service record. His House had run a background check. That meant his question about my father being in the military had been complete bullshit. He probably knew the whole history of my family. He'd manipulated me, and I'd played right into it. Stupid.

"I prefer not to kill children," Mad Rogan continued. "But I have no problems with making them orphans."

True. Every word. He meant it.

Bern blinked.

Mad Rogan drank from his grey kitten mug. "Besides, considering your daughter's skill with a firearm, she's likely to shoot me before you do."

My mother turned to me. "What happened?"

"I don't want to talk about it," I said. I was trying very hard to pretend that it hadn't happened.

"Nevada . . ." she began.

"No," I said quietly.

A dark stain was spreading through Mad Rogan's Henley over his ribs. "You're bleeding."

He looked down at himself and frowned.

"Let me see." I got up.

"It's nothing."

"Rogan," I said. "Lift up your shirt."

He pulled his Henley up, exposing his side. A folded paper towel covered his lower ribs, held in place by duct tape.

"What is this?" I demanded.

"It's a bandage," Bern said.

"No, it's not."

"Yes, it is," Grandma Frida said. "Sometimes you cut your finger and you wrap the paper towel around it real tight, slap some duct tape on it, and good to go."

"Your father used to do this," Mom told me. "I swear, it's like every man is born with it, or they must take some secret class on how to do it."

I waved my hand at them. "It's a paper towel. With duct tape! Where did you get the duct tape?"

Mad Rogan shrugged. "In the cabinet under the sink in your bathroom. I thought it stopped bleeding."

"Well, it didn't. When did you even get this?"

"I got hit by some debris during the blast," he said.

"Did you clean it?"

"I showered," he said.

"Right." I glanced at my mother. "Okay, the two of you will have to postpone trying to figure out who is the harder hardcase until I fix this." I got up and pulled a med kit out of the kitchen cabinet.

My phone vibrated in my pocket. I pulled it out and flicked it on. A text from an unknown number. I sighed. Of course.

I put the phone on the table and tapped the text message. A picture of me and Mad Rogan circling the tower. In the picture, my face was pale, my mouth pressed into a hard line. I looked like I was trying not to cry, which was so strange, because at the time I wasn't anywhere close to crying. Mad Rogan's face was turned away from the camera, his head tilted as he looked up at the second-story windows.

A second text popped under the first. It said, *"Whos the guy?"*

Rogan focused on the phone. "Pierce."

I texted back, *"Where are you?"*

"Outside ur house."

My heart hammered. Mad Rogan leaped up and took off for the door. My mother *moved*. I hadn't seen her go that fast since she left the Army. Grandma Frida dashed to the motor pool, Bern ran to the Hut of Evil, while I chased Mad Rogan. I caught up with him by the door, slipped into my office, and tapped the keyboard. A grey thermal camera image filled the screen, split into four parts, each section of the screen showing the view from a different side of the house: the parking lot and street in front of the motor pool at the back of the warehouse, the trees to the right, the street to the left, and the front door, with Mad Rogan's Range Rover parked next to my car.

I held my breath. Nothing.

Mad Rogan leaned over me. His chest brushed against my right shoulder.

On the screen the night spread outside the house, a charcoal painting came to life. Nothing moved. No cars passed the house. If my mother put a bullet through Adam Pierce's heart, we could kiss the agency good-bye. If he came to burn us to death . . . he shouldn't be able to burn us to death. Hellspawn was a higher-order spell. It would've tapped him out the way Mad Rogan was now tapped out. At least I hoped it had.

The intercom on the phone flashed white. I pushed it.

"Three people in the building across the street," Bern said quietly. The image on the monitor zeroed in on three white human silhouettes on the roof of the warehouse to the north. One of them lay in the familiar sniper pose.

"Those are mine," Mad Rogan said quietly.

We waited. Trees rustled gently in the night breeze, barely visible on the screen.

My phone buzzed. Another text.

"Ma'am, this is the police. The call is coming from INSIDE YOUR HOUSE."

Asshole!

"Did I freak you out?"

Gaaaah!

I pushed the intercom. "Just got another text. I think he's screwing with us."

"Sit tight," Mom said.

I typed *"Asshole"* on my phone.

"Heh. Tell your new friend I said hi."

On the screen the Range Rover exploded. Thunder punched the door and wall with a huge, invisible fist. The warehouse shook.

The intercom lit up. "Do you have the kids?" Mother asked.

"Yes," Bern said. "They're with me."

Flames billowed out of the Range Rover's metal carcass, bright white. Going out there was out of the question. We'd all make lovely targets silhouetted against that fire.

We sat, and waited, and watched the Range Rover burn until the fire department barreled down our street in a blaze of glory, lights, and sirens.

"Take your shirt off." Now there's something I never thought I'd say to the Scourge of Mexico.

Mad Rogan pulled his shirt off, and I tried my best not to stare. Muscles rolled under his tan skin. He wasn't darker than me, but I tanned to a reddish gold, while his skin had a deeper, brown undertone to it. He was perfectly proportioned. His broad shoulders flowed into a muscular, defined chest that slimmed down to the flat planes of his hard stomach. *Handsome* or *athletic* didn't do him justice. Dancers or gymnasts were athletic. He had the kind of body that should've belonged to a man from a different time, someone who swung a sword with merciless ferocity to protect his land and ran across the field at a wall of enemy warriors. There was a brutal kind of efficiency about the way muscle corded his frame.

I hadn't even realized how large he was. Because all those suits streamlined him and his proportions were so well balanced, he looked almost normal-sized. But now, as he sat in my kitchen chair, dwarfing it, there was no way to ignore it. The sheer physical power of him was overwhelming. If he grabbed hold of me, he could crush me. But I didn't care. I could look at him all night. I wouldn't go to sleep. I wouldn't need to rest. I could just sit there and stare at him. And if I looked long enough, I'd throw caution to the wind, reach out, and slide my hand over that powerful muscle. I would feel the strength in his shoulders. I would kiss . . .

And that was about enough of that.

Underneath all of that masculine, harsh beauty was cold, the kind of cold that could stab a helpless man with a knife, feel the tip of it scrape the bone, and do it again and again and not be bothered by it. That cold scared me. Mad Rogan, unlike other people, rarely lied. I didn't know if it was because he knew I would call him on it or if it was simply his way. When he said he would kill you, he meant it. He didn't make threats or promises, he stated facts, and when he wanted something, he'd do whatever he had to do to get it.

I opened the med kit and pulled out gauze and medical tape.

The fire department was gone, having drowned the sad remains of the Range Rover in fire-retardant foam. It was almost surreal how quickly their questions had stopped after Rogan had given them his name. My mother insisted on staying in the crow's nest she and my Grandmother had installed while I'd gone to talk to Bug. The kids had gone to bed. Grandma Frida had too. One of Mad Rogan's men had come to personally take responsibility for failing to prevent the explosion. When Arabella was about two or three, she didn't like to be in trouble. She didn't want anyone to be mad at her, and the suspense of waiting until the exact nature of the punishment was decided always proved too much for her, so when she would do something bad, she would announce, "I'm going to punish myself!" and march off to her room to be grounded. I saw that precise look on the man's face as he stared at Mad Rogan in quiet desperation. He would totally punish himself if he could.

He was gone now, and the warehouse had fallen quiet.

I crouched to take a better look at Mad Rogan's so-called bandage. "I'm going to pull it off now."

"I'll try not to cry."

I rolled my eyes, sighed, and yanked the duct tape off. He winced. A shallow gash cut across his ribs on the right side, more of a scrape than a deep cut, but it was three inches long, and it had bled. At least it wasn't a gaping wound, so we could get away without stitches. I got the saline solution and clean rags.

"Sorry about your car." I squirted the saline solution into the gash and blotted it.

"We agreed on full disclosure," he said. "When were you going to tell me that Pierce is obsessed with you?"

"He isn't obsessed with me."

"He called you to let you know he was starting his fire-works today. He claims he's in lust. Then he texted you to make sure you saw him blow up my car. That's twice he notified you before he did anything he views as impressive."

I smeared antibiotic ointment on the cut and placed a gauze pad over it. "Adam is a flake. He's impulsive and he likes people to reassure him he is cool and awesome. I'm a young woman, I'm attractive, and I indicated that I wasn't impressed by his shenanigans." I began to tape the cut. "He discussed bringing me home with him to meet his mother just so he could see the look on her face. He got a giggle out of it. It's not obsession, it's . . . passing fancy, or whatever people call it."

"These are things I need to know," he said. "I can use this. If I'd known this, I would've handled today differently."

"Funny how it's always 'I' with you. It's never 'we.' " I taped the other side of the gash.

"What did you do that would make him infatuated? Did you kiss? Did you hold hands?"

His voice had taken on a distant tone, but there was a slight edge of heat to it.

"I gave him a peck on the cheek. It wasn't sexual. He was trying to get me to run away with him, and I didn't want to rebuff him so hard that he'd slam the door shut. I still have to bring him in."

"Then why is he infatuated?"

"I don't know why," I said, exasperated. "Probably because I'm chasing him and I said no. He can't comprehend that I'm chasing him because MII will throw my family out on the street. His House has been on top forever and he can't even picture someone doing that to them, let alone try to understand what it would be like. He probably thinks that I'm pursuing him because I'm secretly fascinated with the glittering jewel that he is."

Oops. Said a little too much. I didn't really want Rogan to know that Montgomery held us by our throat. There was no telling what he would do with that information. I straightened. "Look, right now there are two people in this kitchen. One is an overindulged, filthy-rich Prime, and the other is me. You have more in common with Adam than I do. Why don't you tell me why he's doing things?"

Mad Rogan looked at me, his eyes clear and hard. "I'm nothing like him."

On that we could agree. Rogan was nothing like Pierce. Adam was a teenager in a man's body. Rogan was a man, calculating, powerful, and stubborn.

Bern walked into the kitchen at a near run and stopped. I realized that I was standing about two inches from a half-naked Mad Rogan, who was looking up at me.

"Should I come back later?" Bern asked.

"No," I said, stepping away from Mad Rogan. "He was interrogating me while I patched him up, but we're finished."

Mad Rogan glanced down at his side. "Thank you."

"You're welcome."

Bern put a laptop on the table. "I found it."

On the laptop, a video feed played an image recorded with the regular camera at the front door. The time stamp said 20:26. Twenty-six minutes after eight. It had to be just a few moments after we arrived.

A pair of teenagers came skating down the street on their boards, one in a blue shirt and one in black. They looked like typical Houston kids: dark hair, tan, about fourteen or fifteen. They shot by the Range Rover and kept going. The clip stopped with the kid in a black shirt holding a cell phone to his ear as he rolled off.

Bern clicked the keys. The image rewound in slow motion, and I saw the kid in blue bend ever so slightly as he jumped over the curb and toss a small object under the Range Rover.

"Is that . . . ?"

"It's a bomb," Bern confirmed. "He must've remotely detonated it."

"He used children to place a bomb?"

"Yes," Bern confirmed.

"Children?" My mind couldn't quite wrap around it.

"And one of them called him to report." Mad Rogan's eyes iced over.

I sank into a chair. "What if it had detonated early? Who hands a bomb to kids? And for what? To make a lousy point?"

Mad Rogan tapped his phone. "Diego? He used children. Yes. No. Just let me know."

He hung up.

Two young boys had skated by our house, holding a bomb. What if one of them had fallen? What if someone had been in the car? What if one of us had gone to the mailbox? Then we would have had more dead bodies. The death count for today would have been more than six. Six was more than enough, especially because three of those six deaths happened because of me.

My chest hurt. I killed people today. I took their lives. They would've taken mine, but somehow that didn't seem to matter right now. My grandmother barely survived. My house had almost been burned to the ground, then two children threw a bomb under a car parked next to it. It all crashed down on me like an avalanche.

"Are you alright?" Mad Rogan focused on me.

"No," I said.

Bern was looking at me too. "I can make tea," he said. "Would you like some tea?"

"No, thank you." I turned to Mad Rogan. He was a Prime, and right now we couldn't afford to pass up on whatever protection he could offer. "Can you do any magic at all, or are you completely dry?"

"It's coming back," he said. "I'm not helpless."

"Can you stay the night?" I asked.

"I can," he said.

"And if Pierce shows up or something happens . . ."

"I'll take care of it," he said.

True. He meant it.

"Thank you," I told him. "I'll see you both in the morning."

I left the kitchen and went to my room, almost running. I closed the door, sat on the bed, and pulled my knees to my chest. There was a big, gaping hole inside me. It was growing bigger, and I didn't know how to close it.

A knock sounded on my door. It was probably my mother. For a moment I considered pretending that I didn't hear her. But I wanted her to come in. I wanted her to hug me and tell me everything would be okay. "Who is it?"

"It's me," my mother called.

"It's open."

My mother walked in carrying a tablet. She was moving slower than usual. Her leg was really hurting and I felt it because she climbed the stairs. She sat beside me on the bed and swiped her hand across the tablet. A video clip came on. It had been taken with someone's phone. On-screen, Adam Pierce, his phantom spikes and claws glowing, belched fire. The side of the tower where Rogan and I had our little adventure loomed on the right.

The front entrance of the tower blew out with an ear-splitting thunder. The building shook. A man gasped, "Holy shit!"

The video switched to a view of a hand. Whoever had been filming had grabbed his phone and hightailed it out of there.

"Were you inside?" Mom asked.

I nodded. "Adam was a diversion. While he was spitting fire, a team went into this building to retrieve some sort of trinket hidden in the wall. We stopped them."

"Do you want to talk about it?" Mom asked.

I shook my head.

"Can I help?" she asked softly. "Can I do anything?"

I shook my head and leaned against her. She put her arm around me. I wouldn't cry. I was twenty-five years old. I would not cry.

"Rogan's people are analyzing the jewelry we found," I said, my voice sounding dull. "I sent a picture of it to Bern. He's looking too. There is something really big and nasty going on, Mom. I feel like I'm on the edge of it. It scares me. I scared myself today."

"You're doing what needs to be done," Mom said and hugged me to her. "Remember the rules: we have to be able to look ourselves in the mirror. Sometimes that means doing terrible things because there is no other choice. Are you doing the right thing?"

"I think so. It's just spun out of control so fast. Pierce was willing to burn down a building to get that thing. He gave a bomb to a kid Leon's age. Who does that?"

"Someone who needs to be stopped."

"I keep thinking, if MII didn't get involved and call me into their office, this would be happening to someone else. We would be watching all this on TV and going, 'Oh my God, isn't that crazy?'"

"You can't go there," Mom said. "That's how you'll drive yourself nuts. Trust me on this: wondering, What if this didn't happen? never helped anybody. It just drowns you in self-pity and makes you less alert. There is no backing out now. Nevada, view it as a job. As something you have to do. Get the job done and come home."

"I think Rogan is using me as bait," I said.

"Use him back," Mom said. "Throw him at Pierce and let him take him down."

"What if he kills Pierce?"

"Bigger problem if Pierce kills him," Mom said. "But if he kills Pierce, it becomes a matter between House Pierce and House Rogan. Let them sort it out. Your primary objective here is to survive. Then to bring Pierce in, if possible."

I rested my head on her shoulder. "I'm going to need more ammo."

"How was the Ruger?" my mother asked softly. She'd figured it out.

"I hit my target," I told her.

 **Chapter 11**

I awoke early. The sun hadn't risen yet, but the sky had turned a pearly, pale color. I peeled Band-Aids off my face and arm, shook a few drops of lavandin and rose geranium into the oil warmer, lit a candle under it, and took a long shower. I was still clean, but a shower usually made me feel better. I stood under the cascade of hot water, hoping to wash away the remnants of yesterday. I'd dreamed of shooting people. In my dreams I killed them again and again, each bullet punching their heads in slow motion, the blood blossoming like a revolting red flower. It hadn't been like that at all. The whole firefight had probably taken three or four minutes, if that. In the dream, my gun had sounded like thunder. In the lobby, it had sounded dry, like a firecracker. Boom-boom. A life ended. Boom-boom. Another one down.

I let the water run over me and tried to figure out how my mother survived it. How could she look through the scope, squeeze the trigger, and end someone's life and do it again and again and still hold it together? I wanted to ask her about it. Was there some secret to it?

But two years had passed since my mother went to her last group meeting. She was better. Stirring up old demons wouldn't do her any good. I had to deal with it on my own.

I stood under the shower until the guilt got the better of me. Using up all the hot water wouldn't be cool. My sisters and cousins still had to shower. I got out, wrapped a towel around my hair and another around my body, and looked at my reflection. The shallow cuts on my face and arm had survived without bleeding. The cut on my ribs was worse. I smeared an antibiotic ointment on it. Wincing and making sucking noises didn't seem to make the pain any less. I slapped a Band-Aid on the gash and another one on my arm, just in case that cut decided to open up and make a mess.

If only I'd had some paper towels and duct tape lying around. I rolled my eyes. What the hell had he been thinking? He was what, a multimillionaire? And he bandaged himself with a paper towel and duct tape. How did he even know what duct tape was? Maybe he had his own Prime version at the house, stitched with gold and studded with diamonds, just in case he gave himself a paper cut.

I laughed under my breath, snorted, and laughed some more. Standing here, dripping wet, and laughing like a loon. Perfectly mentally fit.

I pulled the towel off my hair, reached to put it on the hook by the window, and stopped. My bathroom window had a view of the motor pool, and from this angle, I could see the entire expanse of Grandma Frida's kingdom. Vehicles covered with canvas and racks with parts stood by the walls. In the middle of the polished concrete floor, Mad Rogan was drawing a magic circle with chalk. It started as a large pentagon, with a two-and-a-half-foot-wide circle at each corner. Lines sectioned the pentagon into separate parts, with glyphs running along the border of the design. It looked flawless, the pentagon sides straight, the circles round. It must've taken him years of practice.

Mad Rogan finished the last glyph and straightened. He was wearing the same Henley and pants he had on last night. He stretched, raising one leg, than the other, and hopped in place, as if jumping an invisible rope. For a moment he stood, barefoot, in front of the pentagon, then he stepped across the line and stopped, facing my side of the warehouse, his eyes closed, his arms at his sides.

The Key. I'd read about it. It was a ritual some of the greater Houses used to recharge. Mad Rogan had expended all of his magic, and now he would try to get it back. Somewhere Adam Pierce was probably doing a very similar thing. People had different opinions on what the Keys actually did. Some said they replenished magic, some said they just realigned the magic user to make the best of it. I'd seen some YouTube videos of it, but none of them were of good quality. The Keys were a well-guarded secret. Each was unique to the House that had developed it.

Mad Rogan raised his arms, his elbows bent, his hands wide open, his eyes closed. I leaned against the side wall. A variation of the mage pose. Okay. So far not that exciting.

Rogan turned his right arm to the side, flexing his back, stretching his chest, simultaneously stepping sideways into the circle with liquid grace, as if his whole body suddenly opened. He spun within the chalk boundary, shockingly fast. His foot shot out, hammering a devastating high kick to an invisible opponent. His hands sliced through the air, right, then left, like blades ready to cut down an attacker.

The outline of the circle began to glow pale blue.

Mad Rogan turned, leaped, spun, and moved into the second circle. His rigid fingers rolled into fists and blades transformed into hammers as he threw quick, hard punches. His long kicks turned short and vicious, his speed and strength melding into pure power. He was graceful, like a dancer, but brutal and efficient, like an assassin backed into a corner.

The second circle glowed. Sweat broke out on Mad Rogan's face, yet a serene, calm expression claimed his face. He rolled into the third circle. His right hand shot up, fingers bent. I'd seen this exact move yesterday when he'd hit the fake firefighter in the face. He must've stopped short, because if he had done it the way he was doing it now, he would've driven the cartilage of the man's nose straight into his brain.

There was a fluid, magnetic grace in the way he moved. All those muscles I had been admiring yesterday were just a by-product of his journey toward his goal. And the goal was power. Raw, lethal power. All of him, his incredible strength, his blinding speed, his flexibility, dexterity, and stamina blended together to achieve an almost feral savagery. Tiny hairs stood on the backs of my arms. It was like watching a god of primal human violence dance, and I couldn't look away. If only I could have him all to myself. What would it feel like to walk up to him, put my hand on his shoulder, and see all that condensed violence turn into lust?

All five circles glowed now. He landed in the pentagon, back in the same mage pose. The glow flared brighter, then vanished, as if sucked into him. Mad Rogan stepped out, wiped the sweat off his forehead with his forearm, grabbed a bottle of water sitting on the nearest covered vehicle, and drank.

I let out a breath I didn't know I was holding and shivered. My left foot sparked with tiny points of pain—it had fallen asleep. I hopped, grabbed my towel before it slid off me, and leaned back to glance through the window. He still stood there. The sun had risen, and golden light spilled into the warehouse, drawing long rectangles on the floor. It washed over him, making his tan skin glow. I couldn't see his face, just the sharp angle of his cheek, warmed by the sun.

If I'd been next to him right now and he'd reached for me, I would have let him do anything he wanted right there, on the hood of some tank.

I was in over my head. I exhaled and tried to drown out the need pulsing through me. Mad Rogan was off limits. He was from a different world, he had different standards, and he promised to make me an orphan if my mother threatened him again. Okay, that last one did. I was all good now.

I moved away from the window.

I had to get a grip. Nothing but trouble would come from messing around with Mad Rogan. He and I needed to catch Adam Pierce, bring him to his family, and go our separate ways.

When I came downstairs, Mad Rogan was nowhere to be found. I tracked Grandma Frida in the garage. She was leaning against the track vehicle she'd been working on and drinking her morning tea.

"Something else, wasn't he?" she asked me quietly.

"You saw me watching him?"

She nodded, reached over, and brushed a strand of hair

from my face. "When did you get so grown up? When did I get so old?"

"You're not old, Grandma. You could probably kick my butt."

She sighed. "Be careful, Nevada. That's a very dangerous man."

Tell me about it. "I'm not planning on hanging out with him one second longer than necessary."

Grandma Frida gave me an odd look.

"What?"

"Does he know that?"

"Yes, he does. I told him. This is a purely professional arrangement."

Grandma Frida shook her head and sipped her tea. "How is the investigation going, Sherlock?"

"Well, we found a weird doohickey made of jewels and almost got ourselves blown up."

"What does it have to do with Pierce?"

I shook my head. "I have no idea. But they are connected somehow. Where is Mad Rogan?"

"Bern came and got him."

The less contact Mad Rogan had with my cousins and sisters, the better. "I guess I'll go find them, then."

"Guess so," she said. "Watch your back, Nevada."

"Always."

"Because he isn't Kevin."

I turned on my foot. "Really, Grandma?"

She waved me on. "Go!"

She was right. Mad Rogan was as far away from Kevin as you could get.

A minute later I climbed the five steps to the Hut of Evil. Bern sat at his workstation. Mad Rogan stood behind him. Three screens in front of Bern showed the inside of Bug's digital jungle lair in all its glory. Bug himself sat in front of the center monitor, petting Napoleon, who sprawled on his lap. His face was relaxed. Not twitching. No jumpy eyes. He was high as a kite on Equzol.

How in the world had Mad Rogan conned him into linking up to Bern's system like this? Usually Bug was too paranoid. In the two years I'd known him, he wouldn't even give me a phone number.

". . . not bad for a home system," Bug was saying.

"Is that a Strix T09x server behind you?" Bern asked. Bug nodded.

"Nice. With Talon-M7?"

"Look again," Bug said.

"How much Equzol did this cost you?" I murmured to Mad Rogan.

"You don't want to know," he said.

Bern zoomed in on a piece of convoluted computer equipment. "Can't be."

"See it and weep." Bug held out a dog biscuit in front of Napoleon. The dog opened his mouth and patiently waited until Bug put a biscuit into it.

Bern frowned. "How did you get this? M8s are scheduled for release in two months. M9s shouldn't even be in production yet."

"That's what they want you to believe. They're waiting for the Stryker chip to drop. When the M8s go on sale, the price will go through the roof, and then they'll be worthless in like a month, because the M9s with the new Stryker will flood the market. Dickfuckers."

"You keep using that word," Mad Rogan said. "You realize it doesn't make sense?"

"Why?" Bug startled.

"You can't fuck a dick," Mad Rogan said.

"But you can fuck with a dick," Bug said.

"Then it's redundant," Bern said.

This was the kind of argument that could go on for hours. "Bug, did you find something?"

Bug rolled his eyes. "No, I'm sitting here talking to you assholes, Major excluded, because I'm a social butterfly and I just love y'all so much." His fingers danced across the keyboard. "Turns out that First National stores two months of their security footage and dumps it to a remote server every night. I've gone through it and voila!"

Security footage of the inside of the bank filled the left monitor. A light rectangle slid across the screen and singled out a slim woman walking across the polished floor. Platinum blond hair, well dyed, white blouse with a chunky gold necklace, grey skirt, shockingly bright red belt, pair of red pumps, and designer bag. A banker met her, and the camera caught her face as she turned. She was about thirty, with large grey eyes, framed by long false eyelashes and a thin mouth. Pretty overlaid with a polish of money.

"Meet Harper Larvo," Bug announced. "Twenty-nine years old, father Phillip Larvo, mother Lynn Larvo, both in real estate. Not affiliated with any House. Attended Phillips Academy Andover, then Dartmouth, where she managed to squeak by with a degree in art history—I've seen the transcript, it's not pretty. Harper's a harmonizer, like both of her parents and her grandfather."

Harmonizers in magic terms had nothing to do with music. A talented harmonizer could walk into a room and make it take on an entirely different mood just by rearranging a few objects. As talents went, this one wasn't that rare. Harmonizers usually worked as interior designers, florists, fashion consultants, any sphere where something had to be coordinated to be esthetically pleasing.

"Harper rates as Notable, but she's really not far from Average," Bug said. "Which is something, but not remarkable. Her parents are Notable too, her grandfather was a Significant. Her family banks at Central Bank. All of their accounts are there and have been for fifty years. So what is she doing here? There is no trace of her opening an account. Furthermore, my sweet little chickies, Harper is more or less unemployed. She interned at a fashion magazine, worked on the Black and Red Hotel in Dallas with some Sullivan dude who is supposed to be famous, and she's affiliated with a couple of charities, but mostly she parties and looks pretty. Like a butterfly. Useless and famous for nothing."

Half a dozen images popped on the screen. Harper with a champagne flute. Harper lying on a table, prettily kicking her feet. Harper at some sort of photo shoot poised on a couch and pouting at the camera.

"And my favorite," Bug announced.

An image filled the screen. Harper giggling, her hair, bright yellow blond, pressed against Adam Pierce, who was looking hot and bothered in his trademark leather. He had one arm around her.

"When was this?" Mad Rogan asked.

"Four years ago," Bug said.

The video resumed and we watched Harper and the bank employee walk to the elevator. They moved slowly, the banker speaking and moving his hands, as if explaining. The doors of the elevator opened, and they disappeared from view.

"And down they go to the safe-deposit box room," Bug announced.

"She got the grand tour," I guessed. "All she had to do was tell them she was interested and set up an appointment, and they showed her the bank, including the safe-deposit vault, where she could've marked the right box for Gavin."

"Do you have her number?" Mad Rogan asked.

"Yes, Major. Sent to your phone."

When Bug said Major, he said it in the way people usually say sir. Until now, I would've sworn Bug had no idea what word respect even meant.

Mad Rogan swiped his phone and held it to his ear. "This is Mad Rogan. Meet me in the Galleria by the fountain at Nordstrom in an hour."

He hung up and looked at me. "Would you like to come?"

"Sure."

"Front door in fifteen minutes." He turned around and strode out.

I glanced at Bug's face on the monitor. "When I met you, you told me you'd rather drink sewage than work with a Prime or anyone from the military again."

Bug bristled. "So?"

I pointed with my thumb over my shoulder. "He's a Prime and ex-military."

"You don't understand," Bug said. "He's . . . he's Mad Rogan."

"Oh spare me."

He waved at me and Bern. "Kid, I'll be moving soon. If you want the M9, you can have it."

"That's mighty big of you," Bern said. "What's the catch?"

"No catch. I'm getting something better, so don't go thinking I'm being nice. It just saves me from having to torch all this junk."

The screens went dark.

"Did Mad Rogan just recruit Bug?" I asked.

"Appears that way," Berg said.

We stared at each other.

"Did you get anywhere with the ornament?" I asked.

"No. It's an odd shape. I got a hit on a Japanese dragonfly brooch, but I don't think that's it," he said. "The pattern is slightly wrong."

"Will you please keep looking? I know it's like looking for a needle in the haystack, and I really, really appreciate it."

"Of course," he said.

"I just don't trust Mad Rogan. We need to figure this out."

"Don't worry," Bern said. "We'll get it. Here, I've got something for you."

Bern opened a drawer and pulled out a Ziploc bag containing a metal doohicky. "Found this on your car. A standard GPS transmitter."

That's how Mad Rogan had known I'd gone to meet Adam Pierce at the arboretum. I sighed.

"Are you okay?" Bern asked.

"Yes," I lied. "I'm going to get dressed." And get my gun.

"Nevada," he called after me. "That M9 would be really nice! Do you have a problem with it?"

"If you can make a deal with Bug, go for it. Just try not to owe him any favors you can't repay."

I stepped out the front door of the warehouse and did a double take. Mad Rogan waited in the driver seat of the perfectly intact Range Rover. It had been a charred wreck only a few hours ago. It couldn't be the same Range Rover.

I saw him looking at me through the window. His eyes were very blue this morning. A by-now familiar feeling zinged through me, two parts lust, one part alarm, and the rest frustration with myself. The impact of all that masculinity should've faded by now. I should've become inoculated and immune. Instead he again knocked my socks off.

Chains, I reminded myself, as I got in. "Do you have more than one Range Rover?"

"I have several," he said, his voice calm.

"So I guess it's not a big deal that Adam blew it up?"

"I have several because I like them."

I looked at him. His jaw was set. His mouth was a straight, hard line. His eyes under the dark eyebrows had acquired a cold, steel-like hardness and I saw anger in their depths. Not the loud, ranting kind of anger, but a bone-chilling determined fury. My instincts screamed at me to get out of the car. Get out now and back away with my hands in the air.

"That particular Range Rover was the one I liked best," Rogan said, his voice and expression still calm and pleasant. "When we find Pierce, I'll take it out of him."

Out of him? If this wasn't personal for him before, it was definitely personal now. "We need Adam Pierce alive," I reminded him. "You promised me."

"I remember," Rogan said. His tone suggested that he really didn't like it. Maybe I would get lucky and Adam would lay low today, because if Rogan ran across him now, he might murder him and really enjoy it.

I buckled up, and the Range Rover rolled onto the street. It would take us about forty-five minutes to get to the Galleria. "Do you know Harper Larvo?"

"Never met her," Rogan said.

"Then what makes you think she would even show?"

"I know her type."

"What type is that?"

"The failed vector."

I glanced at him.

"Her grandfather was a Significant," he said. "He had three children. All of them are Notable. And all of their children are either Notable or Average."

"How do you know?"

"I checked the House database while Bug was talking. I didn't mention it at the time, because Bug was doing an excellent job, and it was his moment to shine. You have to let your people take pride in a job well accomplished and recognize them for it. You will get better results."

Everything Rogan did was driven by efficiency, even his treatment of his employees. Happy employees worked hard and were more loyal, so he took the time to recognize them for their achievements. I wonder where I stood on that recognition ladder. He probably considered me his employee. Well, I wasn't his employee, and the only thing I wanted from him was Adam Pierce, preferably hog-tied.

"In approximately seventy percent of the cases, magic passes from parent to child without a significant change in power," Mad Rogan said. "A few descendants, about three to five percent, show a sudden uptick. The rest lose magic with each generation. You can see traces of this pattern within the same family. Even if both parents are Primes, there is usually a variation in power among their children. You asked me once why I was expected to have no more than three children. This is the other reason. If the first child is a Prime, there is a good statistical chance that the second child might not be. Still, most Houses prefer that the head of the House have at least two additional children. You know what they're called?"

"No."

He glanced at me, his face grim. "Backup plan. The

Houses war with each other. We don't always have the best life expectancy. Do you know why Adam was conceived?"

"No." I wasn't sure I wanted to.

"Because Peter, his brother, was a late bloomer. The full extent of his magic didn't manifest until he was eleven. They thought he was a dud, and that left only Tatyana, his sister, as the Prime of the House. If someone managed to kill her, House Pierce would be without a Prime. So they hurried on with making another baby just in case."

"This sounds so cynical. And joyless."

"It often is," Mad Rogan said. "If the fading magic effect persists over two generations, that particular bloodline becomes a failed vector. Each generation is weaker than the previous one. The Houses fear one thing and one thing only: losing power. If I'm a failed vector, whoever marries me does so knowing her children will be less magically powerful than she is."

The pieces came together. "Nobody will touch Harper with a ten-foot pole."

"Exactly. Her grandfather had strong magic, and that afforded her entrance into society. She probably appeared as a fresh, wide-eyed debutante, sure that she would meet the love of her life and marry into a powerful House. Over the years she realized that men date her, fuck her, but always leave her. She's twenty-nine. By now the bloom has worn off the rose. She knows the facts, she knows a match with any of the Houses is impossible, but she still wants it desperately. She watched her grandfather be a part of the power circle, she watched her parents wield a fraction of that influence, and she'll do anything to claw her way back to the top. I'm an unmarried male Prime. I'm powerful, handsome, and filthy rich."

"Also humble and self-deprecating." I couldn't help myself.

"That too," he said without blinking an eye. "She'll show. She can't pass on the chance I might get smitten."

"That's really sad. I'm really glad I'm not a Prime, because the lot of you are a bunch of sick bastards."

Mad Rogan gave me an odd look. "Power has a price. We don't always want it, but we always end up paying. You held power over life and death yesterday. How does it feel?"

"I don't want to talk about it." *I'm not going to have a heart-to-heart with you.*

"The first time I killed someone, and I mean an up close, personal kill where I watched the life fade out of his eyes, I waited. I'd read all the books and watched all the movies, and I knew what was supposed to happen. I was supposed to feel sick, throw up, and then deal with it. So I stood there, waiting, and I felt nothing. So I thought, maybe it will happen next time."

"Did it?"

"No," he said.

"How many people did you kill?"

"I don't know," he said. "I stopped counting. It was a hard war."

His words kept rolling around my head. He shared something private and personal with me. He probably wouldn't understand, but I felt the urge to tell him about it anyway. I had to tell someone.

"It feels like I lost a part of myself," I said. "There is a big hole inside me, like something has been violently ripped out. I was brushing my teeth today, and I thought of those two men and the woman. They will never brush their teeth. They'll never go to breakfast. They'll never say hello to their mother. They won't get to do any of those simple things. I caused that. I squeezed the trigger. I realize that they were trying to do the same to me, but I feel guilty and I mourn for them and for me. Something is gone from me forever. I want to be whole again, but I know I will never get it back."

"What happens if instead of Harper we walk into an ambush and someone points a gun at you?" he asked.

"I'll shoot him," I said. "It will be bad later, but I'll deal with it. It would help if I knew why. Why are they willing to kill? What's so important that Adam will burn a whole office building just to provide a distraction?"

"That's a good question," Mad Rogan said.

"All of it—the bank, the office tower, the team of people—it seems too complicated for Adam." It had been nagging at me ever since I'd seen the team of fake fire-fighters go into the tower. "He doesn't like to work. This whole thing is well organized and carefully planned. He doesn't strike me as a guy who would bother with that much planning."

Mad Rogan changed lanes with surgical precision. "I learned a long time ago to only employ the best. I choose my people carefully. They're competent, well trained, and diligent, and right now they are scouring the city. I have considerable resources at my disposal. I have contacts among people who run Houston's underworld."

I didn't want to know how he got them.

"I'm not telling you this to aggrandize myself. I'm establishing the frame of reference. When I want someone found, they are brought to me within hours." Mad Rogan glanced at me. "I can't find Adam Pierce."

For a moment the calm mask slid and I saw straight into him. He wasn't just frustrated. He was furious.

"He's moving through the city like a ghost," Mad Rogan said. "He appears and disappears at will."

Now I understood why he had zeroed in on me. Everything his people had done failed, and here I was, buying T-shirts for Adam Pierce.

"Do you think he is being cloaked by an illusion mage?" I asked. Really strong illusionists could distort reality.

"Not by one mage. He is being cloaked by a team. Cloaking a moving target takes a coordinated effort and a special training. The team we took down in the tower had that kind of proper training." Rogan grimaced. "Pierce wouldn't have connections or the knowledge to put an op of this size together. He doesn't have the finances, he doesn't know the right people, and even if he had somehow managed to acquire financial backing and contacts, nobody would take him seriously."

He was right. "It wouldn't even occur to Adam. He isn't a team player. Someone else must be pulling his strings." Anxiety washed over me. "Who could have that much influence over Adam? His own family can't control him."

Mad Rogan's face turned grim. "I don't know. Maybe Harper can tell us."

We rode in silence.

"I want some justification for having ended the lives of these people," I said quietly. "I want to know why."

"I promise you, we will find out why," Mad Rogan said.

I didn't need my magic to tell me he meant it.

The Houston Galleria was the largest mall in Texas. It had hundreds of stores—Nordstrom, Saks, two separate Macy's—and an ice rink, open year round. It was built in the late '60s by Gerald D. Hines, who in turn had gotten the idea from Glenn H. McCarthy, Houston's legendary wildcatter and oil man, known as Diamond Glenn. Since its opening in 1970, the mall had undergone several expansions. We were heading into the newest wing, Galleria IV.

The mall sprawled before us, two levels of stores, all glass, pale tile, enormous vaulted skylights interrupted by white arches. We strolled through it casually. I'd gone for the jeans and blouse again, and I'd brought along my favorite purse, tan leather, light, small, easy to fit over my shoulder, with a modified front compartment that let me pull out my firearm in a fraction of a second. I was carrying a Kahr PM9. At five and a half inches long, it weighed about a pound with the 6-round magazine. It had no hammer, so it wouldn't catch as I pulled it out of my modified purse, and it had an external safety selector, which made me feel better. My Plan A for when things went wrong was to run away without shooting anyone. Plan B was to show the gun and make the person back off, in which case the last thing I wanted was an accidental discharge. Only Plan C involved actually firing the firearm, and considering where we were, I would have to be very sure I could pull the trigger without injuring an innocent person.

Mad Rogan strode next to me. He wore a grey suit with a black shirt he'd left unbuttoned at the collar. The clothes he wore were neither elaborate nor showy. They just fit him with tailored precision and were exceptionally well made. We should've coordinated better. We didn't exactly fit together, but the Galleria was home to an odd crowd. Young mothers walked with babies in their strollers, mingling with scene teenagers with blue, purple, and pink hair. In front of us, two middle-aged women in expensive pantsuits, their faces smoothed by illusion magic into near plastic perfection, ducked into a store, narrowly avoiding a collision with a man in a ball cap and paint-smeared shorts.

A young woman passing us glanced at Mad Rogan and slowed down. We kept walking, and I saw her reflection in a mirrored display. She was still looking at him in that appraising female way. A couple of men walked out of the store on the right and paused, giving Mad Rogan the same appreciative look. The younger of the two winked at me.

On second thought, no matter what we wore, people would still notice. Mad Rogan wasn't the most beautiful man in the Galleria, but that masculine . . . aura? Air? Whatever the heck it was, it rolled off him. It was in the set of his shoulders, in the way he walked, as if there was nothing he couldn't handle. It was in the slight roughness of his skin. In the hardness in his eyes. In a sea of generic illusion faces, he stood out, and people zeroed in on him.

We passed a gift shop selling bouquets of flowers arranged in crystal vases. The middle bouquets held carnations, big, frilly blossoms with gentle pink in the center and pale, wide borders along the petals' edges. I loved carnations. They were delicate but surprisingly resilient. When roses withered in the vase, carnations still bloomed. And I loved the scent, the delicate, fresh, slightly spicy fragrance.

"What is it?" Mad Rogan asked.

I realized I had glanced at the flowers for a second too long. "Nothing. I just like carnations."

The fountain by Nordstrom sat on the first floor, a round basin with plants rising up in a tight arrangement in its center. A ring of white underground lights surrounded the plants, glowing gently under the water. A blond stood next to the fountain. She wore a dress made of intertwining, shimmering dark-purple braids, which formed a complex latticework over her shoulders. I had no idea how she managed to even get into that dress, but I had to give it to her, the woman knew how to pose. She stood relaxed but bending back a little, one foot turned inward and pointing toward the other in that slightly awkward pose fashion magazines liked. The dress fit her like a glove, just a quarter inch too loose to turn from form-fitting to vulgar. Her figure was perfect, her waist slender, her legs tan and toned, her breasts and butt curvy but not too big. She'd dyed her hair from platinum to soft strawberry blond, and it fell in ringlets over her shoulders. Her makeup was fresh and flawless. Too flawless. Harper had had herself spelled before she came to meet us. Nothing too obvious, but human skin typically had pores.

"How can I make it easier for you to tell if she's lying?" Mad Rogan asked quietly.

"Yes or no answers are best," I said.

Mad Rogan stopped by the sitting area just short of the fountain and sat. I sat next to him.

Harper walked toward us, slowly, like a cat, her golden, high-heeled, strappy sandals making a slight clicking sound on the tiled floor.

"Rogan, I presume." Her voice matched her—throaty. She slid into the chair across from Rogan and put one long, tan leg over the other, exposing a dangerous amount of thigh. She eyed him up and down in a slow, blatant appraisal and smiled. "I like."

This wouldn't go well.

Harper gave me a quick but thorough once-over and turned back to Rogan. "What can I do for you, *Mad* Rogan?"

He leaned back against his chair. "When you marked the safe-deposit box in the vault of First National, did you know Pierce intended to blow up the bank?"

Straight for the jugular. Okay, then.

Harper smiled. "You called me here to talk about Adam? I would much rather talk about you. What have you been doing all these years?"

"I'll ask again: did you know Pierce would set the bank on fire?" Rogan asked.

"And if I don't answer?" Harper raised one eyebrow. "Will you do things to me? They say you're a tactile." She glanced at me. "Is he a tactile?"

"I don't know," I said. I had no idea what a tactile was.

"Oh. You haven't had sex." Harper's blue eyes brightened. "Don't feel bad. I imagine he doesn't go slumming very often."

Slumming? Cute.

Harper looked me over with a critical eye. "The dye job isn't bad, but the rest needs help. Especially the shoes. I'd give you pointers, but I'm afraid it wouldn't do much good."

In that moment I got Harper's number. She was one of those women who judged other women's worth by the kind of men they were with. I came with Mad Rogan, and she wasn't sure at first if I was competition or not. Now she realized we weren't a couple, but she demolished me just in case. This was actually sad.

"Answer my question," Mad Rogan said. His eyes had turned darker. He was getting annoyed.

"I dated a tactile once," Harper purred. "The Ramirez branch of the Espinoza family. He wasn't on your level, but it was . . . an experience. He could take my clothes off with his mind. Can you?" She tilted her head. "Can you take my clothes off without touching me?"

Mad Rogan leaned forward, his grim mask suddenly cracking into a smile. "Sure, sweetheart."

Uh-oh. I'd heard that tone of voice before, just before Peaches went splat.

"Show me," she said. "And then I'll tell you about Adam."

Wow. Here was a dangerous Prime she'd known for all of thirty seconds, and she went right to making out. God, she must really have been desperate. I felt a little embarrassed for Harper Larvo.

Mad Rogan leaned back and smiled. He looked at her as if she was already naked and he owned her. Harper smiled back, showing white teeth. And why exactly did I develop a sudden urge to throw some of that fountain water on both of them?

Harper gasped.

"Did it feel something like that?" Mad Rogan asked.

She gasped again, drawing her breath in sharply. Her cheeks flushed. Something was clearly happening. I had no idea what, but she seemed to enjoy it.

The braids crisscrossing on her shoulders slid, moving against each other on their own. They unwound, turned, left, right . . . Harper swallowed and her eyes opened wide, her pupils growing larger.

"Touch me again," she breathed.

Another braid, weaving in between the others. Was he actually going to undress her right here? I followed their movement. Oh no. He wasn't taking her clothes off, like she thought. He was braiding them into a noose around her neck.

"Don't you dare."

Mad Rogan ignored me.

"I mean it. Stop."

"Don't interfere," he said.

"If you're too embarrassed, you can go wait by the fountain," Harper murmured and glanced back at Rogan, her eyes half closed. "I wouldn't have expected you to employ a prude. You're an interesting man . . . full of . . . oh my God . . . surprises."

The braids twisted again.

"Rogan!"

Harper leaned forward, stretching like a limber cat ready for a stroke of her owner's hand. Her words came out in quick, breathless bursts. "Give her a hundred bucks, tell her to buy something so she'll leave us alone . . . More, Rogan. More . . ."

The noose snapped tight, clamping Harper's neck. She gasped for breath, her mouth gaping.

"You can't just strangle her."

"Of course I can," he said.

Harper clutched at her dress, clawing at her neck, trying to get it off her throat.

I pulled a gun out of my purse and pointed it at Mad Rogan's leg. "Let her go, or I'll shoot you."

Mad Rogan turned to me. "You would shoot *me*?" He looked genuinely puzzled.

"To save her life, yes." Even if it meant he would crush me a moment later. "Let her go."

Harper's face turned bright plum red. She struggled, her back rigid.

Mad Rogan looked at me. Looking into his eyes was like staring straight into the dragon.

I took the safety off my Kahr. "Please let her go."

The noose on Harper's throat fell slack. She fell back into her chair, gulping air in hoarse breaths. Tears welled in her eyes.

"Look at me." Mad Rogan leaned forward. Menace and contempt dripped from his words. "Did you know Adam would blow up the building?"

"Yes!" Harper gasped. "Yes, I knew, you sick fuck!"

True.

"Do you know what was in the deposit box?"

"No!"

True.

"Do you know what was in the building next to the one Adam burned yesterday?" I asked.

"No!"

True.

People were looking at us. Blood swelled in the scratches on Harper's neck where she had clawed at herself.

"Do you know what Adam is planning?" I asked.

She glared at me. "You think Adam is planning something? Adam just wants to burn shit! He's just a glorified O'Reilly's cow. He's a means to an end. You have no idea what's coming. Soon the Change will happen, and the only thing that will matter will be whose side you were on. I've earned my place. I was on the right side. I will be on top. You, you fucking bitch, you'll rot in hell with this fucking pervert! I hope you two fucking suffer."

Harper jumped to her feet and ran away, sobbing. A large cityscape billboard hanging from the second-floor bridge moved slightly, turning up as she came toward it, about to peel off the bridge. If it fell on her . . .

I put my hand on Mad Rogan's arm. "Don't."

The board stopped. Harper ran under the bridge and deeper into the mall, her cell phone to her ear. I thumbed the safety back on and put the gun away.

"You would have shot me over *her*?" Mad Rogan asked.

"You can't just kill people."

"Why not?"

"Because it's morally wrong. She is a person, a living, breathing human being."

"Morally wrong according to whom?" he asked.

"According to the majority of people. It's against the law."

"Who is going to tell the law?" he asked. "I could've snapped her neck and shot her up on those arches above us. Nobody would find her for days until pieces of her started to fall down."

"It's still wrong. You can't just kill people because they annoy you."

"You keep saying 'can't,'" he said.

"You shouldn't." It was like talking to some alien creature.

He leaned back and examined me. "I've helped you and protected you. More, you need me to apprehend Pierce. So you have both an emotional and a financial interest in maintaining a working relationship with me. I'm important to you. She insulted and belittled you. She's a completely useless human being. In five years she will still be doing exactly what she's doing now, flitting from club to club, supplying tabloids with gossip, and bitching to her friends about her mother, except the clubs won't be quite as nice and the tabloids won't mention her quite as often. She contributes nothing."

"Are you trying to make me feel guilty for protecting her?" I asked.

"No, I'm trying to understand. You're not annoyed at her."

"I'm annoyed at the people who taught her that her only goal in life should be attaching herself to someone with better magic. I'm annoyed by her because she thinks that having a little bit of money lets her belittle other people. But I'm not threatened by her in the least. Rogan, I own my own business. I'm good at my job. I'm successful enough to keep the roof over our heads and be respected by my peers. My family loves me unconditionally. And when some strange man calls me and orders me to be somewhere, I don't drop everything and rush over. I'm free. I make my own life and my own choices. I'm not desperately trying to earn the approval of people who think I'm worthless because I don't have enough magic or because I'm failing to meet their expectations. Don't you think that if Harper was honest with herself for a moment, she would wish she were me?"

"You're giving her too much credit. She can change her life any moment she wants to," he said.

"You still can't kill her."

"Yes, I can. I wasn't necessarily going to just yet, because I wanted information, but your argument that I shouldn't is baseless. You do realize she participated in an arson that resulted in a man dying?"

"You can't kill her, because it's against the law. Because you live here in this country and its laws apply to you no matter how much magic you have. We let police handle things. We have a justice system. Because killing random people just because they did something you don't like makes you the bad guy."

His lips curved. A light, amused spark flashed in his eyes, and Mad Rogan laughed at me.

I threw my hands up and got to my feet. "I'm done talking to you."

He got up, chuckling. "We could've gotten more out of her if you had let me choke her a little longer."

"I think we got about as much as we were going to. You humiliated her. I'm guessing you were making out somehow and then you nearly killed her. She'll be scarred for life."

"And if she tried to choke me?"

"I would've shot her. I might have warned her first. I don't know." I frowned. "So, we know she is involved. She doesn't know what's in the deposit box."

"They probably told her just enough to get her on board," Mad Rogan said. "Still, we could've gotten more."

I shook my head.

"What?" he asked.

"Rogan, I am not an idiot. By now you probably bugged her car and her house, cloned her phone, and slipped spyware into her computer. You terrified her, and you know she will snitch on you to whoever handles her and your people will be in on the conversation."

He laughed again.

I pulled out my phone and texted Bern to ask him to search the net for some mention of the Change. Then I paused. She'd said Adam was just a glorified O'Reilly cow. I wondered if she'd meant O'Leary. Did someone call Adam that and she misheard, maybe?

We moved toward the nearest exit. The crowd had thinned out. It was just me and him.

"What's a tactile?" I really shouldn't have been asking him that.

His face blank, he didn't answer.

I must've made him uncomfortable. "Never mind. I understand it's probably personal. I shouldn't have asked."

"No, I'm just thinking of the best way to explain," Mad Rogan said. "My father survived nine assassination attempts. House Rogan always had its share of enemies. If we can see a threat, we can deal with it, but one can't always see a sniper hiding in the dark. My father was obsessed with compensating for what he perceived as weakness. He wanted a child with telepathic magic in addition to his own telekinetic powers, so after careful consideration, he found my mother. She had a minor telekinetic talent and she was also a very powerful empath. My father had to go all the way to Europe to find the right combination of genes."

"Where was your mother from?"

"Spain. She was Basque. My father wanted me to have a secondary talent and be a telekinetic sensate, someone who senses when they are being watched or targeted. But my telekinetic magic proved to be too strong, so instead I'm a tactile. I can make you feel touched." He paused. "It would be easier if I showed you. Do I have permission?"

Yes. "No." Being touched by Mad Rogan wasn't a good idea.

We kept walking. What would it be like?

"Does it hurt?"

"No."

How would it feel?

Would it feel . . . oh hell.

"Okay." I stopped. We were in front of a small alcove. Nobody was around. If I made an idiot out of myself, nobody would notice. "Just once."

A soft burst of heat touched the back of my neck. I'd never felt anything like it before. It was as if someone had touched me with a heated mink glove, but the touch wasn't soft, it was firm. It felt . . . it felt . . .

The heat slid down my neck, fast, over my spine, setting every single nerve on fire before melting in the small of my back, its echoes pulsing through me. My body sang.

He'd strummed me like I was a guitar. I wanted him and I wanted him *now*.

"That was . . ." I saw his eyes. Words died.

All the hardness had vanished from his eyes. They were alive and heated from within. "You want me."

"What?"

The magic warmth slid over my shoulders, melting into pure pleasure.

"I feel the feedback." He took a step toward me, grinning. "Nevada, you're a liar."

Uh-oh. I backed up. "What feedback?"

"When I do this . . ." The heated pressure zinged from my back up my ribs. I gasped. Oh dear God. ". . . what you feel loops back to me. I'm partially empathic."

"You didn't mention that." My heart was doing its best to break through my chest, and I couldn't tell if it was alarm, lust, or some weird mix of both.

He grinned, coming closer. "The hotter you are, the hotter I am. And you're on fire."

My back hit the wall. He closed in with an almost terrifying intensity. His muscular body boxed me in.

"Rogan," I warned. In my head, a song played over and over, singing to me in a seductive voice, *Rogan, Rogan, Rogan, sex . . . want . . .*

"Remember that dream you had?" His voice was low, commanding.

"Rogan!"

The delicious warmth danced around my neck.

"Where I had no clothes?"

The warmth split and slid over me, over the sensitive nerves in the back of my neck, over my collarbone, around my breasts, cupping them and sliding fast to the tips, tightening my nipples, then sliding down, over my stomach, over my sides and butt, down between my legs. It was everywhere at once, and it flowed over me like a cascade of sensual ecstasy, overloading my senses, overriding my reason, and rendering me speechless. I hurtled through it, trying to sort through the sensations and failing. My head spun.

He was right there, masculine, hot, sexy, so incredibly sexy, and I wanted to taste him. I wanted his hands on me. I wanted him to press himself against the aching spot between my legs.

His arms closed around me. His face was too close, his eyes enticing, compelling, excited. "Let's talk about that dream, Nevada."

I was trapped. I had nowhere to go. If he kissed me, I would melt right here. I would moan and beg him, and I would have sex with him right here, in the Galleria, in public.

A spark of pain drained down my arm, driven by pure instinct. I grabbed his shoulder. Feathery lightning shot out and singed him.

Agony exploded in me, cleansing like an ice-cold shower.

Rogan's body jerked, as if struck by an electric current. It lasted only a second, and I didn't push as hard as I could have. I was learning to control it.

Rogan whipped back to me, his eyes feral. His voice was a ragged growl. "Was that supposed to hurt?"

"It was supposed to get your attention." I pushed him back with my hand. "You were getting really excited."

" 'No' would've been sufficient."

"I wasn't sure." I pushed from the wall and headed toward the exit. "I said 'once.' That was more than once. I wanted you to stop."

"I was encouraged by you breathlessly moaning my name."

I spun on my foot. "I wasn't moaning your name. I was shrieking in alarm."

"That was the sexiest throaty shrieking I've ever heard."

"You need to get out more." My cheeks were burning.

"Shockers take six months of training and still occasionally kill their users. Why did you implant them in the first place?"

"Because you kidnapped me."

"That's the stupidest thing I've ever heard."

"Mr. Rogan," I frosted my voice over. "What I put into my body is my business."

Okay, that didn't sound right. I gave up and marched out the doors into the sunlight. That was so dumb. Sure, try your magic sex touch on me, what could happen? My whole body was still keyed up, wrapped up in want and anticipation. I had completely embarrassed myself. If I could fall through the floor, I would.

"Nevada," he said behind me. His voice rolled over me, tinted with command and enticing, promising things I really wanted.

You're a professional. Act like one. I gathered all of my will and made myself sound calm. "Yes?"

He caught up with me. "We need to talk about this."

"There is nothing to discuss," I told him. "My body had an involuntary response to your magic." I nodded at the poster for *Crash and Burn II* on the wall of the mall, with Leif Magnusson flexing with two guns while wrapped in flames. "If Leif showed up in the middle of this parking lot, my body would have an involuntary response to his presence as well. It doesn't mean I would act on it."

Mad Rogan gave Leif a dismissive glance and turned back to me. "They say admitting that you have a problem is the first step toward recovery."

He was changing his tactics. Not going to work. "You know what my problem is? My problem is a homicidal pyrokinetic Prime whom I have to bring back to his narcissistic family."

We crossed the road to the long parking lot. Grassy dividers punctuated by small trees sectioned the lot into lanes, and Mad Rogan had parked toward the end of the lane, by the exit ramp.

"One school of thought says that the best way to handle an issue like this is exposure therapy," Mad Rogan said. "For example, if you're terrified of snakes, repeated handling of them will cure it."

Aha. "I'm not handling your snake."

He grinned. "Baby, you couldn't handle my snake."

It finally sank in. Mad Rogan, the Huracan, had just made a pass at me. After he casually almost strangled a woman in public. I texted to Bern, "Need pickup at Galleria IV." Getting into Rogan's car was out of the question.

Ahead of us a grey SUV slid into a far parking spot and spat out three people, two men in cargo shorts and T-shirts, and a woman in a sundress. They began walking toward the mall and us. They were moving deliberately, with a purpose, each step measured.

My instincts whined at me. "Rogan. Three people ahead."

"I see," Rogan said.

The sound of a car engine made me glance over my shoulder. A blue sedan drove down our lane and came to a stop. The doors opened and an older man with short greying hair, wearing khaki pants and a white shirt, jumped out on one side, while a woman in a white dress got out of the other.

Time stopped. Things happened all at once in the space of a tiny, pressure-filled second.

The hood of the car tore off, slid sideways like a Frisbee, sliced into the woman, and kept flying.

I pulled my gun.

The man clapped his hands, and twin sparks of blue lightning hit Rogan straight in his chest.

I fired two shots. Bullets ripped into the lightning mage's face, blowing two wet, red holes in his skull.

Rogan went down like a cut tree.

The top of the woman's body tipped back, a huge gash opening up at her waist like a gaping red mouth. She fell.

I fired two more shots into the windshield.

The car reversed. Its wheels rolled over the woman's twitching body.

I spun and squeezed the last two shots at the three people sprinting to us. They ducked behind the cars.

I grabbed Rogan's legs and yanked him into the narrow space between a black Tahoe and red Honda.

Someone pushed Play on the invisible divine remote. Suddenly time sped back up. I pulled a spare magazine out, released the old one, and snapped the new one in on autopilot. Six rounds. The lightning mage and the woman were down, but the other three and the driver of the car remained. Six bullets, four people. The math wasn't in my favor.

Fear twisted inside me like a living animal. Rogan's legs and arms shuddered, locked up in spasms. Please, God, don't let it be permanent.

If we stayed here, we were sitting ducks. They would

come for us, and I had no idea what sort of magic they had. Bullets wouldn't be enough.

I had to draw them away.

I put my gun down and pushed Rogan, trying to slide him under the Tahoe. His body barely moved. He was so heavy. I pushed against the asphalt. Rogan slid an inch. Another inch. What the hell was he eating for dinner, lead bricks? I pushed with everything I had. Finally he slid under the car.

I grabbed my gun, crouched low, and ran along the line of cars toward the mall, punching the car hoods. One, two, three . . . come on, the line was all SUVs, Cadillacs and BMWs, someone had to have the alarm on . . . Four, five . . . I needed the noise. I punched another hood, a beat-up orange Pontiac Aztek with a mangled bumper. The car alarm shrieked and wailed in outrage. Really? All those cars and someone put the alarm on an Aztek? Oh well, good enough. I kept moving, sucked in a lungful of air, and screamed, "Help! Help me! Help!"

Follow me, you bastards.

"Help!"

An old, white-haired man with wire-rimmed glasses leaned out between the cars, his ruddy face puzzled. He wore dark dress pants, a white shirt, and a dark tie with red and gold stylized flowers on it. He was holding a Star-bucks coffee cup in his right hand.

"Are you alright?" He started toward me.

He had to be a decade past sixty. Why couldn't I have gotten a younger Samaritan?

"It's not safe!" I waved at him. "Get out of here!"

"What's going on?"

"Get out—"

The old man tossed the contents of the cup at me. A

ball of crinkled copper wire flashed, reflecting sunlight, and smacked me in the chest. The wires shot out of the clump, catching my arms, legs, and throat, and yanked me off my feet, dragging me to the side between the cars. The wire strands whipped, twisting around the bike racks on the SUVs and stretching my arms. I hung between an SUV and a small tree growing in the grass divider, my toes barely touching the ground. The wire loop around my neck squeezed, cutting off my air.

The old man walked out between the cars, the wires stretching from the cup in his hands.

"Shhh," the old man said. "Don't struggle, it will make it worse."

He touched his hand to his left ear. An earpiece. Didn't see it before. His hair had hidden it. Stupid, stupid, stupid.

"I have her." He took his hand from his ear and looked at me. "Give me the gun."

I wheezed, trying to suck some air. He wasn't getting the gun from me. He would have to take it.

"Come on." The old man held his hand under my right fist. "Just let it go. Be a good girl."

No, I don't think so.

The old man squeezed the cup and the wires tightened, cutting my throat. I tried to scream but managed a hoarse hiss instead.

"Always has to be the hard way, doesn't it? Fine." He reached over, on his toes. His hand closed over the barrel of the Kahr.

I dropped the gun and clamped my fingers on his wrist. Pain rolled down my shoulder, and I let it blossom into agony. The feathery lightning gripped him and the old man bent back, his spine rigid. His eyes rolled back in his head. Foam bubbled up at his mouth. I let go and he fell to his knees, landing facedown on the pavement.

The wires fell. I crashed to the ground, dug my nails at the metal noose around my neck, and pulled it loose. Air. Sweet, sweet air. Bright red stained my fingers. My blood. The wire must've cut me.

I had to move. The others were coming. I glanced up.

A silver sedan hurtled toward me through the air. I saw it with crystal clarity, every single detail plain, as if I were looking at an enormous HD image: the oblong headlights, the tinted windows, the shiny hood, the top of the car as it turned before crushing me. No time to run. No time for anything.

I'm dead.

I jerked my arms up in reflex.

The sedan froze six inches from my fingertips. It groaned, the metal twisting, and shot up and back, revealing Mad Rogan. He was incredibly, monumentally angry.

The car flew over him, aiming for the attackers. The woman in the sundress tried to dodge the sedan. It smashed into her, sweeping her from her feet.

I yanked the rest of the wires off my ankles and wrists and got up.

The sedan bounced on the woman's body, screeched, scraping the asphalt, spun, and slapped the taller of the two men. He crashed down and the sedan rolled over him, pounding him flat. The vehicle bounced and flew at the third man, who was wearing a dark blue T-shirt. The man leaped up, like he had wings, and perched atop the sedan, standing on one foot, perfectly balanced.

"Are you okay?" Mad Rogan ground out.

"I'll live," I croaked and grabbed my gun.

The sedan jerked six feet into the air, rotating. The man ran over the spinning car as a lumberjack during a logrolling competition, leaped at the parked row of cars, and dashed toward us, running across the cars like they were solid ground.

I sighted him and squeezed the trigger. The windshield of the white truck to the right cracked. The bullet hit him dead center and ricocheted into the windshield. Lovely.

"A wind mage." Mad Rogan clasped his hands together and jerked them apart. Two hoods flew off the nearest cars and flew at the mage. The aerokinetic dodged with room to spare, as graceful as a ballet dancer, and punched the air. Mad Rogan leapt right. A foot-long gap sliced the asphalt next to me. The second gap split the pavement two inches closer to Rogan's foot. Holy shit.

The hoods shot back to us and hovered like shields.

Anything small would bounce off the wind mage. Anything heavier would be too slow to hit him. Catch-22.

Mad Rogan held out a chalk. "Draw an amplification circle around me."

I grabbed the chalk. Amplification circle was magic 101. Small circle around the mage's feet, larger circle around him, three sets of runes. I'd just never tried to draw one on the asphalt while a wind mage was throwing invisible air blades at us.

The hood directly in front of Rogan split with a screech. A bright red line swelled across his chest. He grimaced. The hoods spun around us, faster and faster.

I finished the smaller circle. It wasn't perfect, but it was round.

Something pelted the hoods, sounding like hail. The mage couldn't see us, but we couldn't see him either.

I finished the second circle.

Another hail of air blades, this time from the right. The aerokinetic had us pinned.

I drew the runes out. "Done."

A tiny puff of chalk escaped from the lines into the air. Rogan flexed, his arms bulging. A vein shook in his neck.

The hoods kept spinning. If I were a wind mage, I'd try to get a drop on us . . .

I looked up. A graceful figure soared above us in the sky.

"Up!" I yelled.

The aerokinetic raised his arms. We were wide open.

A Greyhound bus smashed into the wind mage. I caught a glimpse of him, pressed against the bus' windshield like a bug, his eyes wild. The bus crashed into the pavement in front of the mall, sinking three feet into the ground but remaining half upright.

Mad Rogan smiled, like a smug cat who'd just gotten away with stealing something off the counter. "Wind mages. They're all fancy dancing until you drop something heavy on them."

I stared at the bus like an idiot, still holding the chalk in my fingers. A car tire was heavy. He had dropped a damn bus.

My wrists and ankles were bleeding. My knees too—I must've scraped myself trying to draw the circle. So far today I'd seen a woman almost die, I'd shot a person, I'd killed another person with my shockers, I'd been strung up on wires and almost crushed by a car, and now I was bleeding all over the place. If I could, I would punch today right in the face.

Bern's black Civic pulled into the parking lot and swerved to avoid the bus.

Mad Rogan looked down at my chalk lines. "This is

the lousiest circlework I've ever seen. Were you drawing with your eyes closed?"

That was it. I threw the chalk at him, got up, marched to the Civic, and got inside. "Drive, Bern. Please."

To my cousin's credit, he said nothing about the blood, the bus, or Mad Rogan. He stepped on the gas and drove straight home.

 **Chapter 12**

Bern drove with steady surety, obeying all traffic laws and regulations. Leon and Arabella both had their learner permits. Five minutes in the car with one of them behind the wheel was enough to turn my hair white, but riding with Bern was completely stress free. He had made a simple calculation: the cost of a speeding ticket in Houston ranged from $165 to $300 and would bump up his insurance. He didn't have $165 to spare.

Three cop cars, their sirens screaming, barreled down the opposite lane. Good. As far as I was concerned, Mad Rogan could deal with them and leave me the hell alone.

"Remember you told me about how the Great Chicago Fire wasn't started by Mrs. O'Leary's cow? Your professor had some sort of alternative theory about it?"

Bern gave me a funny look. "Did you see the bus halfway in the ground?"

"I don't want to talk about the bus."

"Okay," Bern said in a soothing voice. "We don't have to talk about the bus. We can talk about the cow instead."

"Is there any chance we could talk to your professor?"

"Professor Itou? Sure. I think he has office hours today. I'll check when I get home. Why?"

"Something Harper said. She called Adam a glorified O'Reilly's cow. I think she meant O'Leary."

"She might have been using it figuratively," he said.

"Sure, but I just want to tug on that string and see where it leads. It was so random and out of nowhere."

"No problem, I'll take care of it," he said. "MII called. Twice. Sounded annoyed. They want you to call them back."

Figured. House Pierce wasn't happy about Adam setting an office tower on fire, so they likely leaned on Augustine Montgomery, and now he would lean on me. Crap rolled downhill.

I would have to call Augustine Montgomery. I wasn't looking forward to it.

The cuts on my neck and wrists turned out to be shallow. Catalina helped me clean up and put Neosporin on them. I didn't get much of a chance to recuperate. Bern came back with Professor Itou's office hours, which were between two and four. I fixed my makeup and hair, put on a business suit—not one of my expensive ones but the simple middle-of-the-road grey—then we jumped into the car and drove to the University of Houston.

We found Professor Ian Itou in his office in the history department. He had someone with him, so we sat in the hallway, twiddling our thumbs. Students hurried back and forth, dragging their bags and overly caffeinated drinks. Everyone seemed so young. I wasn't that much older, but for some reason I felt ancient. I was probably just tired.

Even when I was in college, people seemed young to me. I had a full-time job. For me, going to college meant get in, sit in class, turn my stuff in, and get out as soon as I could. I went to one fraternity party, and that was because I had a crush on the guy in my Criminal Justice Organization and Administration class. He had huge brown eyes and freakishly long eyelashes. Every time he blinked, it was an experience. We went on three dates, agreed that this was a bad idea, and parted ways. Eventually I ended up dating Kevin. He was a great guy, and he made my sophomore and junior years awesome. I was so comfortable with him. He just had this way of putting me at ease, and he almost never lied to me. We talked; we hung out; we had good sex and did all of the things that two young people in love usually did. I thought I would marry him. Not that he asked or I did, but back then I could see myself being married to him. It wasn't a wildfire, high drama, heart-pounding-excitement kind of relationship. People started telling us we were like an old married couple three months after our first date. Kevin was just solid, like a rock. Being with him was so easy. No pressure.

My mother didn't like him. She thought I was settling because Dad had died less than a year before and I wanted stable and normal. At the time it didn't feel that way. Then, in our senior year, Kevin got accepted into a graduate program at CalTech. He invited me to move with him to Pasadena. I told him I couldn't. My family was here, my business was here, and I couldn't just abandon it all. He said he understood, but he couldn't miss this opportunity. Neither one of us ended up being that upset about it. There was no ugly breakup, and there were no tears. I was bummed out about it for the first few weekends, and then I moved on. Kevin was in Seattle now, working for an engineering firm. He was married and he and his wife had twins six months ago. I had looked him up on Facebook. It made me a little sad, but mostly I was happy for him.

The point was that, while I was in college, I didn't do all those typical things. I was never in a sorority. I didn't belong to any clubs. If I came home at dawn, it was because there was some surveillance involved. People spoke about their college "experience," and I really had no clue what it was all about.

I glanced at Bern. "Hey. You know, if you want to join a fraternity, you totally can."

My cousin's shaggy eyebrows crept up. He reached over and carefully put his hand on my forehead. Checking for fever. "I'm worried about you."

I pushed his hand off. "I'm serious. I don't want you to feel like you have to miss out on anything."

He pointed at himself. "Programmer and cybermagician. We don't join fraternities. We hide in our lairs in darkness and bloom under the glow of computer screens."

"Like mushrooms?"

"Just like that. Except that mushrooms don't bloom. They produce spores."

The door to Professor Itou's office opened and a girl with a dark ponytail walked out, waving a stack of papers. She glared at us. "He can take his B and shove it. A B! It was the best essay in the class!" She stomped down the hallway.

Bern caught the door before it closed. "Professor? I emailed you earlier?"

"Come on in," a cheerful male voice called.

Professor Itou was about my height and about fifteen years older, athletic, with a compact, powerful build and hooded dark eyes. He seemed full of energy as he shook my hand and sat behind his desk, poised against a massive bookcase filled to the brink. His expression was cheerful.

"What can I do for you, Ms. Baylor?"

"I was hoping to find out more about your theories regarding the Great Chicago Fire. Bern mentioned that you didn't think the cow had started it."

Professor Itou smiled, threw one leg over the other, and braided his fingers on his knee. He looked like someone had just told him a really funny joke and he was still inwardly chuckling over it.

"It's not something that's often talked about in historians' circles. In fact, my research into it has actually made me an object of not so gentle mockery. Academics." He opened his eyes wide in pretended horror. "Vicious beasts. They'll rip your throat out if you aren't careful."

Bern grinned. I could see why my cousin liked Professor Itou. This one academic clearly didn't take himself too seriously.

"I'm armed," I told him. "And if we get in trouble, we can put Bern in front of the door. He can hold off a whole hallway of academics. Nobody will get in."

Professor Itou's eyes sparked. "Are you sure you want the full account, because I'm not asked about this that often, and once I start, I will get giddy and might not stop for a while."

I pulled out my recorder. "Yes, please."

"Prepare to be amazed." Professor Itou leaned back. "First the basic facts. It's 1871 and the summer is very dry. Chicago, which was mostly wood, bakes in the heat, drying up until it becomes a tinderbox. It's Sunday, October 8, 1871. Night has fallen and everyone is in bed. A few minutes after nine o'clock, Daniel 'Pegleg' Sullivan sees a fire through the windows of the barn belonging to his neighbors, Patrick and Catherine O'Leary. He sounds the alarm and runs to save the animals. Firefighters are notified, but they had spent the day before putting out a large fire and they're tired. They go to the wrong neighborhood, and by the time they find the right house, the fire is blazing. They try to put it out and fail. For two days Chicago burns, until on October 10, rains finally smother the fire. Three hundred people are dead, over a hundred thousand are homeless, and the heart of the city is burned to the ground. The official cause of the fire was never determined. Later a *Chicago Tribune* reporter writes about the fire, claiming that a cow owned by Mrs. O'Leary kicked a lantern, knocking it into the hay. Mrs. O'Leary becomes a social pariah and dies a few years later, heartbroken, according to her family."

Professor Itou leaned forward. His face took on a conspiratorial expression. He motioned me closer. I leaned toward him.

He lowered his voice and said softly, as if telling me a great secret, "The cow didn't do it."

"No?" I asked.

"No. The reporter admitted later that he added the cow for dramatic purposes. At the time, it fed right into anti-Irish attitudes. Here is another interesting detail: a study of the street proves that Pegleg Sullivan couldn't have seen the fire from where he had been standing."

"He lied," Bern said.

"Exactly!" Professor Itou stabbed the air with his index finger, triumphant. "The Chicago fire was the subject of my undergraduate senior thesis. I have a somewhat obsessive personality, so I obtained a copy of an archived map of Chicago and was busily re-creating the spread of the fire on it by means of painting the buildings with a brush dipped in coffee."

"Why coffee?" I asked.

"At the time it was the only dye available to me in large quantity. I was a poor college student, but I always had coffee. It was a required food group." Professor Itou crossed his arms. "As I was mapping out the fire, a roommate of mine, silly practical mortal that he was, came to the kitchen in hopes of using the table for the mundane purpose of making himself a sandwich. He was a pyrokinetic, and he noted that the pattern of the initial burn was eerily consistent with burn rings that occur when a pyrokinetic employs concentric fire. Meaning someone had burned Chicago in circles. The fire had spread north and south, against wind direction. Furthermore, the velocity of the burn indicated presence of magic. Entire neighborhoods had been engulfed in moments."

Late nineteenth century. The trials of the serum that brought out magic abilities were beginning, but it wasn't common knowledge yet. It was possible that some early pyrokinetic made it to Chicago. "But why deliberately burn the city?"

Professor Itou raised his hand. "That's the question I asked myself. I will spare you the full explanation. Here is the short version: the British military was administering serum to some of its officers in an effort to maintain its grip over the Commonwealth. One of these officers was Colonel Rudyard Emmens. The colonel had spent most of his service to the British Empire in "the Orient." Unfortunately I could never quite figure out which part of the Orient. Eventually he retired to Chicago. We do not know for sure what his talent had been, but we do know from his personal journals that it had to do with fire. He was very conflicted about it. He was equally disturbed that these "hellish" powers had passed to his only son, Edward. At the time of the Chicago fire, Edward was eighteen. Here's an interesting account: according to a noted Chicago historian, the center of the city remained extremely hot for almost two days after the fire died down. When firefighters were finally able to enter the steaming wreck that was Chicago, they found Edward Emmens in the middle of it. He was exhausted, dehydrated, and smeared in soot but otherwise unharmed."

Only a pyrokinetic mage could stand in the middle of an inferno and survive. "Was he a Prime?"

"You would think so, but no." Professor Itou grinned. "His magic was classified as Notable later in his life."

"That seems an awful lot of power for a pyrokinetic mage of Notable rank," I said.

"Indeed." Itou turned around, peered at the bookshelves, and pulled out a red book. "David Harrisson, one of Chicago's twenty-six police lieutenants at the time, took a particular interest in this occurrence and in the causes of the fire. Nobody knows what he actually found, because the powers that be seemed to have suppressed his investigation, but years later he began publishing crime fiction under the pseudonym John F. Shepard." Itou flipped the book open. " 'The Devil's Fire.' A short story about a young man who steals his father's prized African artifact and uses it to burn down Boston."

He showed me the page and snapped the book closed.

"There exists a deathbed confession by one Frederick Van Pelt, detailing how he and three other young men met with Edward Emmens, who had taken a magical object from his father and was going to show them wondrous things. They met up at a barn whose owners were known to call it an early night, and they paid a local man to keep watch. He claimed that after the fire, the magical object was broken into three pieces and each piece was hidden away."

I put two and two together. "So let me make sure I got it. Rudyard Emmens brings home some sort of artifact with him from somewhere in Asia. Then years later, his son uses it to impress his friends, loses control, and burns down Chicago?"

Professor Itou looked at me for a long second and smiled. "Yes."

"How did it go with the senior thesis?" Bern asked.

Professor Itou's eyes got really big. He waved the book around. "Funny you should mention it. I got terribly excited. I had all my sources. I worked for weeks. I had written a paper that would've made angels weep. I was the last to present my thesis before a panel of professors. They listened to me, nodded, and offered me a full graduate scholarship. Guaranteed admission, BA to PhD track, all expenses paid. Just one small thing—my thesis couldn't be published. It wasn't in the public's interest."

"They bribed you," I guessed.

He leaned forward and tapped the book on the table to underscore his point. "And I took it. Back then I took it because I was poor and had no choice. Now I would've taken it for a completely different reason. The existence of amplification artifacts has been debated for years. We know that some people develop magic powers without the serum, and we know that magical objects can be created, so there is a possibility that an item which makes your magic stronger does exist. If such an artifact could be found, only tragedy would come from it. If it could be controlled, it would be given to a Prime and turned into a devastating weapon. If it couldn't be controlled, any attempt to do so would result in a natural disaster. It's best for this theoretical artifact to stay hidden. It is a lesson for us and a legacy of Colonialism. Stealing another nation's treasures never turns out well."

Edward Emmens was a Notable, a third-tier mage, and he had burned down Chicago. Adam Pierce was a Prime. If he managed to get his hands on such an artifact, he would go nova. Cold worry squirmed through me. Would anything be left after he was done?

"Do you know what it was?" Bern asked. "The artifact?"

Professor Itou shook his head, his face mournful. "No. I've tried to find out over the years, but I've failed. We don't even know where it came from. We know it was most likely of Far Eastern or possibly Middle Eastern origin, but the cultural heritage of both is so rich and varied. It's like looking for a needle in the proverbial haystack."

I pulled out my phone and showed him a picture of the jewelry. "Could it be something like this?"

"Possibly." Itou frowned and spread his hands. "Remember, we're talking about Orient, meaning 'East,' an outdated term by modern standards, which took on different meanings through the years. In the 1800s, this term came to mean mostly India, China, and the Far East, but we can't discount the Middle East. The Orient Express, for example, went to Istanbul. I could probably tell you more if I could get my hands on the Emmens family documents, but the family's descendants refuse to speak to me. It would take someone with a lot more clout than I can scrape together." He exhaled and waved his arms. "I've let it go."

"What does this jewelry look like to you?" I asked. It never hurt to ask . . .

"An old TV antenna?" Itou frowned. "I'm afraid I'm not much help."

"Thank you so much for the information. One last question: is there anyone in your department we could talk to about the artifact?" I asked.

Professor Itou grinned. "Magdalene Sherbo would be the one. Unfortunately she is currently in India as part of her educational outreach. We could try emailing her, but her email access is sporadic, and she is notorious for not checking her account. You might get an answer in a month or so. I once sent her an invitation to my wife's baby shower. Two months later, she replied that she would love to come just as I was sending pictures of the baby to everyone with an email account." He chuckled.

"Could we have her email address just in case?" Bern asked.

Professor Itou jotted an email address on a yellow sticky pad and handed it to Bern.

"Thank you again," I said.

"Is the artifact about to surface?" he asked.

"I believe so," I said.

All humor drained from Professor Itou's face. He took out his wallet and extracted a photograph. On it a woman of Asian descent, her dark hair loose, stood next to two boys against the backdrop of a massive tree. The boys looked a lot like Professor Itou, with the same smart, mischievous sparkle to their eyes.

"This is my wife and children."

"Your family is beautiful," I told him.

"We live here, in the city. If the artifact is uncovered and someone attempts to use it here, in Houston, people will die. The Great Chicago Fire left three hundred people dead. The population density within our city is many times that of Chicago on the cusp of the twentieth century. If this artifact falls into the wrong hands—and really there are no right hands for it—the casualties will be catastrophic."

He slid the photograph toward me. "You have discovered something potentially devastating and you can't just walk away now. You have a moral obligation to them, to me, and to your own family. By virtue of possessing this dangerous knowledge, you are now partially responsible for our survival. Please keep that in mind."

We left his office and walked across the evening-sun-drenched parking lot to our car.

"Do we go to the authorities?" Bern asked.

"If we do, we'll only get one shot at convincing them this is serious. If we're right and Adam wants this artifact and somehow gets his hands on it, it could mean mass evacuation. They're not going to do something like that without some serious evidence. Right now all we have is a theory from a never-published senior thesis and a picture of some sort of jeweled doohicky. I'm all for going for broke, but we have to have something to go with."

"So what now?" Bern asked.

"We go home and do our research." In the morning, if all else failed, I would ask Rogan to see about getting the documents from the Emmens family. Professor Itou was right. The family wouldn't speak to him or me, but they would speak to *Huracan*.

I looked at my family gathered around the kitchen table. My two sisters, my two cousins, Mom and Grandma Frida. I'd just explained in broad terms the story of the Great Chicago Fire and the artifact that could be tied to it.

"I need your help searching for the artifact," I said.

"I have homework," Catalina said.

Arabella glared at her. "Seriously? Can you not be so anal once in your life?"

Lina bristled. "Are you going to let her talk to me like that?"

"I'll write you whatever excuse you want," I said. "But we are short on time, and I really need your help." I pushed the laptop toward them. "This is a map of the British Empire in 1850, when Emmens was probably in the military service." I put the phone with the picture of the jeweled thing next to it. "This is what we're looking for. It's probably a part of something else, some sort of artifact. We each are going to take a region and try to look for an artifact that resembles this. Catalina and Arabella, you take China. Leon, India. Bern, Egypt. Mom, Turkey and Arabia. I'll take the Far East. Grandma Frida, pick a team if you want. And not a word about this to anyone. No Facebook, no Instagram, and especially no Herald."

They scattered.

I holed up in my office. It was nice and quiet. I put a candle under my oil warmer, dripped in some rose geranium, and went to work.

Needle in the haystack was putting it mildly. I tried image search. I tried historical search. I looked through Wikipedia and online museum galleries.

Nothing.

Eventually my head began to hurt. I pushed away from the desk, rubbed my eyes, and glanced at the clock: 9:17. I'd been at this for two hours, and I had exactly nothing to show for it.

At least the artifact part, if that's what it was, was safely locked up somewhere in the bowels of Rogan's dragon cave.

A ghostly memory of him touching me flickered across my skin. What the hell was wrong with me? I'd almost made out with him in the Galleria. After what he had done with Harper, I should've run for my life instead. It was one thing to be attracted to bad boys, something I usually didn't suffer from. It was another to be attracted to bad men. Mad Rogan was a really bad, bad man. If he wanted something, he bought it, or persuaded you to give it to him, or just simply took it. I had to make sure he didn't want me. Because if he decided he did, it would be on his terms, and I wouldn't like it.

No, I would like it, which was even worse. If Mad Rogan suddenly appeared in the middle of my office, picked me up out of this chair with those hard, muscled arms, carried me into a bedroom, and threw me on the bed, at least 50 percent of me would be totally fine with whatever followed. It would be awesome. Just to see him naked, to see that honed, powerful body, to touch him, would be the highlight of my adult romantic life.

The other 50 percent of me would be livid. That jerk. No "Thanks for saving my life." No "Are you okay?" No acknowledgment of a near-death experience. Oh no, no, he decided to critique my chalk drawing while I sat there on the pavement, bleeding and trying to catch my breath. I'd had it with all of them. I'd had it with their fires and their flying buses and exploding buildings. Had it.

It made total sense that Mad Rogan, a man who was rich, handsome, athletic, and a Prime, would turn out to be a self-centered bastard. What made absolutely no sense was why every time he said my name or looked at me, I needed ten seconds to snap back to reality.

It wasn't just the physical pleasure or the intoxicating mental thing he'd done today. It was that terrifying, single-minded intensity he radiated when he focused. I just felt, with some sort of feminine intuition, that when he had sex, he committed to it completely. He would have sex the way other men made war. I wanted to be the only thing in the entire world he cared about, even if only for a few minutes. I wanted all of him, mind and body, to be mine.

And that was the sticking point. Mad Rogan would never be mine. I wasn't the kind of woman he would eventually settle down with. It wasn't even a matter of me not having money. I lacked the right pedigree. Primes married for magic. My magic wasn't on the same level as his, and it definitely wasn't the right kind. His power was primarily telekinetic, and his telepathy was slight. He would look for a telekinetic or a telepath. My magic was primarily will based and didn't fit neatly into any category. I could get Mad Rogan only if he actually fell in love with me. The concept of being in love probably wasn't even in his vocabulary.

If I threw myself at him, he probably wouldn't turn me down. He would've made out with me in the Galleria. I was young and pretty, and he was an unattached man. Well, I assumed he was unattached. If he was attached, it probably wouldn't stop him. There was an ugly thought.

Realistically, the only thing I could hope to get out of any relationship with him was a couple of nights of glorious sex.

God, it would almost be worth it.

No, no, it wouldn't be. I knew myself well enough. I would get attached to him. It would be so hard not to—everything about him was exceptional. People like that just don't come into your orbit that often. If I jumped into that deep water, I would drown. I didn't want to drown. I couldn't afford to drown. I had a family, a business . . .

The phone rang.

I jumped up.

It rang again. I grabbed it. "Yes?"

"Finally, Ms. Baylor," Augustine's clipped voice said.

Oh crap.

"What can I do for you?"

"I've reviewed the press coverage of recent events this morning. Perhaps I wasn't clear at our last meeting. What part of 'Apprehend Adam Pierce and deliver him to his House' did you not understand?"

Oh you ass. "The part where I do this with no resources or assistance from MII."

"House Pierce is unhappy. They are now financially liable for an expensive office building and are the target of several prospective lawsuits."

"Perhaps they should've considered that possibility when they discovered Adam was a Prime. If they hadn't raised a spoiled, immature egoist, they wouldn't be in this mess."

"Ms. Baylor."

Someone pounded on the front door. "One moment," I said. "I'll be right back."

I marched over to the door and checked the monitor. Mad Rogan.

I swung the door open.

Mad Rogan stood at my doorstep, holding a bouquet of carnations. The ones in the store had been frilly and delicate pink blossoms. These were huge, heavy blooms, crimson, glossy, so dark toward the base of their petals that they were almost black, with a border of bright scarlet at the edges. They looked dipped in blood. He might as well have brought me a fistful of rubies.

His eyes looked smug.

I looked at the flowers, looked at his face, and shut the door.

No, wait.

I opened the door, took the carnations from him, shut the door, and locked it. There. I'd had a near-death experience, and confiscating the carnations would make me feel better. I marched back into my office and pushed the button on the phone.

"I'm back."

"You put me on hold." His voice could've frozen the Gulf of Mexico solid.

I smelled the carnations. Oh wow. "Yes. Someone was at the door. It could've been Adam."

I looked for a vase to put the flowers in. The only thing I had was a tall, decorative glass full of marbles because the office needed some knickknacks. I emptied the marbles into a drawer, opened a bottle of water I kept for clients, poured it into the vase, and set the carnations into it. Perfect.

"I don't think you understand the severity of your situation," Augustine said.

The warehouse shuddered. The entire structure vibrated for a second and stopped.

"In the last forty-eight hours, my house was the target of an arson. Then a car exploded in front of our door."

The warehouse vibrated again. Mad Rogan was shaking my house. Damn it.

"I've been almost strangled, almost crushed, and almost buried alive. I understand the severity of my situation."

Shake. Shake.

"Adam publicly embarrassed his House. This matter now involves not just you . . ."

Shake.

". . . but the reputation of the entire firm and . . ."

"I'm going to have to put you on hold for just a second."

"Ms. Bay—"

I marched to the door and opened it. Mad Rogan smiled at me. I jerked my hand toward my office. He walked in. I locked the door behind him. Mad Rogan stepped into my office and landed in a chair. Instantly my office shrank. There had been space before, and now there was Rogan.

I pushed the button again. "I'm back."

"My patience is at an end," Augustine said with diamond-sharp precision. "I have to report to House Pierce, and my report, apparently, will say that you've made no progress. You're making MII look incompetent."

I'm shaking in my slippers. "Why don't you tell them the truth: you assigned this case to me because you expect me to fail. When I do, you will take my business and write it off."

"I'm trying to give you a chance to keep your business," Augustine said.

"She'll have to call you back," Mad Rogan said.

"What?" Augustine asked.

"I said, she'll have to call you back, Pancakes. She's busy right now." He pushed the disconnect button.

He didn't just hang up on Augustine. Yes, yes, he did.

"Pancakes?" I asked.

"When he was trying to enter the Arcana Club at Harvard, one of the initiation trials was eating the most food. That year, it was pancakes. He won and got admitted, but it took six months before he could walk by pancakes without getting sick." Rogan smiled. "He'd smell them and run out of the room."

"Well, Pancakes owns the mortgage on my business. You just hung up on my boss," I said.

"He was talking in circles. He'll get over it."

"You know what your problem is? 'You' as in Primes, in general?"

"I think you're about to tell me." Mad Rogan leaned forward with rapt attention.

"Your problem is that nobody ever tells you no. You think you can do whatever you want, enter wherever you want . . ."

"Seduce whoever we want." He grinned, a wicked, wolfish smile.

Oh no, we are not veering off the highway onto that road. "You play with people's lives. When cops show up, you wave your hand and make them go away. Because you are Primes and the rest of us are, apparently, nothing."

"Mhm," he said. "The irony of this is so rich, it's simply delicious."

"I don't see what's so ironic about it."

"I'd tell you, but it would ruin the fun."

"Could you be more smug?"

He leaned on his elbow. "Possibly. I see you liked the flowers."

I got a sudden urge to set the carnations on fire. "They are gorgeous. It's not their fault you brought them." I leaned over the table. "Mr. Rogan—"

"Mad," he corrected. "Mad Rogan."

"Mr. Rogan, here are some boundaries. You're using me as bait for Adam Pierce. I'm using you as a means to capture Adam. I think you're a dangerous man."

"So formal," Mad Rogan said.

"Here is the informal version: we have to work together, and when we're done, we will go our separate ways. Don't bring me flowers. We don't have that kind of relationship."

He laughed. It was a genuine, amused laugh. "You're really mad at me."

I was mad as hell, but saying it would be admitting that I'd let myself get emotionally involved, and he didn't need to know that. "No, I just don't want to compromise our professional relationship. It's late and I'm tired. If you don't have anything to tell me about Adam, please leave."

"Thank you for keeping me alive earlier today," he said. "I should've acknowledged it. I didn't. In my defense, your circlework really is terrible."

I opened my mouth to tell him where he could shove his circlework, when someone knocked on the door. What was it with the visitors tonight?

I went to the door and checked the monitor. Augustine Montgomery, wearing a silver suit, his glasses perched on his perfect face, his pale hair styled into a razor-precise haircut. Seriously?

"Who is it?" Mad Rogan came up behind me and peered over my shoulder. He was standing too close to me.

I didn't want to let Pancakes in, but he still owned us. I unlocked the door.

Augustine stared over my shoulder, his eyes like ice. "What are you doing here?"

"I dropped in to borrow a cup of sugar," Mad Rogan said.

"You shouldn't be here." Augustine looked at me. "He shouldn't be here."

"You got here rather quickly," Rogan said.

"I was driving when I made the call."

Behind Augustine, an elegant silver Porsche sat in a parking spot, all alone. We'd moved all of our cars inside, given that we couldn't just order a brand-new one if one of them blew up.

"You might not want to park there," Mad Rogan said. "I parked there yesterday and my Range Rover exploded."

Augustine opened his mouth.

If we kept standing here with the door open, sooner or later my mother would come to investigate. If she realized that Augustine Montgomery—the cause of all our misfortunes—had appeared on our doorstep, she would shoot him. Just out of principle. Not to mention that we were sitting ducks here, lit up by the floodlight. The last thing I wanted was to have them both here at the same time, but I had no choice.

"Come inside," I growled.

I led them both to my office. Augustine saw the flowers, blinked, and turned to Mad Rogan. "So you decided to involve yourself in this because of Gavin? Why the sudden concern for your relatives? So unlike you, Connor."

Mad Rogan peered at him. "Why are you wearing glasses? I know for a fact that you have perfect vision."

Here we go. This would end in them unzipping themselves to see who was bigger.

"You should've stayed retired." Augustine's voice was dry.

"And what's going on with your hair?" Mad Rogan raised his eyebrows. "That's a huge amount of illusion. What are you hiding up there? Are you prematurely balding?"

Augustine turned to me. "You have no idea who you're dealing with. This man is extremely dangerous."

Mad Rogan reached out toward Augustine's hair, but lowered his hand. "I'd touch it, but I'm afraid I might cut myself."

"Listen to me." Urgency vibrated in Augustine's voice. "You need to limit your association with this man. We exist in a fragile balance, and the core of that balance, the thing that restrains us, is our family. He feels no obligation to his family or anyone else's. He has no restraint. You have no idea what kind of things he is involved in."

And that, exactly that, was the problem with Primes. That right there.

"She needs to limit her association with you," Mad Rogan said. "You're trying to take her business."

Augustine pulled off his glasses. "I may be putting her at risk financially, but you would take her life, if it was convenient, and make jokes about it later."

Actually, Augustine was sending me after Adam Pierce, which was pretty much a death sentence.

Augustine kept going. "You have no code, Connor. You know nothing about duty or honor or self-sacrifice . . ."

Rogan moved, brutal and blindingly fast. Augustine's back hit the wall, and Mad Rogan drove his left forearm into his neck, pinning him. His eyes turned cold and merciless.

"You spent your time after college sitting in a comfortable office learning the family trade." His voice was precise and so filled with menace that the tiny hairs on the back of my neck rose. "This was your grand, self-serving sacrifice. You sat here, wrapped in your luxurious cocoon and wallowing in self-pity, while I spent six years starving and bleeding in a fucking jungle where all the money in the world couldn't buy you a gulp of clean water. I did this so people I'll never know could go to sleep in peace. What do you know about sacrifice? You never watched someone's head explode from a bullet, then brushed pieces of human being off you and kept going. So how about you shut the fuck up?"

The room turned dark. Black bulges slid along the

walls. Fear drained down my spine. Every instinct I had screamed at me that whatever was in the walls was bad and dangerous, and if it broke out, I needed to run.

"Don't push me, Connor," Augustine ground out. "You'll fucking regret it."

A violent, deranged light flared in Mad Rogan's eyes. "Let's test your theory about killing and jokes. I've got a good one just for this occasion."

The bulges split. Ropy black tentacles shot out of the wall, flailing. If it was illusion, it was the best I had ever seen. Panic crushed me, chaining my feet in place. I shuddered in its grip. What the hell kind of magic was this?

Things rose into the air as Rogan sorted through my possessions, looking for a weapon.

No. This is my house. You will not wreck my house and put my family at risk.

The icy vise of panic broke. "That's enough," I barked.

The two men startled. Augustine frowned. "How . . ."

"What the hell is wrong with both of you? This isn't some bar you can wreck. This is my place of business. This is my home! There are children sleeping less than a hundred feet from this room."

The darkness vanished like a candle flame snuffed out by a draft. Rogan let go of Augustine.

"I don't know which one of you is worse. Are you out of your minds? You're both selfish, spoiled pricks."

"Nevada?" my mother said behind me.

I glanced over my shoulder. My mother stood in the hallway with Grandma Frida next to her. My mother carried a shotgun. Grandma Frida carried her phone.

"Why are you screaming at an empty room?" my mother asked.

It had to be Augustine's illusion. I glared at Augustine. "Drop it."

He grimaced. Grandma Frida gasped. I had a feeling she and my mother just saw Mad Rogan and Augustine Montgomery suddenly pop into existence in my office.

"Get out of my house," I said.

My mother chambered a round with an unmistakable metallic click.

The two men marched out of the office. Grandma Frida raised her phone and snapped a picture. The door closed. I landed into my chair.

My mother looked at the carnations. "Is there something going on that I should know about?"

I shook my head and picked up the phone. "Bern? Tell me you recorded all of this."

"I've got it," he said. "I saved a hard copy and offloaded it onto two remote servers."

"Good," I said. If there was ever a question as to why I needed to slap both of them with a restraining order, at least I would have plenty of evidence. Primes or not Primes, no judge would deny me a restraining order after viewing that.

Someone knocked on my bedroom door. I opened my eyes. I was sitting in bed, slumped against the pillow, my computer on my lap. I glanced at the electronic clock. Wow. 5:30 a.m. I'd moved to my bedroom after midnight, when my eyes had started glazing over. I must've fallen asleep. It had been a long day.

"Come in," I called.

The door swung open and Bern entered, carrying a stack of papers. "Hey."

"Hey."

"The kids printed out some stuff." He put it on the bed. His eyes were bloodshot, his face haggard.

"Were you awake all this time?"

He nodded. "I'd gone over some things. It's not Egypt, Japan, or China, I can tell you that. Leon did some research on India, but he conked out, so . . ." He yawned. "You . . ." He yawned again.

"Get some sleep. I've got India."

He sat down on the trundle bed. It used to be mine when I was much younger. Sometimes, when my sisters and I would watch a movie in my room, they would pass out on it.

"I'll just sit here a minute," he said.

"Sure."

I leafed through the papers. Printouts of articles about various artifacts. Some weird doodle. A picture of a knight holding a shield against a gout of flame. "Not bad." I turned to show it to Bern. He lay asleep on the trundle.

Poor guy.

I tapped my keyboard to wake the laptop up. Right. India.

Leon's notes listed the search strings. India, artifact, Emmens . . . over thirty-five searches. I blew out some air. He was very thorough.

Let's see, what did the guy say before the explosion? Something about gateway to enlightenment, or door to enlightenment . . . I typed in *Indian artifact enlightenment*. The search engine spat out image results. Lots of things about Native Americans and United Native Tribes. Let's see, what about Hindu artifact enlightenment? Hmm, pictures of flowers, ancient palaces, mosaic, an illustration of some deity with four arms sitting on a pink flower, a metal statue of a deity with an elephant's face, a photograph of some beer cans and empty soda bottles . . . how did that get in there? This was a wild-goose chase. I kept scrolling. City with a river lapping at its walls, a piece of quartz, another deity, blue this time, with white stripes across his forehead . . .

Wait. Wait, wait, wait.

I clicked the picture. An illustration of a beautiful man with blue skin and one hand raised looked back at me. Two white stripes marked his forehead, forming oblong outlines. I grabbed my phone and pulled up the picture. The exact same shape. My heart sped up. There was something else sitting on top of the outline, but the image was too small to figure out what it was. I clicked the link for the image's page. A site selling antique beads.

I typed so fast that my fingers flew over the keyboard. Hindu god blue skin. The search engines spat out the images. No, no, no, yes! Exact same picture. I clicked it. Dead website. Damn it.

I kept scrolling. Another one, something about a video game. I clicked the image. Shiva. I had a name. Dozens of articles popped up. Shiva, supreme god of Hindu mythology. Chief attributes include a snake around his neck, a third eye . . . A third eye!

I clicked the images search and forgot to breathe. Here it was, a statue of Shiva with a jeweled ornament on his forehead: two oblong stripes of pale jewels forming a base for a crimson outline of an eye positioned vertically, with a radiant jewel in its center, where the iris would be. There were dozens of different photographs.

I kept following the trail of bread crumbs. *Lord Shiva, he of three eyes, his right eye is Sun, his left eye is Moon, his third eye is Fire*. Fire? *Once when a god of love Kamadeva distracted Shiva during meditation and Shiva opened his third eye. Fire poured forth and consumed Kamadeva . . .* Oh, this wasn't good. More sites. When Shiva opened his third eye in anger, most things turned to ashes. Shiva the Destroyer. Shiva the Universal Teacher, whose third eye destroys ignorance. Shiva, who once revealed his infinity to other gods in a form of a pillar of fire.

It all fit. Emmens must've found this artifact on one of the statues of Shiva, and it turned out to be the real thing. If Adam Pierce got hold of it, he too would become a pillar of fire, and all of us would burn with him.

"Nevada?" My mother stood in the doorway.

"Shh." I pointed at Bern.

She came in and sat next to me on the bed.

"How's it going?" she murmured.

"We found it."

I let her read the article. Her face grew darker and darker.

"Is that what Pierce wants? To burn everything?"

"I don't know," I said. "I think you should take the kids and Grandma and leave the city for a few days."

Mom looked at me. "Would that make it easier on you?"

"Yes." I braced myself for an argument. I just wanted to make sure they wouldn't burn to death.

"Okay," she said. "I'll pack up, and we'll take a trip."

"Thank you."

"Whatever will take a load off your shoulders." My mom paused. "Are you planning on working with Mad Rogan?"

"Yes. He's still the only hope I have of bringing Adam in."

"Nevada, how rich is Mad Rogan exactly?"

I frowned. "I don't know. Bern looked into him. His

words were 'scary rich.' Probably a few million, I'd imagine. Or maybe a few hundred million."

My mom had a very neutral expression on her face. "And he's unattached?"

"I don't know, actually. He strikes me as the kind of person who has a very liberal interpretation of that word. Why do you ask?"

"Look outside your window."

I got up and snuck to the window, trying not to wake Bern. Brilliant red carnations filled the parking lot. Some bright red, some dark, almost purple, they rose from planters—hundreds, no, probably thousands, illuminated by small red lights thrust between the planters, blending together into one giant beautiful carnation flower.

I closed my mouth with a click.

"They arrived around two," Mom said. "Two trucks with flowers and eight people. Took them almost three hours—they just left a few minutes ago."

"That's crazy." What was he thinking?

"It's none of my business, but are the two of you involved?"

I spun to her. "No. No, we are not."

"Does he know that?"

"He knows. I told him specifically not to bring me flowers. That's why he did it. He probably thought it was funny."

My mother sighed. "Nevada, even if he got these carnations for a dollar apiece, there are about five thousand of them down there, not including the labor and the time of the night. He must've given them enough money to drop everything and do this. That's not a joke. That's probably the price of a decent used car."

"He probably dug it out of his couch." I pictured Mad

Rogan fishing for change in an ultramodern furniture. "I should've told him not to give me car parts. He would've brought a whole tank just to be contrary. Grandma would've loved it."

"It's your life," Mom said. "I just never pictured you with someone like Mad Rogan."

Oh no, not the unsuitable boyfriend lecture. I winked at her. "Who did you picture me with?"

She frowned, stumped. "I don't know. Someone tall. Athletic."

I giggled. "That's it? That's all you want from your son-in-law? Because Mad Rogan is tall and athletic."

My mom waved her hands, flustered. "Someone like us. Normal. Money and magical pedigree, it's a curse. Trust me on this."

"Mom, I have no plans on doing anything with Mad Rogan." I leaned against the window. "He kidnapped me and chained me in his basement. He doesn't even understand no. The last thing I want to do is get emotionally or sexually involved with him. The man has no brakes, and that kind of power . . . it's like . . . like . . ."

"A hurricane," Mother said.

"Yes. Like that. I'm going to mind my p's and q's and keep him at arm's length if I can."

"What the heck are we going to do with all those carnations?"

"I don't know." I grinned. "We'll figure something out."

My mother shook her head and left.

I opened the window and looked at the sea of red below. The air smelled like flowers, a delicate but slightly spicy scent promising wondrous things. They were so gorgeous, my carnations. I didn't know why he'd given them to me. It was probably a trap or some sort of manipulation. Maybe it was an apology. I had no idea, but I was sure that no matter how long I lived, no man would ever give me five thousand carnations again. This was a magical thing that could happen only once, so I stood there, breathed in the scent, and let myself dream.

 **Chapter 13**

I walked into the shark fin building of Montgomery International Investigations armed with my laptop, phone, and Bern. My cousin surveyed the ultramodern lobby as we made our way to the elevator. He didn't seem impressed.

"Think Mad Rogan will show?" Bern asked.

"I hope so." I'd texted him before we'd left the house: "I know what Adam's trying to do. Meet me at MII in Augustine's office at nine." He hadn't replied. We needed Rogan. This was now too big for me and Bern, and I wasn't sure where Augustine's loyalties lay. He and Rogan clearly had some sort of problem, but I was sure that Rogan wanted to get his hands on Adam Pierce. For all I knew, Augustine might have been helping Adam and whoever his mysterious backers were the entire time.

The elevator brought us to the seventeenth floor. I checked my phone. Three minutes before nine. When we emerged from the elevator, the receptionist met us at the door and led us down a corridor.

She glanced at me. "I understand you're working with Mad Rogan."

"Yes. Did he arrive?"

"Yes, he did. Have you set your affairs in order? You know, in case."

Bern's eyes got really big.

"My aunt and uncle run a funeral home," she said. "Let me know if you need any help. It pays to be prepared. That way you're not a burden on the family."

Before I could say anything else, the hallway ended and we stepped into the ice-painted privacy of Augustine's office. He sat behind his desk, his hair, clothes, and the rest of him impeccably perfect. Mad Rogan was in a chair across from him, drinking coffee. His muscular body was clad in a dark suit that fit him like a glove. Well. They hadn't ripped each other's throats out.

I looked around the office.

"What are you looking for?" Augustine asked.

"Blood and severed limbs."

"What you witnessed last night was personal," Mad Rogan said. "This is business. We're remarkably civil when it comes to business."

"We?"

"The heads and heirs of the Houses," Mad Rogan said. "Your message made it seem like you've had a breakthrough. We both want Adam Pierce, so we're willing to put our differences aside. Besides, if we were going to brawl, we wouldn't do it in corporate headquarters."

"Precisely," Augustine said. "We observe all necessary formalities before murdering each other."

Okay then. I put the laptop on the desk and opened it to the picture of Shiva's third eye. "I think Adam Pierce is planning to destroy Houston."

It took me about twenty minutes to explain the Great

Chicago Fire, Emmens, Shiva, and the legend of his third eye.

"I believe that this amulet wasn't destroyed. I think it was separated into three pieces, and Adam's trying to re-assemble it. We have a piece, Adam has the piece he re-trieved from First National, and there is still a third piece out there somewhere. If I'm right," I said, "we're now re-sponsible for this knowledge. I think I'm right. I asked my family to leave town. I also called Professor Itou and suggested that his family leave town as well."

Augustine sighed. "Ms. Baylor, are you trying to start a panic?"

"No, I'm paying back the man who helped me. I've gone with this as far as I can go. I'm at a dead end. If I take this to the authorities—and I have no idea who and where these mysterious authorities are—I probably won't be believed. The Emmens family, if anyone is still alive, is unlikely to speak to me." I pushed the laptop toward them. "This is now yours. You're both Primes. You're re-sponsible for Houston."

Rogan and Augustine looked at each other.

"Do you have it on you?" Augustine asked.

Rogan reached into his inner pocket, produced an object wrapped in silk, and passed it to Augustine. Au-gustine unwrapped the silk and lifted the section of the amulet we'd found. He positioned it in a beam of light, and the quartz stones shone as they caught the sun.

"You're right," Augustine murmured. "Considering its worth, it's probably the real thing."

"I wouldn't think quartz was worth that much," I said.

"It's not quartz," Rogan said.

"These are uncut diamonds," Augustine said. "Excellent quality. Each of these would be about one point seventy-five karats after being cut. I'd estimate a twenty- to thirty-thousand-dollar range per stone."

There were at least a hundred diamonds. I nearly choked.

"You're thinking Lenora?" Augustine asked.

Lenora Jordan, Harris County District Attorney? Lenora Jordan, my high school heroine who bound crim- inals in chains? She would be the only Lenora I knew who was in a position of authority. "Did you mean Lenora Jordan?" I tried to keep excitement out of my voice and failed.

Mad Rogan glanced at me, then looked back at Augus- tine. "You know her. She'll take it."

"If it's an amplifier, you can't keep it anyway." Augus- tine passed the jeweled piece back to Rogan. "The Houses won't stand for it. They'll come for you with pitchforks, tear the artifact from your dead body, and then fight to the death over it. Even you can't fight all of us."

Rogan grimaced. "Do you want Emmens or Lenora?"

"Emmens," Augustine said. "Lenora always disliked you less. Also House Pierce will have to be told." He looked like he had gulped a mouth full of sour milk. "Ugh. This will be a joyous experience, I'm sure. I'll also have to put my people onto Pierce."

"I don't understand," I said. "I thought you tried to avoid dealing with Adam?"

Augustine sighed. "Like you said, I am a Prime of a Houston House. The welfare of the city is my responsi- bility."

I looked at Rogan.

"If Adam burns an office building or two, it's some- what annoying," Rogan said. "If he burns downtown or any of the financial centers, the economic impact on the Houses will be enormous. Every major local House and many families from out of state own property in the city. Aside from the immediate financial hit, the blow to the reputation of affected Houses would be catastrophic. Our people, our retainers, would die in huge numbers."

"Nobody would do business with a House that can't protect its own employees," Augustine said.

"If this happens," Rogan said, "the Houses will look for a scapegoat, and Augustine here was charged with apprehending Adam Pierce."

"But so is the Houston PD," Bern said.

"We expect Houston PD to fail," Augustine said, his voice dry.

"Your record as a top-notch investigative outfit might fool House Pierce, but it wouldn't stand up to an enraged National Assembly," Mad Rogan added. "They'll figure out exactly what Augustine tried to pull, and they'll tear House Montgomery to pieces."

Augustine's face rippled slightly, as if his illusion tried to slide off his features. He bared his teeth. "They'll try. I'm going after Emmens. We'll know where the third piece is in twenty-four hours."

"Have fun." Rogan rose.

"You too." Augustine looked at me. "Are you going with him to see Lenora Jordan?"

"Yes," Rogan and I said at the same time.

"Don't joke with Lenora, don't volunteer information, and keep your answers short," Augustine said. "If you get locked up, you're responsible for your own bail."

We exited the building together, Bern, Rogan, and I. Bern and I turned left, Rogan turned right.

"Nevada," Rogan said. "My car is this way."

"We'll follow you."

"Do you want to meet Lenora?" he asked. "If so, you ride with me."

I wanted to meet Lenora Jordan. Half of my high school time was spent idolizing her.

"You should go," Bern said. "I'll follow you and post bail if I have to."

Mad Rogan winked at me. Somehow that bastard figured me out and was now dangling Lenora like a carrot on a stick. Must've been the way my voice spiked when I said her name.

Control, control . . . I gave Rogan my best business smile and started walking toward him. "Thank you so much for your generous offer."

Mad Rogan chuckled. A tantalizing, feather-light heat washed over me, dancing on my shoulders, and an exhilarating mixture of warmth and pressure rolled down my neck. I almost jumped. Breath caught in my throat. I quashed the urge to stretch against that phantom touch like a cat.

"Do it again, and I will hurt you."

The phantom touch slowly melted away and part of me wanted to follow, wherever it was going.

Mad Rogan was walking next to me with that same confident stride that had made me notice him back in the arboretum, and I knew precisely where he was and how much distance separated us. My whole body was focused on him. I wanted him to touch me. I didn't want him touching me. I was waiting for him to touch me. I didn't know what the hell I wanted.

"Did you like the carnations?"

I reached into my pocket and handed him a small red card. "Texas Children's Hospital is grateful to you for your generous donation. Thanks to you, every one of their rooms has beautiful flowers this morning. They think it might be at least partially tax deductible, and if your people talk to their people, the hospital will provide the necessary paperwork."

Mad Rogan took the card, brushing my hand with his warm, dry fingers. The card shot out of his hand and landed in the nearby trash bin.

My skin tingled where he'd touched me. This was some kind of torture.

A black Audi sat in a parking spot about twenty feet away. A wide, elegant car, it seemed to imply power and quiet aggression. It was the kind of car a rich man would buy when he decided his adolescent-dream Maserati was too flashy.

"Is that an A8 L Security series?" His Range Rover was armored. I seriously doubted the Audi wouldn't be. Most Houses owned several armored cars. That's what kept Grandma Frida in business.

"It's an A8 customized." Mad Rogan touched the car door and the engine purred in response. "I've made some modifications."

Of course he had. I slid into the leather passenger seat. The cabin was surprisingly roomy, all sophisticated lines and sleek design, clean, elegant, and efficient. Nice.

Rogan pulled out of the parking lot. The car practically glided. The luxury aspect of the car didn't do that much for me, but the quality was really nice. Grandma once told me that it took almost five hundred man-hours to assemble one of these, and it showed. He drove it well too. No matter what they tell you, a high-performance luxury car didn't handle like a typical sedan, and an armored luxury car didn't handle like one either.

"Did you want something more maneuverable for the city?" I asked. Not that there was anything wrong with the Range Rover.

"Yes. You never know, we might encounter squirrels." The Audi slid into traffic.

"We should have sex."

I must've misheard. "I'm sorry, what?"

He glanced at me. His blue eyes were warm, as if heated from within. Wow.

"I said, we should have sex. You and me."

"No." Alarm made me sit up straighter.

"What do you mean, no?"

"I mean no. Has it been so long since you heard the word that you might have forgotten what it meant?" Okay, that was probably rude. I had to keep this as professional as possible. Calm, just very calm and firm.

"I'm attracted to you." His voice was confident and assured, as if this whole conversation was simply a formality and he knew he would win in the end. "I know you're attracted to me."

Just had to rub it in, did he?

"We're both consenting adults. Why wouldn't we have sex?"

Because you're dangerous as hell, you scare me, and because it would be mind-blowingly good. Which would mean I would want more and more and I really, really can't afford to fall in love with you. "Because we don't have that kind of relationship."

"I'm suggesting we change our relationship."

"That's not a good idea."

He glanced at me again, his face slightly wolfish. He was giving me just a hint of that intensity, a tiny glimpse of what it would be like. It was more seductive than Adam stripping completely naked. I had to be careful, so, so careful . . .

"I think it's an excellent idea," Mad Rogan said.

"I don't even know you. I don't trust you."

"You trusted me with your life just yesterday," he said.

"We were in a life-threatening situation and it was in your interests to keep me alive. By the same criteria, the men with whom you served trusted you with their lives daily. Did you all have sex as well? It must've been an interesting army unit."

"So you want seduction? Dinners, flowers, gifts?" His voice hinted at a mild disapproval.

"No."

"Seduction is a game," Rogan said. "You dazzle, entice, and finally seduce. Both parties know what is happening, but they go through the motions anyway. If you pay enough of the right commodity—attention, flattery, money—you will get the desired result. I thought you were above the game."

"I don't want to play the game."

"You want me, Nevada. You thought about it, you imagined it, and you probably touched yourself while you pictured it."

Oh my God. He just went there.

"Have sex with me, Nevada. You will enjoy it."

"Do you know what I want? I want a human connection. I want to be in bed with someone who is worth being with."

"And I'm not?" A dangerous intensity crept into his voice. I might have pushed things a little too far.

We shot out onto Franklin Street. The rectangular tower of the Harris County Criminal Justice Center loomed on our right. Bridge Park, with its iconic *Riding*

Cowboy statue, was on our left. The street was filled with parallel-parked cars. No spots except for the short space between a blue Honda and a red sedan on the opposite side of the street by the park. Rogan couldn't possibly be aiming for it. We were coming in way too fast. This was an armored vehicle, not a stunt car.

Rogan was looking at me instead of the traffic.

We barreled down the road. The Audi cut into the opposite lane, right in front of a giant pickup. He was still looking at me and not the street.

"Rogan!"

He braked, his gaze on me. Tires squealed as the car's rear slid. My heart jumped into my throat. The Audi spun 180 degrees, and we skidded into the parking spot inches from either car's bumper.

The truck driver laid on the horn, and the massive vehicle roared away in outrage.

I exhaled.

Rogan pushed a button, turning off the engine.

"I want an answer," he said.

"You are the man who kidnapped me, chained me in his basement, and almost strangled a woman he barely met because he found her annoying. That's your resume." Okay, that probably wasn't entirely fair, but I owed him for the car stunt. "I realize that this is strange for you, because ninety-nine percent of the time, your name, your body, and your money do the trick and women fall over with their legs spread if you look at them for longer than ten seconds. I'm not one of those women."

I got out of the car and started across the parking lot. He caught up with me. I risked a glance at his face. Mad Rogan was smiling. Something I said must've been really funny.

"Do I have any redeeming qualities?" he asked. A charming, self-deprecating dragon. No, not buying it. That charm could tear in a split second, and then there would be flame and sharp teeth.

"Not running over the squirrel was in your favor."

"Mhm. Good to know." He smiled wider.

Uh-oh.

"Don't do it."

"Don't do what?"

"Every time you smile like that, someone dies. If you attack me, I will defend myself."

"Of all the many interesting things I'm thinking of doing to you, killing you or hurting you is not on the list." He winked at me.

We walked into the justice center and got into an elevator. Two men carrying laptop bags made a beeline for us, trying to catch a ride. Mad Rogan gave them a flat look. Without a word, the men simultaneously changed their direction and angled to the elevator on our left. The doors closed and the cabin slid upward.

This was really happening. I was going to see Lenora Jordan. Lenora who bound criminals in chains. Who wasn't afraid of any Prime. Who . . .

What if she was just like them? Just like Augustine or Pierce? I wasn't sure I could handle it. That would be crushing.

I opened my mouth.

"Yes?" Mad Rogan asked.

"If she isn't what she appears to be, please don't tell me."

"She's exactly what she seems," he said. "Law and Order is her god. She's a zealot, and she prays to it sincerely and often. She's impartial and resolute, and crossing her is stupid."

The doors slid open. We walked out into a busy hallway. People moved out of our way, almost unconsciously.

"Even for a Prime?" I asked.

"Especially for a Prime. She holds the office with the blessing of the Harris County Houses. We put her there because even we recognize the need for oversight."

We stopped before a door. Mad Rogan held it open for me. I went through and stopped before the receptionist's desk. A Native American woman in her forties sat at the counter. She had a wide face with large dark eyes and a full mouth. She looked at Rogan with a kind of get-back stare that would've stopped an enraged dog.

"Behave yourself," she said.

Rogan turned left and opened the door. I followed him into a large office. It was well furnished, with a heavy desk of reclaimed old wood and several comfortable chairs. Behind the desk, heavy bookcases lined the wall. Between the bookcases and the desk stood Lenora Jordan. She looked just like her billboard image: strong, powerful, and confident. She wore an indigo business suit. Her curly black hair was pulled back from her face into a thick, elaborate plait. Her skin was a rich brown, and her face, with big eyes, a wide nose, and full lips was attractive, but what you noticed first about her was the complete assurance with which she held herself. This was her kingdom, and she ruled it unopposed.

Lenora Jordan crossed her arms. "I was about to issue you a formal invitation to visit my office."

"Really?" Mad Rogan said.

"Really. How long did you expect to rampage around the city unchecked? There must be a very compelling reason that explains why you're blowing up businesses and dropping buses on people in public. I'm eager to hear it." She turned to me. "Who are you?"

Lenora Jordan was talking to me.

"This is my associate, Ms. Baylor," Mad Rogan said.

"Can your associate speak for herself?"

"Yes, I can," I said. What do you know, my mouth moved and words came out. I hadn't thought they would. "Nice to meet you."

Her gaze pinned me down. "My office has been trying to identify a young female who has been accompanying him on his reign of havoc. Are you that female?"

"Yes."

"How are you involved with him?"

"I've been tasked by my parent company to convince Adam Pierce to surrender himself to his House."

Lenora Jordan's eyebrows rose.

"MII," Mad Rogan said.

"What are your qualifications for this job?" she asked.

"I'm expendable," I said.

Lenora frowned. "Sounds like Augustine. Okay, let's hear it. All of it."

We sat down, and Mad Rogan and I took turns explaining the situation. When we finished, Lenora held out her hand. Rogan produced the artifact and placed it on her palm. The DA studied it for a long moment.

"Have your people reached any conclusions?" she asked.

"It's magic. It's inert. It's indestructible," Mad Rogan said. "We dipped it in acid. We blowtorched it. I couldn't break it."

Lenora's eyebrows rose again. "You personally?"

Mad Rogan nodded.

She turned the piece of jewelry in her hands. The diamonds caught the light, glowing weakly. "This doesn't fit Adam's MO. He's impulsive and impatient. Last year he set a bouncer on fire because he tossed Adam out of the club. Then Adam got roaring drunk, high, and partied until dawn so hard that when we came to get him in the morning he barely remembered the incident. What we have here is complicated and done in stages. It took careful planning and preparation. To what end? Ms. Baylor, has he said anything to you?"

"He enjoys setting things on fire and embarrassing his House, his mother especially," I said. "He didn't give me the impression that there was anything larger going on, but clearly his actions are part of some complicated plan. He also led me on, because as long as I kept reporting back that he and I were communicating, House Pierce sat on their hands."

"The attack on your family is the only thing that doesn't fit." Lenora tapped her nails on the desk. "And he hasn't contacted you since in person?"

"No."

"Someone is controlling him," Lenora said. "Why? He could've quietly gathered the pieces, but instead he is creating a huge public spectacle every time. For what purpose is this being done?"

"It's classic destabilization," Mad Rogan said. "People don't feel safe, law enforcement appears incompetent, and public sentiment toward the Houses plummets. It reminds people what we can do if we choose to disregard the law. Most people find that uncomfortable."

That was a surprising analysis, coming from him.

"Nobody is above the law, Rogan," Lenora said. "Not even you."

"So you tell me," he said.

She sighed. "I will check with Homeland Security to see if any of the anti-Houses terrorist groups could be involved. But it would take a hell of a personality to rein in Adam Pierce and make him follow a plan. Many have tried and failed."

"Lenora." Mad Rogan leaned forward. "He needs this trinket. He has at least one, possibly both, although I doubt it."

"He would've made another production out of getting the third piece," I agreed.

"He will be coming for it," Mad Rogan said.

"Are you questioning the integrity of my office?" Lenora asked him. Her voice was amused, but her eyes weren't.

If she looked at me like that, I'd probably get out of my chair and hide behind it. Mad Rogan didn't even blink.

"I'm trying to account for all possibilities. If he gets the three pieces together, he will become a pillar of flame. If his current pattern is consistent, he will do it somewhere public. In front of this building or in front of House Pierce. Somewhere where population is dense."

"I count on you to make sure this doesn't happen," she said.

"But if it does, there will need to be an evacuation," Mad Rogan said. "You and I both know how difficult it would be."

"You want me to issue a terrorist alert." Lenora leaned back. "You do realize that the advisories are not given lightly. There is a great deal of weight and planning that comes with it. I have to coordinate with the Office of Homeland Security, National Guard, and FBI. Not to mention the Houses will lose their collective minds."

"It's your call," Mad Rogan said. "But keep in mind: this is real. It's happening. I don't want us to be caught unawares."

"I'll think about it," Lenora Jordan said.

We made it outside without being arrested.

Mad Rogan looked at the building and shook his head. "What?"

"The next time we see that trinket, Adam Pierce will be wearing it."

"I think she'll take good care of it."

"Not as good as when it's locked in one of my vaults."

We started across the street.

My phone beeped. I glanced at the text message. *Arrived in Austin. Checked into hotel. Tell Rogan thank you for escort.*

"Did you send an escort with my family?"

"Yes. They're a target."

"How did you know they would be leaving?"

"My people saw them load up, called me, and I told them to follow."

Duh. "Thank you."

"You're welcome. I plan to hold them hostage until you sleep with me."

I stumbled.

He turned and gave me a brilliant, impossibly handsome smile. "Just kidding."

Damn it.

"Have lunch with me," Rogan said.

"No."

"Nevada, you should have lunch with me. Somewhere public where we could be easily seen. It would also help if you pretended to enjoy yourself. Throw your hair back and smile. Perhaps even giggle girlishly."

I paused. "Baiting the hook for Mr. Pierce?"

"Yes."

It wasn't a bad idea. I didn't mind being bait if it netted me Pierce, not even a little bit. "Bern . . ."

"Do you think your cousin would rather sit in a car, watch you, and risk being fried by that half-baked lunatic, or play with Bug's new setup in complete safety at my compound?"

My phone rang as if on cue. I answered it.

"Hey," Bern said. "Do you still need me? I've got an invite from Bug, and there are some people here with an armored Range Rover. They're saying Mad Rogan told them to pick me up."

I looked at him. Mad Rogan stepped close to me, his big body too near, the look in his eyes too heated. I smelled a hint of sandalwood and vetiver, mixed with an almost harsh, peppery scent. He bent down, arresting, his eyes so blue. My heart beat faster.

He smiled a slow, predatory grin. "Resistance is futile."

"You are not assimilating me." I stood my ground and raised the phone to my ear. "Bern, if you want to go with them, go ahead."

"You sure?"

"Yes." Mad Rogan already had my family covered in Austin anyway. At least Bern would be protected.

I hung up and looked at Mad Rogan. "I'll go to lunch with you. But I'm not giggling."

Casa Fortunato turned out to be a small restaurant at the intersection of Crawford Street and Congress Avenue, only a few blocks from the justice center. It had a small outdoor area facing the Minute Maid ballpark. The day was hot and humid, and the last thing I wanted to do was sit outside. That's why anyone who had any sense ate underground in Houston's tunnels. They started out as an underground passage between two movie theaters and grew over the years to connect to just about everything, with their own restaurants and rest areas. On a hot day, downtown looked almost deserted. Unfortunately, if we sat underground, Adam Pierce would have no chance of noticing us. It was highly unlikely he would enter the tunnels, where he could be cornered.

We walked to a table with bright yellow, blue, and white Spanish tile, and Mad Rogan held the chair out for me. I hung my canvas bag on the chair and sat. The canvas bag contained a Baby Desert Eagle, .40SW, with a 12-round magazine. After the last brush with Adam's crew, I didn't want to take chances, so I'd upgraded my firepower. I was turning into Dirty Harry. BDE was as big and bad as I wanted to be. Eventually it would all be over and I could go back to my normal business of tracking cheating spouses and insurance fraud. It might be less exciting, but it rarely required me to fire a gun within city limits.

The familiar, sick feeling sucked at my throat. I had killed someone. I really didn't want to think about it. Eventually I would have to deal with it one way or another.

The waitress appeared with a dish of salsa and a plate of still-warm chips and took our drink orders. Two ice teas, fake sugar.

I pretended to be engrossed in the menu. What to order? Something not messy. Baja tacos with shrimp looked good. I put the menu down.

"What do you think of Lenora Jordan?" Mad Rogan said.

"I think she's awesome. I want to be her when I grow up."

"You want to be the DA?"

"No, I want to . . ." I struggled to put it into words. "I want to be where she is professionally but in my own way. I want to be confident and respected for what I do. I want to earn a reputation. I want it known that the Baylor Investigative Agency stands for something. My father started it, and I'd like to make sure the name means competence and quality. What is it you want?"

He leaned back. The sunlight played on his face, sneaking in past a tree on the corner. His skin seemed to almost glow, highlighting the strong lines of his face, the powerful nose, and the hard chin. He shrugged. "I haven't thought about it."

The waitress returned with our drinks, took our order—I got Baja tacos and he got crispy tacos with ground sirloin—and disappeared again.

His phone beeped.

"Excuse me." Mad Rogan raised it to his ear. "Yes?"

There was an odd kind of contrast between a man who crushed people out of existence and the one who had perfect dinner manners. Somehow the raging Prime and urbane millionaire were one and the same, and it completely made sense, except that the mundane part of him made the violent part even scarier.

"When?" Mad Rogan asked. "Tell him to meet me here."

He hung up and glanced at me. "I'm sorry, I have to take care of some business. It can't wait, but I'll keep it short."

"Not a problem. I'll busy myself with being seen and tossing my hair. Would you like me to twirl it on my finger while biting my lip?"

"Could you?"

"No, sorry." I grinned at him.

"Tease," he said, and my mind went right into the gutter. I dragged it out, kicking and screaming. Professional. At least try to stay professional.

"So you have no goals?"

"No, I have short-term goals," he said. "They're not particularly challenging."

"Why?"

Mad Rogan took the lemon wedge off his glass and deposited it onto his appetizer plate, as if it had been some sort of offending bug. "Well, let's see, what do men in my position usually want?"

"More money?" I sipped from my glass.

"I'm worth one point two billion."

I choked on my tea.

He waited until I got my coughing under control. "I have investments, and I own several corporations that make money mostly without my involvement. At some point more money is just more money. Some Primes go into research, but it never held any particular interest for me. Occasionally I may improve a spell if I want to accomplish a specific purpose, but I find the idea of dedicating myself to it boring."

"Professional goals?"

Mad Rogan shook his head. "I'm excellent at only one thing: destruction on a massive scale. Been there, done that, got a lot of fatigue-colored T-shirts. I've reached the pinnacle of that career."

Our food arrived. That was fast.

I bit into my taco. Delicious. "Why did you get out of the army?"

"Do you ever regret mortgaging the business?"

I saw how it was. An answer for an answer. A piece of shrimp slipped out of my taco and landed on my plate. Smooth move.

"Oh God, yes. We should've sold it as soon as we knew Dad was sick. We would've gotten more money and started the treatment earlier. The experimental therapy was working, it's just that by the time the mortgage went through, my father was too far gone. But I was very green at that point, and running the business with an established name seemed like a better option. Had we sold it, I would've built it back up by now under a different name. But hindsight is twenty-twenty. My mother got a little bit more time with my dad, and he got a little bit more time with us. I have to be content with that." I realized he was looking at me oddly. "What?"

"It wasn't what I was asking, but I guess I got my answer anyway." He tilted his head. "I got out of the military because we were winning the war. When I started, Belize was in ruins and Mexico threatened half a dozen nations in South America. We had to hit hard to turn the tide of war, so I hit hard."

Now that was the understatement of the century.

"Years later, the coalition had beaten back Mexico and pacified the region. In the end they didn't even deploy me. Having me in the area was enough to force the other side into retreat. When the conflicts began to die down, the chain of command on our side started talking about going into Mexico. I realized I was a factor in that decision and I resigned my commission, because as much as I enjoy flexing my magic, it was time for someone else to rebuild what I had wrecked. Even if the Mexican Initiative hadn't been an issue, I would've left. The army has no use for me in peacetime. I'm bad at paperwork, and I can't teach others to do what I do. I'm a killer. So I got out."

"And now you're a Prime without a cause."

"Yes. Most things are not a challenge." He leaned forward, focusing on me. "When I find a challenge, I devote myself to it."

Was that about me? Because I wasn't a challenge. I was a human being. I opened my mouth to tell him that, but he glanced over my shoulder at the parking lot. I turned and looked behind me. A grey Ford Escape pulled into a parking space. It was an older vehicle, with at least ten or twelve years on it. The man who stepped out was in his midtwenties, fit, with broad shoulders and short blond hair. He carried a manila folder and was wearing an ill-fitting black suit, the kind that was probably bought years ago and hung in the back of a closet, wrapped in plastic, extracted solely for funerals, weddings, and job interviews.

The man approached us. Mad Rogan rose. The man offered him his hand. "Troy Linman, Major."

They shook.

"Sit," Mad Rogan said.

Troy sat next to me. "Ma'am."

Ex-soldier. I'd bet every dollar in my wallet on it.

Troy passed the manila envelope to Mad Rogan. Rogan opened it and scanned the contents. "Eleven Bravo?"

"Yes, sir."

Infantry. Some MOSs, military occupation specialties, translated well to the civilian world. Anything in 68 category, medical, was good. Or 91B, wheeled vehicle mechanic. Eleven Bravo wasn't one of those MOSs. It was the backbone of the army, but in the civilian world, there wasn't much you could do with it.

"Why did you get out?" Mad Rogan asked.

Troy hesitated. "I was coming up on my reenlistment. My wife was six months pregnant with our second child, and she didn't want me to reenlist. She didn't say anything, but I put two and two together. I was kind of done too. I wanted to get out and try civilian life. I wanted to come home every night."

"How is it going?"

"We do okay," Troy said.

His flat voice told me that they weren't doing okay. Not at all.

Mad Rogan pinned him with his stare. "The background check says your house will be repossessed tomorrow, so I'll ask again, Mr. Linman. How is it going?"

I couldn't see Troy's right hand, but his left had rolled into a tight fist. "I work third shift in a tire-retreading plant and deliver pizza in the evening. My wife works days while I watch the kids. She's a payroll processing clerk. I've been applying everywhere, trying to get a job, any job that would let me work in the daytime. Anywhere with a decent paycheck wants a degree."

I'd heard this story so many times from so many people that I could guess what he would say next.

"I tried to apply to be a tollbooth operator. They want someone with a bachelor's. What the hell does a tollbooth operator need a bachelor's for? Army would pay for me to go to college, but I can't afford to take the time off. We've been trying hard for two years. We just get deeper and deeper in the hole."

"Did Santino explain what's involved in working for me?"

Troy nodded. "Yes."

"My rules are simple," Mad Rogan said. "Be where

you're told to be when you're told to be. The first time you lie to me will be the last day you'll work for my House. If you try hard but fail, it won't be counted against you. Being lazy and sloppy will get you fired. Getting high or drunk will get you fired. Being in debt will get you fired."

Troy opened his mouth, his face stoic.

"I'll take care of your foreclosure," Mad Rogan said.

"With all respect, Major, I came for a job, not charity. I want to work and provide for my family."

"It's not charity," Mad Rogan said. "House Rogan owns all of the loans of its employees. Home, auto, college, anything else. When someone else holds your loan, you become a security risk. I don't like security risks, so I take care of my own. People who work for me do get hurt. Your medical is covered, your life isn't. You have a family, so take that into consideration. I pay well, so take some of that money and buy yourself a decent life insurance policy."

Mad Rogan fell silent.

Troy swallowed. "Am I in?"

"You're hired."

Troy's face went white. He stopped breathing, and for a moment I thought he would pass out. He could deal with rejection. He must've braced himself for it so he could get up from this table and walk away with some dignity. But the relief of acceptance was too overwhelming. His entire life had been riding on Mad Rogan's words, and now he couldn't process it.

I reached out and touched his hand. "It's okay."

He looked at me, stunned.

"It's okay," I repeated. "He hired you. Your home is safe. You're okay. Breathe, Troy."

Troy inhaled deeply.

Shivers ran down my spine. I finally realized just how dangerous Mad Rogan was. Most Houses had their private armies, but Mad Rogan took it a step further. For Troy it wasn't just a job. It was a chance to be a man again, to be appreciated for his skills and to provide for his family. It was a new life, and Mad Rogan had given it to him. That's what he did. He found ex-servicemen at their lowest, gave them a chance to matter, and rewarded them for it. I now understood perfectly the man who had reported to Rogan after the Range Rover had blown up. Rogan didn't just own them financially. He owned their souls. They thought he was God.

"When do I start?" Troy asked.

Thunder rolled down the street. I jumped off my chair. It came from behind Mad Rogan and to the right. He sprinted, clearing the fence. I ran out of the eating area into the parking lot and caught up with him at Franklin Street, Troy at my heels.

Smoke billowed from the justice center. The thick plume of it poured out of the eleventh floor, rising up. Oh no.

Something shot out of the window directly under the smoke and plummeted to the street. What the hell?

The thing charged down Franklin Street, running toward us on all fours in powerful leaps, half hidden by the vehicles. Something fast and as big as a pickup truck.

"You start now, Mr. Linman," Mad Rogan said and ran toward the thing. As I pulled my gun out of my purse, Troy Linman yanked off the jacket of his suit, threw it on the ground, and ran after Rogan. I chased them, gun in hand.

The thing cleared the small sedan in its way and landed on the street, out in the open. Shaped like a cheetah with the head of a dog, it was made of metal. Sections of thick pipes sat where its bones would be, and chains wound around the metal skeleton. There was nothing holding it all together, nothing except magic and someone's will. I'd never seen anything like it. Small animated objects, yes, but this, this was incredible.

The beast slowed and raised its head. A small bright spark shone in its long jaws.

"It's got the artifact!" I yelled.

Mad Rogan stopped and brought his arms forward. The beast fell apart, sliced in four sections. The pipes and chains crashed to the ground and scattered.

"Find the animator!" Rogan walked toward the metal debris, moving cautiously. The pipes and chains slid apart in front of him, skittering across the pavement. He was sorting through it, looking for the artifact. Troy grabbed a loose pipe that had rolled to our feet and brandished it.

I spun around. An animator mage had to be within a short distance of his or her creation. On our left was a pay-to-park lot, complete with a toll bar and an automated payment booth. Directly in front of us, across La Branch Street, a ten-story parking garage blocked out a chunk of sky. Both were a bad idea for a quick getaway. In a moment, the area would be swarming with bailiffs, marshals, and cops. There was no way to escape quickly through the parking garage or the crowded parking lot. I turned. On our right, an empty square lot took up the entire block. It held only two cars; it had to be a tow-away zone. The animator wouldn't risk parking there either.

"What are we looking for?" Troy asked, hefting the pipe like a club.

The pipes on the far left shivered.

Rogan turned . . .

The metal debris flew to him, clamping around him with terrible force, trying to crush him. I jerked my gun up. Rogan vanished behind the cage of metal pipes. Chains wrapped around the pipes and squeezed. Metal groaned, sliding and moving. Shooting it would do nothing. I could hit him by accident.

Troy ran at the shifting pile of metal.

"No! We can't help him. We have to find the animator!"

The metal cage fell apart, as if it had exploded from the inside. Troy froze in the middle of the street. I saw a glimpse of Rogan's furious face. The metal debris clamped him again and squeezed. He would have no bones left if I didn't hurry.

"What are we looking for?" Troy yelled.

Rogan's power was incredible. To go toe to toe with him would take a Prime. "A luxury armored car."

He turned left, I turned right, scanning the street. A big black Cadillac Escalade was parked on La Branch next to the vacant lot, facing us. Two people sat, one in the driver's seat, one in the passenger's.

The debris exploded, rolled on the pavement, and clamped Mad Rogan again.

Around me vehicles swerved, rushing to avoid Mad Rogan and the explosion of magic around him. Anyone with half a brain would get the hell out of here. Especially anyone in an Escalade.

"Troy!" I raised my gun and walked straight at the Escalade.

The driver didn't move. He saw me coming straight for him with a firearm and he didn't move. We'd found the animator.

Out of the corner of my eye I saw the metal fall apart, clamp Rogan, and fall apart again. Time slowed, stretching. An armored Escalade meant a reinforced hood, radiator protection, and RunFlat inserts, rubber strips embedded in tires. Even if I shot the tires to pieces, the vehicle could still drive off at sixty miles per hour and keep going. The windshield was bulletproof. A round from Baby Desert Eagle wouldn't penetrate. But it would still crack the outer shelf of the glass. I didn't need to kill the Prime inside. I just needed to obscure his vision enough to keep Mad Rogan alive.

Time restarted. I squeezed the trigger and fired six shots in a tight pattern right in front of the driver's face. The gun spat bullets and thunder. The windshield cracked, each bullet striking the glass and forming a round burst of cracks, as if someone had taken a handful of ice from the wall of a freezer and pressed it against the windshield. I could barely see the driver.

I fired six bullets at the Prime's side of the windshield, ejected the magazine, and slapped the second one in. Twelve rounds left.

Troy ran by me, leaped onto the hood, and swung his pipe at the windshield, putting the weight of his whole body into it. The glass cracked but held. He bashed it again. The windshield bent inward. Another solid whack and he would get through.

The Escalade roared into life and shot backward. Troy slid off, rolled on the pavement, jumped to his feet, and chased the huge black SUV. The Escalade turned the corner of La Branch, still in reverse, and sped up the street parallel to Franklin. I ran through the empty lot after it. The Escalade made a sharp right onto Crawford. The driver was circling the parking lot in reverse. If he made another right, it would put him straight on a collision course with Mad Rogan.

"Troy!" I turned right and cut across the parking lot, running at full speed.

The Escalade turned onto Franklin. Mad Rogan was still fighting the metal debris.

I squeezed every drop of effort out of my muscles. Air turned into fire in my lungs. Hot pain stitched my side.

The Escalade sped straight at the metal clump surrounding Rogan.

I fired at the tires, trying to slow it down. Four bullets ripped into the rubber.

The metal clump of the pipes and chains fell apart. For half a second Rogan stood completely exposed. The Escalade rammed him. There was a crunch, a sickening crunch. Oh my God.

Rogan flew across the pavement, fell, and lay still.

I lunged between him and the Escalade and fired point-blank at the rear window. Eight, seven, six . . .

The passenger door swung open. The pipes jumped up, re-forming into a beast, a shield between me and the car. I kept firing. An arm in a suit sleeve reached down and swiped something off the ground. The sun reflected on a thick gold ring just before the door slammed shut.

Last round. I fired.

The SUV snarled and sped up Franklin Street.

Rogan.

"Drop your weapon!" someone roared behind me.

I raised my hands in the air, slowly lowered my gun, and let it fall from my fingers. Something bit me from behind, right between the shoulder blades. My body locked up, as if I'd jumped under an ice-cold shower and every muscle had gone rigid at once and stayed that way, numb, hot, and painfully itchy. I fell on my side. My head bounced off the pavement. Three men in marshal uniforms jumped on top of me.

Tased, I realized. They'd Tased me.

The men wrenched me up. Someone forced my hands behind my back, and I felt the cold metal of cuffs on my wrists.

Ahead I could see Lenora Jordan stopped by a pile of metal. Where was Rogan?

Four people in uniform dragged Troy forward. He was bent over, his skin scraped bloody from falling on the asphalt.

Oh my God, oh my God, oh my God, please don't let Rogan be dead.

The metal heap shivered.

The marshals dropped me, and I went down on my knees, hard. There were cops and marshals and bailiffs everywhere I could see, and every gun was pointed at the metal heap.

The pile of pipes and chains exploded. Rogan staggered up. His expression was terrible.

"Stand down," Lenora ordered.

Two dozen people simultaneously lowered their firearms. Rogan turned to her, his face contorted by dark rage. For a second, I thought he might kill her.

"Issue a fucking alert, Lenora," Mad Rogan growled.

Chapter 14

"He probably has two broken ribs," the female paramedic told me. "It's likely an incomplete fracture, but the only way to find out for sure is to take an X-ray. We've relocated his shoulder to its proper place, but he's refusing further treatment."

She glanced at Mad Rogan sitting on a stretcher. He had what could only be described as the Look of Rage on his face. The first responders were giving him a wide berth.

"He really should go to the hospital," the female paramedic said. "Really."

"Have you told him that?"

"Yes, but . . ."

I waited.

The female paramedic leaned closer. "He's *Mad Rogan*. The DA said I should talk to you about it. She said you could make him see reason."

If the clouds split open and an archangel descended onto the street in all of his heavenly glory and tried to make Rogan see reason, he would fail miserably and have to pack up his flaming sword and go back to Heaven in shame. I had no idea what gave Lenora the idea that I could do any better.

Well, if none of them could scrape enough courage to explain to the Scourge of Mexico that he needed to go to the emergency room, I guess I'd have to do my best. "Thank you so much. I'll take care of it."

I walked over to Mad Rogan. The female paramedic trailed me.

"Your ribs are broken," I informed him.

"You heard her," he said. "It's an incomplete fracture."

I held out my hand.

Mad Rogan looked at it.

"Give me your keys, Mr. Rogan. I'm taking you to the hospital."

I became aware of the sudden quiet around us.

"This is ridiculous," Mad Rogan growled.

"Broken ribs can be life-threatening." I cleared my throat. "I need you to function, so let's fix this. Which part of going to the hospital is upsetting?"

His eyes narrowed. "It will take forever. I'll get there, sit for two hours, then someone will X-ray me and tell me, 'You have broken ribs.' Then they'll give me two ibuprofens and send me home."

"This is almost the same argument, word for word, Leon used last year after he decided it would be a grand idea to ride his bike down the stairs."

"It's a perfectly good argument." Mad Rogan bristled. "What's wrong with it?"

"Leon is fifteen years old. You're twice his age."

"Are you implying that I am elderly and decrepit?"

"I'm implying that you should know better. You were hit by an armored vehicle going at least twenty-five miles per hour. Before that you were compressed by half a junkyard's worth of metal. You could be bleeding internally. You could have a concussion. You are supposed to have more sense than a fifteen-year-old boy who wanted to get on YouTube."

"I've been injured before. I know it's not serious."

"I'm sorry, was your official designation sixty-two-alpha in the Army? Were you an emergency physician?"

"I've had training."

I nodded. "Do you know who else had training? All these paramedics around you." I nodded to the first responders. "Raise your hand if you don't think Mr. Rogan should go to the hospital."

Nobody moved.

"See? Please let them do their job."

Mad Rogan leaned forward. A muscle in his face jerked. He caught it, but it was too late. I saw it. He pronounced every word with quiet menace. "I'm not going to the hospital."

"Okay," I said. "Is there another place with X-ray equipment and medical personnel where you would be willing to go?"

"Yes. You can take me to my family physician." He reached for his pocket, slowly and gingerly pulled out the keys, and put them in my hand.

"Thank you for your cooperation."

Three minutes later I was driving an Audi through the crowded streets of Houston. Mad Rogan sat in the passenger seat. His breathing was shallow. Troy shifted in the backseat. His left leg was broken when the Escalade hit him during its final escape. He also refused to go to the emergency room.

I changed lanes, sliding the Audi neatly in the short space between two cars. It handled like a dream.

"Maybe I should drive," Troy said.

"She knows what she's doing," Mad Rogan said.

I sniffed.

"What?"

"The fragrance of a genuine compliment from Mad Rogan. So rare and sweet."

The radio came on. "This is an emergency broadcast. The Secretary of Homeland Security received credible evidence of a possible terrorist attack on the city of Houston . . ."

Lenora had issued the alert. Hopefully downtown and the other business centers would begin to empty.

"Take the exit in two miles," Mad Rogan said. "Did Leon make it down the stairs?"

"Yes, he did. He rode the bike straight into the wall and the handlebar cracked his ribs. He also managed to hit his head and get himself a serious concussion for his trouble."

My Leon was in Austin with my sisters and out of harm's way. But the city was full of Leons and Arabellas and Catalinas, and Adam Pierce now had another piece of the artifact. For all we knew, he already had all three. He would burn the city down. And now another Prime was involved. What was happening? Why?

I felt like the further we went, the fewer answers I got.

Mad Rogan's family physician practiced out of a three-story building that had no sign. It looked like a perfectly nondescript office building with tinted windows and its own small, private parking lot. There were only three other cars there, all three dark SUVs.

I parked and dipped my head to look at the building through the windshield. No signs of life.

Mad Rogan was getting out of the car. I stepped out

and opened the door for Troy. "I'll see if I can get a stretcher or a chair."

Mad Rogan punched a code into the keypad.

"I think I can manage," Troy said.

"It's okay, I'm sure we can wrangle up something . . ."

The tinted double doors swung open. Three men and two women emerged, pushing two stretchers with practiced efficiency. Behind them, a huge Hispanic woman followed. She wasn't fat but large, tall, at least six feet, and powerfully built, with broad shoulders and strong-looking arms left bare by her dark green scrubs. Her dark hair was pulled back. Her features, like everything about her, were large: dark eyes, strong nose, and big, full mouth. You knew she smiled often and the smile would be bright. She looked around forty.

She looked at Mad Rogan. "What did you do?"

Mad Rogan opened his mouth.

She turned to me. "What did he do?"

"He got hit by a car," I said.

The woman pivoted back to Mad Rogan. "Why in the world would you do a stupid thing like that?"

Mad Rogan opened his mouth again to say something.

"Don't you have an army of badasses to keep this exact thing from happening?"

"I . . ."

The woman turned to me. "What kind of car was it?"

"An armored Escalade," I said.

"Well, at least it was a nice car." She turned to Mad Rogan. "Who would want to ruin their nice car by hitting you with it?"

Mad Rogan sucked in a slow breath and let it out.

"Got you in the ribs, huh." The woman waved. "Load both of them up."

"I can . . ." Mad Rogan started.

She pointed to a stretcher. "Down."

I felt the distinct urge to do whatever she said and do it quickly.

Mad Rogan lay down on the stretcher. The team wheeled Troy and him into the building.

"I'm Dr. Daniela Arias," the woman said to me. "Come inside. You can wait in our waiting room."

I followed her in. I didn't really feel like I had a choice.

Most waiting rooms I visited had rows of semi-comfortable chairs, a TV, and, if you were lucky, a Coke machine. This waiting room should've been in some luxury hotel. A huge floor-to-ceiling aquarium took up one wall, and small schools of silver fish with bright red fins swam back and forth, darting in and out of an elaborate white coral at the bottom. Plush couches occupied the room, some in the corner, arranged into a semi-private ring around an obligatory fireplace, others in front of an enormous flat-screen TV, hooked up to what had to be every gaming system known to man. To the left, a large stainless steel fridge with clear glass doors showed off rows of water, orange juice, and Gatorade on one side, and deli meat, yogurt, salads, and plastic bowls filled with cut vegetables and fruit on the other. I was encouraged to "help myself." I helped myself to a bowl of raspberries. They were ridiculously delicious.

I was on my third bowl—I had earned it—when Daniela Arias walked through the door.

"He will live," she said.

Oh drat.

"He would like to see you."

I made myself put the raspberries down and followed her down the hallway.

"Is he in pain?"

"I've given him something that will get him through the next six hours. But if he twists the wrong way, he'll feel it. He has two cracked ribs, and his shoulder is severely bruised."

He wasn't dead. That was all that mattered.

"What about Troy?"

"Broken leg, a nice clean fracture. He'll be sent home with a bonus. So what's your story?" Daniela asked. "Were you in the service?"

"No, ma'am. My mother was."

"How did he rescue you?"

"I'm not employed by Mad Rogan. We just happened to work together."

"I see."

"Were you rescued, ma'am?"

"Yes," she said. "I served for ten years, six of them in South America. Then I finally got out, because I was ready for civilian life. I went to work for a med-first urgent care clinic. Some urgent clinics offer good service. The one I worked for was all about money. When I got into medicine, I did it to save lives. So if I knew that a certain drug was needed, I prescribed it. If a treatment was required, I administered it. Even if I knew the patients might not be able to pay the deductible."

"The owners didn't like it?" I guessed.

"No. All doctors write off some patients who can't pay, but the owners decided I was writing off too much. They talked to me, then they threatened me. They expected me to fold, but I didn't tuck my tail between my legs and slink away. I was paid a salary based on what they thought I would make. Then insurance refused to pay a few times, some deductibles weren't met, and I ended up owing the clinic money. Normally the clinics would push those moneys out to the next quarters, but they didn't. They demanded that I cover what the insurance didn't, and when I couldn't, they went after me in court. I sold my house, emptied all of my savings, and then I declared bankruptcy. Then Mad Rogan found me, paid off my settlement, gave me a chance to practice medicine, and made my life a hell of a lot better. So if you do anything to hurt him, I will put a bullet in your brain." She smiled at me and opened the door. "Go in."

I walked through the door and heard the lock click behind me. I stood in a beautiful hotel room. Directly opposite the door, a thick, grey curtain framed a floor-to-ceiling window presenting a view of Houston. On my right, a giant bed stood against the wall. It was high enough, and the metal and plastic frame in which it rested was complicated enough, for it to serve as a hospital bed, but right now it looked more like a bed in some upscale suite, complete with snow-white blanket and rows of pillows. Further on the right, a small kitchenette hugged the wall. Across from it near the curtain stood a rectangular glass box. It took me a second to realize it was actually a shower with several nozzles, with water still beading on the inside of its walls, and that Mad Rogan stood next to it, barefoot, wearing jeans and a plain white T-shirt, and that his dark hair was damp.

Mad Rogan had just taken a shower. He had stood in that glass box, naked, with water running all over him. I'd probably missed a naked Rogan by mere minutes.

My imagination painted him nude, the golden skin damp, hard, smooth muscle rolling on his arms as he ran his hand through his hair . . . heat spread through me. I was flushing. I knew I was flushing.

We were locked in a room together. The room had a bed. Why did my heart speed up?

". . . male."

What?

Mad Rogan grimaced. "No, I didn't see his face. I saw his hand as he bent down."

He was on the phone. This wasn't good. I was observant. It was one of my professional skills, something I practiced, but also something that came naturally to me. He was standing right there with his phone to his ear, and I completely didn't see it. I just saw his eyes, and his jaw, and the strong line of his neck, and the outline of a muscular chest under the T-shirt. I saw an enormous dark bruise creeping up the left side of his neck and a dozen small cuts and bruises on his arms. But I didn't see the phone. The thought of him in the shower short-circuited whatever power of observation I had.

Okay. This had to stop. This was now actively interfering with my ability to do my job. I had to not think about him in the shower. Or being in the shower with him.

"Yes, I'm sure, Augustine," Mad Rogan said into the phone. "He didn't caress my cheek softly with his calloused fingers, but I saw a male hand."

"He wore a ring," I said.

"Wait." Mad Rogan put the phone on speaker. "What kind of a ring?"

"A thick gold ring. It looked like a school ring."

"Did you happen to notice what finger the ring was on?" Augustine said through the phone.

"Index finger."

"Are you sure?" Augustine asked.

"Yes," I said. "I thought it was odd, because school rings are usually worn on the ring finger of the right hand."

"Not if it's a Zeta Sigma Mu frat ring," Rogan said.

"What kind of fraternity is that?" I asked.

"Magic. Notable and above only," Augustine said.

"That frat ring is worn on the index finger because the ancients believed that ring fingers had a vein going through them that led straight to the heart," Mad Rogan said. "Magic is an analytical art and must be free of constraints of the heart, so you wear the ring as far away as possible from the ring finger. Which would technically mean the thumb, but thumb rings are too impractical."

"There are eight animator Houses in the country," Augustine said. "Possibly more. I don't like it. I don't like that more than one Prime is involved in this. The stakes just skyrocketed. Okay, I'll call you when I get him."

Mad Rogan hung up the phone and looked at me. "He found Mark Emmens, the great-grandson of the original Emmens. He is seventy-nine and of sound mind. Augustine is personally bringing him to MII."

"Great."

"He's hexed."

"What do you mean, hexed?"

Mad Rogan tossed the phone on the bed. "Every member of the Emmens family is placed under a powerful compulsion that prevents them from speaking about the artifact."

"You can do that?"

"Not me personally, but it can be done. It's very rare and requires months of preparation. Apparently the Emmens family considers it their sacred duty to protect the location of the artifact."

I frowned. "So how does it help us?"

"You'll have to break the hex."

"Me?"

"You."

I spread my arms. "I have no idea how to do it. You've used Acubens Exemplar on me. Can't you do something like Hammer Lock to break through the hex?"

"I'm a weak telepath. My telepathy is the by-product of my being a tactile, and besides, Acubens Exemplar took weeks to set up. It was left over from another venture I was involved in. Using it completely drained me. Of the two of us, you have much better chances."

Great.

"Rogan, I don't know how. I will try my best, but I don't know how to do it."

He sat on the bed. "You'll likely have to tap into the same place you did when you interrogated me after your grandmother nearly died during the arson."

Sure. Piece of cake.

"Nevada?"

"I can't. I'm not sure what I did or how I did it."

"Okay." Mad Rogan leaned forward. "Let's try to figure this out. When you exercise your power, do you make an effort?"

"Not really."

"What happens when your magic misfires?"

"It doesn't."

He paused. "You never had a false positive?"

"No."

He looked at me. "Are you telling me that all this time you've been tapping your passive field, and it has never misfired?"

"I don't know what that means."

His expression went blank.

Silence stretched.

I felt stupid standing there. "Rogan?"

"Hold on. I'm trying to figure out how to condense thirty years of being a Prime and learning magic theory into twenty minutes of explanation. I'm trying to put it into words you'd understand."

I shook my head.

"What?"

"I realize that I'm ignorant and it's frustrating for you, but it would be nice if you didn't imply that I was an idiot."

"You're not an idiot. I'm trying to explain how to fly a jet to someone who's never seen a plane before."

I sighed and sat in a chair. "Well, when you find the words my stupid self can understand, you let me know."

"Are you at least going to try to learn, or are you just going to sit over there and pout? It's unlike you."

"Rogan, you don't know anything about what I'm like."

He slid off the bed and crouched by me. No wince, no frown. Whatever painkillers the good doctor had given him must've been really strong. He focused on me completely, the same way he did when he asked me a question and waited for an answer. It was almost impossible to look away. If he ever fell in love—which probably wasn't possible, given that he was likely a psychopath—his would be the kind of devotion people fantasized about.

"You'll hurt your ribs," I said.

"What's the problem, Nevada?"

I wanted to lie. I had a strong, almost irresistible urge to make up some bullshit. Except there was no vital reason for me to do it. I just wanted to protect my ego and my pride, and that really wasn't good enough to justify a lie. "Have you ever written a paper last minute for school or college?"

"Sure."

"And then someone reads it and tells you it's sloppy

and you shouldn't have waited till the last minute, so you get mad at that person. But really you're mad at yourself."

"Are you mad at yourself?"

"Yes. It's my magic. There is a lot of it, apparently, and it's strong, and I never did anything with it. I got by, because it was enough. I never tested myself. I read about all of the spells and circles, but until that day with you, I'd never drawn one on the ground, and I can't even tell you why. It never occurred to me. I just thought that being a human lie detector was my limit. I don't like having my nose rubbed in it."

He nodded. "Okay. We got it out in the open. Here it is. This is your moment to be angry at your own laziness and wallow in self-pity. A moment is all you get, because any minute Adam Pierce might set Houston on fire. Take a few minutes for your pity party. Would five be enough?"

"You're an asshole."

"Yes, but I'm a very well-trained asshole. I'm offering you the use of my expertise. So suck it up, get over this bump, and let's go. Are you with me?"

You know what? No: if he ever fell in love, it wouldn't be great romantic devotion. It would be an exercise in frustration and lust, and at the end of it his significant other would strangle him.

I couldn't let Houston burn. "Yes. I'm with you."

He stood up, wincing slightly, and sat back on the bed. "Magic acts in two ways, passive and active. Let's take an aquakinetic, a water mage. A water mage always knows where the nearest source of water is. The question is how?"

"He feels it," I guessed.

"Yes. Some part of his magic scans his surroundings independently of his will. If you ask their kind to concentrate on pinpointing the water, most of them surprisingly can't actually make that effort. It happens subconsciously. That's called a passive field. They can't turn it off either. An aquakinetic in the desert will become fatigued much faster than anyone else in his party. Why?"

"Because he's constantly scanning for water and not finding any?"

Mad Rogan nodded. "It's similar to a cell phone. If you take it to an area where there are no towers, it will continuously roam, looking for a signal and draining its battery. Passive field. If the aquakinetic decides to manipulate water by drawing moisture from the air or a water source, that manipulation will require an active effort on his part. That's called an active vector. If we stick to the cell phone, passive field is the phone looking for a signal. Active vector is you actually making a call."

"So when I can tell that people are lying, it happens because they're in my passive field." That meant that when I'd locked him down to ask if he was responsible for arson, it had been the first time I'd actually actively used my power. Ugh. No, wait. I also resisted his spell when he kidnapped me. Maybe I could draw on that.

"Yes." Mad Rogan rose. "I'm forty-five years old."

My magic clicked. "Lie."

"Turn around," he said.

I turned around, facing away from him.

"My mother hated me."

Click. "Lie."

I turned around. He backed away into the kitchenette area.

"Are you testing range?" I asked.

"Yes."

"I can save you the trouble. If I can see you and/or if you're close enough for me to hear you, it works. Phone calls, TV broadcasts, and Skype sessions don't, so there has to be some physical proximity. It works better if I can see you and hear you at the same time. Direct eye contact works best."

He approached me and stopped about a foot away, looking directly into my eyes. "Ask a question and try to compel me to answer."

I strained, focusing on him. Something simple that required yes or no. On some neutral topic. "Have you ever been married?" Oh yes. This was totally neutral.

Nothing.

We waited another ten seconds.

"Let's try something else." Mad Rogan rummaged through the kitchenette's drawer and came up with a piece of chalk. He offered it to me. "Draw an amplification circle."

I took the chalk from him, walked to the wide, clear part of the room, crouched, and began to draw the circle on the floor.

"Wait." He walked over to me and knelt behind me. "This is one of those cases when size doesn't matter."

Ha-ha.

"A small circle that's perfectly drawn will have more power than a large, sloppy mess. Here, let me show you."

He covered my hand with his.

I felt the heat of his hand, the texture of his fingers, and excitement shot through me, an apprehensive thrill, part hope, part alarm. His other arm braced me.

Oh my God. Where did all of the air go?

"Extend your arm. Don't lock your elbow." His hand slid up my arm to my elbow, setting off a chain reaction that rolled all the way up my arms into my back in a splash of shivering heat. My mind desperately tried to reassert control, while my body moaned in my head. *Touch me. Again. Touch me more.*

"Place the chalk down." He was directly behind me, talking into my ear.

The world shrank. I was suddenly hyperaware of every inch of space between us. The air became charged, as if he'd been a thunderstorm. Anticipation grasped me. My ears tuned out everything except his voice. His hand caressed my arm. His knee brushed against my thigh, and I almost jumped.

"It's like a compass. Your body is the frame, and your arm with the chalk is a pencil."

The timbre of his voice had changed. He was breathing deeper. His hold on my arm widened, shifting. "Hold it firmly. Now, turn."

I pivoted on my feet, drawing a near perfect arch on the floor.

"Good."

My hand bumped into his leg. I let go of the chalk and looked up. We were face-to-face.

His eyes, normally cold and merciless or sardonically amused, were a hot blue, drowning with an intense male need. They lured me in, promised me things that made my head spin, and I didn't care if those things were lies.

He moved forward, fast, his arms catching me, and he sealed my mouth with his. His tongue thrust between my open lips, caressing, making me open wider for him, and seducing me into tasting him. A phantom fire spilled over the back of my neck, sliding over my throat like warm amber honey, slipping deep into my flesh, into my veins, and my skin all but sizzled with lust in its heated wake. The liquid warmth rolled down slowly, dripping into the valley between my breasts, then sliding along their tops to the sides, then under the breasts. My nipples tightened in anticipation. Suddenly the fire sped up, cupping my breasts with velvet pressure. It squeezed gently, lathing my breasts, and finally seared my nipples with tiny explosions of heat. My body collapsed under the onslaught of pleasure. I gasped into Rogan's mouth.

His hand was in my hair, cupping the back of my head. His other hand lifted me to him, hard across my back, effortlessly supporting my weight. His chest flattened my nipples. The time at the mall was just a tiny taste of his magic. This? This was heaven, or maybe hell, I didn't know and I didn't care. I wanted more.

The insanity-inducing liquid heat pooled under my breasts, sliding down my body, slowly, ever so slowly, tracing the sensitive nerves in my back and igniting them one by one until my whole body hummed with near ecstasy . . . he drank me in, like nothing else mattered, and I let him.

The heat crept down, lower and lower, winding in ribbons of pleasure around me. Pressure built between my legs, aching need and shuddering anticipation. The heat pulsed inside me, building and building.

He kept kissing me, the onslaught of his tongue relentless.

Oh my God. I couldn't stand it. I couldn't . . .

He thrust into my mouth. The velvet warmth drenched me. Pleasure was a river and I drowned in it, overwhelmed by the throbbing rush of ecstasy and delirium. My body contracted, so hard it almost hurt and I cried out, my hips arching up on their own.

The pressure between my legs broke into a cascade of aftershocks. I slumped against him, into his arms, and floated in a haze of bliss.

He held me to him and kissed me, the brush of his lips on mine almost tender.

Someone banged on the door. "Sir? Sir?" Daniela.

The reality slammed into me like a train. I made out with Mad Rogan and I came. I had a mind-numbing, life-altering orgasm that I would remember until the day I died, and he didn't even take my clothes off. Oh no. No, no, no. I covered my face with my hands.

"What?" Mad Rogan snarled.

"You're not answering your phone, sir. I have Augustine Montgomery on the line."

"I'll call him back," Mad Rogan said.

"He says it's urgent."

"I'll call him back," Mad Rogan repeated, steel in his voice.

I heard retreating steps. His arms were still around me.

"Nevada?" he asked. "You okay?"

I'd shot my professional integrity in the face. I'd made a complete fool of myself. I'd made out with *Mad* Rogan. But worst of all, he'd given me a tiny taste of what it would be like to be with him. It was magic. It would be a drug that would be addicting from the first moment, and like a drug, it would consume me and leave me hollow. And he would leave me. I couldn't have him forever. He was a Prime, he looked after his own interests first, and the moment I became boring or tiresome, he would walk away. Just thinking about it hurt.

"Nevada?" he repeated.

Get a grip. I took my hands off my face, pushed away from him, reached for the bed, and handed him his cell phone.

He took the phone from my hand and tossed it over his shoulder with a dismissive flick of his wrist. The cell phone thudded into a wall and fell on the carpet. He reached for me.

"No," I told him.

"Why the hell not?"

"It's unprofessional and dangerous. This didn't happen."

"It happened."

"No."

"It happened. I was there. And you liked it."

"No."

"You melted." A male, self-satisfied smile touched his lips. "Like spring snow."

"I don't know what you're talking about."

We stared at each other.

"Fine," he said. "You had no idea it could be this good. Nobody in your past was ever that good and you know that nobody in your future will ever be this good. You've had a taste and you want more. You want sex. Dirty, naked hot sex. It's floating through your head as we speak. You think you can imagine what it would be like. Trust me, you have no idea. I haven't even started. So run from it, think it over, pretend it didn't happen, it doesn't matter. I'll allow it for now. The more you fight, the more irresistible it will become, until one day I'll motion with my hand and you'll come running."

My fingers closed about something hard. I tossed it at his face. The chalk hit him square in the forehead. He blinked.

I got to my feet and marched into the bathroom to compose myself.

Chapter 15

Either Mad Rogan's cell phone was shatterproof, or he had an identical supply of them, because when I came out of the bathroom, he was holding one to his ear, listening. He was also wearing shoes. We were leaving.

Mad Rogan beckoned to me and headed for the door. I followed, and we walked out of the room, down the hallway. Rogan moved fast, and I almost had to jog to keep up with him.

"Okay," Mad Rogan said. "I need you to be there in ten. Can you do it?"

He hung up and sped up. "Augustine called. A police cruiser sighted Pierce driving into the city on South Freeway. They radioed it in three minutes ago."

"Did he explode the cruiser into a fireball and then laugh dramatically?" I broke into a run.

"He ignored them, and then an armored vehicle following him rammed the cruiser and rolled it off the road."

We burst out of the doors into the light.

Adam wasn't taking the opportunity to make a statement. He was heading into the city on South Freeway, which would put him straight into downtown, and he was conserving his energy. He was about to hit Houston like a meteor. This had just turned into a race.

"Keys." Rogan held out his hand.

I put them into his palm. He clicked the locks on the Audi and we got in.

"He doesn't have the third piece." Rogan reversed and stepped on the gas, and the Audi shot out of the parking lot like a bullet. "He made a huge production out of getting the first and the second, so he'll make a production out of getting the third one. He knows where it is. We don't."

The radio came on. "This is an Emergency Broadcast. The Secretary of Homeland Security received credible evidence of a possible terrorist attack on the city of Houston. The risk of terrorist attack has been raised from elevated to imminent. Evacuate the downtown area. I repeat, evacuate the downtown area. If you're unable to exit via vehicle, seek shelter in the tunnel system. The main entrances are . . ."

Mad Rogan turned it off. We wove in and out of traffic at a breakneck speed. A flood of cars clogged the street going in the opposite direction. Everyone in our lane was either turning onto side streets or trying to turn. People fled out of downtown.

"Mark Emmens has one daughter," Mad Rogan said. "His wife and sister are deceased, and so is the sister's husband. The daughter and her husband are accounted for. According to Augustine, nothing unusual has taken place in their life, but Mark's grandson Jesse Emmens disappeared from his dorm room at Edinburgh three months ago."

"His grandson's last name is Emmens? Was there a son, too?"

"No, Mark's son-in-law took the Emmens name. The Emmens family is respected and their name has more recognition. Jesse Emmens was gone for forty-eight hours, then he was dumped in front of the dorm unharmed, but with no memory of what had transpired while he was missing. The block on him was so strong that it took him twenty-four hours before he could remember his own name."

"Did Jesse know the location of the artifacts?"

Mad Rogan nodded. "He was hexed as well. Someone had broken him, so it can be done."

And it would be up to me to do it. I still had no idea how.

"You can do it," Rogan said. "This could've gone a lot differently if you had received proper instruction."

"If I had received proper instruction, people like Augustine would force me to become their own personal lie detector." And now, no matter if I succeeded or failed, it would happen anyway. Assuming MII survived whatever Adam was about to unleash.

"Can Augustine compel you to do it under the terms of your contract?"

"Yes."

"I can buy your contract."

"No, you can't. Any sale of our mortgage requires my consent, and I won't consent to it."

He grinned. "You don't want to work under me?"

"I'm not even going to dignify that with an answer."

"Do you have a copy of the contract?"

"I have it on my phone."

"Read me the provision that forces you to take MII's cases."

Ten minutes later we pulled into the parking lot in front of the blue glass shark fin of the MII building. A flood of cars rolled out in the opposite direction. People hurried out of the building, their faces pinched with worry. Augustine was evacuating MII.

Augustine's receptionist met us in the lobby. Her makeup was still impeccable, her clothes still fit her perfectly, but her hair was now malachite green. "Follow me, please."

She hurried to the elevator at a near run. We followed her. She pushed the button for the fifteenth floor. "We were able to capture an image of Adam Pierce coming into the city via street-level cameras before the entire network went off line. He was riding his motorcycle, which was preceded and followed by two black BMW X6 SUVs."

The elevator chimed, signaling a stop. The doors opened and the receptionist rushed down the hall. "The recordings indicate that street-level observers did not see either Pierce or the SUVs. The police forces have set up blockades on every major roadway into downtown."

Someone was cloaking Adam Pierce. Another powerful magic user. This was getting more and more complicated by the minute. Whoever these people were, they were organized and powerful, and they planned in advance. None of it boded well for Houston.

What did they want? Why? Why was this even happening? It made no sense.

The receptionist stopped before a door and held it open for us. We walked into a wide room. The floor was black, not glossy, but not exactly rough. The same paint covered the walls. Blackout shutters blocked the windows. The only light came from six glass tubes, positioned vertically like columns, from ceiling to floor, three on one side of the room and three on the other. Each tube was about a foot in diameter and filled with clear liquid. Hundreds of bubbles floated up through the water, their ascent slow and hypnotic, backlit by purple lights embedded inside the tubes, making the entire arrangement glow with gentle lavender light.

In the wide space between the tubes stood a chair. An old man sat in it, holding a carved wooden cane in his left hand. He wore a suit, and his hair was white and wispy, like cotton. Age marked his face with deep wrinkles, but his hazel eyes looked at me with sharp, alert intelligence. Augustine stood next to the man. At the far end of the room, five people sat at computer stations below a big flat-screen TV. The light from their displays illuminated a little of the wall behind them, highlighting swirls of chalk dust. Now the odd color of the floor and the walls made sense. This was a spell room, painted entirely with chalkboard paint.

"Mr. Emmens," Augustine said, "allow me to introduce Connor Rogan and his associate."

"A pleasure," Mr. Emmens said.

"I need an amplification circle drawn," Mad Rogan said, "with two focal points at forty-five and one hundred and thirty-five degrees."

A woman jumped up from one of the terminals, ran over, and began drawing on the floor.

"Excuse me." Augustine smiled at Mr. Emmens. "I need to speak to my colleague."

He drew Mad Rogan aside. I followed them, because I didn't know what else to do.

"This isn't going to help and you know it," Augustine murmured. "He was hexed by Cesare Costa at birth. You're not strong enough to break through. This will take a Breaker Prime. There are two of them in the country, and they're both on the West Coast. We have minutes."

"Ms. Baylor would like to renegotiate her contract."

Augustine pivoted to me. "Now?"

"Now," Rogan said. "She would like one word added to provision seven. It should read MII may NOT compel Baylor Investigative Agency to assist, etc."

"Why would I do this? This is against my best interest." Augustine frowned. "What's going on here?"

"You will do this because the wind is blowing south," Mad Rogan said. "No matter where in downtown Adam starts his party, this building will be hit by his fire, and you know it. Your House will lose millions. One word, Augustine. Consider the stakes."

Augustine locked his jaw.

"Don't be petty," Mad Rogan said.

"Fine." Augustine swiped a tablet from the nearest desk. His long fingers danced on it. He showed me the tablet. It read, "Addendum One," listed the paragraph, and showed the correction. Augustine pressed his thumb to the screen, signed it, and held the tablet out. "Fingerprint."

I added mine to his. The screen flashed.

"Done," Augustine said.

"You're on," Mad Rogan told me.

I took a deep breath. Augustine watched me like a hawk.

Mad Rogan walked me to the circle. "Take your shoes off," he murmured.

I took off my tennis shoes and slid the socks off. He held my hand and helped me step into the circle.

"Relax," Mad Rogan said. "Let yourself interact with it."

I stood in the circle. It felt strange, as if I'd somehow been balancing on the surface of elastic liquid. I had the odd feeling that if I jumped, it would bounce me up like a trampoline. Trouble was, I had no idea how to jump.

Mr. Emmens nodded to me. "Before we get started,

I've been warned that answering a direct question about the location of the object may kill me. I want to tell you where it is, but if you force me to disclose the exact location, I will die before I can help you and you will never find it in time. I don't mind giving up my life for the city. It is the duty of my family. I ask you only not to waste my life. I don't want to die answering the wrong question."

"I understand." My magic filled the circle like a dense vapor. The surface of the "liquid" was placid under me. Somehow the two had to interact.

"We're wasting time," Augustine said.

"Do you feel the circle?" Mad Rogan asked, walking behind me.

"Yes."

Slowly, he circled the chalk line and stopped on the left of me. "Do you feel your magic filling it?"

"Yes."

"Do you know what Pierce plans to do?"

"He wants to burn the city down." Where was he going with this?

"The artifact made Emmens into a Prime." Mad Rogan's voice was cold. "It will make Adam Pierce a god of fire. He can melt steel now. It melts at 2,750 degrees Fahrenheit. The artifact will double that. A house fire never burns higher than 1,200 degrees Fahrenheit. Adam Pierce will burn at five times that, maybe hotter. At 2,192 degrees, concrete will lose its structural integrity and turn into calcium oxide, a white powder. At 2,750 degrees, stainless steel within the buildings will melt. The downtown will be a nightmare of molten metal, crumbling concrete, flames, and noxious, poisonous gasses. It will become hell on earth. Thousands of people will die."

I swallowed. Anxiety rose inside me.

"Pierce just crossed Dreyfus Street," one of the people at the terminal announced. "The cameras have gone out. We lost him again."

He was staying off the main roads to avoid Lenora's roadblocks. Even with traffic, it would take him only twenty minutes to get downtown.

"The problem with 'thousands' of people," Mad Rogan said, "is that it's not personal."

He took Augustine's tablet and tapped it. The big flat-screen on the wall flared into life. A silver van was parked in front of an elaborate, ultramodern building—2 Houston Center, corner of MacKinnley and Fanin streets. It was a really distinctive building, all black glass, right in the middle of downtown.

Mad Rogan handed the tablet back to Augustine and raised his phone. "Bernard?"

"Yes?" my cousin's voice answered through the phone.

"I need you to step out of the car and face the building."

No. My body went ice cold.

The passenger door of the van opened. Bern exited the van and turned to the building. The camera zoomed up on his face.

Everything else disappeared. All I saw were Bern's serious blue eyes, wide open on the screen.

Adam was less than twenty minutes away. Bern would die. And Mad Rogan knew it. He knew it, and he'd parked him there.

I heard my own voice. "Get out of there. Get out of there!"

"He can't hear you." Mad Rogan put away the phone.

"You bastard!"

My magic punched into the circle, smashing it. A cloud of chalk dust shot up from the circle's boundary.

Augustine dropped his tablet. The circle bounced back, and power flooded me.

"There it is," Mad Rogan murmured. "It's not fear or anger. It's the protective impulse."

"He's nineteen years old!" My magic raged and my voice matched it.

"Then you better do something to save him."

My magic snapped to him.

"Not me." Rogan pointed at Mr. Emmens. "Him."

I pivoted. My magic grasped the old man into its vise. He paled. The circle fed me more power. I stared into his eyes. "Is your name Mark Emmens?"

"Yes."

True.

My magic locked on him. He was enclosed in a barrier, like a nut in a shell. It was old, thick, and strong. I felt his life, shivering inside, both protected and bound by the shell. The two were connected. If I broke the barrier, the light of his life would perish with it.

"Do you know where the third piece of amulet is hidden?"

He tried to resist. I punched the circle with my magic. Power bounced into me. I grasped the invisible barrier with my magic and strained to wrench it apart. I didn't need much. Just a gap. A small opening.

The shell resisted.

I didn't have time for this. Bern would die.

I pulled the power from the circle. It kept coming and coming, as if I pulled on a rope, expecting only a foot or two, but it kept going, and now I was pulling it with both hands as fast as I could. The influx of power slowed. I punched the circle again and the flow sped up. I focused it all on the shell.

It shuddered.

More power.

I felt light-headed.

Another tremor.

The shell cracked. In my mind, I saw light spilling from inside it. I thrust my magic into it like a wedge and kept it open.

"Yes," Mr. Emmens said.

He had answered my question. I made my mouth move. "Is the third piece in your possession?"

"No."

"Is it hidden on the property you own?"

"No."

"She's going to die," Augustine warned. "She's pulling too much power."

"She's fine," Mad Rogan said.

It hurt now. It hurt as if something had stabbed me in the stomach and I was trying to pull the knife out inch by inch. But my magic wedge held.

Think, think, think . . .

Bern's face looked at me from the camera. I had to save him. He was just a boy. He had his whole life ahead of him.

Adam Pierce was going downtown. The piece had to be here. In the center of the city. It wouldn't be in a bank or in a building, because the Emmens family wouldn't want to repeat themselves.

"Is it on the property you used to own?"

"No."

The pain was clawing at me now, hot and sharp.

"Is it on the property your relative owns?"

"No."

"Is it on a property your relative used to own?"

"Yes."

That *yes* nearly rocked me.

"Search the records," Augustine barked.

The five people at the computer terminals typed furiously.

"Was that property sold?"

"No."

If his relative no longer owned it but it hadn't been sold, what the heck could've happened to it?

The world swayed. I was about to pass out. I clung onto consciousness, desperately struggling to stay upright.

"Frederick Rome," one of the computer techs reported. "His daughter's ex-husband, from her first marriage, used to own a building on Caroline Street. It was lost in a divorce settlement and awarded to his second ex-wife."

Augustine spun to me. "Ask if it was lost in a legal action."

"Was the property lost as a result of a legal action or awarded as a settlement?"

"No."

Tiny red circles swam in my eyes. My magic was ebbing. I was barely holding on. I forced my brain to work through the haze of pain and fatigue. It was downtown. There was nothing downtown but big businesses owned by Houses, government buildings, and . . .

Government buildings.

"Is it on municipal land?"

"Yes." Mr. Emmens came to life.

"Was the property donated to the city?"

"Yes." Mr. Emmens nodded.

The techs typed so fast that the clicking of their keys blended into a hum.

"Patricia Bridges," the middle technician called. "Married to William Bridges, maiden name Emmens."

Mr. Emmens smiled.

"William and Patricia Bridges jointly donated a parcel of land to the city of Houston, provided that the land may never be sold or built upon but used instead as a place for the free people of Texas to gather as they see fit."

The Bridge Park. Directly across from the justice center. My magic was quaking under pressure. I had just enough time left for one last question.

"Is it in a monument that includes a horse?"

"Yes," Mr. Emmens said.

The shell snapped closed, crushing my magic.

Mad Rogan grabbed me and pulled me out of the circle. The pressure and pain vanished. I felt light-headed again.

His gaze searched my eyes. "Speak to me."

"I hate you."

"Okay." Mad Rogan let go of me. "You're fine."

He handed me the phone. I grabbed it. "Bernard, get out of there! You don't understand, Pierce is about to burn down downtown!"

"I know. I volunteered," he said. "Did you do it?"

Oh you idiot. "Yes! Get out of there. Don't bother with the van, go down into the tunnels."

On the screen my cousin ran down the street.

I turned to Rogan. "Don't ever ask my family to volunteer for anything."

"Don't you want to know what it is?" Mr. Emmens asked.

We gaped at him.

"The hex covers what it does and where it is, but not what it is," he explained. "It's a forty carat green flawless diamond. The color is the result of natural irradiation."

"I have to go," Rogan told me.

"I'm coming with you." I would see this to the end.

I would get through this and punch Adam Pierce in the face while Rogan dug the last piece of the artifact out of that horse.

"Fine. Keep up." He turned and ran. I spun to Augustine. "I need handcuffs."

One of the computer techs opened a drawer and tossed a pair to me, together with keys.

"Thanks!" I caught them and chased Rogan down the hallway.

"Stop," Augustine yelled.

I turned.

"You're a drained battery. You have no magic left. What could you possibly do to Pierce?"

"She can shoot him in the face." Rogan mashed the elevator arrow.

"If Rogan fails to stop him, you'll die," Augustine called out.

The doors swung open.

"If he fails, we're all dead anyway," I told him and ducked into the elevator with Mad Rogan.

Two lanes of traffic filled Caroline Street. The cars in both lanes faced south, away from downtown. Nothing moved. The cars were abandoned. Their owners must've gone into the tunnels.

Mad Rogan took the corner too sharp. I grabbed onto the door handle to steady myself. The Audi jumped the curb and landed on the sidewalk. The side of the vehicle scraped against the building. Mad Rogan stepped on the gas. We barreled down the sidewalk, the Audi screeching in protest as the stone scraped the driver's side. Ahead a lamppost loomed. I braced myself. The post snapped off and flew aside.

"Try not to kill us," I squeezed through my teeth.

"Don't worry. Wouldn't want to disappoint Adam."

Before us Congress Avenue was completely clogged with cars. The green trees of the Bridge Park shivered in the breeze just beyond the traffic.

The Audi slid to a screeching stop. I jumped out, my Baby Desert Eagle in my hand, and ran ahead, between the cars. The park occupied a single city block. I saw the bronze statue of the *Riding Cowboy* through the trees. The horse's head was gone, melted into a puddle of cooling metal goo. Next to the horse stood Adam Pierce. The third eye of Shiva sat on his forehead: three rows of uncut diamonds crossed by a vertical eye shape studded with bloodred rubies. In the middle of the eye shape, where the iris would be, an enormous pale green diamond shone in the sun, like a drop of pure light somehow captured and faceted and set among the lesser stones.

I sighted Adam Pierce, aimed for the center mass, and fired. The bullets punched the space near Adam and fell harmlessly to the grass. I kept firing, walking straight at him. My gun spat the bullets, the sound too loud in my ears.

Boom. Boom. Boom.

Click.

I was out.

I lowered the gun. We stood face-to-face, Adam and I. Directly around him, the grass lay flat. He was in a magic circle, not one drawn with chalk but one made by the third eye of Shiva.

"Null space," Adam said, his voice quiet. "You're too late."

"Why? Why, Adam? Thousands of people will die. Don't you care? Don't you care even a little bit?"

"Look around you," he said. "You see all this? It looks good, but once you look deeper, you'll see the rot. All of it is rotten to the core."

"What are you talking about?"

"The establishment," he said. "Their so-called justice system. Justice. What a joke. It's not justice; it's oppression. It's a system designed to shackle those who can to those who can't. The rot is everywhere. It's in the politicians, in the businessmen, and in the courts. There is no repairing it. There is only one way to get rid of it. I am going to purify the downtown."

"There are people down in the tunnels, normal ordinary people, Adam. They have nothing to do with your rebellion."

"They have everything to do with it." He faced me, his eyes completely lucid. "They are dragging us down. They prevent us from taking what is rightfully ours. You see, we bought into this entire bullshit utilitarianism. We had it pounded into us that good is whatever benefits the majority. Well, I don't give a fuck about the majority. Why should I care about their laws and their needs? If I have the power to obtain and to keep the object of my desire, then I should be able to do so."

"And if someone stronger takes it from you?"

He spread his arms. "So be it. Now you're getting the picture. I'm illuminating the rot. I'm a freedom fighter. I'm freeing us. I'm severing the chains."

"The way you tried to free me from my family?"

He nodded. "I thought you'd understand, but you weren't ready. You either have the power or you don't, Snow. Power is action, and today I choose to act. I will turn this place to ash, like a rotten forest, and watch the new growth stretch to the sun. I will be remembered."

"So you want this to be your legacy? You want to be the one who burned alive thousands of people? Families? Children? Listen to yourself. You can't be this monster."

He raised his finger to his lips. "Shhh. Save your breath. The old world is about to end, and you have a front-row seat."

We'd failed. We'd failed so miserably. Everything was over. There was nothing we could do now.

"I liked you, Snow," he said. "Sorry you won't get to see it. No hard feelings?"

There was no reasoning with him.

"Hello, *Mad* Rogan." Adam stretched *Mad* into a three-syllable word. "We meet at last. How does it feel to come up second best?"

"Nevada," Mad Rogan said. "Come here."

"I almost feel sorry for you, man." Adam grinned. "You had a chance to be invited to the party, but your own cousin made you into a patsy instead. God, that's got to suck."

Mad Rogan took me by the hand and pulled me to him, leading me away from Adam.

We were going to die. Houston would burn. It was over.

"Nothing to say, oh Great One? Come on, Scourge of Mexico!" Adam called. "Look at me when I'm talking to you. I'm about to incinerate your ass."

Rogan glanced at him. "It's your party. You're wearing the tiara. Try to be a gracious host."

Adam's face flushed.

"Fuck you!" He stabbed his index finger in our direction. "Fuck you, man. Fuck both of you."

"Kids these days." Mad Rogan shook his head. "No manners."

Rogan halted in the middle of the lawn. I stopped with

him. Everything seemed so bright. The trees were such a vivid emerald green, the sky so blue. I could see every blade of grass around us.

"I don't want to die," I whispered. I realized I was crying. I was supposed to be stoic or strong, but all I could think about was how much I loved being alive. I'd barely gotten to do anything with my life. I would never get to see my sisters grow up. I would never fall in love and have a family. I wouldn't even get to say the proper good-bye. I'd just pecked my mom on the cheek. I . . .

"Stay close to me," Mad Rogan said. "You'll feel the boundary around us. No matter what happens, do not cross. Do you understand, Nevada? You can't enter null space, but you can exit it, and if you try to do it while I'm active, it will shred you into a bloody mist."

I swallowed.

"Once I begin, I may not be able to stop," Mad Rogan said. "I won't know where you are. I won't hear you. I won't see you. Do not leave the circle. No matter what happens, you'll be safe here. Do you understand?"

"Yes."

He pulled me to him, my back against his chest, and he locked his arms on me. Magic pulsed out of him. Wind stirred the grass around us.

"Won't work," Adam called out. "Whatever you're doing, it won't work. I'll burn through it."

"Let's dance," Mad Rogan said. His voice sounded strange, deep and distant.

Nothing happened. His arms were still around me. He didn't move.

Seconds dripped by, slowly, so slowly.

Across from us, faint orange light rose from Adam's circle. It flared up, like phantom flame, and died down, then flared up again and faded once more. Adam Pierce opened his mouth. His voice was no longer his own. It was a voice of something ancient and terrible, a roar of a volcano come to life. "I AM FIRE. BURN FOR ME."

The wind died. It was there one second, and now it was gone. I could still see it rustling the trees and the grass, but I felt nothing. A strange calm came over me, as if an invisible wall cut us off from the world. I felt it about two feet in front of me, curving into a circle about seven feet wide. It was so peaceful here. So quiet.

Mad Rogan's hold loosened. His arms slid up my shoulders. I turned. His eyes turned unnatural turquoise blue. His face looked serene.

"Rogan?"

He was looking into the distance. He didn't see me.

His feet left the ground. His body floated a foot up in the air. His arms opened, loose by his sides. The grass outside the circle bent away from it, as if a blast wave ran across it.

In his circle, Adam Pierce's fire shot up, spinning around him, solid and four feet high now. He was looking straight at me, and his eyes were pure fire. Hair rose on the back of my neck.

The circle around me pulsed. I didn't hear it, but I felt it. It reverberated through me, echoing in my bones, not painful, but not pleasant either. The trees around us collapsed, severed at the root. The Riding Cowboy slid sideways and crashed down.

The circle pulsed again. The Harris County Criminal Justice Center quaked. To the right, the huge tower of the Harris County civil courthouse shuddered.

What was Rogan doing?

The circle pulsed again, like the beating of a titan's heart.

The Justice Center slid forward and broke apart. For a fraction of a second, pieces of it hung in the air, as if deciding whether they should obey the pull of gravity. Hundreds of glass shards hovered, catching the sun. Thousands of chunks of stone floated, motionless. Between them, the inner guts of the building showed, fractured, all of the three hundred and twenty-five feet of its height torn and left on display. It was as if the entire enormous structure had turned to glass and some deity had smashed it with its hammer.

The massive building imploded. Tons of stone, glass, wood, and steel crashed to the ground. It made no sound as it fell. My brain refused to accept that it made no sound. I kept straining to hear it, but it didn't come.

To the right, the Civil Courthouse swayed and shattered. Two dust clouds boiled forth, heading straight for us, boulders of broken stone flying among the dust. I crouched, hands over my head.

The pain never came. I raised my head.

Chunks of stone littered the ground around us. None had landed in the circle. Above me, Mad Rogan levitated. His face glowed from within, the brilliant turquoise of his eyes bright, like stars. He looked like an angel.

I glanced at Adam. The fire had engulfed him, turning into a pillar. It climbed higher and higher, spinning, ten; no, eleven; no, twelve feet high.

The circle around me pulsed again. The force minced the rubble into dust, pushing it back, sweeping it against itself. Behind the park, Harris County Family Law Center disintegrated. Across Congress Avenue, the juvenile justice center fell apart, spitting out a car-sized boulder. It hurtled through the air. Oh my God.

Don't leave the circle.

I clenched my hands into fists.

The boulder smashed against the circle and bounced off.

The circle pulsed again and again, each wave pushing the rubble out and up, crushing it into powder, again and again.

Rogan was building a wall. If he could contain the fire, it wouldn't spread.

The pillar of fire was fifty feet tall and climbing.

The pulse from Mad Rogan toppled the next circle of buildings. Their remains joined the wall.

The pillar of fire shot up another twenty-five feet.

The wall gained another ten.

They kept racing, growing taller, wall, pillar, wall, pillar.

The pillar had to be over a hundred feet high. I couldn't tell if the wall was higher.

The pillar of flames flashed with white. A ring of fire exploded outward, racing toward me. The fallen trees vanished, instantly turned to ash.

I braced myself and held my breath.

The fire splashed against the circle and swallowed it. I was alive. The air around me wasn't any warmer. I couldn't even smell the smoke. The air tasted fresh.

The fire rolled toward the wall. Please be tall enough. Please be tall enough.

The flames splashed against the barrier and came up thirty feet short.

I held my breath. It could still burn through.

All around me an inferno raged, and within its depths Adam Pierce stood, glowing with golden light, wrapped in flame, the stolen artifact on his head blazing like an angry sun.

The street turned black and glossy. The pavement had

melted into tar. The *Riding Cowboy* had melted too, its metal slipping into the slowly moving river of asphalt. The grass under my feet remained intact.

The circle kept pulsing, compacting the wall.

The fire battered against the barrier. The outer layer of concrete chunks turned to white powder.

Please hold. Please.

Minutes passed, sliding by. I sat. I couldn't stand anymore. My heart was tired of beating too fast. My whole body shook from anxiety. I felt punched all over.

The wall began to glow with eerie light. The concrete had turned into calcium oxide, which was now melting and producing the same kind of light that had illuminated the stage productions before the electricity took hold.

The fire raged and raged, eating at the wall.

All those people in the tunnels. If the wall broke and the fire ravaged downtown, they would suffocate from the smoke. If they didn't cook alive first.

The wall to the left stopped glowing. I peered at it. The fire still burned, but the concrete and stone of the wall no longer lit up.

My mind struggled with that fact. I was too shell-shocked to process it. Finally, pieces came together in my head. The wall stopped glowing, which meant there had to be a space between it and the magic fire. Adam had grown the pillar of fire as wide as he could. Rogan could hold him. The blaze was contained.

Relief washed over me. A sob broke free, then another. I realized I was crying.

Bern wouldn't die in the tunnels. The city wouldn't di—

Another pulse rolled through me. The circle was still pulsing. The buildings beyond the wall were quaking. Oh no. Rogan was still going. If Adam didn't burn downtown, Rogan would level it.

I jumped to my feet.

Rogan was three feet off the ground now, his face glowing, floating so high that he seemed inhuman and unreachable.

If I disrupted what Rogan was doing, the circle might collapse. We would both be incinerated. I would die. I would kill Rogan. The thought squirmed through me in a cold rush. I didn't want him to die.

If I didn't find a way to disrupt him, the entire downtown would collapse onto the tunnels. Instead of being burned alive, all those people would be buried alive.

Our lives for Bern's. For the countless lives of the people inside the tunnels, for the lives of children trusting in their parents, for the lives of those who loved each other, for the lives of those who'd done nothing to deserve to die.

It wasn't even a choice.

"Rogan!"

He didn't answer.

"Rogan!!!" I grabbed his feet. I couldn't move him an inch. He was held completely immobile.

I pounded his legs with my fists. "Rogan, wake up! Wake up!"

No response.

I had to get to him. If only I could get to his face. I gathered what little magic I had left.

The circle pulsed again. As that pulse reverberated through me, I pushed against it the same way I had pushed against the amplification circle, sinking everything I had into that push. Something snapped inside me. My feet left the ground and I floated up and locked my arms around

Rogan. It wouldn't last, my instinct told me. I had seconds before my magic ran out and gravity would drag me down, and I had no power left to do it again. This was my one and only shot. I had to wake him up.

His expression was so serene, his eyes wide, his mouth slightly open. He wasn't here with me. He wasn't even on this planet.

I took a deep breath, closed my eyes, and kissed him. All of my wants, all of my secrets, and all of the times I'd watched him and thought about him and imagined us together, all of my gratitude for saving my grandmother and for protecting Houston and its people, all of my frustration and anger for putting my cousin into harm's way and for having no regard for human life, I poured all of it into that kiss. It was made of carnations and tears, stolen glances and desperate, burning need. I kissed him like I loved him. I kissed him like it was the only kiss that had ever mattered.

His mouth opened wider beneath mine. His arms closed around me. He kissed me back. There was no magic this time. No phantom fire, no velvet pressure. Just a man, who tasted like the glory of heaven and the sin of hell rolled into one.

My feet touched the ground and I opened my eyes. He was looking at me. His irises were still turquoise. His skin still glowed. But he was here now, with me. The circle was still up, and rivers of tar and fire flowed past us while Adam burned in his own hate.

"You have to stop," I whispered. "You've won, but you're wrecking the city."

"Kiss me again and I will," he said.

An hour later, Adam finally stopped and fell to the ground. Rogan kept the circle up. Everything was too hot.

I sat with him in the circle and watched the asphalt solidify slowly. At some point I dozed off, slumped against Mad Rogan.

When I woke up, Rogan's eyes and skin had stopped glowing. A helicopter had flown over us twice. Then a crack appeared in the wall. We couldn't hear it, but we saw it happen. A torrent of water gushed in, instantly evaporating when it touched ground scorched by Adam. But the water kept coming. The aquakinetics must've tapped Buffalo Bayou for the water supply.

The world turned to steam. It took another hour before the water began to stay, and another hour before we decided we probably wouldn't boil alive. Rogan let go of the power that connected him to the circle. The water flooded in, reaching my ankles. It was warm, at least a hundred degrees, but it didn't burn me. We waded toward Adam Pierce. He lay on his back. His circle must've collapsed at some point, because water lapped at his hair and bare chest. He looked no worse for wear. The artifact was still on his head.

Mad Rogan slipped it off and passed it to me. "Hold this for a second." He leaned over Adam's prone body and shook him by his shoulder. "Hey, buddy."

Adam's eyes opened. "Hey," he said, his voice hoarse.

"Sit up." Rogan helped him up, a smile on his lips. "You okay? Everything working as intended?"

Adam stared at him, confused. "Sure."

"You know who you are?"

"Adam Pierce."

"You know what happened here?"

"Yeah." Adam got to his feet. "I burned it down."

"And you're not hurt? Nothing's broken?"

"No."

"Oh good." Mad Rogan sank a vicious punch into Adam's jaw. Adam fell to his knees, his mouth bloody. "How about now, Adam? Anything hurt now?"

Adam surged from his feet and swung at Rogan. His fist whistled by Rogan's face. Mad Rogan hammered a punch into Adam's gut with his left hand, while his right landed a hook to Adam's face. Adam went down.

"Have some more." Rogan punched him again, hard, his fist like a sledgehammer. Adam threw his arms in front of his face.

"You whiny little piece of shit," Rogan growled. Another punch. "We don't kill civilians. We don't show off in public and scare people." Another punch. "We don't abuse our power, you fucking moron. You're a disgrace."

"Rogan! That's enough." I grabbed him and pulled him off Adam.

Adam rolled to his hands and knees. I kicked him as hard as I could right in the stomach. He fell and curled into a ball.

"You almost killed my grandmother. You used kids to deliver a bomb to my house." I kicked him again. "Flirt with me now, you sonovabitch! See if I'm impressed."

Behind me Mad Rogan was laughing his head off.

Adam staggered back up. I swung, turning my body into it, the way my mother taught me. My punch connected with his gut. Adam exhaled sharply and rolled down. I kicked him again. "Bet you wish you wore a shirt now, huh? Need something to mop up the blood with?"

Mad Rogan picked me up and carried me a few feet away from Adam. "Okay, that's enough. You have to have something left to turn in to his House."

"Let me go!"

"Nevada, you're still under contract."

I pulled away from him and marched over to Adam. He jerked his hands up.

"Get up," I growled. "Or I'll get Rogan to beat you and then drag your body to your family by your hair."

Adam got to his feet.

"Hands in front of you, wrists together," I barked.

He put his hands out. I slapped the handcuffs on him, and we marched him across the flooded street to the gap in the wall.

We walked through, Mad Rogan first, then me dragging Adam. The street outside was crowded. People stood with cameras. I saw Lenora Jordan. Next to her stood a tall, prim woman with a haughty expression on her face. Christina Pierce, Adam's mother. Perfect.

I hauled Adam in front of her and kicked the back of his knee. He went down to his knees. I pulled the keys out of my pocket and dropped them next to him. "Adam Pierce, surrendered alive to his House, as requested. MII will expect prompt payment."

She stared at me. If she'd been a spitting cobra, my face would be dripping with venom.

I turned around and walked away, from the wall, from the crowd, heading down the street amidst the rubble. Most of downtown was still standing. I could hardly believe it.

A familiar figure squeezed through the crowd and ran to me. I opened my arms and hugged Bern as hard as I could.

I sipped my Angry Orchard cider and tapped a lug wrench against my leg. The garage doors were open, and Grandma Frida's workshop was flooded with bright morning light. The big industrial fans created a cooling breeze.

A week had passed since Adam Pierce had tried to turn downtown into a burned-out wasteland. I knew that MII had received a payment from House Pierce, because they'd applied our fee against our loan balance. Augustine hadn't returned my phone call acknowledging the receipt of paperwork. He was probably still sore because Mad Rogan had outmaneuvered him on our contract. I had spoken with his secretary. Her name was Lina, and she'd passed along a message: the third eye of Shiva had been returned to India, where it belonged. Professor Itoh had been right. Stealing another nation's treasures never turned out well.

I'd had several requests for interviews, all of which I'd turned down. A couple of people had proved persistent, and I'd referred them to MII and its lawyers. They'd stopped calling. I wasn't looking for fame, nor did I want to drum up clients by hitting the talk-show circuit. I would much rather Baylor Investigative Agency be synonymous with quiet professionalism.

There had been a formal inquiry. I had no idea how it had gone, because I hadn't been required to testify. Whatever testimonies House Rogan, House Montgomery, House Pierce, and Lenora Jordan had provided must've been sufficient. I still had no idea who was behind all those people helping Adam. All I knew was that they'd locked him up in Ice Box, a subterranean, maximum-security prison somewhere in Alaska. It was designed to hold magic users. He was awaiting trial. I probably would have to testify at that proceeding, unless he pled guilty.

Gavin Waller had been found. The news reported that Adam Pierce had stashed him away in a motel room with a week's worth of food and drugs. Gavin spent the week terrified that he would be found by authorities and executed on the spot. Twenty-four hours after the events downtown, Mad Rogan had brought him to the police station. The leading detective on the arson had publicly speculated that the only reason Gavin had survived at all was that Adam had been busy with his end-of-the-world plans and had simply forgotten the boy.

I hadn't heard from Rogan. All in all, that was a really good thing.

It was Saturday, and I was helping Grandma Frida with her latest project. One of the Houses had commissioned a hover tank from one of the other armored car garages. The tank neither hovered nor tanked very well. They'd sunk a lot of money into it and had finally ended up selling it for scrap. Grandma Frida had bought it, and we were pulling it apart for spare parts. She'd gone into the house to get a sandwich, and she'd been gone for ten minutes. I sipped my hard cider. She'd probably gotten distracted.

Someone stepped through the garage doorway. I squinted against the light. Mad Rogan.

He wore a dark suit. It fit him like a glove, from the broad shoulders and powerful chest to the flat stomach and long legs. Well. A visit from the dragon. Never good.

He started toward me. The track vehicle on his left slid out of his way, as if pushed aside by an invisible hand. The Humvee on his right slid across the floor. I raised my eyebrows.

He kept coming, his blue eyes clear and fixed on me. I stepped back on pure instinct. My back bumped into the wall.

The multiton hover tank hovered off to the wall. So that was the secret to making it work. You just needed Mad Rogan to move it around.

Rogan closed in and stopped barely two inches from me. Anticipation squirmed through me, turning into a giddy excitement spiced with alarm.

"Hi," I said. "Are you planning on putting all of this back together the way you found it?"

His eyes were so blue. I could look into them forever. He offered me his hand. "Time to go."

"To go where?"

"Wherever we want. Pick a spot on the planet."

Wow. "No."

He leaned forward slightly. We were almost touching. "I gave you a week with your family. Now it's time to go with me. Don't be stubborn, Nevada. That kiss told me everything I needed to know. You and I both understand how this ends."

I shook my head. "How did this encounter go in your head? Did you plan on walking in here, picking me up, and carrying me away like you're an officer and I'm a factory worker in an old movie?"

He grinned. He was almost unbearably handsome now. "Would you like to be carried away?"

"The answer is no, Rogan."

He blinked.

"No," I repeated.

"Why not?"

"This is a long explanation, and you won't like it."

"I'm all ears."

I took a deep breath.

"You have no regard for human life," I said. "You saved the city, but I don't think you did it because you genuinely cared about all those people. I think you did it because Adam Pierce got under your skin. You hire desperate soldiers, but you don't do it to save them either. You do it because they offer you unquestioning loyalty. You rescued your cousin, but you had been content to ignore the existence of that whole branch of your family. Had you stepped into Gavin's life earlier, perhaps he would've never met Adam Pierce. You don't feel that rules apply to you. If you want it, you buy it. If you can't buy it, you take it. You don't seem to feel bad about things, and you offer gratitude only when you need to overcome some hurdle. I think you might be a psychopath.

"I can't be with you, no matter how crazy you make me, because you have no empathy, Rogan. I'm not talking about magic. I'm talking about the human ability to sympathize. I would matter to you only as long as I had some use, and even then, I would be more of an object than a lover or a partner. The gulf between us, both financially and socially, is too great. You would use me, and when you were done with me, you would dismiss me like a servant and I would have to go back to pick up the pieces of my life, and I'm not sure there would be anything left of it or of me by that point. So no, I won't go away with you. I want to be with someone who would if not love, then genuinely care, for me. You are not that man."

"Pretty speech," he said.

"It's the only one I've got."

"I know what's really going on here. You're scared to step into my world. Afraid you can't hack it. Much better to hide here and be a big fish in a very small pond."

"If that's the way you see it, fine." I raised my chin. "I have nothing to prove to you, Rogan."

"But now I have something to prove to you," he said. "I promise you, I will win, and by the time I'm done, you won't walk, you'll run to jump into my bed."

"Don't hold your breath," I told him.

All of his civilized veneer was gone now. The dragon faced me, teeth bared, claws out, breathing fire. "You won't just sleep with me. You'll be obsessed with me. You'll beg me to touch you, and when that moment comes, we will revisit what happened here today."

"Never in a million years." I pointed at the doorway. "Exit is that—"

He grabbed me. His mouth closed on mine. His big body caged me in. His chest mashed my breasts. His arms pulled me to him, one across my back, the other cupping my butt. His magic washed over me in an exhilarating rush. My body surrendered. My muscles turned warm and pliant. My nipples tightened, my breasts ready to be squeezed, ready for his fingers and his mouth. An eager ache flared between my legs. My tongue licked his. God, I wanted him. I wanted him so badly.

He let me go, turned on his toes, and went out, laughing under his breath.

Aaargh! "That's right! Keep . . . walking!"

I threw the wrench down.

"Now that was a kiss," Grandma Frida said from the doorway behind me.

I jumped. "How long have you been there?"

"Long enough. That man means business."

All my words tried to come out at once. "I don't . . . what . . . asshole! . . . screw himself for all I care!"

"Aww, young love, so passionate," Grandma said. "I'm going to buy you a subscription to *Brides* magazine. You should start shopping for dresses."

I waved my arms and walked away from her before I said something I would regret.

 **Epilogue**

He parked the car, got out, and looked at the house. A typical suburban home, a cookie-cutter traditional on a square of mowed grass. A dime a dozen in any subdivision. He walked to the door and tried the handle. Unlocked. Tom had said it would be.

He had left Thomas Waller with Daniela. By now Thomas was likely sedated. His teenage son had been arrested and charged with murder. His wife had disappeared. Then he'd gotten an email from her, and the contents of it had broken the last shreds of resolve Thomas had. His hands had been shaking when they'd spoken.

He walked through the house to the kitchen. A brand new laptop waited for him on the kitchen island, its box still nearby. Tom had followed the instructions in his wife's email to the letter.

He checked the time. 6:59 p.m. He set his phone to record and placed it on the table behind him.

The clock on the screen blinked. 7:00 p.m. A blue icon flashed, indicating an incoming call. He tapped the icon.

Kelly Waller's face filled the screen. "Hello, Connor."

He hid his fury. "Why?" he asked.

"Because I hate you. I wanted you to know this. I hate you so much. If I could get my hands on you, I would grab you by the hair and I would hit your face into this island until it turned into a bloody mess. I would burn you. I would skewer you. I would vent my rage for days."

That told him nothing. Ten years ago, when he had reached out to her through his mother and offered a college fund for Gavin, she had turned him down. She made it painfully obvious she wanted nothing that had the Rogan name attached to it. At the time he'd wondered if it was pride. Now he realized it had been hate, but he still didn't understand it. "Why?"

"Because they loved you and praised you. Because you're magic and I'm not, and I will never be good enough. I want to destroy you. I want to rip you apart with my hands, but I lack the strength, so I found some people who are a lot more powerful than me. I sacrificed my son for my revenge. But you failed me, Connor."

Her face shook for a moment, distorted by anger. "We knew Adam was a loose cannon. We needed additional insurance, and who would be better than you. The Scourge. The Huracan. We knew there was a chance you would stop Adam but we counted on you destroying Houston in the process. You were doing it. I saw the buildings quake, and then you stopped. How is it you stopped, Connor? You could never stop your magic in the higher state, not since you were a child. Once you start the ascent, you continue until all of your power is exhausted. Not even your mother could reach you. What did you do? What happened? Is this some recent skill?"

He didn't answer.

"How is it that between you and Adam, you couldn't

do such a simple thing? No matter. We counted on it, and you and Adam both disappointed us. We will find a different path."

We. Us. Here it was, the secret force that drove this entire plan. She knew about it. All he had to do was find her and rip that knowledge out.

"I wanted to tell you this: you have no idea what's coming. It's big. You can't stop it no matter how hard you try. It will undo you. When you lie dying and broken, I want you to remember this moment and my face. Remember me, Connor. This is only the beginning."

The laptop went dark.

He stood, looking at it. A month ago he'd had no goals, only the minutiae of annoying tasks that had occupied, rather than challenged him. Now he had two.

He had to crush whoever was behind his cousin and Adam Pierce. He'd fought for this country and the safety of its people because he believed in it and in them. The system wasn't perfect, but it was better than most of what he saw outside of it. This city belonged to him. They would realize soon enough what kind of enemy he made. That was his first goal. As to his second . . .

He closed his eyes for a lingering moment and conjured a memory. Nothing existed in the ascent. It was a place of magic and power, calm but completely empty. He entered it to access the apex of his power, but within it there was no joy and no sadness. No cold, no warmth, only serenity. It was a prison and a palace all in one.

And then he had felt her. She was warm and golden and she tore through the sterility of ascent and reached for him. She kissed him and as she shared all of her fears and wants, he felt alive. He had shrugged off the cold serenity for her, and the world around him bloomed. He felt like an addict who, after abusing a narcotic for years, somehow found himself sober, wandered through his house, opened the front door, and saw a beautiful spring day.

He wanted Nevada Baylor. He wanted her more than he had wanted anyone in a long, long time, and he would get her. She just didn't realize it yet.

What's next for Nevada and Rogan?

———

Keep reading for a sneak peek from
ILONA ANDREWS'
second Hidden Legacy novel.

———

I stood in the private executive bathroom of Montgomery International Investigations and slipped a big black boot onto my left foot. The boot was almost knee high, charcoal opaque leather, and it looked like something out of a historical movie. Augustine Montgomery leaned against the marble vanity and watched me wedge my heel into it.

When you saw Augustine for the first time, he took your breath away. His face wasn't just handsome, it was perfect in the way the greatest works of Renaissance art were perfect. His skin was flawless, his pale blond hair was brushed with surgical precision, and his features had a regal elegance that begged to be immortalized on canvas or, better yet, in marble. His beauty had that cold air of detachment. If he had somehow traveled to the sixteenth century and met Michelangelo, the angel statue would've looked completely different. Augustine Montgomery specialized in illusion, and he was a Prime, the highest rank of magic user, which meant he was capable of remarkable things. There was no telling what hid under that remarkably perfect facade. The only thing human about him were his thin-rimmed glasses and his eyes. Shrewd, smart, they gave away his real age—he was around thirty—and they told you he would be a dangerous man to cross.

Lina, his receptionist, surveyed me with a critical eye. Unlike Augustine, she didn't have the benefit of being an illusion Prime, so her perfect makeup and unnaturally scarlet hair were the result of hours of daily preparation.

"This is a terrible idea, Ms. Baylor," Augustine said.

I wasn't going to argue. I'd had better ideas.

"Let me explain why this is a terrible idea."

"Let me" was a figure of speech. I really had no choice about it, since I was relying on him to make this happen.

"If you do this once, even if it is completely anonymous, they will expect you to do it again. And when you won't, they will become unhappy. That unhappiness will breed discontent. Eventually one of them will let it slip out: there is a magic user who can extract the truth out of all of our criminals, but she is too selfish to help us."

I stomped my foot into the right boot.

"This is why Primes do not engage in the day-to-day operations of society. We are only people. We can't be everywhere at once. If an aquakinetic puts out one fire, the next time something goes ablaze and he fails to be there, the public will turn on him."

I straightened. "I understand."

"I don't think you do. You're about to do something that's technically illegal. Yes, I can't think of a more worthy cause than saving a child, but you are still breaking the law."

He was wrong. I understood completely. My morning had started completely differently. I had received a payment from a client and then ended up sitting in my car in front of the New Justice Center looking at my tablet and reading the news article about the most hated man in the city of Houston.

His name was Jeff Caldwell. He was in his late forties, neither handsome nor ugly. If you met him on the street, you wouldn't pay him a second glance. He worked as a support specialist for Harris County Transit, which meant that when people with disabilities applied for curb-to-curb service, he was the one who reviewed their applications. He had a perfectly ordinary family, a wife who was a schoolteacher, and two children, both in college. He had no magic and wasn't affiliated with any of the Houses—powerful magic families that ran Houston. His friends described him as a kind, considerate man.

In his spare time, Jeff Caldwell kidnapped little girls. He kept them alive for up to a week at a time, then strangled them to death and left their remains in parks, surrounded by flowers. His victims were between the ages of five and seven, and the stories their bodies told made you wish that hell existed just so Jeff Caldwell could be sent there after he died. Last night he had been caught in the act of depositing the tiny corpse of his latest victim, and he'd been apprehended. The reign of terror that had gripped Houston for the past year was finally over. There was just one problem. Seven-year-old Amy Madrid was missing. She had been kidnapped two days ago from her school bus stop, less than twenty-five yards from her house. The MO was too similar to Jeff Caldwell's previous abductions to be a coincidence. He had to have taken her, and if so, it meant she was still alive somewhere.

Jeff Caldwell refused to talk.

Police scoured his house. They questioned his family, his friends, and his coworkers. They pored over his cell phone records. They interrogated him for hours. He kept his mouth shut.

I could make him talk. Ten minutes with him, and my magic would crack him like a walnut. There was only one problem. Doing that would be announcing to the Houston PD that I was a Truthseeker.

If I'd been a member of a prominent family or a retainer of one of the Houses, such as House Montgomery, the power and influence of such a magic dynasty could have shielded me from the consequences of exposing my magic. But I wasn't. I was twenty-five years old, and I ran Baylor Investigative Agency, a small, family-owned investigative firm. I had no wealth, no power, and no pedigree. I was a nobody.

If I walked into the police station, declared that my name was Nevada Baylor, and wrenched the truth from Jeff Caldwell, a couple of hours later I would get visitors from Houston PD, Homeland Security, FBI, CIA, private Houses, and anyone else who had need for a talented, 100 percent accurate interrogator. Truthseekers like me were rare and valuable. My life would become hell, and they would keep pressure on me and my family until finally I broke and went to work for one of them as a human lie detector. If the government didn't strong-arm me into it, one of the Houses would.

I liked my life exactly the way it was now. I liked my job, I loved my family, and I even loved our odd house. But if one of my sisters had been kidnapped, and some woman I didn't know could find her, I would do everything in my power to convince her to do it. I would cry, I would beg, and I would offer her anything she wanted if only she could bring my sister back. Right now Amy Madrid's parents were probably begging and crying, trying to convince a monster to return their child. And I was that other woman, sitting in my car, while somewhere Amy Madrid was slowly dying of thirst and hunger.

I'd been walking to the New Justice Center, about to

destroy my life, when Augustine Montgomery had called my cell. Technically, MII owned Baylor Investigative Agency. We had mortgaged our firm to pay for my late father's medical bills. Augustine Montgomery had a client for me. He could no longer compel me to take his cases, thanks to a renegotiation of our contract, so I'd declined. But he had insisted. The client was his friend and had asked specifically for me. We'd struck a deal. I would talk to the client, and Augustine would make sure I could anonymously interrogate Jeff Caldwell. Which is how I'd ended up in the corporate bathroom, putting on this disguise Augustine had procured for me. It was the only way he would let me do it.

Lina handed me a charcoal black mask that looked like a ski mask and a ninja hood had a baby. I pulled it on, making sure to tuck in any loose strands of hair, and looked in the mirror. The mask hid my face and my blond hair completely. All you could see were my brown eyes and a narrow strip of tan skin around them.

"Hold your hands out," Lina said, picking up a pair of elbow-long charcoal gloves. "You can't put these on by yourself."

I raised my hands and she tugged the gloves on me.

"Nevada," Augustine said. "Don't do this."

"I have to," I told him. I couldn't get the photo of Amy Madrid out of my head.

"You don't."

"Mr. Montgomery, when my father was still alive, he set up three rules for our agency. We stay bought once a client hires us. We try to avoid doing illegal things. But most important, at the end of the day we have to be able to look our reflection in the eye. I have to do this. She is just a little girl. She is slowly dying somewhere."

Augustine sighed. Lina turned to the dark garment bag hanging from the hook on the wall, unzipped it, and took out a long green garment. "Arms."

I raised my arms again. She slid the garment on me. I was wearing a cape. Dark, forest green, it hid me from head to toe. Lina pushed the Velcro closed on my chest, pulled the deep hood onto my head, and stepped back.

I couldn't even tell if I was a man or a woman. "What is this?"

"It's a costume from Alley Theater's stage production," Lina said.

"Congratulations," Augustine said, his perfect face twisting in disgust. "You are now Sir Dougal MacLagain, 'the Scottish Highwayman.'"

Lina opened the bathroom door.

"Showtime," Augustine said.